Room for a Lodger

Also by Sally Worboyes

Wild Hops
Docker's Daughter
The Dinner Lady
Red Sequins
Keep on Dancing
Down Stepney Way
Over Bethnal Green
At the Mile End Gate
Whitechapel Mary
Girl from Brick Lane
Banished from Bow
Down by Tobacco Dock
Where Sparrows Nest
Time Will Tell
Jamaica Street

SALLY WORBOYES

Room for a Lodger

HODDER

My thanks to Luigi Bonomi and Amanda Preston
for being there when I most need them.

I

On a bitterly cold late Friday afternoon at the beginning of January 1970, seventeen-year-old Cathy Jackson shivered as she wrapped her scarf twice around her neck to keep her long wavy hair dry as well as using it as a buffer against the chilly air. She reminded herself in her usual way that springtime would soon come around. She had hardly been able to ignore the miserable weather since her desk at work, in an old-fashioned office, was on the third floor of a dowdy building by a window and her view was a grey sky and drab buildings opposite. All a touch joyless, to say the least. But Cathy was not down-hearted, because she had walked away for the last time from the company where she had been employed for two years.

The head office of E. Gottard & Sons, in Clerkenwell, a highly successful business with moneyed directors at the helm, was out-of-date and, once inside the building, anyone could be forgiven for losing sight of what was happening in the outside world during the nine-hour stretch of business from 8.30a.m until 5.30p.m. The company rules which commanded silence were part and parcel of the place. At Gottard's the ladies had never been allowed to wear stiletto heels and were expected to don sensible twin-sets and black or grey skirts, as if time had not moved on. Not so far away in the City, however, the mini and the flowing maxi-skirt with knee-length boots created a colourful scene to brighten any dull day. Most of London during this time, with the swinging sixties over and a new decade beginning, was an exciting, lively place in which to work. Fashion designers were pushing the boundaries with the new, all colours clashing, reminiscent of the gypsy look.

Arriving at Smithfield meat market on her way to Farringdon station, where she would catch her train homeward bound, the place was eerie and quiet and she could hear the heels of other women echoing on their way through the back route to the station. The hustle and bustle of the busy market had come to an end by this time of day and the place was now a stark contrast to the early mornings. Then, she had to make her way through and around the busy porters everywhere, in their slightly blood-smeared white coats and hats, who lost no time, when carrying a half carcass of lamb or pork on one shoulder, competing with one another as they announced their best prices. This was a scene that she was going to miss.

Once on the platform, Cathy looked across to a mainline train on its way to Bishops Stortford and smiled back at the company secretary from Gottard's, in his black bowler hat and smart grey overcoat, as he looked over to where she was standing, smiled farewell and tipped his hat. Remembering the good times at work as she waited for her train, Cathy was too pre-occupied to take notice of what her colleagues, in whose foot-steps she had walked to the station, were complaining about: the minimum fare on the underground was to rise from six-pence to one shilling. But as far as she was concerned more important things were happening at all levels. Deaths from Asian flu were rising, Mick Jagger of the Rolling Stones had been publicly shamed and fined for possession of cannabis, the FA had suspended Manchester United's George Best for disreputable behaviour and Labour MP Will Owen had been charged under the Official Secrets Act for passing on under-cover information! More exhilarating than all these, though, were the ongoing reports from the previous summer when Neil Armstrong, commander of the space ship Apollo II, stepped off of the lunar module Eagle on to the moon and spoke to television viewers while walking about on the surface of fine powder with Buzz Aldrin. While they were there the two men collected samples of dust and rock and took pictures of the lunar landscape.

It was no wonder that people felt a need for excitement in their own lives. Cathy had certainly had enough of working in the chief accountant's office within a dull, dry-as-dust company. Even so, during her walk from work she had been filled with mixed emotions – euphoric one minute and worried the next – in case she had made a big mistake in leaving the familiar for the unknown, even though deep down she knew that this was a move for the better.

Lady Luck had been on her side when the employment agency Brook Street Bureau sent her for an interview one lunchtime. She had got through with flying colours, and had felt so right in the lively surroundings. Now she was thrilled by the new life ahead of her, working for Johnson's newspapers in Moorgate at almost twice the pay she had been getting.

In the autumn, at the age of forty-eight, Jim, Cathy's dad, had suffered a massive heart attack while at work in the London docks. But after being in hospital for eight weeks he was now back at home and looking better, even though he could not afford to forget to take even one of his twice-daily heart pills and was under strict orders that going back to work was not an option. To make up for his loss of wages Cathy's mother, Alice, had taken on full-time work at Woolworth's in the Bethnal Green market. Jim meanwhile, was doing his bit by taking over light house duties. He also found himself reaping the reward of his past generosity, when he had insisted that his widowed mother-in-law, Molly, Cathy's much-loved nan, move in with them.

Molly had taken the attic room of their tenement house soon after her husband had passed away some five years earlier. Short and nicely rounded, she was a bit of a live wire with her urchin haircut, bleached back to the blonde it had been before she went a dark grey. At sixty-nine she was good for her age: each morning she took one teaspoonful of cod liver oil followed by one tablespoonful of honey. Taking on the role of house-keeper in the family's changed circumstances, she left Jim to do little other than pick up a few groceries, set and light the small coal fires and make a pot of tea now and then. His main duty as far as she was concerned was to study the racing pages of the daily paper, so that when they each had a little bet on their fancied horses they would stand a better chance of picking a winner. Alice disapproved of gambling for no other reason than she thought it to be a mug's game with everyone a loser. Cathy remained completely neutral should a small family dispute break out, because she had her own life to live: she let both generations above her in the pecking order get on in their own sweet way. All in all, the new domestic routine kept Jim's pride at a respectable level now that he was no longer the bread-winner. And privately, Molly was not too upset that he had had to give up work, because, apart from anything else, he was very nice company for her.

With a renewed sense of having done the right thing in leaving Gottard's after experiencing waves of doubt on her train journey home, Cathy was pleased to have met up with her next-door neighbour, Rosie, who had stepped out of the carriage next to her own and called out to her. Once outside in the crisp fresh air in Bethnal Green the girls linked arms.

'I can't believe I've done it, Rosie,' said Cathy. 'I've actually left my job!'

'People do it all the time.' Rosie chuckled.

'I know, but it just feels so weird. A bit like the day when you walk out of the school gate for the last time.'

'Ah . . . now that I *can* relate to. A kind of an ending that I was only too ready for – but someone else would be using my desk that I'd kept all my little secrets hidden in.'

'Something like that.' Cathy squeezed her friend's arm and quietly laughed. 'I won't be going back to miserable old Gottard's any more. As from this Monday, *I shall be working with journalists*,' she said, using a mock posh voice.

'Well, don't get your hopes up. You might not like it – you might feel like a fish out of water,' warned Rosie as they arrived in Tillet Street, tucked away behind the fire station.

As soon as Cathy turned her key in the door she could smell an oxtail stew on the stove. Once in the passage, she could hear her nan in the front room bending her dad's ear about oxtail being tastier than stewing steak, and him trying to get a word in by saying that she should buy a skirt of beef from the butcher's in Cambridge Heath Road to try. Cathy's mother was in the ground-floor bathroom, enjoying a soak after an eight-hour stint at Woolworth's.

Quiet as a mouse, so that she could go into the kitchen and make herself a cup of Nescafé and have five minutes by herself, Cathy crept along the passage. But she couldn't help smiling as her nan called out to her, 'I 'eard the door go and you come in, so you can stop creeping about! Get yerself in 'ere and tell us 'ow you got on. Did you give in and stop there, or 'ave you got your cards?'

Cathy pushed the door into the living room open wide and said, 'Mind your own business, Nan. I'm a career woman, not a little girl.'

With an eyebrow raised, Molly looked directly into Cathy's face, 'Oh, right, you've done it then. Good job an' all. Fucking slave drivers. Should 'ave given you twice as much as you was earning. Did they make you an offer at the last minute, or what?'

'They wasn't that desperate, Nan,' she said, then glanced at her dad who was resting in the armchair next to the glowing fire and smiled at him. 'All right, Dad?'

'Not so bad, love. Not so bad. The old pensioner's getting on me nerves, but what can you expect?' He leaned back in his chair, a smile spreading across his face. 'You did it, then? Well done, love. It was time for a change, and your mum will be really pleased for you as well.'

'I might be a pensioner but not *old*. I'm sixty – that's not old!' insisted Molly.

'Sixty-nine,' said Jim. 'And that's why you shout so much – because you're going deaf. First sign of it, that is. Shouting all the time just because *you* can't hear properly.'

'I don't shout. I raise me voice now an' then, that's all,' sniffed Molly, her voice a touch above a whisper. 'And the only reason I do that is because you're the one that's hard of hearing, Jim – not me. Put the kettle on for us, Cath, would you, love?'

'I'm not hard of hearing,' insisted Jim, rising from his chair. 'And *I'll* make a pot of tea, if you don't mind. That's *my* job.' He squeezed Cathy's arm and gave her a wink. 'Tell your nan all about it and get it over with in one, eh?'

'I couldn't care less if she tells me or not,' said Molly, tonging a lump of coal on to the fire. I don't need to know all the ins and outs and who said what to whom. Fetch us in a couple of slices of bread to toast by the fire, Jim, while you're at it.'

'With or without St Ivel cheese spread, your majesty?' said Jim, baiting her.

'With. Even if it sticks in my throat.'

'Sticks in your throat?' said Cathy, dropping down on to the small sofa. 'Cream cheese? Never!'

'Forget it, Cath,' said Jim, giving her a wry smile. 'She's been reminiscing again. Did you want a bite to eat, love? Or you gonna wait for dinner?'

'Just a cream cracker for me, please, Dad. And a scraping of spread. I'm watching my waistline. I've got all those young male journalists to think about now.'

Jim left the room and went into the passage, calling out as he made his way to the back parlour and the kitchen: 'Reporters might not be all they're cracked up to be, love! You can't go far wrong with a docker. And you don't need to slim down!'

'Bloody la-de-da cow,' whispered Molly, miles away and staring into the flames in the small, ornate black grate.

'Who?' Cathy kicked off her shoes and curled her legs under her. 'Who's rattled your cage?'

'One of my brother-in-law's tarts. Soon after the LCC gave us a tram on route 77, which meant I could go back and forth to see my sister whenever I felt like it, as well as catching it to go to work. Well, I caught something on that day all right. Caught the look of guilt on your uncle's face.'

'Well, come on, then. Out with it. Give us the low-down,' said Cathy as she tore off a strip of newspaper and pushed the tip of it into the flames of the fire to light her cigarette.

'The adverts for St Ivel cheese that went right along the side of that bus. I should think they sold a lot of cream cheese after that. Cheap advertising. I bought some straightaway, so it even worked on me. It was a lot creamier than it is today, though.'

'If you say so.' Cathy drew on her cigarette and blew a smoke ring.

'My sister couldn't 'ave been no more than twenty-eight, give or take a year. I'd gone on the new tram to pay her a little visit. We went up the market to get some cheap curtain material – and that's when she saw the pair of them. Her old man sitting in a café, opposite a good-looking tart and sipping a cup of tea. It was 'is lunch break from the bottle factory where 'e worked.' Molly raised her eyes to meet Cathy's and slowly shook her head. 'Broke 'er bloody 'eart, that did.'

'You mean they were together?' Cathy grinned. 'Blimey. What didn't you lot get up to in the old days, eh?'

'They was sitting there as if they'd known each other for years, sipping tea, gazing into each other's faces. Bastard! He hardly ever said a word to my sister . . . always quiet and moody indoors.'

Pursing her lips, Cathy tried not to laugh. She leaned forward and patted her nan's hand, saying, 'It must 'ave been hurtful. You're right. Men can be bastards, can't they?'

Molly slowly raised a hand and pointed a finger at her granddaughter. 'Don't you let your father hear you swearing! I'll cop the blame for it, you can bank on that.'

'Sorry, Nan. It slipped out. Although it *is* in the dictionary, so it's not exactly swearing, is it? Not if it's in there.'

'I might forget myself sometimes but I never swear in front of you, Cathy.'

'No . . . of course you don't, Nan. So what did that woman do once she saw you gawking at 'er?'

'We went inside and stood by the table, and I looked into

the woman's face while my sister glared at her old man with a look to kill. She fucking well blushed like she was guilty all right. And you could see the guilt in his eyes as well . . . He was too good-looking for 'is own good, my brother-in-law. Not any more, though. Ugly as a pig now. He never wore well, but then 'andsome young men don't. It's the ugly ones that improve with time. Well . . . them that can't get any uglier do, anyway.'

'And what's all this got to do with St Ivel cheese spread?'

'The woman was spreading a little of it on to a dainty little cracker, that's all. La-de-da cow. Now I can't eat it without seeing 'er face.'

'Fair enough . . . Anything happened down our street today?' Cathy lay back, stretched her legs and drew on her cigarette. 'Did the tally man go into Mrs Woods again? For a bit of the other? It *is* Friday.'

'No. And only because she knows I saw it last week and let her know it with no more than a look . . . So . . . you've left your job and you can work your way up to be on one of them magazines. Well done, Cathy. I never thought you 'ad it in yer. You've got gumption – and you got that from me.'

'Of course I did! And I love you to bits and love getting the little snippets of gossip from you.'

The sight of her dad coming into the room with freshly made tea in their old familiar brown teapot, and sliced bread to toast on a long fork by the fire, was touching. She knew he had to put on a brave face because he was no longer the one bringing home the keep and was having to get used to fetching and carrying to make up for it. She would like to have pleased him and have toast spread with melting butter and cheese – but she would be having a proper meal at the usual time of half-past seven and liked to keep an eye on her figure. Her two sisters, a few years older than herself, were proud of their full curvy shapes, but big breasts and small waists didn't suit the current trend as far as Cathy was concerned. The look now was long, lean and flowing.

'Don't let me forget to switch on the telly later on, will you,

Molly?' said Jim, passing her a cup of tea. 'When it's time for Vera Lynn. I'd hate to miss that programme.'

'I've scribbled a note and sellotaped it on the back of the kitchen door.'

'Not a programme about the war again,' complained Cathy. 'Why can't you lot bury all that? I would 'ave thought you'd want to.'

'It's not about the war, love. It's about her life. And she *is* my sweetheart!'

'It'd be a sorry bloody thing if we did let it be forgot,' said Molly, sipping her tea. 'Men died fighting to keep this country free from Hitler!'

'Sorry, Nan,' said Cathy, looking into the flames of the coal fire and filling her mind with her own thoughts. For some reason she was beginning to feel a touch sad as it sank in that she wouldn't see any of the people she had worked with again and that they would no longer be part of her life. Not only her friends and colleagues, but the Italian family who ran a café opposite Gottard's. A place where she and the other girls had gone for their freshly made tomato and cucumber sandwiches and breathed in the wonderful smell of coffee from the beans grinding in the little machine or percolating nearby. Even now she could almost catch the aroma that filled the air as she thought about the good-looking Italian lad who helped his parents run the establishment, and had tried once or twice to ask her out but had never quite plucked up the courage. She had almost asked him when they were going to go for a drink, but in the end didn't because it wasn't really the done thing. So she had left the area knowing she wouldn't see him or his lovely family again, even though she said she would go back now and then for her favourite lunch of home-made pasta. She knew that such promises were hardly ever kept. So, deep in her thoughts with various snapshots coming to mind from her time as Gottard's, she ate her snack and let her dad and nan's conversation go over her head.

Her thoughts slid from the shy, handsome Italian lad in the

café to his spitting image, Paul McCartney, who had married
the heiress Linda Eastman the previous year. The news of the
couple's engagement had broken her heart, but she was over
all of that once the band of gold had been slipped on to Linda's
finger, as were a million other fans who knew then that they
had lost any chance of catching Paul for themselves. The reality
of the difference between her world and that of the Beatles
kicked in when George Harrison had been arrested for illegal
possession of cannabis. To make matters worse, this had
happened on the same day that Paul got married. She looked
across to her nan as the old woman's voice drifted through her
thoughts.

'Your dad's going on about Vera Lynn again, Cathy.'

'I wasn't going on about her, Molly. I just reminded you not
to let me forget, that's all. We're fortunate to have her giving
an interview, really. She's famous.'

'Of course she is. The woman's a saint. She kept our peckers
up,' agreed Molly.

Cathy, leaning back in her chair and closing her eyes for a
five-minute doze before she got herself ready to go out, let out
a sigh when she heard her neighbour, Henry, calling her name
from the back garden. But at least it gave her a chance to
escape before Molly went on about the war.

Cathy knew that nineteen-year-old Henry, who lodged with
Rosie and George, the childless couple living next door, was
harmless enough – although she sometimes wondered about
his mental state, especially when she saw him in the back yard
practising his own version of kung fu or karate, or in deep
meditation while sitting cross-legged for an hour or so on a
patch of grass. Her family, no different from others in her
street, couldn't help but feel for Henry, who had no close
friends of his own age other than the postman who brought
him mail from his pen-friends around the world. But Henry
took care of the local newspaper delivery round, getting up at
the crack of dawn seven days a week, so knew quite a few
people casually – and this seemed to suit him fine. He also

had a regular job in the corner shop which he helped run with efficiency, keeping everything ship-shape and always opening up at eight-thirty after his paper round. Easing the back door open, Cathy smiled at him.

'Ah, Cathy . . . I just wondered if your mother's had any mail delivered from China,' he said. 'Only I've been expecting a letter and it should have arrived by now. I have a feeling I might have put the wrong number on my return address on the left-hand corner of the letter I sent.'

'No, Henry,' she replied. 'I saw no post other than what I think is a letter from my sister to Mum.'

'But your sister visits regularly,' he said. 'Why would she want to send a letter? Do you think you could just check the envelope for me, Cathy? I don't want to be a nuisance but it *is* important.'

'I *know* it's from one of my sisters. From Ava.'

He nodded slowly as if deep in thought. 'Well . . . if you're sure, then I'll ask Leo and Becky if it's been put through their letterbox by mistake . . . Oh, and how did it go today? Did the company arrange a little farewell drinks party for you? Or should I say cocktail party? I think that's what people call that kind of a thing, isn't it?'

'I wouldn't know,' said Cathy. 'But no – nothing was arranged. Hugs all round from my friends, though. Hugs and promises to keep in touch. You know the sort of thing.'

'Of course. Yes. Well, never mind. You can look forward to Monday and beginning a new life. This is the thing. You mustn't let it get you down just because no party was arranged.'

'No. I didn't even expect it, to be honest. It's an archaic firm.'

'Archaic?' said Henry, doing anything he could to make conversation. 'That's an interesting old word for you to come out with. Archaic. I like that. And will you have to work the same hours in your new job? Or longer? Or shorter?'

'I won't have to be in so early in the mornings. I'll get an extra half-hour in bed,' she smiled. 'Anyway . . . I'm about to run a bath, Henry.'

The hint escaped him. 'Most people appreciate a little extra time in bed in the mornings, it seems. I like to be up and about myself. I much prefer morning to evenings, for some reason. All most people want to do, from what I can gather, is throw the alarm clock against the wall when it goes off.' He cupped his chin and looked into her deep blue eyes. 'You will let me know if my letter from China has been put somewhere for safe keeping, won't you? It's a particularly nice pen-friend, that one.

'I will definitely let you know. I promise. Anyway . . . I must run the bath and wash away the city grime.' She hated herself for not giving this poor soul more of her time – but it was Friday night, after all, and she did have something to celebrate with her girlfriends. She had left her boring job.

'Just one other thing before I go. Do you find any ice on the inside of your bedroom window when you wake up on cold mornings?'

'No, Henry, I don't,' she said. 'My curtains are lined and that does the trick.'

'I ask you this,' he said, cupping his chin again, 'not because it's a problem for me, but it might be for the old couple next door. I keep my dressing gown under the bedclothes and put that on before I get up. It's nice and warm by then. It was a gift from Rosie and George. The Christmas before last.' He paused, thoughtfully, and then said, 'You will let me know if your mother wants to change her daily paper from the *Mail* to the *Mirror*, won't you? It wouldn't be a problem. I'll arrange it at the shop. Both are the same size, so it should go through the letter box with no trouble.'

'I'll tell her, Henry,' said Cathy, showing a hand and leaving him to go back to Rosie's.

Back inside the kitchen, Cathy leaned on the closed back door. She had known Henry since childhood and had played with him along with other children of their age in the street – games such as Tin Tan Tommy, Chase, Knock Down Ginger and, when there were only the two of them around, marbles.

At that time Henry hadn't seemed that different from the rest, except that he argued more than the others did about the rules of the game and seemed to think he was being singled out as a nuisance when this wasn't necessarily the case. Gradually the neighbours, old and young, realised that he was more sensitive than the run-of-the-mill boy, and as time went on he withdrew into his own private world, hardly ever playing outside.

Henry had little idea how a normal family was run and had often sat by himself on the doorstep, rain or shine. Sometimes he had been left alone in the house when his family, who had never treated him properly, had gone out for the day and not taken him with them. The comics he read he knew off by heart, having read them over and over. The lonely child had now developed into what was seen as a solitary person who liked his own company. Nothing could have been further from the truth, however, because in reality he wanted to have friends, but those of his own age backed away once he started to lecture them about nothing of consequence.

Pouring herself a glass of water, Cathy wiped all thoughts of her sad neighbour from her mind. She had known him long enough to realise that there was little she could do to help him other than to chat over the garden fence or invite him in for a game of cards now and then. She felt sure that if she were to let him come with her and her friends to the young people's pubs at weekends he would be out of his depth and regarded as odd, even though he was quite handsome – tall, slim but muscular, with lovely soft hazel eyes and sandy hair. It was his inner self that was the problem, and at the end of the day this was all-important when it came to being out and about town. Even the nicest of lads or girls could be cruel when it came to an oddball.

Cathy wandered back into the front room and sat down by the fire to smoke another cigarette. She let her nan's ramblings go over her head in her usual way and thought about asking Henry to join her and her friends on one of their quiet midweek evenings out for a few drinks, down by the river at the Prospect of Whitby, where it was more relaxing. She told herself that she might just do this, one day.

'I don't think anyone from my sister's street was killed, Jim,' said Molly, 'but she never really got over the bombing.'

'Best forget it all then, eh, love,' said Jim. 'And pray that we won't 'ave to go through another war.'

'Seeing is believing, and I 'ope I shan't be around should it repeat itself. I'd sooner be dead and buried. Hanbury Street, Spital Street, South Tenter Street – even the Whitechapel church was hit. I don't know what God made of that. Whitechapel, Aldgate, Mile End and Bethnal Green – you name it. It was raining bombs. Why they 'ad to pick on us poor fuckers in our 'umble little dwellings I do not know. You'd think that even the dopey Germans would 'ave seen sense in blowing up the big posh houses in the posh roads up West if they were after Members of Parliament.'

'Yeah, all right . . . that'll do. Cathy doesn't wanna hear all of that. Our little girl's starting her new job on Monday, don't forget. I bet she'll end up writing one of them magazines 'erself.'

'She ain't a little girl, Jim,' sniffed Molly. 'She's old enough to get pregnant.'

'Cheers for that, Nan. I love it when you get straight to the nub of it.'

'I could 'ave had been one of them poor bastards,' she murmured. 'One of the poor sods on them stairs in the underground at Bethnal Green. That was my station, don't forget. I was in and out of there going to Mile End, to work. I'm lucky to be alive.'

'Well, thank God for it then, eh, Nan?'

'But then the East End was a disaster wherever you went. Talk about piss on the poor. One hundred and seventy people, crushed to death. Seventy-eight feet below ground in a tomb. The underground's a recipe for disaster! You'd think they'd 'ave more sense at the top. They should 'ave built all railway tracks above us instead of beneath the ground. You'd have thought they'd 'ave thought of that, wouldn't you? Eh? You would, though, wouldn't yer? They get paid a lot more'n we do. Fucking morons.'

'Right,' said Cathy, having heard enough. 'I think Mum's out of the bath, so I'll go and run one for myself and wash and roll my hair, ready for a fucking good night out.'

'Oi, oi!' snapped Jim. 'Watch your tongue, young lady! That bar of carbolic is still in the cupboard under the sink. I've not had to use it on any of my three daughters yet – but don't think I won't wash your mouth out with it, Cathy.'

'I'm only parroting Nan, Dad. And since we could all be blown away any day if it takes some lunatic's fancy I might as well go all out and burn the candle at both ends. Right, Nan?'

'Yeah, all right. Point taken. I won't talk about the war no more. And if I 'ear you using that language you'll feel the flat of my hand on your arse. And don't forget to put a shilling in the electric meter if you're gonna have a bath! I might want one later and I don't want the immersion tank to be full of lukewarm, thank you very much.'

'Good,' said Jim. 'That's you two sorted out, then. I'll have my bath in the morning.' He leaned back in his chair and closed his eyes. 'Talking about the war don't do my heart any good whatsoever.'

'I shouldn't think it would do. Fucking Hitler wiv 'is fucking Vls is enough to give us all an 'eart attack. Grove Road, Becton and Canning Town. They all took a good bashing as well. Flying bombs. Doodlebugs. No warning . . . just a flash in the sky. And now, just when we're getting used to things being on the up, what do they do? They take *Mrs Dale's Diary* off the fucking air! After twenty-one years! Bollocks to them country bumpkin Archers! I ain't listening to that. They can keep the carrot crunchers out of my living room.'

Cathy left them to it and slipped away, leaving her dad to take the brunt of it. She knew he would be all right, that he could let it all go above his head. He was a good actor when it came to her nan, and if truth be known he enjoyed the stories that she came out with – fully embellished, of course. Turning away, she heard her nan talking about her even though the door was closed.

'She's too soft, that one, Jim. Can't bear to hear about the war? Needs to harden up a bit, if you ask me.'

Normally Cathy would have left it at that and pretended not to have heard – but not today, when her life was at a turning point and she was in high spirits. She turned the highly polished brass knob, opened the door and stepped back inside the room, saying, 'You're right, Nan, and that's just what I'm gonna do. So you can expect me to answer you back from now on. Okay?'

'You'll get a right-hander if you do – saucy mare.'

'Not from you I won't. You're too old and slow.' With that Cathy was out of the room.

'Well,' said Molly, 'if this is 'ow she's gonna be just cos she's chucked in 'er notice, I can see a few rows going on under this roof!'

'Leave her be,' said Jim. 'She's a good girl and it's time she stood up to you. She's not your little granddaughter any more. She's a young woman with a mind of 'er own.' He leaned back in his chair and winked at his mother-in-law. 'Well go on, then. You were in full flow, so let's have the rest of it.'

'You have to nip it in the bud, Jim, I'm telling yer. Once they start to think they're independent and don't need us—'

'Molly – she's going on eighteen! You was a married woman by then, from what you told me . . . with a bun in the oven.'

'I still never cheeked my grandmother, though. When I think of all I've bin through and she talks to me like that. Me and my friend 'ad to be taken to the London Hospital, you know. Suffering from shock, we was. We got there just in time for dinner and out again before they started taking blood. I wasn't gonna give any of mine. I needed it. My friend knew all the timetables. She got two meals a day at times. Had to part wiv a bit of the red stuff for that. A pint of blood for an 'ot dinner. I'd sooner go without. Well, you never know, do you? When you might need every bit of blood you've got. I wouldn't want no one else's red stuff running through my veins. I'd sooner bleed to death, thank you. I wouldn't put on a pair of someone else's knickers or use their toothbrush, would I?'

The sound of the doorbell stopped her short. 'Well, whoever that is they can sod off. That dinner's nearly ready and I'm not letting that stew go one extra. I like a bit of leftovers for next day breakfast, you know.' She stood up to answer the door, still talking as she went. 'Coming round at this time when most people are in the middle of their dinner.'

Jim leaned back in his chair and sighed with a smile. He knew his mother-in-law better than his wife did. Molly loved it when someone arrived out of the blue before she dished up a meal with an extra plate on the table. Her loud, happy singsong voice drifted in through the open doorway of the sitting room and made him smile. She was welcoming one of his mates from the time when he was working in the docks. One of the young lads, Johnny Dean. Jim recognised his voice and knew that, beneath whatever excuse he would give for his impromptu arrival, his youngest daughter was the reason for the call. He liked this lad a lot but he had been born and bred into a family of gamblers and, just like his elder brothers, on payday Johnny sometimes gave his wages to the betting shop before he had even reached home.

Jim leaned back in his chair and put his feet up on an old and comfortable padded footrest and waited for the good-looking chap to make his entrance. And make it he did, with a certain glint in his eye.

'Hello, Jim. How's tricks?'

'Not so bad, son, not so bad. How's your luck?'

'All right, as it happens. I backed an outsider and it came in at twenty to one.'

'Very nice, son, but did you put it all back?'

'Not this time. I've learned my lesson. Put your winnings in your pocket and walk away.'

'Good lad! Well, sit down, then, Johnny and take the weight off your feet. Cup of tea, son?'

'Wouldn't mind . . . but I've got a couple of bottles of stout in the car . . . if you're allowed?'

'Course I am,' beamed Jim. 'Go and get 'em . . . my throat's parched. There's not a drop of anything in this place.'

'I've got a half bottle of Scotch but—'

'No, son. No. Best not. Doctor's order. Ale's fine.'

'Right, I'll just nip out then . . . Cathy about, is she?' he enquired, all innocent.

'Yeah. Not long in, though.' She left her job today. Starts work at a publisher's in the City on Monday.' He could hardly stop himself from grinning, so proud was he of his youngest daughter.

'Good for Cath,' the young man replied, and then, 'Right. Won't be a tick.' In no time he was back inside with two bottles of brown ale and shaking off the cold air. 'It's cold enough to freeze the balls off a brass monkey out there, Jim,' he said, making himself comfortable in the armchair by the fire opposite his old workmate. He used the edge of the black iron fireplace to ease the metal top off each bottle. 'All right if I go through to the kitchen to get a couple of glasses?'

'Course it is. You know the way, son – should do by now. Ask Molly to get a couple out of the kitchen cupboard.'

'Right. Won't be a tick.'

Jim couldn't help smiling. The young docker, all smartened up in his Italian suit and polished shoes, wasn't here to see him – but he was pleased with the company and he liked the lad. He liked him a lot. Nice-looking, too – but didn't go too heavy on the aftershave. Chuckling to himself, he put the bottle to his lips and enjoyed his first taste of beer for a few days as he pictured Cathy arm in arm with this young man who, he reckoned, was on the verge of asking her out.

Johnny was as confident as the next man when he was

working down the docks, and looked a Jack the Lad when he was out with his mates in the East End pubs on a Friday and Saturday night – but as soon as he came into Cathy's realm, the eighteen-year-old was like a different person. Soft and silly, and grinning from ear to ear. Jim reckoned he would be a good catch for his daughter if only he could kick the gambling.

Coming back into the room, Johnny handed Jim a glass and then sat himself down. 'Did you hear about the bit of trouble at East India docks?'

'No, son – I'm a bit out of touch. Not another strike, I hope?'

'Yeah. Looks like the men will come out over the governors taking on freelance labour.'

'Silly buggers. They should have known the men would have gone potty over this. There'll be murders over it if it's not nipped in the bud. Most of 'em grew up in the back streets of the docks and wharves. It's in their blood.'

'That's just it. And it's growing, Jim, not easing off. Another wharf comes out on strike, and another follows.'

'Unofficial strikes, though, son. Unofficial.'

'I know, but I don't think it'll stop there. It's spreading right through London. They gave another dead man's job to an outside man . . . and if that's not adding fuel to the fire, I don't know what is. I don't reckon many of them casuals 'ave got union cards. And poor old Alfie Blake wasn't dead and buried a day when they gave his job to an outsider. The men are livid over that alone. If there is an all-out strike – which is on the cards if the mood of the men is anything to go by – it'll cause a lot of trouble at the top and right down the line.'

'Bastards. If you ask me, the Import Trades Committee can't wait to break the trade union. Trouble is, son . . . if the union push management too hard with their demands it could mean the end of the London docks.'

'No way. That'll never 'appen, Jim. Nar . . . there'll always be lorry-loads of stuff coming out of the docks and going to the markets. Stands to reason. Import and export. That's gonna grow rather than shrink, surely?'

'We'll see, son,' said Jim, all thoughtful. 'We'll see.' And then, changing the subject, 'Has anyone been round to see if Alfie's missus is all right?'

'Must 'ave done, Jim. There was a good turn-out for the funeral, and a good collection was taken round to 'er afterwards.'

'Good. That's the way it should be. Us lot sticking together when needs must.'

'Absolutely.'

'So . . . you out tonight, then? You look smart in that suit, Johnny.'

'Well . . . it's Friday night. Gotta look the business for the girls at Kate Odders.'

'I thought your favourite pub was the Black Boy on the Mile End Road, son.'

'Not always. Friday night at the Two Puddings on my home ground in Stratford, and Kate Odders or the Black Boy on a Saturday night. And if we've not got enough birds to make a good party go wiv a swing it's outside the Blind Beggar at turning-out time.'

'Then you can stroll through the groups of girls and take your pick.'

'That's right. Trouble is . . . there's so many parties going on that the birds can pick and choose.'

'And then it's a quick two quid whip-round from the lads and off to one of your chum's mum and dad's house who've gone away on 'oliday?'

'Something like that.' Johnny chuckled. 'Not always, though. Sometimes it's an engagement or a birthday . . .'

'But it makes no difference so long as one way or another you can rock and roll wiv the girls.'

'That's a bit out-of-date, Jim,' Johnny replied with a laugh. 'Rock and rolling to Elvis Presley? No way.'

'I don't know why you don't ask our Cathy out,' sniffed Jim. 'I know she'd be in safe hands with you, son. And between you me and the gatepost,' he said, winking, 'I think she's a bit soft on you.'

'Nar,' said Johnny, smiling and soppy again. 'She don't wanna waste 'er time with a docker. No. It's a white-collar worker for your daughter, Jim.'

'Don't you bet on it, son. I'll lay a dollar on 'er saying yes if you ask 'er out.'

'All right,' said Johnny. 'Put like that, I can't back off, can I?'

'No. And d'yer know why? Because you and me and old Molly are peas in a pod. We love a little gamble. I bet you a two-bob bit she'll say yes.'

'You're on,' said Johnny, his blue eyes sparkling.

'And speaking of laying a bet . . . our Cathy's against gambling. Fiercely against it. So if you've a mind to start courting her, which I for one would like to see, you're gonna have to give up the gee-gees.'

'I will do. Once this winning streak is over. I'll quit once I'm well ahead, don't you worry.'

'Good intentions, son – but I've heard it all before. A cousin of mine lost everything at the dog track, you know. Had to sell his little Mini motor car in the end – and would 'ave sold 'is mother too if he could 'ave found a punter.'

'Well, that's a compulsive gambler for you, Jim. Not me, though. I know when to quit.'

Jim slowly shook his head. 'Famous last words, Johnny. Famous last words.'

In the back room, which was linked to the kitchen, three generations of women, Cathy, her mother Alice and her grandmother, were involved in a conversation. Alice, a small-framed woman with short brown soft curly hair and blue eyes, and wearing a paisley pinafore over a plain camel-coloured jersey dress, was telling Molly about something that she had heard from one of her other daughters. Gang fights between youths of Johnny's age, in and around Bethnal Green and Hackney, were growing fiercer: a lad of sixteen had been badly beaten up and seriously cut with a broken bottle, just a ten-minute walk away from where they lived. The most popular weapons were old-fashioned knuckle dusters as well as bicycle chains and even meat choppers. Some of the trouble was centred on local pubs where the young drank, and youth clubs where junior boxing matches and dances were held. Places that young Cathy sometimes liked to go to with her friends.

Her two elder sisters, Ava and Marilyn, independent and living away from home, shared a spacious attic flat in a large, converted Victorian house close to Victoria Park in Hackney. They came regularly to see their parents, their nan and their younger sister and still treated the place as if it were home, helping themselves to food from the cupboard or fridge. But they nearly always left a five pound note or two hidden in a blue china milk jug that was never used. This was for their mother to spend on herself without Jim, their very proud and independent dad, knowing anything about it.

The girls not only enjoyed a well-paid unlawful living but had generous boyfriends, part of the local gangster fraternity with whom Johnny sometimes drank in the Grave Maurice in Whitechapel. Both Cathy and her nan listened while Alice related, word for word, the conversation she had had on the phone with her second daughter, Marilyn. Having heard enough, Molly cut in. 'Yeah, all right, Alice. We do read the local papers, you know. Your girls broadcast it as if they're angels or nuns. They need a good slap on the arse, the pair of 'em. They've started to nick jewellery as well now, you know.'

'No, they've not. They shoplift for their clothes up West, that's all.'

'Yeah, right – ring the other bell, I'm deaf,' said Molly. 'I know where the pair of 'em will end up if they carry on the way they're going.'

'Don't worry about them, Mum,' said Alice. 'They're not exactly putty in anyone's hands, are they?'

'Which is exactly what I'm saying. They're getting as hard

as nails and living the role of gangster's molls! Fucking drama queens, the pair of 'em. Should 'ave gone on the stage.'

'Our Marilyn said she *saw* the knife fight, Mum – not that she was *involved* in it. She was there when the trouble broke out. In the doorway of the Green Gate, having a drink. Where madam here, as young as she is, goes with her mates.'

'I've only been in there two or three times, Mum.' Cathy smiled. 'And I didn't think much of it. It's for the likes of Marilyn and Ava and their flash boyfriends.'

'All I'm saying, Cathy, is that your sisters, your *elder* sisters, told me to tell you to keep at arm's length when you're out for a night, that's all. Stay out of old Bethnal Green for a bit. Until things have blown over. And keep a distance between you and the Repton Club.'

Cathy raised an eyebrow as she drew on her cigarette. 'Now you *are* going too far. And Marilyn knows I don't go to the dances there any more. I stopped once I started work.'

'But you do like to watch a boxing match there now and then.'

'So? It's called sport! And look how many good boxers come from our little patch. Ted Lewis, Jack Berg, Teddy Blacock. East End boys. Ask Dad. He's seen them fight. Reckons they were born with "World Champion" written across their fore-heads. And anyway, I've only been to a few local fights – and only then because of the atmosphere.'

'Yeah. And the good-looking Jack the Lads in the audience,' said Molly.

'That as well, yeah. You'd love it, Nan. Being there with all the fans round the ring shouting their favourite on. It's a bit of fun, that's all.'

'Fun? Trouble in the making, more like it,' complained Alice. 'Some of the wrong sort go to boxing matches. Villains.'

'That's going a bit over the top, Alice,' retorted Molly. 'Its Bethnal Green you're talking about – not fucking Chicago! You've been listening to your would-be gangster daughters for too long. Who do they think they are? The two queens of the patch? Silly mares. And another thing,' she added quickly before Alice could get in. 'Last week you was going on about the snooker clubs and 'ow dangerous they've got! Johnny's in the front room wiv your 'usband – ask 'im if it's too dangerous to go outside our front door. He's always up the club playing snooker. As are a lot of blokes that we know. And I've not heard of any one of them being shot or knifed!'

'All the girls were saying was that our Cathy should be aware of the trouble spot, that's all. And one in particular.'

'And which one might that be?' Molly asked.

'The old cinema in Bethnal Green Road. It's notorious for fights and protection racketeers and getting worse. A different sort are running the gambling club behind the little Bingo Hall now.'

'You've bin watching too much television,' said Molly before she started to laugh. 'You're getting as melodramatic as your girls.'

'So big old locked double door covered by thick drapes separating old ladies who play bingo from villains gives us nothing to worry about, then? Is that what you're saying?'

'Yeah. That's about the long and short of it, Alice. We're living in the East End, darling. You should read your 'istory books, sweetheart. It's a lot safer for ordinary people to walk about in the back streets now than it ever was. Crime, violence, drug dealing . . . opium dens in Chinatown – it was part and parcel for centuries! Before I was even a twinkle in my father's eye. My own grandmother used to smoke opium with the Chinese down by the docks. She liked the Chinese – got on well with 'em.'

This was too much for Cathy, who cracked up with laughter. 'I'd love to have known your grandma, Nan. She sounds like a real character.'

'Not really. She wasn't any different to me. All right, she was on the game at fifteen, but she was fussy. And a stunner. No fourpenny trick for her. Oh no. She danced with the best of 'em, did your great-great-grandmother. The rich and wealthy came into the music hall in Aldgate to watch her performance and then go into her boudoir. She knew what she was doing. Canny mare. Your sisters have got my grandmother Eliza's blood running through their veins all right.' Molly glanced at Alice and added, 'And you're worried about a billiard hall and a bit of gambling. Do me a favour.'

'But Mum has got a point, though, Nan. The Mile End snooker club has been in the East End papers lately.'

'Yeah? And that's probably been going on since the thirties. Go and ask Johnny in the front room what he thinks. He was jumping on a bus from Stratford East before he'd turned thirteen to sneak in and watch a game of snooker. His dad and uncles 'ave been going there for years, and a more astute family you couldn't wish to know. If it was a bad trouble spot they wouldn't go there. It's a Mickey Mouse gambling sport, that's all.'

'I didn't hear Johnny come in,' said Cathy, speaking before she thought and sounding more charmed over it than she would like the others to have picked up on.

'That's because you were miles away – daydreaming about your new job, no doubt,' said Molly. And then, grinning at Cathy, added, 'I think I can see the look of love in those eyes. Bit soft on 'im, are yer?'

'No, Nan. I just said that I didn't hear anyone come in, that's all.'

'All right. Don't get aerated or we'll be thinking you've taken a secret shine to 'im. You could go and ask him what he thinks about the snooker club. Stop your mother from worrying.'

'No, that's all right, Nan. I'm fine where I am. And if I want to go in the front room I'll go.'

Molly turned to Alice. 'Well, go on, then. You go and ask him.'

Alice knew there wasn't any point arguing with her mother when she was in this mood, and Cathy certainly wasn't going to give her nan food for thought. She liked Johnny – of course she did. Who wouldn't? He was tall, blond and blue-eyed. But he would hardly be interested in her, she thought. And it was true: he did play in snooker tournaments at the club with his pals. And on the surface, so far as this family was concerned, Johnny was a lovely unassuming chap.

The club in the Mile End Road, like others in and around East London, had a good atmosphere but more and more shady characters had drifted in from Hackney, Bethnal Green and Shoreditch and this had tended to change its local clubbiness and taint the ambience. Young men turned up who without a doubt had been influenced by one American gangster movie too many. There was always a new set of villains coming along, following in the footsteps of their heroes such as the spivs of the forties and fifties who had worked the clubs in the South, North, and West of London as well as the East End. Local lads, flash twin brothers, had run the East End for more than a decade before, after the longest-ever Old Bailey trial, they were found guilty of murder and locked up for life.

Cathy's sisters had enjoyed a drink with the twins in the past. In the Kentucky Club in the Mile End Road, celebrating the gala premiere of the film *Sparrows Can't Sing*, they had rubbed shoulders with film stars and gangsters under the star-spangled ceiling. By then the fame and power of brothers Ronnie and Reggie Kray from Bethnal Green had spread and they were seen as celebrities themselves. The one good thing for the traders during and after the murder trial following the shooting in the Blind Beggar pub was the surge of tourists that came into Whitechapel, as they had when Jack the Ripper hit the headlines nearly a century earlier. The East End had suddenly become a fashionable place for the pilgrims again.

Letting her mum and nan argue the toss as to whether her sisters were inching further into the criminal fraternity or not, Cathy got ready for a long soak. She couldn't believe that she wouldn't be going into that grim and stuffy office building as usual on Monday, but walking up the wide staircase of a large modern structure with wide picture windows to begin a new life. She couldn't wait to celebrate with her girlfriends.

'I'll dish my own stew up a bit later on, Nan,' she said as she stubbed out her cigarette in the glass ashtray.

Just as she was leaving to run a bath she saw Johnny coming along the passage, and giving her a lovely smile which took her by surprise. He looked a touch embarrassed as he said, 'I don't suppose you fancy coming out with me for a drink, do you, Cath? Celebrate the fact that you're changing jobs? What d'yer reckon?'

'I would, Johnny,' she replied, 'but I've got to get ready for a night out with my mates. They're calling round about half eight.'

'So?' He glanced at his Rolex wristwatch. 'It's not late. You can spare twenty minutes to come and 'ave a short with me. Come on – don't be boring.'

'What – and Nan's local's not boring?' she said, smiling and showing her perfect white teeth.

'Not really. It's a nice old-fashioned pub with a publican who just happens to sell the best pint of beer I've tasted yet.'

This new and gallant approach from a man she had always secretly had a crush on was sending a warm thrill all the way down to her toes. 'All right, then. Why not? But I warn you . . . I packed in my job today after two years so I might start to shed a tear or two.'

He gave her a cheeky wink. 'I've got a clean hanky and a broad shoulder to cry on.'

'Oh, for Christ's sake! Get yourselves going before I cry my eyes out,' said Molly. 'You'll 'ave us all in tears at this rate. You're as bad as them slushy old black and white films.'

'Thanks, Nan!' said Cathy facetiously as she grabbed her coat off the armchair. 'Lead the way, Johnny. I do need a drink, as it just so happens!'

When she heard the front door slam shut behind them, Molly grinned and gave Alice a wink. She was pleased as punch to see the pair of them going out together. 'I thought that daft sod would never ask her out. Love's young dream or what?' A silence fell between the two women, who were both thinking similar thoughts: that it was a shame a lad such as Johnny had to be born into a long line of heavy gamblers.

'They're only going for a drink,' murmured Alice. 'And in that old smelly local. Hardly romantic.'

'Oh – listen to it. Who just tried to drum into madam that she should stay away from pubs and clubs? All that rubbish about gangs and villains.'

'I wasn't talking about our local. And anyway – some of it was true.'

'Half of it might have been, but not much has changed since you was 'er age, Alice. Since you was fifteen you was always out dancing with the spivs and flaunting your good looks. Cathy's got a sensible head on them shoulders. Not her sisters, though. They're the ones you should worry over. Too used to places like the Double R Club with its classy flock wallpaper and furniture to suit the villains.'

'Oh, so you've been in there then, Mum, have you?' said Alice, tongue in cheek.

'Yes. I 'ave as a matter of fact. To do a bit of cleaning when a mate of mine had the flu. She 'ad a right cushy little number, I can tell you. Cash in hand and twice as much as you'd get paid anywhere else. I hung about till seven o clock one time, out the back, polishing where it didn't need to be polished, just so I could 'ave a look at the celebrities. It was like Hollywood *and* Las Vegas at times.'

'Don't exaggerate. My Marilyn and Ava go in there and they reckon they've seen better in the back and beyond of Soho.'

'I'm sure them two will have done. You'll have hard core criminals for sons-in-law if you're not careful. Villians and flash boys with more money than sense. Your daughters are getting too used to the high life, Alice.'

'They're old enough to know their own minds. And they rely on no one. My girls make their own way and pay their own rent.'

'Yeah . . . from nicking gear from the posh stores up West.'

Coming into the living room, Jim looked pleased with

himself. 'Bit of a turn up for the book, innit?' He jerked a thumb over his shoulder and raised an eyebrow. 'Never thought he'd ask 'er.'

'I s'pose you egged 'im on,' said Molly.

'I never had to. He's been soft on 'er for a while.' Jim glanced at his watch and smiled. 'Vera Lynn's on the telly in ten minutes' time. I've bin looking forward to this all week.'

'So've I.' Molly smiled. 'We'll eat our stew while we're watching it. How's that suit yer?'

'Suits me fine,' said Jim. 'What about you, Alice love? You gonna watch it?'

'No. I'm going into the other room to listen to a bit of light music on Three. Vera Lynn reminds me of the war and I'd prefer to leave all that behind, thank you.'

'She's gonna be talking in between the bloke playing records, love,' said Jim. 'About her *life*. Not the *war*.'

'She still makes me think about it, and I don't want to. I'll listen to the wireless while I eat. Fetch mine in, will you, Mum?' With that Alice swanned out of the back room.

'La-de-da cow,' whispered Molly. In truth she was glad that her daughter was opting out of watching. She could be a wet rag at times. 'Switch on and let the telly warm up while I dish up, Jim.'

Quietly sighing, Jim relaxed back in the small armchair by the tiny fireplace. He had no intention of turning the box on until his wife was content and settled with her dinner in the front room. Keeping her happy was high on his list of priorities now that she, the person closest to his heart, was the breadwinner. He was happy enough to sit and think about Vera Lynn and cast his mind back to 1939, when he had fantasised about her being his wartime sweetheart, because she lived then in Barking, close to his brother and sister-in-law's family.

'So I'm to take her dinner into her, am I? On a silver plate if I can find one.'

'No. An old tin one'll do.

'I should cocoa. We might not be rich, but scorn the day when we 'ave to eat off anything but bone china.'

'My brother used to live close to Vera Lynn.'

'I know that, Jim. You've told me before – and more than once.'

'He got himself one of them Amardian Homes. They were fairly new at the time. In 1939 they offered a bright sunny kitchen, a spacious lounge, three bedrooms and a tiled bathroom for a down payment of a pound note and weekly payments of thirteen shillings and sixpence. A lot of money to stretch to in those days. But my brother, being the clever Dick in the family, got himself a mortgage from the bank and never looked back. He wasn't only buying his own house but living a stone's throw away from the lovely Vera Lynn.'

Thinking about his own missed opportunities, Jim didn't hear the tapping on the back door. But Molly did. She could see Rosie's lodger Henry from next door through the back window and beckoned the lad in, murmuring, 'He needs a good sunshine holiday, that one. Pale as a ghost.'

'Who?' said Jim.

'Who d'yer think? There's only one lad who can step over the back fence into our yard.'

'Back garden, if you don't mind,' said Jim, a smile on his face as he nodded hello to Henry as he came in through the kitchen.

'I wanted to ask you about your daily paper, Jim. Whether you want to change from—'

'No, that's all right, son,' Jim cut in, having been asked this question many times before. 'But come and take the weight off your feet.'

'Shall I dish you up a bit of my stew, cock?' said Molly. 'I've made plenty.'

'No, but thank you all the same. I shall be eating supper soon. I've opened one of those tinned meat pies that Rosie and George like. It's in the oven now. We're having it with tinned peas and mashed-with-butter potatoes.'

'That sounds lovely, son,' said Jim, giving Molly a warning

look before she went on about fresh meat and vegetables being healthier, as was her wont.

Henry lowered himself into the armchair opposite Jim. Then, cupping his chin thoughtfully, he said, 'I have some news to upset you. I think you should prepare yourself. Take a deep breath and count to ten.'

'Oh,' said Jim, wondering what might be coming next. Bad news from this young man was a first. 'And what might that be, Henry?'

'Some of our neighbours have suffered a tragedy. Becky and Leo have lost their beloved pet. Their cat, Pongo, has passed away.'

'Oh, no!' said Molly, wiping her hands on her paisley pinafore. 'They loved that animal as if it were a child. I 'ope it never got run over. It's them bloody motor bikes zooming around.'

Henry showed her the flat of his hand and spoke quietly, saying, 'Let's not jump to conclusions, Molly. The cat did not meet with an accident in the street. And furthermore I have buried it in their garden. This is what they wanted.' He looked from Molly to the stove. 'I must say that stew does smell quite delicious. Perhaps you could give the recipe to Rosie?'

'It's not a recipe, son – it's down-to-earth stew,' said Jim. 'Chuck it all in a pot and wait.'

'Cheers for that,' said Molly. 'It's good to know I'm no more than a robot.'

'I'm sure your son didn't mean—'

'Son-in-law, if you don't mind, Henry. If I 'ad 'ave had a son he'd have been good-looking.'

Henry smiled and then said, 'I wish I wasn't the bringer of bad news, but at least I can tell you that Rosie and George's dog is fine. I left it fretting by the fire. The hound knows by instinct that his friend the cat is dead. You might have heard him crying earlier.'

'No, I never,' said Molly. 'But that's because these walls, unlike them flats they keep building, are fairly soundproof.'

'They played together all the time. The mongrel and the cat. But then I expect you knew this.'

'Course we did,' said Molly. 'Stop talking like that, Henry. Be normal.'

'Molly . . . I have not long since buried a pet. A pet that I was very fond of. I've managed to soften the blow for the old couple, and I was trying to do the same for you. Now would you like me to tell you something which I thought a bit strange?'

'No . . . that's all right, son. You keep it close to your chest,' said Molly.

'I found a small gold cross in our garden last week,' he continued remorselessly. 'While I was digging horse droppings into the rose beds. I think it might have been an omen. For the old couple's cat, I mean – which is why I felt that *I* should bury it. I placed the cross just beneath the earth so that nobody could see it. But now I'm wondering if the cross might belong to one of you. If so, I'll fetch it.'

'No, none of us lost a cross, Henry,' said Molly, 'and we're all sorry about the cat. But then again, it has been slow for ages and on death's doorstep. So it was time.'

'Yes, I agree. I dug the grave good and deep.' Henry studied the palm of his hand and the blisters. I should have waited until we had had a storm, I suppose. Torrential rain would have softened the ground. It was rock-hard.'

'You're a good lad, Henry. Thoughtful.' Jim gave him a fatherly wink and then rested back in his chair, now hungry and ready for his stew. He didn't want to make the lad feel as if he was in the way. But then neither did he want to get into a one-sided conversation with him about life and the universe, which he felt might be on the cards. He had heard it all before. His glance at Molly was a clear message that she ought to dish up dinner.

'Well, son – if you're not hungry, I am,' said Jim. 'So if you'll excuse us . . .'

Henry nodded and glanced out of the small back window.

'I think we'll need to trim that ivy next year, Jim. Clip it right back.'

'Ah, now that's more like it,' said Molly. 'Common sense. I've been telling Sir, here, to give it a clip for a while. If you see Becky tell 'er I'm sorry about Pongo, and that if I hear of any kittens going spare I'll let her know.'

'Yes, I will – and that's a lovely thought.' Henry cleared his throat and nudged his glasses back on to the bridge of his nose. 'I don't suppose Cathy's about, is she?'

'No, son,' said Jim. 'She's popped out for twenty minutes. Why? Did you want to see her about anything in particular?'

'No. I just wanted to tell her about the cat. She thought a great deal of Pongo.' He turned to Jim and gave him a studious look. 'And you're sure you're happy with your usual newspaper?'

'Yes, son. Quite content, thanks.'

Smiling amicably at his neighbours, Henry gave a polite nod and left the way he had entered as Molly shook her head despairingly. 'He must drive Rosie and George to distraction.'

'He's lonely, Molly. You know that. Lonely and harmless,' said Jim, a touch sorry for the lad.

An hour had flown by in the small pub on the corner of the street and Cathy was on her second port and lemon. She was listening to Johnny telling her that he wanted to find a bachelor pad so as to get away from his two sisters, who did little in the evenings other than watch television, munch chocolate and talk about the characters in *Coronation Street* as if they lived just around the corner and were best mates. 'I know this sounds a terrible thing to say, Cath, but I think if I lived away from home I might, just *might*, begin to see a side of them that I could take to.'

'Oh, come on. You don't mean that.' Cathy laughed. 'They're your sisters. Your flesh and blood.'

'I know – but they get right under my skin. Maybe I'm using it as an excuse for wanting to move out.'

'We'd all like a place of our own, if truth be known,' she

said. 'Providing we can come back for Sunday dinner and to collect our clean, ironed washing.'

Johnny laughed softly and then smiled, to set Cathy's heart beating a touch faster. He had the deepest blue eyes she had ever seen, and yet his hair was so blond as to be almost white. 'We'd best be on our way, or you won't have time to put on your glad rags to go out with your mates.'

Cathy raised her eyebrows as she checked her watch. 'I can't believe the time! It's flown by.'

'If I see you in the Black Boy I'll buy you a drink. I've seen you from across the crowded bar before, but couldn't quite pluck up the courage to move in on you and your mates.'

'Well, perhaps you will now.' She smiled. 'Come on. We'd best get back.'

Having left Jim and Alice to watch television together, Molly went round to her neighbour Rosie with a half-price, half bottle of brandy that they liked to use to spice up a decent cup of percolated coffee. She wasn't just giving Alice and Jim some time and space to themselves – Henry's news about the cat had upset her a bit. Like all her neighbours in this row of terraced houses, she had got used to the pet always being around like one of the family. She would also be able to see more clearly from Rosie's back yard, in the glow of the kitchen light, the place where the cat had been buried and to say a little private farewell.

At the door Molly smiled and asked, 'All right if I come in for a minute, Ro?'

'Of course it's all right. You don't even have to ask, Molly – you know that.'

'Well . . . the three of you might 'ave been eating your supper.'

'No. Come through. I've just washed up and George is out with his mates. Hackney Wick and then on for a jar or two. Henry's in his room reading.' She closed the door behind her friend and followed her along the passage. 'With a bit of luck

George might back some winners. I saw a fantastic spring outfit in Carnaby Street on my way home from work.'

Once in the back room Molly sank into a comfortable fireside chair and relaxed. 'Our Cathy's said something about going to that street for a browse around. That's your doing. I hope the stuff's not too dear, that's all.'

'More than we'd pay in Roman Road market – but then, you wouldn't get the same clothes there.'

'No, I shouldn't think you would do. They're good enough for me, though.'

'Anyway,' said Rosie as she filled her smart chrome kettle in the adjoining kitchen, 'it doesn't look as if I'll be having any children, Molly. The fertility drug doesn't seem to be working and I've only got a few more months before I'm taken off it. So what else am I gonna spend my money on other than nice outfits?'

'I could do with a new frock if you fancy treating me. I know you and George must 'ave it stashed away. Just like them granddaughters of mine. The gangster's molls.'

Rosie smiled. Her friend could brighten a sorry day without even trying. And since Rosie had lost her own gran she couldn't have wished for a better surrogate one than Molly. And as for Henry, she had taken him in not because she needed the rent money but because she felt sorry for him. Apart from the good salary she earned as a freelance stage manager, sometimes on small West End productions, her husband George made a decent living managing his own secondhand car business in Whitechapel. He also did a little bit of other business on the side with no questions asked because no answers would be given.

This couple, both in their thirties, could easily afford to live in a smarter area but neither wanted to. George, though always in made-to-measure suits and wearing gold cufflinks, could not risk appearing too affluent in case new and perhaps jealous neighbours who didn't know him had a quiet word with the law. But then George was an East End boy through and through, and had no desire to live among people who weren't his own kind. He was also fond of Henry and enjoyed treating him now and then, sometimes coming home with a smart shirt and tie for the lad when he had been shopping for himself. At the age of twelve Henry had been abandoned by his family and left to fend for himself, which as far as George was concerned was the cruellest thing that could have happened to him.

The couple were genuinely fond of the lad and had always seen him as a lonely soul. Besides, Rosie knew what it felt like to be unloved herself because her own mother had not cuddled her as a child. Instead she had been cherished and treasured by her grandmother, Harriet, who had always been there for her as well as her brother Tommy, her only sibling, who had been killed when in his late twenties. At the time it had all but destroyed Rosie.

Now, however, Rosie was happy and content in her modernised Victorian terraced house which she and George had painted white throughout – a fantastic contrast with the rich red fitted carpet. Her home was a place that both Cathy and her nan saw as somewhere they could come and go as if they were family. They loved the ambience, the antiques, pine furniture and the brass chandelier in the hall which cast a gentle light on the lovely old framed pictures. Molly also loved the familiar smell of beeswax polish and percolating coffee. Not that she always drank coffee. Tea was Molly's usual beverage.

Resting her head on a feather cushion propped on the fireside chair, Molly, with all thoughts of the cat on hold, said, 'I should think your granny Harriet would be proud as punch of you, darling, if she could look down from up there and see the way you've done this place up.'

'I know. I just wish she was here to see it.'

'Never mind. She lived life to the full.'

'You know what she wanted more than anything, Molly?' she said, handing her a cup of coffee spiked with a little brandy. 'To be a great-grandmother. I was the only one who could oblige – and I turned out to be barren.'

'Oh, don't use that word "barren". Anyway, you can always adopt a couple of kids.'

'I know. And that's just what I intend to do.'

'Oh, well now, that would be lovely!' Molly was thrown by this news. She sipped her coffee, then said after a few moments, 'You're a dark horse, you are. Fancy springing that on me. I think it's a smashing idea, but you wanna get a move on. How old are yer?'

'Thirty-one this year.'

'Is that all? I thought you was older than that. Well, that's it, then. That's the next step for you. You'll make good parents, you and your George. Even if he *is* a gangster.'

Rosie laughed. 'He's not a gangster.'

'No, course he's not. And nor are them thieving granddaughters of mine. I wish one of *them* would get up the spout. Then they'd know what was what. They must think they're film stars, the way they swan around.

'I've got a lot of respect for people who take on little orphan Annies – or orphan Alfies, as the case may be. You know what was once my secret dream? To run a lovely big old children's home in one of them ancient buildings that are standing empty all over the East End.'

'They're all gonna be turned into luxury flats,' said Rosie.

'Tell me about it. It makes my blood boil. *Our* buildings in *our* area that *we've* been paying rates for over the decades, and they close 'em down and sell 'em on. Greedy bastards. We need them buildings for the next generation. They soon shout the odds when kids hang around on the streets because there's nothing to occupy their minds. Vultures. That's what they are. Vultures at the top of the tree with no thought for the working classes at the bottom.'

'Molly . . . we've been down this road before. Think about the lovely new skyscrapers they're building instead. I wouldn't mind living in one. Big spacious rooms and picture windows. Up in the sky with the birds.'

'Yeah, right. A nice skyscraper that looks like a hospital.

Horrible things. You can't beat having your own back garden. I wouldn't feel safe in one of 'em. If those Irish labourers cut corners after a drink over the top while they're working, the whole fucking lot could come a cropper later on. It's all very well 'aving posh bathrooms and kitchens, but if the foundation ain't bang on – you're in the graveyard pushing up the daisies with the bricks and rubble.'

Amused by her friend, Rosie drew on her cigarette to make smoke rings. 'You should have gone on stage, Molly.'

'I've never been off it, sweetheart. Life is one big stage. Didn't anyone tell you? Oh, and by the way, Henry buried Becky and Leo's cat this afternoon.' Shifting in her seat, she rubbed her aching back. 'He seemed a bit depressed over it.'

'I know, he told me. He's a sensitive lad, is Henry. Becky and Leo loved that pet and he knows it. We'll all miss old moggy. Maybe we should treat the couple to a kitten?'

'They're too old to look after one now, Ro. Best leave it be . . . God, my shoulder blade hurts. I think I'll go back and run a nice hot bath. You won't mind if I take my brandy back with me, will you?'

'Why would I after all this time? You never forget to take it back with you!'

'Just testing.' Molly smiled as she pulled herself out of the comfortable armchair to leave Rosie to herself, her dreams of adopting children and her posh house with wall-to-wall carpet. All was well in that household, as far as she could tell . . . and with luck there would soon be the sound of the pattering of a poor little orphan's footsteps.

Not long after Molly had gone the sudden crashing of breaking glass made Rosie go cold. Quickly but cautiously she went to her street door and opened it, to see in the glow of the street lamp three lads of about fourteen yelling insults in the narrow quiet turning outside her Jewish neighbours' home. Seeing Rosie glaring at them, the boys turned away. The next to appear on her doorstep was Molly, who looked from the smashed window to the lads and shook her fist as she shouted, 'You little bastards!'

'Watch your language, foul woman!' came the phoney theatrical reply. 'You wouldn't like a brick through your windowpane, would you?'

'I take it you're happy to live next door to the poor Jew?' retorted another.

'Come back down this street again, you little bastards,' said Molly, 'and your arse will feel the heel of my boot! You should be *ashamed* of yourselves!'

'Leave it,' advised Rosie. 'They're the sort who come back for more if they get that kind of response, Molly.'

'Tell the old Jew born in a workhouse to keep away from our family! She's nothing to do with us! Take the brick as a warning!'

'Bastards,' murmured Molly, too angry to yell at them further. She cursed herself for not being younger and able to chase them off. 'Hung, strung and quartered – that's what they deserve. Posh little bastards.' She turned to her old Jewish neighbour, who was now standing in her doorway and trembling. 'I bet you they're from the college, Becky. Little sods.'

'No,' said Becky, her face tightening as she tried so desperately to stay calm. 'They're not from the college. Leave it be.' She slowly shook her head and sighed. 'All I wanted was to find my family. It doesn't matter. None of it matters.'

Baffled by this, Molly eyed Rosie who simply shrugged. She had no idea what her neighbour was talking about either. 'Go back inside, Becky, and I'll come in once they're well and truly out of sight,' she said.

'Don't make a fuss. I don't want any trouble,' mumbled Becky as she nervously glanced along the street. She then covered her face with her shaking hands, doing her best and managing not to break down.

Once inside the Hanovitches' passage, with Rosie following, Molly held the old lady's arm and walked her slowly into the back room as Becky's resolve not to cry broke and tears trickled down her lined, sagging cheeks. She was repeating over and over, 'I didn't mean any harm. I don't want anything from anyone.'

'That's all right, sweetheart,' whispered Molly. 'They won't be back, don't you worry.' What she didn't say was that she had picked up a train ticket that one of the lads had dropped. It would seem that the boys had come in from Buckhurst Hill, on the fringe of Essex. This she kept to herself for the time being.

'I think I know who they might be,' said Becky's husband Leo. 'This isn't the first time. Once before they banged on the knocker after they had pushed a disgusting note through the door. I won't even tell you what it said. I screwed it up and chucked it on the fire before Becky saw it. All she wanted for God's sake was to find her family.' He tried to hide the fact that his own hands were trembling. 'After years of searching this is what happens. I never heard such a thing.'

'Don't you worry, Leo!' Molly raised her voice slightly in the usual way when speaking to the old boy, who was partially deaf. 'I've seen their faces. I'll make sure the little bastards won't come back again.' She went quiet for a moment and then said, 'What do you mean? Years of searching?'

Leo flapped a hand and shook his head. 'Leave it be, Molly. Leave it be.'

Rosie, who believed that if anyone could get the truth out of the old couple Molly could, went through to the back to make a pot of tea. She manoeuvred around Leo's slim-line walking frame, an aid that he occasionally had to use when his legs were playing up in damp weather. Rosie's husband George had had it made specially by a friend who worked in the local metal foundry – it was light enough for Leo to manage, and took up little space once folded and leaning against the kitchen wall. Resting against the sink, Rosie folded her arms and forced herself not to show her emotions. She was not only angry but upset for the couple. Half-watching Molly and Leo through the open doorway, she busied herself filling the kettle in the small, crammed kitchen with its flowery linen curtain at the window to match the one across the larder doorway. Molly had run them up for Leo and Becky on her small hand sewing machine. The once spacious walk-in larder now housed a small white toilet suite, and the full-length curtain gave it absolute privacy. The old outside lavatory had just a couple of years previously been ripped out by George and a friend, and the little brick building was now in use as a storage shed for garden tools and everything else but the kitchen sink.

All things considered, the old couple's home was spotless, and the only smell in the air was that of Dettol and oil of lavender. Fortunately, in this area the welfare service was excellent and old people such as Becky and Leo had regular home helps coming in to clean their houses as well as having Meals on Wheels deliver hot dinners daily. Still wondering why anybody would want to throw a brick through the window, Rosie made a mental note to buy her old neighbours an electric kettle to make things a bit easier for them.

Next to the sink was a free-standing cupboard with a Formica surface and electric points within easy reach. A portable battery-powered radio stood on the windowsill for use inside the house and out in the garden when they were enjoying spring and summer days on their deckchairs. In this household the sound of the wireless was part of their way of life – more so than the television. Hoping the couple wouldn't notice, Rosie switched off the radio because she personally couldn't bear the intrusion of invisible strangers constantly talking in the background.

The sound of Becky weeping in the adjoining room was upsetting, even though she could hear Molly assuring the old folk that George would have the window repaired in no time and that meanwhile she would get Henry to tack a piece of hardboard over the broken pane.

'I don't care about the window,' said Becky. 'We hardly use the front room these days. We're happy in here . . . in our snug by the fire.' Her eyes fixed on the floor, she slowly shook her head. 'That my own flesh and blood should do such a thing. It doesn't bear thinking about, does it? I feel ashamed of them.'

Rosie glanced at Molly and said, 'What are you talking about, sweetheart – your own family? They were twits from the college bored out of their brains, weren't they? Too much time on their hands – that's what that was all about, wasn't it?'

'No. I don't think so.' Becky, more at ease now that she was settled back in her fireside chair, drew wispy grey hairs off her face. That face, which had been beautiful when young, was now lined and pale. But even at her age she always wore a little rose-pink lipstick and Yardley's face powder. Her soft silver-grey hair was swept back with tortoiseshell combs.

'I told her not to bother!' said Leo, hunching his shoulders and waving his hands. 'I said she should leave things be. If they wanted to find her they could have done so years ago. Who bloody well needs relatives, in any case? We've got good friends and neighbours and you can't ask for more than that. Why suddenly want to see bloody relatives? Sod them. Leave them be.'

'Be quiet, Leo,' said Becky. 'Give it a rest.'

'Ask Molly and Rosie. Go on. Ask them.' The old boy looked from his wife to his neighbours. 'Would you give a toss if you never saw any of your relatives again?'

'I should say I would,' Molly replied. She glanced at Becky's face, full of misery, and saw that she was trying not to shed any more tears. Lowering herself to her knees so she could look into the poor soul's eyes, she took her old neighbour's bony hands and squeezed them, saying, 'What is it, sweetheart? What's brought all this on? It can't just be the broken window. Windows get smashed by kids every day of the week all over London.'

'She's been trying for bloody years to find her half-brother and sister. I told her not to bother. I said—'

'Shut up, Leo! I'm talking to Becky, not you,' interrupted Molly.

'All I'm saying is that it wouldn't bother me if I never saw any of my family again – so why must she look for hers?' Leo sniffed.

'That's because yours come and go all of the time. You've often got one of your brothers or cousins to play dominoes or cards for pennies.'

'I don't know why *you're* getting your knickers in a twist, Molly,' Leo sighed. 'It's not *your* bloody window that's been broken. You won't have to foot the bill for it.'

'No, and neither will you. The council will fix it, as well you know. So shut up for five minutes and let Becky speak. It'll make a nice change.'

Used to her husband, and letting most of what he said go in one ear and out the other, Becky spoke in a whisper. 'I just needed to fill in the blank spaces, Molly. That was all. Find my roots.' She looked into her friend's face and smiled faintly. 'I have a brother and a sister living in Buckhurst Hill that I knew nothing about until I made it my business to. I looked into things. For myself and no one else.'

Lost for words – unusual for Molly – she peered at the old woman. If it was true, and Becky had suddenly found out about a family, what did this have to do with boys throwing a brick through her window?

Becky and Leo gradually relaxed in Molly's company and privately thanked God for this woman, this neighbour . . . this saint who spoke her mind no matter what and never cut anyone with her words. Molly was one of the best friends they could have wished to have as a neighbour. But even she couldn't make up for what had happened. The broken window was giving Becky a clear message: 'Stay out of our world . . . you old Jew.'

Back from the pub, and having made arrangements to see Johnny later on in the Black Boy, Cathy, with big rollers in her shoulder-length hair and still wearing her housecoat after her bath, was getting ready for a night out. On the surface she looked quite calm, but inside she was glowing. She and Johnny had strolled to the pub, chatting quietly about Cathy leaving her job. She had told him how apprehensive she was, deep down, about going into a world she knew nothing about, and he had said that it didn't matter – if it was horrible, all she had to do was leave. He made it sound so easy and matter-of-fact that she wondered why she hadn't seen it in the same light herself. She realised, while sitting in the quiet little pub with Johnny, that her anxieties had probably come from the fact that she had only ever worked for one company and that the regime at Gottard's was so rigid and archaic. Johnny had managed not only to put her mind at ease but to make her feel confident that she would be fine that coming Monday morning. Outside her house, and not on a social call to see her dad, he seemed so different. He had been easy to talk to, and his lovely, warm, friendly smile just melted her.

Having picked up on all that was happening at Becky and Leo's, Cathy found some strong, thick cardboard in her dad's shed to cover the broken windowpane and keep the January cold out. From the small back garden she could see Henry standing in Rosie's back doorway and knew that he would be only too willing to cut the cardboard and fit it. Not only willing, but flattered to be asked. She waved him over, and he listened intently to Cathy's brief and to-the-point instructions.

'Do we know who did this and why?' he enquired.

'I don't think it's the time for questions, Henry. Let's just do what's necessary, eh?'

'Have you never been told, Cathy,' he said, a touch patronisingly, 'that half a story is worse than having been told the whole of it, no matter how dark or upsetting the piece left out might be? When are you going to stop treating me like a child?'

'I'm not, and it's only a broken window,' said Cathy. 'This is not the time for us to have a debate. Just do what's necessary and fix the cardboard into the window frame for the old couple. The window was broken by kids throwing a brick. It happens. It happens all of the time. It's no big deal.'

'I see. And you think we should let it be. Ignore it?'

'Well, no, but first things first. It needs fixing to keep out the cold air. The freezing cold air. Tomorrow we can discuss it over a cup of tea. It's a Saturday – my day off.'

He looked thoughtfully into her face and then shook his head. 'You seem a bit highly strung tonight, Cathy. Do you think this might be because you went against my advice and left a perfectly good job with no sound reason?'

'No, I don't.' She pushed her face up close and spoke quietly: 'Fix the sodding window.'

She shoved the cardboard into his hands and went back indoors to get ready to escape into the magic of a Friday night out with the girls and to see Johnny and his mates on their pub crawl. She did like Henry, and saw him as a brother figure who sometimes warmed her heart and sometimes irritated her. There were occasions when she felt as if she could strangle him when he wouldn't leave off his innocuous questions to which straight answers couldn't always be found or weren't actually necessary.

'I'll speak to you later, Cathy!' he called out once he was over the fence and in Becky's back yard with the cardboard.

Inside their home, he was taken aback to see Becky in a flood of tears and wringing her hands. He looked from her to Leo, and saw that he too was covering his face. Stepping up to Molly, who was still there, he murmured, 'This is when a shot of whisky or brandy is required. Do you have any in the house?'

His immediate grasp of the situation with none of the usual questions took Molly by surprise. She nodded and said she would go next door and fetch her small bottle of brandy. She could tell by Henry's expression that he knew more than she did as to why a brick had been thrown at the old couple's window, and decided she would find out more later on once she could get Henry to herself for a quiet word. He was the closest person to the old couple, after all was said and done. They had been more like parents to him than his own had been, and she knew that over the years he had talked intimately to Becky about each of their sorry pasts. Becky and Leo had known him since the day he was born.

Henry's parents had not only abandoned him when a boy but shown no affection towards him even as a baby, and since Leo and Becky had lived in the street for all their married life they were well versed in the history of his family. There had been three children before him, and three had clearly been more than enough for his mother to cope with – or *want* to cope with. Henry's father had gone out most evenings to the local pub, leaving his wife to look after their two small sons and little girl. Then Henry arrived in the world, bald and pink and forever crying from hunger or wanting a nappy change. Becky and Leo often heard him wailing pitifully day and night from neglect because his mother had had enough of the paraphernalia that went with new babies. She had told Becky and Leo from the start that she was going to give Henry up for adoption, and sometimes offered him to people in their street.

Had it not been for his excellent lungs and vocal cords when he was a baby he might not have been fed or cleaned all day long. But he had survived it all, mostly because this lovely Jewish couple had not only been there to lend a hand but had taken him in when he was abandoned altogether. The couple had grown to love him and he spent many hours playing in their back garden, or sitting by their coal fire in the winter.

The worst thing of all for the couple in those early days had been when, during the evenings and at night, they could hear him through the party wall crying pitifully in his cot until he finally wore himself out and fell asleep. So in a sense he and Becky had something in common. Rejection. The only difference was that Becky had been born in a workhouse and then placed in a wretched children's home in Bethnal Green, whereas Henry had been ignored by his mother from birth and then left behind when his family moved away from London.

Glancing from Becky to Leo, Henry slowly shook his head and then, addressing Molly, said, 'I think I know who might be responsible for this – for breaking the window. You can leave this to me now.' He knew because the old couple had told him they had been to Buckhurst Hill and why.

'You know?' said Molly. 'Well, don't you think the rest of us should be clued in? Getting a brick thrown at your window is bad enough – but an old couple? If you know who did it, son, I think you're gonna have to let Rosie and George know, don't you?'

Henry gave her a look as if to say, 'You don't understand, so leave it be.' Doing her best to be calm and collected she smiled for the sake of Becky, who was still wringing her hands, and said, 'I'll stop and make you a nice milky drink, shall I?'

'It's all right, Molly,' said Leo. 'We'll be fine. You've been very kind, but we'll be okay now.'

'What about you, Becky?'

Leo looked back at his wife and spoke gently to her. 'Would you like Molly to stay with you, Becky?'

'I don't know,' said the old woman as she lowered herself into her armchair by the small fire burning in the grate. 'I just don't know.'

'Becky, sweetheart,' said Molly, lowering herself to her knees so she could look into this lovely woman's sad face. 'The little sods around this way think it's a new game. You're not the first one, sweetheart. And we can get a new pane put in there first thing tomorrow.'

'I think I'm supposed to feel ashamed about my past – but I'm not. It's not something to be ashamed of. I'm proud of my mother. It must have taken a lot of courage for her to leave me with strangers when I was a baby.'

'Too right,' said Molly. 'Proud, sweetheart, is what you should feel . . . so why are you still tormenting yourself over something that happened a lifetime ago?'

Becky looked into Molly's face. 'My father, whoever he was and God rest his soul, was a Jew, my mother a Christian. But of course you know all of this already. I told you before that I have a brother and sister who didn't even know I existed.'

'*Didn't* know?' said Molly. 'What do you mean, sweetheart? Are you saying that they do now?'

'I told Henry about it and he never said a word to you, did

he? He's such a good boy. Trustworthy.' She lifted her face to look at Henry and smiled softly at him. 'This young man has been more of a son to us than a neighbour. My own family probably never even knew I existed.'

'They do now,' said Leo. 'She wrote a letter. I told her not to bother. But would she listen? Of course she wouldn't.'

'I can't believe that any family would allow the younger generation to throw a brick through the window of an ageing relative,' Becky went on. 'How could anybody do such a thing? I wrote them that I was going on eighty. I didn't ask for anything. I just said I would like to get in touch and meet my brother or my sister. I feel as if I've missed out on my family. Who knows, maybe we would love each other?'

'Their offspring put a brick through the window, didn't they?' said Leo, fed up with it all. 'You're a silly cow at times, you know. Forget it. Who needs those sorts of people? You've got me. And you've got Henry and our friends and neighbours as well as our own daughter's family, even if they do live a million miles away. Who needs brothers and sisters? They're a pain in the bloody neck, in any case. Mine are . . . And Buckhurst Hill – you think the people who live there would be like us? It's a bloody posh area. People with a bit of money live there. It's right next door to bloody Chigwell, where the rich footballers live. Well, one or two of them in any case. Bobby Moore . . . I think.'

'All I wanted was to find my brother and sister,' murmured Becky. 'That's all.'

'I wish to God she'd never discovered that she had a sister and a brother. A waste of bloody time and train fares. We went to Somerset House to look up the surname on her birth certificate a few years back and it became a bloody mission. At least she had one, though. She had a birth certificate. How that came about, God only knows. We went backwards and forwards to that place and spent hours searching volumes until we found the name. A waste of bloody time. What has she got from it? A nasty warning note through the door and then a brick through the window.'

Becky shook her head sadly. 'My mother is dead – of course she is. I'm almost eighty myself, give or take a couple of months. I was born in a workhouse and then placed in that awful children's home. I ran away when I was thirteen, before they could send me to live with a family in the country and be their slave. You wouldn't believe some of the stories we heard about girls who had been sent to such places and by the grace of God managed to escape. After they were beaten, starved and raped. Nobody knows the truth. They should, but they don't.'

'I'm not so sure,' said Leo. 'I don't think I entirely agree with that. Why dish up dirt for dinner? It won't change anything. It still goes on, you can bet your bottom dollar. All under cloak and dagger. Bastards.'

'My mother did eventually marry, according to the records office. She was only fifteen when she had me and twenty when she married after being in service in a big house in the country for five years. And now I have relatives living in Buckhurst Hill in Essex.

We took the train, the underground, from Bethnal Green. They live in a beautiful house, in a very quiet cul-de-sac, not far from the station. We walked along the road looking for the name, which we eventually found on the entrance gate. A big double-fronted house it was, at the end of a tree-lined avenue.

It was beautiful. I didn't knock on the door. I just looked and saw a woman glancing out of a leaded glass window. I was going to turn back, but I didn't. I went up to the porch and pushed my letter through the box. The letter that said who I was and that I would like to see my half-sister and brother. We shared the same mother, after all. We came from the same womb.'

'And?' said Molly.

'Nobody came to the door. It doesn't matter. Nothing matters. Not now, anyway. I believe the lads that came to put a brick through the window are the younger generation. They came to warn me off, I think. I have a brother and a sister, I have nieces and nephews, but they don't want to know. And who can blame them? A poor Jewish bastard from the East End who was born in a workhouse knocks on their door and says she's a long-lost relative? No. I shouldn't have been such a silly cow. I shouldn't have gone.'

'Is there anything you want me to do?' said Molly, gently.

'No, I'll be fine. Henry will take care of things, once he's fixed the cardboard on the window. Henry makes a lovely cup of tea.' There was no more to say, but Molly knew that this was not something to be dropped. Buckhurst Hill was not that far away. Only a train ride on the underground.

Leaving Becky and Leo to Henry, Molly took her leave, safe in the knowledge that they were loved by the lad. The two pensioners had told Molly the story of Henry's sad upbringing when she first moved in with Jim and Alice. They had revealed that, in the beginning, they worried that by interfering in Henry's family business no good would come of it. They had feared that the small, thin child would be taken from his family and put into care. Becky had experienced this herself, and hadn't wanted the little boy to suffer what she had gone through. She hadn't quite been able to forgive herself for not doing more when Henry was an infant and neglected by a mother who seemed to have despised him. Long and skinny, with sunken cheeks, he had not been a baby that his mother had wanted to touch, never mind cuddle. His father hadn't been able to bear the constant crying – or at least this was the excuse he gave for going out every evening to the local for a game of darts. It had not been unusual for him to return home and fall immediately into his bed.

'*Get the little bastard adopted, for fuck's sake!*' was something Becky had heard through the walls between her house and theirs. This and '*Runt of the fucking litter, that one. You should 'ave drowned it at birth.*'

When Henry was a lad the family moved away to live in a brand-new council house on an estate built specially for London overspill in Basildon, and were never seen again. By design and not accident they had 'forgotten' to take Henry with them.

It was at this point that Becky and Leo had taken him in and looked after him as they had looked after their own daughter, their only child, long since married and now living in Canada with a family of her own. Later on, when Henry was sixteen, he decided that it was time to be independent, so he moved back into the attic room of the house next door to the old couple as a paying lodger. In with Rosie and George to the bedroom that was so familiar to him. The attic room where as a child he had lain in the dark for hours on end, waiting for the sun to shine through a gap in the curtains. Henry had learned what it was to be lonely during those times, when he had been left in the silent house by himself.

2

Cathy had had a wonderful Friday night out with her friends, having met up with Johnny and his mates in the Black Boy where he had drawn her into a quiet corner so they could chat by themselves. They had agreed to meet up the following afternoon in Whitechapel at a favourite coffee bar, Luigi's, a place aimed at the young with a great selection of records in the jukebox.

Sitting at their table for two in a corner of the Black Boy, Johnny, clearly besotted by Cathy, was doing little to hide the fact as he smiled into her eyes.

'I know we've both made arrangements for tomorrow night, Cath, but shall we contrive it so we're in the same pubs at the same time?' he said.

Cathy gently laughed at him. 'And you think no one would guess?'

'Not if we plan it.' He smiled. 'We could work it so I don't let my mates down on Saturday night and you can go out with your friends without upsetting them.'

'Why? Why don't we just go out by ourselves? Or would a whole evening with me be too much to take?'

'Course not. I'd love to do that. Much prefer it. But you know what the blokes are like. They picked up on my silly mood last night when I saw you across the bar, and took the Mickey out of me. They don't miss a trick. It's too soon to look like we're courting. Next weekend will be different. It's just tonight that we need to show I've not fallen head over heels.'

Doing her best not to laugh at him, Cathy blushed as she

said, 'Don't be daft! Head over heels? And even if you had . . . what's wrong with that?'

'They'd take the piss out of me. And that's the same with you girls . . . at least that's what us blokes think.'

'No, Johnny. It's not the same with us – no way. If you were to ask me to go out with you tonight just the two of us, I would do. I'd phone my friends, who live just around the corner, and tell them I'm going out with you and that would be that. It won't stop them from going out just because I'm not with them.'

'Fair enough. I suppose we're different, then. My mates would be miffed that I'd let a new girlfriend get under my skin enough to let them down on a weekend pub crawl.'

'Right,' said Cathy, leaning over the small table so that she almost touched his face. 'So which pubs are you and your mates going to, then? Let's start plotting.' She grinned. 'But it had better be a good plan if it's to be you who'll be taking me home tonight.'

'It'll be a brilliant plan,' he said, unable to stop looking at her beautiful face and love-me eyes.

That Saturday evening Cathy spent longer than usual getting herself ready. She was careful with her make-up, not wanting it to look too heavy or too light, and took more time styling her hair. Her final glance in the full-length mirror in her room said it all as far as she was concerned: there was nothing else she could do to improve her looks. What she saw was the best there was, and all she could hope was that among all the beautiful girls out there Johnny would like her the best. He was good-looking and he was cool. On Friday evenings in one of the pubs she had seen the way the girls were all over him. Why had he chosen her, she wondered, when he could have the pick of the crop?

Cathy, no Plain Jane, had had a few boyfriends since her first at fourteen and had thought herself to be in love every now and then, but this time it was different. She had fantasised about going out with Johnny during the visits he made to her dad, when he would sit in the front room for an hour or so chatting. Now he was going to pick her up in his car and stroll into the pub with her, telling his mates that he had seen her walking along and had stopped to give her a lift. Cathy found this kind of subterfuge strange, if not amusing, but when they got down to the finer details, with both of them laughing at the way they might engineer things, it became fun and she saw another side to Johnny that she had not seen before. Especially when he had said, 'This way I've got every reason to give you a lift home after the pubs are shut and we've all been for Chinese supper. My mates can take your mates home in a black cab.'

'It sounds mad, but let's go for it,' said Cathy, believing she had fallen in love.

Jim was chuffed to hear that his younger daughter was going out with the lad he liked and trusted. So, playing a game of rummy with Molly in the back room while Cathy was upstairs waiting for Johnny to knock on the door, he wasn't slow to give his mother-in-law a word of warning.

'If our Cathy wants to go straight out without Johnny coming in to say hello, Molly, you let her have her way. It's a little bit embarrassing for her, him being such a close friend of the family.'

'Yeah, all right, Jim. I don't need you to tell me that. I'm a woman. Our instincts are a lot stronger than men's are. I've not said one word to Cathy about this date. Not even a wry knowing smile on my lips.'

'Good,' said Alice as she came in from the kitchen where she had been pouring batter on to best sausages ready to go in the oven for their evening meal of Toad-in-the-hole. 'Just act natural, Mum.'

'Stone me!' Molly laughed. 'Anyone one would think it's Prince Charles coming to tea. It's only a date! And let's not forget the old saying, "Once a gambler, always a gambler" – and Johnny's from a gambling family! Let's not marry her off with him so soon.'

'Shush,' said Jim. 'Keep your voice down.'

The sound of the door knocker being tapped softly three times shut them all up as they listened for Cathy's footsteps above. 'You should open the door, Jim,' said Alice. 'She might not have heard it.'

'She heard,' grinned Molly. 'She turned her music off a few minutes ago so she'd hear.

'Don't wait up!' Cathy called out before opening the front door and slamming it shut behind her.

'There you are,' said Jim. 'I told you so. She doesn't want us to see them going out as a couple. It's embarrassing. Especially with you trying to cover a silly smile, Molly. Which you would be bound to do and she would be bound to see.'

'Shush, Jim, I'm listening,' said Alice, standing in the passage. 'Ah, good. They've gone by car. That means he doesn't intend to drink too much.'

'Either that or 'e's 'oping to get 'er in the back. Mind you, it's a Mini. But then, I've known men to like it in a broom cupboard,' Molly teased.

'Have you now, Mum?' said Alice. 'Pity Dad's not alive to hear that confession.'

'It's your father I'm talking about, sweetheart. If he saw a cardboard box that was big enough he'd have squeezed me in there.'

'Yeah, all right,' said Jim. 'That's enough of that talk. I won't have it. Not under my roof. I'm going in the front room for a quiet read. Pack the cards away, Molly, I'm not in the mood. I'll listen to a bit of wireless instead. And don't go and bolt the door out of habit tonight, either of you.'

Once he had left the room, Alice came in and sat with Molly at the table. 'See? Pretends he's not overly worried about our little girl, but can't stop 'imself reminding us not to bolt her out. As if we would forget. Men, eh? I still can't fathom them.'

'You never will, darling. Don't even try. They're a God unto themselves. And if you ask me, best it's left that way. The longer they lurk in their own little orbits the better. They always turn out to be damp squibs whether they mean to or not.'

'Jim's not that bad, though, is he?'

'Course he's not. You've got one of the best there, Alice. Think yourself lucky.'

'I do. He's one in a million. A brick.'

Cathy thoroughly enjoyed her evening out with her friends. They went to the young people's pubs, where she and the girls could enjoy a bit of idle gossip while Johnny talked football to his mates. And in the background for all of them was the sound of the jukebox playing the Troggs' 'Love Is All Around', Ava Everett's 'It's in His Kiss', Desmond Dekker's 'Israelites' and Sam and Dave's 'Soul Man'. The most meaningful, where Cathy and Johnny were concerned, was Gene Pitney singing 'Something's Gotten Hold of My Heart'. While this one was playing, Johnny had caught her eye from where he was standing in a small group with his mates. She had seen the expression on his face and the look in his eyes, and the smile that she returned gave him a silent message: '*I know what you mean.*'

Around midnight, after supper in a Chinese restaurant on the Mile End Road, Johnny took Cathy home in his second-hand Mini and parked just around the corner from where she lived. No more than heavy petting had gone on and, even though his breath had been hot on her neck, he had shown absolute respect for her before asking if he could take her out again during the week. Then he said goodnight and left her feeling as if she was in seventh heaven.

Now, just before dawn and semi-conscious, Cathy turned on to her side, curled into a ball and pulled her pillow over her face, hoping to go back to sleep and dream of Johnny. But the words she had heard her nan say to her dad the evening before floated into her mind: 'Once a gambler, always a gambler – and Johnny's from a gambling family.' She switched on her bedside lamp and glanced at the clock: it had only just turned seven-thirty. With the rest of her family asleep and the house silent, she could hear a couple of cats outside screeching at one another, then suddenly going quiet. No matter how hard she tried after plumping up her pillow and snuggling down in the bedclothes, she couldn't get back to sleep even though she was still tired. The more she tried, the more alert she became on this Sunday morning, her one chance for a lie-in. Eventually she gave in and got out of bed to pull on her warm dressing gown, creep out of her bedroom and quietly make her way down the stairs.

When she saw the *News of the World* on the doormat she smiled. Henry was very sweet and always made sure that their house was the first port of call on his Sunday paper round. He knew that her dad was usually the first one up and liked to sit in the quiet with the paper and a cup of tea before he was invaded by females. She was particularly pleased to see it there today because now she had something to read at this unearthly hour. Picking up the paper, she went into the kitchen to make herself a cup of coffee.

With her mug cupped in her hand Cathy curled up in the armchair by the fire, which still had a few embers glowing from the night before, and drew her legs up and under her to keep warm. Flicking through the paper on the lookout for a bit of celebrity gossip, her eye was caught by a quarter-page advert. A company in Aldgate were publicising fantastic colourful embroidered patches for stitching on to jeans, skirts or tops. Inspired by this, she sat in the silent room and imagined creating an outfit to wear when out with Johnny. A soft-coloured, long, flowing, lightly woven cotton skirt to swish around long brown boots, with a matching top from the Roman Road market decorated with these fabulous patches, all topped with a big floppy hat to match and a fabric shoulder bag to blend in. Before she had even thought about having a second cup of coffee, her mind was made up. She was going to use this time when she would normally be asleep to go to Petticoat Lane, where most places were traditionally open for Sunday trading.

Creeping back up to her bedroom, she pulled on her jeans

and a thick roll-neck sweater, then carried her Cuban-heeled
boots to the street door where her old faithful sheepskin coat
was hanging on a hook. Realising that she had not washed or
brushed her teeth so as not to wake the others, she made her
way first to a little tobacconist's to buy a packet of strong mints
to freshen her mouth. Once on Cambridge Heath Road she
found others who were also out and about and waiting to catch
the red double-decker which would stop at Aldgate, a stone's
throw from Middlesex Street, Petticoat Lane, Cutler Street and
Brick Lane. Like Cathy, most were on their way to the longest
lane in Britain, which would be crammed with stalls selling
everything bar the kitchen sink – and possibly even one or two
of those in one of the junk yards. Everything had a price in
that marketplace, where shoppers from all over London went
in search of a bargain from stallholders who auctioned their
wares out loud, each trying to outdo the other. Cruder, of
course, than the auction houses up West where antiques were
sold – but the loud cries from the old die-hard cockney merchants
were just as stimulating.

   The bus ride over, Cathy stepped off the platform to
squeeze her way through the bustling crowd of shoppers, stopping only when she came to a policeman on the beat to ask
directions to the creative fabric company. The friendly officer
knew exactly where it was – in Strype Street, a turning off
Petticoat Lane.

   When she arrived she was surprised to see a crowd of people
on the pavement outside the open heavy double doors with
their polished brass handles. Small, happy groups of different
ages, race and religion, male and female, merged together. She
liked the fact that they were in the same expectant, buoyant
mood as herself and that the advert in the Sunday paper was
obviously a success for this small, Jewish, family-run business.
Still feeling it was too early in the day for conversation, Cathy
stood in the shambolic queue smiling and just pleased to be
up and about. Had anyone told her the day before that her
mind would be on fashion rather than publishing, which she

was to enter into the very next day; she would have said they were crazy.

Smiling at a young Asian woman dressed in traditional clothes, Cathy could see why designers everywhere had suddenly been influenced by such people and why flower power and the colourful new look was growing so fast. The Beatles with their music and way of dressing had brought India's traditional garments to the eyes of the world, influencing people of her own age around the globe. People were even beginning to think like the Fab Four when it came to peace and freedom or thought and prayer.

Easing her way through the busy reception area of the typical early 1930s' building, she heard an echoing, clanking sound coming from the huge machines on one of the factory floors and resounding down the stairwell. There was a friendly atmosphere, with animated conversations going on between members of the public who had seen the advert and others within the trade who had been personally invited to what was clearly an open day event in the heart of the East End. Moving with the flow of people, she felt the adrenalin pumping as she and they followed signs pointing to the upstairs embroidery department, where there were goods for sale to the public as well as a small exhibition of samples on show for the trade.

Another sign which caught her eye told of a second demonstration at which large sheets of shiny metallic material were being cut by machine into tiny colourful sequins. Intrigued, she changed direction and went through an open doorway which led to a narrow staircase and up to where she could see die-stampers operating as they punched out purple, bright pink, indigo, light blue, gold and silver sequins, with each puncher serving a machine which fixed the shiny objects on to cotton thread. Everywhere that Cathy looked she saw sequins of all colours which had been strewn across the floor when a box overflowed. With the exception of one or two machines, all were turning out multicoloured sequined fabric which she thought was stunning. Then, eager to see the embroidery exhibition too,

Cathy left the packed area and went up to the next floor, where patchwork designs were in the process of being made, packaged and sold.

Once she had seen all that was on offer throughout the exhibition Cathy left, and outside in the fresh cold air she drew breath, unable to remember ever having felt so exhilarated. She glanced around, wishing Johnny was there with her to enjoy the buzz of it all and a cup of frothy coffee with her in the nearby café. As a small child Cathy had often come to Aldgate with her dad, holding his hand as they took the route across Cambridge Heath Road and into Three Colts Lane, to go through the animal market and cross over the busy Commercial Street. Then she had thought it a magical place – a place where thousands of people over the decades had packed into the narrow turnings between the sweatshops and old factories, and where stalls still pitched up on every available bombsite which had been cleared and flattened for the market vendors on Sundays and for children to use as a rough playground during the week. It was on Sunday mornings that Aldgate really came alive, the closest London got to compete with a colourful Eastern bazaar.

In Dickens's time, of course, a gentleman could walk through this long market to find his own handkerchief or empty wallet set out on a stall for sale at the other end – thanks to a pickpocket who had been at work. Petticoat Lane and Brick Lane had always been a thieves' paradise where nimble-fingered pickpockets and innocent-looking con artists were as expert in the mid-twentieth century as they had ever been. The only risk for a child had been being squashed or losing grip of the parental hand and getting lost in the sea of legs amid the confusing noise of the street vendors calling out to people in the crowds as if they were long-lost friends. They would use every trick in the book to draw in the punters, and today was no exception. Cathy moved with the throng and, even though she was used to that neck of the wood, was invigorated by the mix of people, the usual cockneys along with the well-heeled folk from more refined parts of London. Then there was the Jewish sector, the Asian and the West Indian patch, not forgetting of course, the Chinese – East London's earliest immigrants. She had seen it all before, but today with this new glow in her heart she was looking at it in a new light.

Standing out in the noisy crowd was the racing tipster and somewhat notorious African Zulu figure with his pink feathers who had named himself Prince Monolulu, and not only came into the Lane on Sundays but travelled on the tube between Aldgate and the Tottenham Court Road during the week. He was a character known sometimes to make the girls shriek by pulling weird and wonderful faces. And in the distance Cathy could just hear the Salvation Army band and the call of the sandwich-board wearers who walked up and down denouncing the Jews for trading on Sunday mornings – the good Lord's day of rest. This was an ordinary scene in the East End.

Cathy's nan, when not going on about the war, had often told her and her sisters tales of this part of London, where women sat outside their street doors rather than inside their dark and dingy homes. The area was a mine of interesting stories, but one in particular that most East Enders knew since it had been passed from one generation to another was that of the infamous Dick Turpin.

In the 1700s, on a bustling Saturday night at the Red Lion Inn in Whitechapel, the innkeeper was looking after a thoroughbred mare for someone who turned out to be the highway robber who, along with a friend, had mugged a gentleman in Epping Forest in order to steal his purse and horse. The gentleman happened to go into the Red Lion a week or so later, and saw his thoroughbred stabled there. He asked the innkeeper who owned the mare and was given the names of the two men. The gentleman immediately booked a bed in order to lie in wait and be there the next morning when the robbers were due to return to collect the horse – *his* horse which *they* had stolen. When they did arrive, the landlord, who by then knew the story in full, tried to arrest the scoundrels.

During the scuffle Dick Turpin accidentally shot his friend instead of the landlord. Turpin escaped, but never forgave himself for the death of his friend. The inn was later used as a knocking shop for drivers en route to the docks.

Molly, who was full of such stories, had once been house cleaner to a Jewish woman in Whitechapel who was a friend of the Bloom family who were reputed to be related to Dick Turpin, so this gave her some credence and something to boast about. Now, of course, in 1970, Bloom's was famous for its salt beef sandwiches. Say Whitechapel, say Bloom's.

On her way home through the back streets, Cathy arrived at the animal market in Three Colts Lane and felt sad when she saw all the penned and caged kittens and puppies, budgerigars and canaries, hamsters and pet mice. Resisting an urge to buy one of the kittens for Becky and Leo, in case they didn't want another pet to replace Pongo, she promised herself that once she was living in a place of her own with a garden she would return to the animal market.

She soon arrived at a lively yard where for decades old junk and secondhand goods had been sold – a place where her dad used to take her as a kid when he was after anything from a wireless to an old pushbike or discarded toy. Even now, as a young woman, she was still easily excited by the buoyant mood of the shoppers. It was a different set of people coming into these cobbled back streets now, and while there were just as many stalls in the open yard as there used to be, most of the stallholders were touting not old tat but bric-à-brac and antiques. The customers were a mixed bunch from the smart and fashionable to the trendy young with their unkempt hair, old jeans and military overcoats from army surplus stores. Most of them were rummaging through boxes of old china and brass ornaments. Cathy strolled through the entrance and squeezed through a gap in the crowd towards a stall where she could see an oil lamp with a beautiful coloured glass shade on a copper stand, similar to one that Molly had once had in her sitting room when Cathy's grandfather had been alive and they had lived in a terraced cottage off the Mile End Road.

Reaching between the dealers searching for bargains, she pulled the lamp close enough to be able to lift it with both hands. To her amazement she saw a familiar crack next to a tiny gap in the red glass. This was her nan's old lamp – the lamp that she had sat and gazed at as a little girl in her grandparents home. 'A fiver to you, dear,' said the stallholder, a man in his late sixties wearing a thick old overcoat and a cap on his head.

'I can't afford five pounds,' said Cathy, choked at seeing a part of her past on a market stall, of all places.

'Blimey,' said the dealer. 'It's not the end of the world, is it, love?'

'No,' said Cathy, avoiding eye contact. 'This lamp . . .' she only just managed to say, 'used to be my nan's. She let it go when my granddad died – once she moved out of their old house and came to live with us.'

'Oh, yeah . . .' The old gentleman grinned as he scratched his ear lobe. 'And where 'ave I 'eard that old story before? Gimme a break, love. If you want it for four pounds I'll let you 'ave it – but only cos you've made me smile on a cold and frosty morning.'

'I'm not telling lies,' said Cathy. 'I'd know this lamp anywhere. This is my nan's table lamp – no question.'

'Is that right? So where'd your nan live then? Before all the world's troubles landed on 'er shoulders?'

'In a little courtyard off Mile End Waste.'

The man, who now had a different smile on his face, looked at her for a few moments and then said almost in a whisper, 'You're not telling me that canny old Molly is your nan, are you? You look too honest. She was thieving before I was, way back when.'

Cathy looked from the lamp to the stallholder and saw a kind of hopeful look in his twinkling eyes. 'Molly is my nan,' she said. 'Believe me or don't believe me – it's up to you. What's the best price you can do on the lamp?'

'Well, well, well,' said the old boy, chuckling warmly. 'So you must be little Catherine.'

'I am . . . but not little any more. Should I know your name?'

'Should she know my name,' he murmured to himself as he adjusted his cap. He then looked into her eyes as his own became a touch watery. 'I'm lost for words,' he said. 'You 'ave jarred me. Molly's lovely little granddaughter Catherine right 'ere in the yard. Well I never.' He turned away from her, pulled a screwed up white handkerchief from his trouser pocket and dabbed his face, in particular his eyes. Cathy wasn't sure whether he was play-acting or not.

'So . . .' he said, clearing his throat. 'How are them sisters of yours doing? Still successful, are they? Still thieving? Because if they are, tell them to come and see me. I'm on this pitch every Sunday. Dear, oh dear, oh dear. How the worms do crawl out of the woodwork every now and then.'

Cathy studied the man's face and vaguely recognised him from the time when he used to call at her nan's with his wheel-barrow, collecting or delivering old junk.' You know my name but I don't know yours,' she said.

'Arthur Wood. And your mum and dad are all right, are they?'

'Mum's fine, but Dad had a heart attack—'

'Ah, no! No! Don't tell me that Jim's . . .'

'Dead?' said Cathy, finishing the sentence for him.

'Ah, don't, love. Don't use that word.' The man was clearly gutted. 'Oh dear, oh dear, oh dear,' he said, wiping his eyes again.

'Dad's all right.' Cathy smiled. 'He very nearly didn't make it, but after a few weeks in the heart ward in Hammersmith Hospital he pulled through. Now he's doing well. Can't go to work any more and has to take heart pills, but he's all right.'

'Is he?' said the man, an escaping tear now rolling down his cheek. 'You're not just saying that to make me feel better, are yer? I know I'm over-emotional at times, but don't you let that affect you. You tell me the truth. Give it me straight from the shoulder.'

Cathy smiled warmly at him. 'I *have* told you the truth. I don't know you well enough to fib. Why would I, anyway? Dad's fine.'

'Honest?'

'Cross my heart and hope to die.'

'Oh, now, don't say things like that! That's what your bloody nan always used to bloody well say! *And* she was always telling me porky pies.' He pushed his handkerchief back into his trouser pocket. 'I hope you're not a fibber as well, because there's nothing worse.'

'I'm not, and nor is my nan. Sometimes I wish she was. But then you must know she always gives it to you straight. Tells it as it is,' said Cathy.

'Well . . . well, well,' said Arthur, slowly shaking his head again and gazing at nothing. 'I *am* pleased that Molly's living wiv yer. Because she was always a very independent woman, you know. Too blooming independent, if you were to ask me.' His expression suddenly changed from sad to joyous. 'You tell 'er you saw me! You tell 'er that you saw Arthur Wood in Cutler Street. You tell 'er that I'm still a rag and bone man at heart and proud of it, even though I now deal in antiques. You tell 'er I'm an antique dealer but I've not changed. I've not got all above m'self.'

'I will,' said Cathy, smiling at this character with his cap on one side of his head, and in the corner of his mouth a roll-up which stuck to his top lip when he spoke.

'Now then,' he said, pointing a friendly finger into her face. 'If you break that lamp on the way 'ome, you'll get a right-hander from me the next time I see you. Right?'

'I told you, I can't afford five pounds.'

'Oh, fuck off. Five pounds? The fing ain't worf a dollar of anyone's money. She robbed me blind, your nan. Blooming old-fashioned lamp like that. And you can tell 'er I said so. Tell 'er I move with the times – I've gone modern. Got rid of all the flock wallpaper as well and painted the lot over in brilliant white. And it looks lovely in my little old terraced house in

Jubilee Street . . . And you can tell your old nan that the stuck-up cow I married ran off three years ago wiv 'er bloke to Walthamstow to live in a place that she reckons to be the suburbs. There are more thieves there than there are in Bethnal Green. And that's saying something.'

'I will tell her . . . but there's something I don't understand,' murmured Cathy, puzzled. 'Nan moved out of her little home five years ago – so how come the lamp's only just come into your hands?'

'Listen to yerself. Talking all posh, but not as brainy as Molly. I've had that bloody thing sitting on a little table for years. Couldn't bear to part wiv it, could I? And whether you want to believe it or not, *Miss Catherine*, this is the first time it's seen the light of day.' The man straightened and pushed his shoulders back. 'I've 'ad it in my little rented house all this time. I don't want it now, do I? Not now that I've gone modern. No – that old fing had to go. Molly can like it or lump it.'

'Well, it couldn't go to a better person, could it?' Cathy grinned. 'You wait till Nan sees this. It'll make her day.'

'Never mind all that slushy stuff,' he said, pushing his shoulders back again. 'We've all gotta move on. It's the nineteen-seventies!'

'Only just,' said Cathy, smiling at him as she backed away, 'only just.' She had her nan's lamp and had met one of her old cronies from the past, and now couldn't wait to get home to see Molly's face when she told her about this old boy in the yard in Cutler Street.

'Course . . . we go back a long way, me and your nan,' said Arthur, all thoughtful. I was born in nineteen-ten, you know! What d'you think of that, then? Eh? Not bad going, is it? I could tell you young people a fing or two.'

'I bet you could,' said Cathy, hugging her lamp to her chest. 'I'd best be off, then. But I'll be back. I'll definitely be back.' She looked around and felt at home. Very much at home. 'I might even have a stall of my own in this yard one day.'

'Oh, fuck off out of 'ere,' he said, waving her away. 'Stall of your own? It's a shop you want, not a blooming stall in a yard by Brick Lane. Go on home out of 'ere – and don't talk to any strangers on the way! And tell Molly to get 'er arse up here and help me out on this stall now and then – she owes me more than one favour!'

'I'll tell her,' said Cathy as she moved off. 'Don't you worry – I'm gonna enjoy telling her.' Leaving the bustling yard with her piece of treasure, she knew that her nan was going to be thrilled to see the lamp even though she would no doubt act the opposite. And she also knew that Molly would be chuffed to get a report on an old friend.

Once out of the narrow back turnings and on to the Cambridge Heath Road, Cathy strolled along an old, worn stone pavement alongside the railway arches where rag and bone men once kept their horses and carts, and where steaming piles of horse manure could often be seen on a cold day. To the other side of her were the Bethnal Green public gardens, and further along in a cobbled street were more arches where an old carthorse belonging to a rag and bone man still hitched up. Further along still was the junior school she had once attended, John Scurr.

Continuing on her way past these familiar landmarks, she wondered what her nan and mother would say when they saw the lamp. They were certainly in for a surprise. Wrapped in her thoughts, thinking about the places she had been to that morning, she felt she was at an exciting cross-roads and that she was somehow meant to remain part of her old world as well joining a new one tomorrow. She had to admit that the yard in Cutler Street had been the best thing that day. Seeing all those stalls laden with bric-à-brac, junk and antiques had got her going, and she couldn't wait to go back on another Sunday. Neither could she wait to get home and tell Rosie about the exhibition she'd been to. But first she wanted to show Molly the lamp and remind her of someone from the past who just might bring a little fun into her life – someone who might take her out for a drink in one of the pubs she used to frequent in her younger days.

Cathy saw in her mind's eye her nan's room, the third bedroom at home, with its cardboard boxes piled up in all four corners. Molly had always been a hoarder, and now Cathy wanted to go through all those boxes and the big old trunk under her bed to see what was hiding inside. She imagined Molly wearing an old leather apron like the one a woman at a stall had been wearing: it had a zip-up pocket across the front where market-trading money was kept. The vision of Molly in Cutler Street behind her own stall calling out to the punters had Cathy chuckling.

Arriving home, she found her mother in a huff as she prepared Sunday lunch. She was so deep in thought that she hadn't heard the front door, and all but jumped out of her skin when Cathy appeared in the kitchen carrying her piece of treasure. 'God help me!' she said, a hand flying to her chest. 'I thought you were a ghost for a minute. Where have you *been*?'

'Down the Lane,' said Cathy. 'I woke up early and couldn't go back to sleep, so I went out. Why? What's the matter? Has something bad happened?'

'I was worried sick, that's what the matter is! I thought you hadn't come in last night. We all thought that. You could have been murdered for all we knew and left under some dark arch bleeding to death!'

'Of course I came home last night. Obviously my creeping about worked, because I never woke you or Nan up. And I do usually, if the pair of you moaning at me in the past is anything to go by. Where is Nan, anyway? I've got a little surprise for her.'

'She's next door with Leo and Becky.' Alice dried her hands on a tea towel and looked from the lamp to her daughter's face, a puzzled expression on her own. 'Why? What do you want Nan for?' She began to whisk her batter pudding mixture energetically. 'And where did you get that? It looks just like one she used to 'ave in the old house.'

'It's the very lamp,' said Cathy. 'I saw it on a stall in Cutler Street amongst all sorts of other stuff, and I recognised it.

When I told the bloke who was selling it who I was, he was really pleased to see me. He said his name was Arthur Wood and that I'm to say hello to you lot. He never charged a penny for it. Said I could have it and to tell Nan to call in and see him at the yard.'

'Well, I never did!' said Alice. 'Arthur Wood.' She stopped whisking the batter and smiled as his face came to mind. 'Now there's a name from the past. Your nan's going to love this. I'm not sure she'll want the lamp back, though. She never did like it. That's why she got rid of it to Arthur in the first place. The wily rag and bone man – as he was known in the old days. How is the old codger?'

'Great. He's got his own stall in Cutler Street and sells bric-à-brac. But his wife left him for another man.'

'Did she now? Well, well. *And* he's got a stall, eh?' Alice started to laugh. 'He's come up in the world. He was a horse and cart man born and bred. At least that's what he used to say when he went out on the rounds. I believe he was wheeling and dealing at the age of seven or eight when his crafty old uncle, Wilkie Collins from Wapping, took him along when collecting door to door. Apparently people couldn't resist little Arthur's angelic face – especially when they saw his backside showing through his ragged trousers. People always managed to find some old bit of junk to give him. They say Arthur's got a fortune stashed away – and that he hid it just so as his wife couldn't get her hands on it.'

'Well, she's gone now, so he can get it out of the bank and spend it, can't he? She ran away to Walthamstow with her lover.'

This was more than Alice could take and she burst out laughing. 'I can't wait to see your nan's face. She's going to love this. Arthur Wood back to haunt us! Well, well.' Then her expression suddenly became a touch more serious and, she added, 'I might say that your nan's not best pleased with you, though.'

'Why not? What have I done?'

'She couldn't remember whether she'd made your bed yesterday or not. She went straight into panic mode. You went out with Johnny last night and none of us waited up, and so that was the last we saw of you. She thought you'd been out all night with that young man. I never thought it for one minute. I was worried about you, though.'

'Oh, Mum! The Sunday paper was on the armchair and not the doormat. That should 'ave told you something. And I never washed up my teacup.'

'I know you didn't, and I knew that you'd slept in your bed – I just didn't know where you'd gone at that time in the morning. Your dad knew you'd been reading the paper.'

'And where's Dad now?'

'Popped in next door to cheer up Leo while Nan comforts Becky. Dad saw her earlier on through the front window, wandering along as feeble as you like and every bit the lost soul. I suppose it's the shock of it all. God knows, the Jews were persecuted enough in the early days – so the old couple were bound to think that's what it was about until they read that note that came through the door. Nobody likes to have a brick thrown at their window. It's the worst thing of all, and those little sods that did it would have known that. I know what I'd like to do to their parents – and they're Becky's family, after all. Because that's who's put them up to it. Members of her own lost family. You can bet your life on it.'

'They won't be back, Mum, don't worry. Nan scared the pants off 'em,' said Cathy. Then after a few seconds she added, 'Did you *really* think I'd been out all night with Johnny?'

She hoped in a way that the answer would be yes, because she fancied staying out at an all-night party in the near future. Getting this idea into her family's head now would be no bad thing. She knew plenty of girls of her age who did so without their parents making a fuss.

'I didn't think you'd do such a thing, Cathy. No,' said Alice. 'Perish the thought that my youngest should turn out to be a slut.'

'Right, well, thanks for that, Mum. That makes me feel a lot better. So . . . you must be really proud of me. Not only a decent and sensible seventeen-year-old, but one who gets up at the crack of dawn on a Sunday morning like a good East Ender to go for a stroll down Petticoat Lane. Nan should give me some Brownie points for that, surely? I mean to say, I could have been out at dawn on the game. I could have been hanging around in dark shop doorways in Brick Lane with a little gold chain around my ankle, ready to do a bit of business.'

Choosing to ignore the sarcasm, Alice asked her daughter why she had chosen to go on her nostalgic visit on a dark, cold winter morning and not in the summer when it was light and sunny before six o'clock. Cathy explained that she had woken up early and couldn't get back to sleep, so read the Sunday paper and saw the advert.

'As it turned out,' she said, placing the lamp on a small corner table, 'I'm really glad I went.'

'Why's that?'

Flopping down on to a kitchen chair, a smile on her face, Cathy replied, 'It was the best thing I've done in a very long time, and a real eye-opener. Honest to God, you'd have loved it in the factory where I went. You should have seen those massive great machines turning out this fantastic sequined material. You know you like a bit of glitter.'

'I do. You could have woken me up.'

Cathy looked across at the big brown teapot. 'Is the tea fresh?'

'I've just made it. Your dad and gran will want a cup when they come in. It's very sad the way Becky's taken this window-breaking thing.'

'She'll get over it. God . . . a fresh cup of tea is just what I need.' What she didn't need was any discussion of sad things. She wanted to hold on to the lovely warm glow that was pervading her. 'Do you want me to pour you a cup?'

'No, I'll wait for Dad. You can put the kettle back on for me, though, so I can top up the pot.'

'Will do,' said Cathy. 'Once I've drunk my tea I'm going to
have a little chat with Rosie about what I saw in that fabric
factory this morning. We could have ourselves a little business
on the side and bring in a few more pound notes.'

Letting that go above her head, Alice heard the front door
open. 'That sounds like them coming in now,' she said. 'I always
know the way Nan gives the door a little kick when she opens
it . . . Prepare yourself for a lecture.'

'Oh?' said Molly predictably, as she breezed into the room.
'Madam has returned then, has she? I hope you realise what
you've put us through, young lady! Your father's been worried
sick and that's not gonna do his bad heart any good, is it? I
wouldn't like to think what he'll say to Johnny when he sees
him. He shouldn't have kept you out all night. We'd have been
banished from Bethnal Green in my day if we'd behaved so
disgracefully.'

'I don't know what you're worrying about, Nan. Me and
Johnny slept in the back of 'is car together as snug as a bug
in a rug. No one saw us because the windows were all steamed
up. All night long we were at it. You'd have been really proud
of me.'

'Saucy mare! So where did you get to at the crack of dawn?'
In truth, Molly was pleased that Cathy had got one over on
her and was proving to be a chip off the old block.

'I went to the Lane, Nan – to see Arthur Wood. He's still
soft on you. He's been keeping something warm for the day
when you might walk back into his life.' She nodded towards
the lamp in the corner. 'He said to give you that as a present
and that he's still in love with yer.'

'What are you talking about?' demanded Molly, not too keen
to have the shoe on the other foot where teasing and tormenting
was concerned.

'Well, that's for me to know and you to find out. You was a
dirty little cow when you was foot-loose and fancy-free, wasn't
yer, Nan?' Cathy gave her mum a sly wink as she clicked her
teeth, because she had clocked that Alice was enjoying the tease

as well. Molly, however, was speechless for a few seconds –
which was a first. She glanced from her granddaughter to the
table and the lamp. 'You'll feel the back of my 'and if you don't
explain where that lamp came from.'

'I'll tell you all about it once I've drunk my tea and had a
ciggy,' said Cathy as she sat on the chair by the fire, put her
feet on her nan's little footstool and lit her cigarette. 'Johnny
really looked after me last night. He took me out to supper. A
Chinese. It was brilliant, and I think I might be in love. Fucking
fantastic, it was.'

'That's enough, Cathy,' said Alice. 'I know you're teasing
your nan, but you might get used to saying that word. It's bad
enough that Nan always uses it.'

'Excuse me?' said Molly. 'Are we talking about me? Because
I *am* in the room, you know. Fucking cheek.' She looked from
Alice to Cathy. 'And where did you go before he treated you
to Chinks grub? To the dog stadium? For a little gamble? A
chance to lose your wages on the races?'

'No,' said Cathy. 'After our meal we went for a coffee, and
after that Johnny brought me home. Door-to-door chauffeur
– can't be bad, can it? I don't know why I woke up early,
though. And I do mean early. Well before the crack of dawn.
Though it was more than worth it – as it turned out. Definitely
worth losing a few hours' beauty sleep.'

'That was nice of him,' said Alice as she attended to the
cooking. 'I always thought he was a good lad. Will you be seeing
him again, love?'

'Yep. On Wednesday. He's taking me to the pictures.'

'So you're officially courting, then, are yer?' said Molly.

'Not yet we're not, Nan. Don't be silly. We're just trying each
other out for size. But I do like him. I like him a lot, as it
happens, and so does Dad – so he could be the one for me.
Who knows? I'm sorry if he's not up to scratch where you're
concerned!'

'What d'yer mean? I like Johnny . . . and I knew 'im before
any of you lot did. But he's a gambler – and there's nuffing

wrong with that so long as you've got no thoughts of marrying 'im.'

'You never knew him before Dad did,' said Cathy, ignoring the name-calling. 'Dad worked with him down the docks.'

'Yeah – but I knew 'im when 'is arse 'ung out of 'is trousers as a kid. When I cleaned at the People's Palace, as did Johnny's mother. You lot are going to have to remember just how far back I go,' said Molly. 'His mother had a terrible life with his dad, never mind her spoilt brat daughters. And she never knew for certain if she was gonna get his wages on a Friday night or a bag of chips to feed the lot of 'em. Gambling's in the blood. Be warned.' The sound of the doorbell cut her soliloquy short.

'That'll be your father back from next door,' said Alice, ignoring her mother's last remark. 'I think we should put a key on a string round his neck. He never takes one with him.'

'Yeah . . . and no doubt you two would like to put a bit of string round *my* neck,' said Molly. As she left the room she tried to ignore the dull ache under her shoulder blade – the one that came every now and then and that she told no one about.

'That was good timing,' said Alice. 'I wish Nan would go down the flipping Lane for a couple of hours and burn off some of her energy.'

The sudden unexpected entrance of Cathy's sisters, Marilyn and Ava, rushing into the room with bulging bags, was worse than the cold wind blowing through. Both girls ignored their mother and Cathy, talking to each other as if no one else was in the room. 'I'll go and get some more, Ava – you shove these behind the armchair before Dad comes in,' said Marilyn.

'What *is* going on?' Alice asked as she placed her hands on her hips, unconsciously imitating her own mother. She glared at both her visiting daughters. 'If the police are on your heels and you've led them straight here I'm gonna be furious!'

'Don't worry about it, Mum. Nan's fetching some stuff in as well.' With that Marilyn scurried out of the room again.

'Don't mind us, will you?' Alice called out behind her. 'We only live here!'

Dropping the bags in their temporary hiding-place behind the armchair and squashing them down, Ava, her black hair pulled back into a French pleat with tortoiseshell combs, her green eyes glistening with joy, offered her mum a radiant smile. She was obviously in her hyper-happy mood. 'Hello, Mum,' she said with enthusiasm, kissed her on the cheek and then did the same to Cathy. 'We just want to get the stuff in and be done with. Then we can settle down and have a nice cup of tea.' Her face lit up. 'There's loads of stuff today.'

'And nothing that'll fit me, I bet,' said Cathy.

'Go and give Marilyn and Nan a hand, babe. You'll love what's in some of them bags.' Ava went into the kitchen and poured herself a glass of lemonade. 'I'm all in, Mum,' she complained. 'Exhausted from being up since five this morning.'

'Doing what, might I ask?' enquired Alice.

'Catching things from a third-floor window. God, I don't think I've ever been involved in anything as exciting as that. Brilliant, it was! My pulse is still racing. I loved it. It was better than the best sex.'

Alice pursed her lips and shook her head, letting the last remark go above her head. 'You're going to get caught one of these days, my girl. I'm telling you. You and our Marilyn will end up in Holloway doing a long stretch.'

'Don't talk daft. We're too clever to get caught.' Ava flopped down into the armchair, and as she relaxed a grin spread across her face. 'It was *so* brilliant! Jackie Finch knows exactly what she's doing. She hides the stuff behind the packing machines in the factory during the week, and then tosses it all out of the window on a Sunday morning when nobody's about – except me and Marilyn. And she gets paid double for going in on the holy day.' Her laughter filled the room as she said, 'And I know you won't believe this, Mum, but we've got pure *cashmere* sweaters for men and women. Fashionable ones with Harrod's and Liberty's labels already stitched on. And not only this, but pure silk blouses as well, all destined for the big stores up West. I reckon we'll make a grand out of this little hoard.

'What colours are they?' said Alice, more interested than she would have been had the jumpers been acrylic. She had always fancied herself wearing cashmere.

'Light blue, navy, red and black. And that's only the jumpers. The silk blouses I'm not so sure about. Jackie said she had six different colours and threw down a couple of gross of each for us to shove into our laundry bags.'

'So you had someone waiting in a van, then? To take them to your flat and load up your car there?'

'No! Course not, Mum. We work on our own, me and Marilyn – you know we do. I parked my car as close as possible to the alleyway and we just kept running backwards and forwards, shoving the lot into the boot and on to the back seat once they were in them cotton sacks. We packed every bit of space with them. I don't think it took us much more than fifteen minutes to load up. It was brilliant.'

Molly shot into the room, dropped two bulging laundry sacks and then looked at her watch thoughtfully before saying, 'Well . . . we don't want to waste any time, do we? It's nearly twelve o'clock, so I'd best get my skates on. I can be done and dusted with a few bob in my pocket and back in time for my dinner. A nice Sunday roast by the telly will suit me fine.'

'Why, where you off to, Mum?' asked Alice, surprised by this previously unmentioned appointment.

'Never you mind! Nosey cow. Your daughters aren't the only ones with a head for business. Anyway, you'll no doubt find out in the fullness of time. I'm not seventy yet, so I'm allowed to have the odd secret rendezvous with an old lover. Sort out twenty-one of them cashmeres, mixed colours. And don't slack. I'll just put on a bit of lipstick and powder before I go and see my old friend. And that reminds me – it's about time you brought some stuff in that I can actually sell. Those Yardley lipsticks are still in the box up there. Who the fuck is gonna want to put purple lipstick on? You got caught with a dog there, girls.'

'Give 'em to the charity shop in Stepney Green. And why twenty-one jumpers, Nan?' demanded Marilyn as she pushed a manicured hand through her short curly red hair and checked her high-cheekboned face in the wall mirror. As she moved closer she saw that her wide, grey-green eyes were a touch bloodshot from too many late nights.

'Because twenty-one's my lucky number – you know it is. Or at least you should do by now. I sometimes wonder if any of you listen to what I'm saying half the time.' The rest of the family went quiet as they all looked at each other, trying not to laugh.

Molly belted upstairs to the bathroom to change out of her everyday slacks and top into the smart black trousers and soft grey jumper she kept for best. Once she had given herself the finishing touch with a pair of pearl clip earrings, she admired her reflection in the mirror and murmured, 'Never too old, Molly girl. Never too old for a bit of romance.'

She was smiling on the surface – but inside she was laughing. Not only was she going to do a little bit of business, she was going to see her old flame Arthur in Cutler Street and possibly shake hands on a deal with him. She was going back out into the wheeling-and-dealing world that she had been missing for several years. Not only that, but she had something to prove to her granddaughters: she might be a pensioner, but she still had gumption.

The final rush, with Cathy, Marilyn and Jim coming into the room with the last of the booty, was too much for Alice. 'That's it now,' she insisted. 'No more. I hope to God none of our neighbours are out there cleaning their windows or washing their cars. We'll end up in the Old Bailey at this rate!'

'Don't be daft, Mum,' said Ava, at twenty-eight the oldest of her daughters. 'Ask us nicely and we might treat you and Dad to a week at Butlin's with the earnings from this little haul.'

'And what about me?' said Molly, coming into the room done up to the nines. 'Don't I deserve a bit of sun, sand and sea?' She dropped a large, empty zip-up shopping bag on the floor.

'Of course you do. You can come with us to Spain to stay in a mate's villa on the Costa del Sol. So long as you're prepared to give us some of your lovely cooking while you're there.'

'What mate? Who do you know with a villa in Spain, you lying mare?'

'Terry Preed.'

'Oh,' said Molly, 'that's sounds all right. He's more like it. Knows what it's all about, does Terry. He robs safes, not fucking jumpers. Yeah . . . I'll 'ave a slice of that. When we going?'

'Probably off in September.'

'September? I could be dead and buried by then! May is when we should go. Before it gets too 'ot and before them cheap package deals are there. The riff-raff. Screaming brats with adults who ignore their kids and get drunk on cheap plonk every night. I ain't gonna mix with that kind of a person at my age. You wouldn't expect me to neither, I shouldn't think?'

'If you ask me, Nan,' said Marilyn, with phoney compassion to torment her, 'an old woman like you should be sitting in a corner knitting baby clothes for when one of us get in the family way. Now what about if we book you into a hotel in Bournemouth? A little place that's quiet and by the sea front. One that caters for the elderly gentlefolk like you. That would suit you better than Spain, wouldn't it?'

'No, Marilyn, it wouldn't. I read the newspapers, darling, which would do you good if you could but read. I'm worldly, sweetheart. I know more about what's going on abroad than you do. So Spain's fine for me, thanks all the same. But *you* might like Bournemouth. *You* can sit all day long by a window that looks out to sea and flick through them women's magazines with lots of pictures for you to look at. You might even meet some wealthy old folk to rob.'

Molly glanced at herself in the heart-shaped mirror on the wall and tousled her soft bleached-blonde hair with her fingers before spraying on a little of Cathy's lacquer. 'But then I don't s'pose it's your fault that you can't read and can't be bothered to learn.' Molly eyed her own daughter for a reaction, but none was forthcoming. Alice had learned long ago to ignore her mother when she was in a baiting mood.

'Where are you going then, Nan? Somewhere nice?' said Ava.

'That's for me to know and you to find out. It's just as well I made a nice big apple crumble this morning. Make sure one of you remembers to put it in the oven twenty minutes or so before you take the joint out. Then make the custard with half milk and half water.'

'Anything else while you're at it?' said Marilyn.

'Yeah. Put twenty-one cashmeres in that 'oldall of mine, if you please. We don't want stolen goods in our 'ome, thank you very much. I'll have sold every one I take with me before the day's out – and with an order for more.'

'To?'

'To my private contacts, Ava. All right? How much you asking a piece? And how many 'ave you got? More than what you've fetched in, I expect?'

'Three times as many, actually. The rest are hidden away in our flat – we thought we should spread the load a bit.'

'Quite right too. A fiver each suit yer?' said Molly, her chin forward.

'We could get a tenner for the cashmeres, Nan. No trouble.'

'If you sold 'em one at time, maybe you could. But I'm talking about the lot of 'em going at once. A nice big order for yer. Now, does a fiver suit you or not?'

'Eight pounds a piece,' said Marilyn, 'and that's cheap. You can make a quid on each one at that price.'

'I'm not thinking of making a penny, Marilyn! I'm doing this to help you, my kith and kin – my daughter and son-in-law, who's got a bad heart and who you're putting at risk by bringing stolen goods into his house. But then, I don't think I really need to remind you of that, do I? Settle for a fiver or I'm not gonna help you out. I could get a nice big order for the lot if you wanted.'

Marilyn looked from her nan to her sister. 'What d'you think, Ava?'

'Oh, let 'er have some. She'll never stop going on about it otherwise. It would be good to get rid of 'em ASAP. And there's plenty more from where they came from, so, yeah, let Nan shift the lot if she thinks she can.' She then turned to her grandmother and asked, 'D'you want a lift to wherever you're going?'

'No, I don't, thank you very much. For one thing I'm not letting you know who my contacts are, and for another there's nothing wrong with my legs. Walking's good for 'em – and you two wanna think about that. Put one leg in front of the other instead of spreading 'em apart all the time.'

That said, Molly opened her bag wide. Then she went back to the mirror and brushed a bit of mascara on to her eyelashes. Make-up she kept for special occasions. The girls, pursing their lips so as not to laugh, looked from one to the other, obviously pleased that their nan was not going to change with age. Without saying another word for fear of laughing and hurting Molly's feelings, Marilyn and Ava filled the holdall with the cashmeres individually wrapped in cellophane.

'Right,' said Molly, checking her watch again. 'I should think I'll be back from delivering old Mother Riley's washing in about two hours. If the joint's cooked before that, dish mine up and put a plate on top. I'll steam it later on.' She picked up her booty and, holding her head high, left them staring after her. It wasn't until she was outside and the street door was closed between herself and her family that she broke into gentle laughter. Molly was as quick as ever despite her age, and as far as she was concerned sharper than her grown-up granddaughters.

All that talk about her going to Spain with them. She couldn't think of anything worse. No. If she was going to go abroad she would go by herself on a lovely cruise to find herself a rich man. Her life as an independent, good-looking woman wasn't over yet by any means. She could afford to wait until she reached seventy and then sail away on a nice big ship with her own spacious cabin and a balcony, waited on hand and foot and with no granddaughters around to cramp her style. It wasn't that long ago that handsome men had been falling over backwards to impress her. Molly had been a stunner – and still was, age, wear and tear taken into account.

Having made her way to Cambridge Heath Road through short cuts, she was feeling on top of the world as she stood on the pavement and waited for a black cab to come along. She knew that the East End cabbies were no fools, and for them Sundays in this area at this time of day meant good business. It was only a few minutes before one turned up and she was soon settled in the back and making the most it. She closed her eyes, giving a clear message to the driver that she wasn't one for idle chit-chat and that if he wanted a sixpence tip he should keep his trap shut until he dropped her off at her stated destination: Cutler Street.

3

The cab set Molly down just before the entrance to the yard where she knew that Arthur would be trading. Before she got out of the taxi she paid the driver his fare plus a tip for a nice comfortable ride, and he gave her eight crisp pound notes for the cashmere sweater she had let him have for his wife.

Continuing to enjoy her buoyant mood, Molly felt as if she was a young woman again, back in her stride doing what she was best at, wheeling and dealing goods she hadn't had to pay for up front. She had been a good fence in the past and didn't think she had lost her touch, and now she was about to find out. Whether Arthur was going to let her run rings around him was something else. He had been in the game for donkey's years, at first running his legitimate rag and bone business as a way of making a living and then as a fence selling packs of cigarettes and cases of whisky beneath his huge bundles of secondhand clothes. The fact that he now had his own stall selling bric-à-brac made her smile, and she couldn't help wondering what might be for sale under the counter.

Looking through the crowd, Molly caught a glimpse of her old chum and smiled to herself. He had worn well and was still a good looker. The trouble was that the sexy bastard knew it. It was those twinkling blues of his that had got the women going in the past – and no doubt still did. Strolling over to his stall and going behind it, she set her bag down and sat on Arthur's chair while he tried to persuade a punter that a pair of candlesticks were solid silver. The potential customer, a woman, trying hard to appear the experienced dealer, was scrutinising the sticks for a hallmark through her own small silver-handled magnifying glass. With lips pursed and a slight frown on her forehead, she looked into Arthur's face and then said, 'I'm awfully sorry to disappoint you – but I think you've been duped if you purchased these believing them to be solid silver. What you have here is top-quality Sheffield plate. I'll give you four pounds for the pair.'

'Four pounds! Do me a favour. My old dad's at home, half blind, and waiting to see what he can get for something that means so much to 'im! They were a wedding present from 'is firm when he was a gardener for a grand house in Essex – in 1890.'

'Oh, dear. Such a pity – but we each have to make a little profit, do we not? Never mind.' She thought about it for a few seconds and then said, 'I suppose I could stretch to six pounds. They are rather sweet.'

'Make it eight and they're yours,' he said. 'Not a penny more or a penny less. I'd sooner put 'em back on the old Welsh dresser with the rest of my dad's silver collection.'

'Oh . . . he has more silver, does he, your father?'

'He's got stacks of it, madam. His mother, my dear departed grandmother, came from good stock and passed it on to him. The only reason he's selling it on now is because he can't bear to think of me reaping the reward once he's popped his cork. I'll fetch some more along next Sunday if you're interested. But I do need ten pounds at least for this pair.'

'Ten? I thought you said eight.'

'Slip of the tongue if I did,' fibbed Arthur. 'I told Father I'd take no less than ten.' He gave her a sexy wink and said, 'We all 'ave to make a little profit, don't we? Ten pounds and they're yours.'

'You're a very clever dealer, sir,' said the woman, smiling. 'I shall buy these from you if you promise to fetch more silver from the collection for me to look at next Sunday. What do you say to that? Do we have a deal?'

'Here's my hand and here's my heart,' said Arthur, pushing his rough hand into her delicate one knowing full well there was no silver at home. 'Ten pounds and they're yours.'

'You drive a hard bargain, sir,' she said, just managing to show a faint smile as she slowly withdrew her manicured hand.

'My father's a very hard man when it comes to his silver,' said Arthur as he clamped his other hand on top of hers in time to imprison it. He then moved closer to whisper into her ear, 'If he believes something to be solid silver, then that's what it must be. There's no shifting him. But the same goes for when he insists that a nice little bit of Georgian silver in his old cardboard box is rubbish and not worth more than a couple of quid.'

'Oh, I see,' smiled the woman. 'I think I've got the picture now. Thank you so much for sharing that with me. I shall pay ten pounds for the candlesticks – if you would be so kind as to throw in that little nail file.' She pointed the tip of a beautiful red-varnished fingernail at the small item on the stall.

'Do what?' said Arthur, peering at the nail file. 'But that's a bit of old rubbish I picked up off the ground. That's not worth a sixpenny bit, sweetheart.'

'Ah.' The woman quietly giggled. 'I was just testing. Well done you for being honest. But I *will* take it, if I may. It will be just perfect for scraping the dirt off the soles of my boots before I get into my car.'

'Fair enough,' said Arthur. 'I'll chuck that in with the candlesticks. I can't say fairer than that, now can I? A tenner for the lot, then. That's dirt cheap, that is.'

The woman raised an eyebrow, pulled a ten pound note from a pocket where she had several more kept for a quick purchase, and waited as Arthur wrapped her goods in newspaper. The fair exchange made, the woman strolled off, doing her utmost not to look thrilled at having picked up what she saw as an absolute bargain.

'If you were to ask me,' said a voice from the back of the stall, 'I would say that those candlesticks are worth three times as much as she paid you, Arthur.'

Spinning on his heels, Arthur broke into a smile when he saw Molly sitting on his chair. 'Stone the fucking crows!' he said. 'It didn't take you long to find me, did it? What do you want, Molly? I hope you're not here after my body – I can see you've put a bit of lipstick and mascara on!' He pushed his shoulders back and roared with laughter.

'You won't think it's so funny my being 'ere when I show you what I've got in my laundry bag.'

'Well,' said Arthur, rubbing his chin and still smiling. 'I've heard it called some names before, Molly, but never laundry.' He pulled his big white handkerchief from his trouser pocket and blew his nose. 'What a bloody sight for sore eyes and a tonic you are. You just couldn't resist it, could yer? Your Cathy told you I was here and you had to come and find out for yourself. Now then, are you gonna buy me a pint for that lamp I give you back, or what?'

'I might do, Arthur. But gimme a minute, will yer. I want to have a little chat with that customer who bought the candlesticks. Admittedly, what I've got hidden away is not antique . . .'

Again Arthur roared with laughter. 'I should think it must be by now, Molly,' he said, pulling her leg again. 'Let's face it – you're no spring chicken, sweetheart!'

Ignoring him, Molly drew her bag close and withdrew a single cashmere jumper, keeping it in its posh wrappings as she slipped it inside her coat. 'Don't go away, Arthur,' she commanded, and then went off on the woman's trail.

She soon found her at a stall on the other side of the yard, admiring old, worn Turkish rugs. Tapping her lightly on the shoulder, Molly kept a respectable distance between herself and the woman, who was wearing a rather expensive-looking, full-length sheepskin coat. As she turned around, Molly saw an expression of warning in her eyes which suited her fine. Speaking very quietly, she said, 'I thought that was very fair of you with them candlesticks and that old boy. Very fair indeed, madam. Now . . . I don't deal in antiques but I do know a lady who has good taste in clothes when I see one. I would have thought that you only wear cashmere and silk, and never put acrylics anywhere near your skin. Am I right?'

'Well, as a matter of fact you are. But I can't say I know what it is you're driving at.'

'Well, I'm not one to waste good people's time. Because time is money and I can see you're a canny businesswoman and that this is a business trip for you and not a tour of the back streets of Whitechapel. Now . . . what I have to sell is more on the personal and luxurious side.' She pulled the cashmere from her hiding place and held it for the woman to see. 'You don't have to feel the quality, madam, just look at the label. I'm asking twelve pounds a piece, and I only approach you because I can see you'll know the price they should be when sold in Harrod's or Liberty's.'

The woman glanced at the label and then looked directly into Molly's face. 'Is this the only colour you have? Black?'

'No. If madam is interested, I do have a colour range of four with me and more than one of each.' Reeling off the colours and sizes, she felt the adrenalin pumping – but she remained as cool as a cucumber.

'I have my car parked not far from here. Fetch the rest and follow me.'

'Certainly, madam. My pleasure.'

Her head held high as usual when in this mood, Molly walked as elegantly as she could back to Arthur's stall, collected her bag and spoke not one word to her old friend, who had one eye on her and one on a customer examining a piece of china on his stall. She made her way out of the yard, met up with the woman again and strolled with her into a side turning where a brand-new green Range Rover was parked.

The woman unlocked the tailgate and asked Molly to place the lot inside. She then leaned forward, counted the cashmeres, closed the door and locked it. There were twenty pieces altogether and Molly had already done her sums. Twenty at twelve pounds each amounted to two hundred and forty pounds.

'I'll give you two hundred pounds for the lot,' said the woman, who was clearly enjoying this East End wheeling and dealing.

'You drive a hard bargain, madam,' said Molly, 'but since

you were so generous with the old man and the candlesticks I'll accept your offer – providing it's cash.'

'Of course I'll pay you in cash. I'm accustomed to this sort of a thing. We each have to dodge the tax man,' said the woman. She pulled a blue linen bag from an inside coat pocket and peeled off ten twenty pound notes from a large wad.

Beside herself, Molly only just managed to stay cool and calm as she discreetly received the money. 'If there is anything particular that you need in the future, such as more cashmere sweaters or silk-lined kid gloves, ask the old boy on the stall to contact Molly – or give him a note to hand over.'

'I shall indeed,' said the woman, thrilled by it all. She gave Molly a farewell nod as she climbed into the driving seat. Walking back to Arthur with her pocket lined, Molly was itching to scream the words '*Fucking brilliant!*' and dance around the stall with him. But she clung desperately to her reserve until the Range Rover had pulled away.

'I don't believe you,' said Arthur. 'You're not here for five minutes and already you're stitching someone up!'

'She got a bargain and she fucking well knew it, Arthur!'

'Yeah? So how come you're looking like the cat that got the cream?'

'Because I know how to deal, sunshine, that's why. Those jumpers were a nice little earner and I don't mind saying so. Anyway, what are you moaning about? Don't think I didn't clock them candlesticks being reproduction and made to look old.'

'So, Molly . . . you coming out for a drink wiv me or what?'

'Call round in the week. You know where to find me. We're still in Tillet Street.' With that Molly was lost in the crowd and making her way back to Cambridge Heath Road to catch another black cab. The only thing she had to decide now was how much she should pay her thieving granddaughters for the goods. After debating the odds she thought she would split the profit fifty-fifty and not charge them for the cab fare to the market and back. This seemed fair. Once in the taxi

she surreptitiously counted the money into two piles – one
hundred pounds for herself and one hundred for her beloved
granddaughters . . . the thieving cows.

On her return to Tillet Street Molly saw Ava's car still parked
by the kerb, which meant the girls were staying for Sunday dinner.
This was no bad thing as far as she was concerned: the more
they still saw this place as home, where they could come and go
and put their feet under the table, the better. The chaps that
Marilyn and Ava associated with were wealthier than the average
local small-time thieves-cum-dockers and this was fine by her,
because Jim got on well with them, they bunged a hundred
pounds into the pot now and then and they also gave her son-
in-law an update of what was happening down by the river.

Letting herself in with her key, Molly bowled into the passage
a happy woman and went into the back room. The table was
not yet laid but Marilyn and Ava were lounging at it, smoking
Sobranie cigarettes and each enjoying a large glass of sherry.

'Comfortable, are you, girls?' enquired Molly.

'No so bad, Nan. Not so bad.'

'Well, I hope you brought that drink with you.' Molly nodded
at the half-empty bottle. 'Because I'm not going to be too happy
if that's my bottle you've nearly got through.'

'Course we brought it with us, Nan. Look in the drinks
cupboard – that'll put a smile on your face . . . with a bit of
luck.'

'Why? What else is in there that wasn't there this morning?'

'Cherry brandy,' said Alice, a smirk on her face. 'What have
you got to say about that, Mum?'

'Very nice, thank you,' sniffed Molly. It was her favourite
drink. 'So you're stopping for dinner? Good. It's about time
you spent a bit of time with us on a Sunday. Your dad doesn't
get to see many people, you know.'

'What have you done with our swag?' asked Marilyn, keeping
her beautiful face straight and her green eyes all innocent. 'You
didn't get accosted, did you?'

Molly raised one eyebrow and looked from Marilyn to Ava. 'Someone 'as to work on a Sunday if we're to keep the coffers full.' She then slipped a hand into her coat pocket and withdrew one of the wads of ten pound notes. 'Here. Get a butcher's at that little bundle. One hundred pounds and I'm not asking for a penny of it. And if you want me to, I'll shift the rest for yer. My contact is very interested in whatever I have on offer. Now then . . . who's gonna make me a nice big cup of tea in my china cup?'

'You've sold them all – and all you've got is a ton?' gasped Marilyn.

'That's not what I said, Marilyn. I said you should look at that bundle – one hundred pounds, and I'm not asking for a penny of it. That's what I said. Why? What's your problem? I've sold 'em, 'aven't I? I've not wasted any time, and it cost me a lot of money in taxi fares. But I'm willing to take on the out-of-pocket expense because of the little bit of spare change I've made. Be thankful for a ton. I was only offered a nifty fifty at first, if you must know.'

'But you took twenty-one cashmeres, Nan,' said Ava. 'You telling me you sold 'em for under a fiver each?'

'I never said that. But I did give one to the cabbie to keep his mouth shut. And what I got for the rest is none of your business. You've got a hundred quid more than you 'ad when you woke up this morning. And I've got fucking blisters on me feet from walking the length of the Lane, punting your gear!'

'Fair enough.' Marilyn grinned. 'We've learnt all we know from you, so we can't really start knocking it now, can we, Nan? At least you've got enough money to come with us to Spain when we go. You can pay your own way – because we know how independent you are.'

'So do you want me to sell the rest of 'em? The rest of the stolen gear you keep under this roof . . . putting your mother and father in danger of a police raid and arrest?'

'We'll have to think about it,' said Ava. 'I'll tell you after dinner.'

'And as for bloody Spain – I'd sooner save up to buy a little cottage on the cheap in the countryside. They say Norfolk is very nice and dirt cheap when it comes to old-fashioned country cottages with thatched roofs.'

'You'd die of boredom, Nan.'

'Maybe so . . . but I'd sooner that than catch a bug in Spain. And I don't much fancy ending my days in the East End either, if you want the truth. Not the way it's going. The sly sods with all the money have every intention of digging up our roots and making them part of the City. There won't be any tiled slate roofs or red brick chimneys left, the way things are going. It'll be high-rise tower blocks wherever you fucking well look. But never mind. I'll soon be dead and buried and you can all look after yourselves while I'm sunbathing on a cloud. The planet will be blowing itself up by then, in any case, with every country chucking nuclear bombs all over the place . . . never mind that every time your mother sprays a bit of that bloody furniture polish she poisons the air we breathe.'

'Nice one, Nan,' said Cathy. 'Trick of the week, that.'

'What?'

'Side-tracking. How much did you get for the cashmeres? Come on. Don't be mean. Tell us. We're all dying to know.'

'I mean to say . . . you'd think the government would want to preserve what we've got instead of bulldozing it, wouldn't you? Soon there won't be any streets left, never mind alleyways and courtyards. There'll just be walkways from one council estate to another, with parades of shops all selling the same fucking fings. All the old 'ouses need is a bit of money spent on 'em. That's all.'

'How much, Nan?' Cathy urged with a smile.

'A tenner each. And none of you lot sitting here on your arses could have done that well.'

'Well . . . you're a ray of sunshine, Molly,' said Jim, coming into the room. 'Your little trip successful, then, was it?'

'Ask your daughters. I've just handed over a ton.'

Jim's face lit up. 'Honest?'

'Well?' said Molly, looking to the girls for a bit of praise. 'Tell your father what I've just done for you, then.'

'She sold twenty-one cashmere sweaters, Dad. For a hundred pounds.'

'Did you now?' Jim was smiling at Molly. 'And how much did *you* make?'

'I beg your pardon, Jim, but I was doing them a favour. I've earned a little bit of pocket money for going, but if you all think I don't deserve it they can fucking well have it back. It's only small change where these two thieves are concerned.'

'Oh, shut up, Nan. You know we're only teasing. How much do you want for going, then?'

'Nuffing. I did it for the love of my family.' She turned her back on the girls and faced Jim to mouth the words: 'A hundred quid for me.'

Jim couldn't help but chuckle. Then, changing the subject, he said, 'As it happens, Molly, you've got a point about the docks. The trade is falling away. Africa and Asia are turning to the States, Germany and Japan. Word spreads across the oceans fast nowadays. Some countries don't want to ship goods to England because of the gossip about the militants among the dockers.' Easing himself into the small armchair by the fire he added, 'The press don't do us any favours – but there we are. They print the stuff that sells newspapers and that's what it's all about. Filling their coffers.'

'At threepence a copy they're not going to get rich, Jim, are they?' said Alice from the kitchen, where she was carving the roast leg of lamb.

'They make a mint on the advertising, love. That's where the money is. Look at our Cathy. She was up at the crack of dawn – and why? Because she saw an advert that got her excited, that's why.' He paused for a moment and then said, 'There's a need for mechanisation down the docks, of course there is. And let's not forget that we were the first to have forklift trucks. In East India Dock in 1946.'

'We've all got to move with the times, Dad,' said Marilyn, drawing on her cigarette.

'I don't entirely disagree with you, love, but I don't see any point in spending millions to modernise the docks. Have you seen the damage the new container ships have caused by running into the locks and scraping the jetties? Damage everywhere. I don't know what the answer is. The East India and St Katherine are running heavy losses now as well, from what Johnny told me.'

'Things change, Dad,' said Ava. When the Conservatives got in, do you know how much they sold some of the dock land for? One and a half million, that's what.'

'I know, love – and what a bargain Taylor Woodrow got, eh? Planners and developers are crawling all over the place now, waiting to buy any site they can get their hands on. But it beats me why they think people are going to want to live down by the docks – down by the smelly river with all them rats running around the warehouses.'

'I wouldn't mind buying one, Dad,' replied Ava as she studied her perfectly painted fingernails for any sign of chipping. 'Be worth a fortune in twenty years or so. There's talk of the Italian ivory house being restored and given a frontage of smart shops.'

'Load of fucking rubbish,' snorted Molly, leaving the room and going upstairs for a ten-minute lie down before dinner was served.

'Anyway,' said Jim, a touch melancholic, 'there's still hope that Wapping and the Isle of Dogs won't be messed about. All we need is for the PLA and the union leaders to sit down together and agree on a policy of modernisation. The port authority's coming out of the red, but the dockers are suspicious of all them new forklift trucks that are appearing – as well as the mechanical pellet system.

'I'm telling you, if the Conservatives get in again in June it could be the end of the docks as we know it. We need Wilson to get elected. I don't care what anyone says. There's a recession already, and it could get worse. And still we'll see our docks taken from under our feet.

'Years ago they blamed Jewish immigrants for taking our jobs and pushing up rents and making everything overcrowded. Load of rubbish. They were and still are good, hard-working people. It's no wonder most of them who made a success of themselves moved out to Clapton and Golders Green. They got no thanks round this way. But they did get bricks through their windows now and then, like next door.'

'Yeah,' said Ava, suddenly interested in the conversation again. 'Johnny told me about that. Bit of a nerve, wasn't it? A touch out of order?'

'Don't worry about it, love,' said Jim. 'Your mum and Rosie next door are taking care of it. The little sods came from Buckhurst Hill, by all accounts. I think a little trip might be planned.'

'And what about Johnny?' Ava grinned. 'He's been walking around like a love-sick puppy, from what my Stanley tells me.' She eyed Cathy, who was laying the table for dinner.

'Bait me all you like, sis, I'm not saying a word.'

'Which says it all.' Ava laughed. 'What a catch, eh? You don't want to let him slip through your fingers, Cath. He's a handsome sod with a regular job, as well as earning a bit on the side now and then. And he's reliable . . . apart from the gambling.'

'Yeah, yeah. So I've been told. But don't you worry – I'll soon cure 'im of that little passion.'

'It's more of an addiction with your Johnny, Cath, but the boys have got a lot of respect for 'im even so. Best contact down the docks in a long while, apparently.'

'He's not my Johnny. We've only just started to go out.' Cathy felt her cheeks burning bright red.

'Johnny might thieve a few things out of the docks now and then, but he's not a villain,' said Jim. 'Take no notice of her, Cath. Your sisters think any bloke who comes into their realm is a bandit.

'Some people earn an honest living, you know, Ava,' Jim went on. 'And that goes for you as well, Marilyn. You're both getting too used to spending your time with villains. And just so we nip it in the bud now, young Johnny does a full eight-hour day down the docks, all right?'

'And a couple of hours in the betting shop.'

'Don't exaggerate! He's a good lad. One of the best there is.'

'Whatever you say, Dad,' said Marilyn, winking at him. 'Whatever you say.'

'You're not too old for a slap on the back of your legs, you know! And don't think I wouldn't do it. My father never stood for any cheek, so—' A long ring on the doorbell stopped him short. 'Now what? It's like a railway station here today, with everyone coming and going.'

'It's probably the boys, Dad,' said Marilyn, leaving the room to open the front door to her bloke and Ava's.

'All right, babe?' said Marilyn's man, Albert, as he crossed the threshold, giving her a wink first and then a kiss on the cheek. 'We were in the area, so we thought we'd pop in to see your mum and dad.' He was carrying a beautiful bunch of flowers to give to Alice.

'That excuse should do the trick – I don't think. It might get past Mum and Dad, but not Nan.'

'Course it will,' retorted Ava's young man, Stanley, who for his part was holding a huge box of chocolates.

'Don't make it sound like a bribe, whatever you do,' Marilyn whispered as she closed the door and followed them along the passage into the back room which was already bursting at the seams.

'Well, look at who the wind's blown in,' Jim greeted them, desperate to get away from the heat produced by the living room as well as the kitchen. 'Come on into the front room away from the women, lads.'

'We're just about to 'ave Sunday dinner,' said Molly, coming back into the room. 'We'll 'ave to do some instant mash if you're stopping. Which I take it you are, since you come bearing gifts of flowers and chocolates. Where's the bottle of champagne, then? You've obviously pulled something off!'

'Nan!' snapped Marilyn, 'The back door's open. Keep your voice down. You never know who's about.'

Molly smiled knowingly. 'It must 'ave been a good one if she's on edge over it. And look at you, Albert – never mind the flowers, cop the expression. The pair of you look as if you're the cats who got the cream. A bank job, was it?'

'Had a little win on the pools, Molly,' grinned Stanley, the half-Jew, half-Italian who looked like Tony Curtis apart from his warm brown eyes that could melt butter on a frosty morning. 'And today we're gonna go and pick up our winnings. Jew's luck, I think they call it. Of course if you don't *want* our gifts, Molly, we can always take them to my mother. She doesn't make such a good roast dinner as you or Alice – but nor does she ask questions. And from the expression on *your* face I think there's a few coming. Am I right, Molly – or am I wrong?'

'I wouldn't know, nor give a fuck what you see in my expression, Stanley. But you can hand over them chocolates because Black Magic just happen to be my favourite. Alice can 'ave the flowers. I prefer to see blooms out in the open where Mother Nature meant them to be.'

Alice pulled her tray of roast potatoes out of the oven and slowly shook her head. 'I'm going to have to peel some more spuds and put them in the pressure cooker. We can have both – some mashed with butter and some roast.' She was talking to herself, but of course they could all hear her.

'It's all right, Alice,' said Albert, smiling. 'We're not stopping for dinner. All right if we pop upstairs and change?'

'Change into what? Two fairy princesses?' said Molly, her face straight. She then glanced at the smart new carrier bag that Stanley was holding and her expression immediately changed. She was smiling now. 'Savile Row, eh? Right . . . so you *have* come into the money, boys.'

'Not yet, Molly,' chuckled Albert. 'Not yet.'

'Go up and change in Nan's room,' said Marilyn. 'Her bed's not a divan, so you can shove your bag and clothes beneath it.'

'All right for us to do that, Alice love?' said Stanley, putting protocol first.

'Course it is.'

'Well, I don't know what is going on,' said Molly, 'but I don't mind if you change your clothes in my bedroom. It's at the back on the middle landing. You don't 'ave to treat me for it when you get back from wherever it is you're going – unless it makes you feel better.'

Laughing at her, the boys went upstairs. Alice, a touch concerned, shoved the tray of roasting potatoes back into the oven and slammed the door, then looked from one daughter to another. 'This is going too far. First you fetch your stolen goods into my home, and now the boys are hiding whatever they've nicked under your nan's bed. What d'yer think this is? The cave of the forty thieves?'

'They won't be hiding stolen stuff, Mum. They're just changing out of their suits and putting something more comfortable on, that's all.'

'Oh. Well, that's different. I just don't want them bringing the law to our doorstep.'

'I shouldn't worry too much about that. It's Marilyn and Ava you should 'ave a word with. They treat this place like a laundry. Stuff in and out all of the time.'

'Yes, Mum,' said Alice. 'And who sells most of what goes out that front door. You!'

'Course I don't. I wish I did – I wouldn't be so poor. I've got no savings whatsoever,' lied Molly. 'But you don't hear me moaning about that, do yer? And as for the men changing, it's my room they're taking over. And if they don't bung me a few quid afterwards there'll be trouble.'

'After what?' said Alice.

'Wait and see, sunshine. Wait and see. They're up to something, or my name ain't Molly. But cheer up. They'll treat you for using the premises – you know they will. And it wouldn't be the first time, would it?'

Alice turned her back on her mother and busied herself plumping up the cushions as Molly turned to her granddaughters. 'They'd better have, anyway. If they don't, you'd best have a word and tell them they can't use this place as and when they like.' She folded her arms thoughtfully.

The shrill, piercing sound of the doorbell brought instant silence and a touch of fear. 'I'll go,' murmured Ava. 'It's someone for the boys, I think.'

The silence persisted in the room as both Molly and Alice eavesdropped until the sound of conversation between Ava and Cathy's new boyfriend drifted through from the passage.

'It's Johnny,' said Ava, coming into the room. 'The boys are having a quiet chat in the passage with him.'

'What in God's name is Johnny doing turning up of a Sunday dinner time? Don't this lot 'ave 'omes to go to?' Molly turned to Cathy. 'Were you expecting 'im today?'

'He never said anything to me about coming round today, Nan, no. Why are they in the passage and whispering? What's going on?'

'They're not whispering!' said Marilyn, a touch edgily.

'Give them a minute or two. Maybe it was the boys he came to see and not you,' said Alice.

'Oh, right.' Cathy shrugged. 'There goes my little bit of love rush. I thought he couldn't wait to see me again.'

'Shush!' said Alice. 'They're coming. Act normal when they come in. We don't want them to think we're talking about them behind their backs.'

'Don't we?' retorted Molly indignantly. 'They ain't gonna rule the roost. I'll behave the way I think fit.'

'Shush, Nan,' whispered Marilyn. 'They won't come over that doorstep again if they think you don't want them in the house. You know that.'

With the women quiet, Albert and Stanley came into the kitchen wearing light brown overalls and flat caps. On this rare occasion Molly was silenced by the sight of them. 'You look like you've stepped out of a Laurel and Hardy film,' she just managed to say.

Used to her, Albert addressed Alice. 'We'll be back in a couple of hours, darling. You sure it's all right by you to leave our Sunday clothes upstairs?'

'Course it is,' said Alice. 'Did you want me to put a bit of dinner on steam for you both?'

'No, thanks. We'll grab a Chinese once we've done and dusted.'

'Once you've done and dusted *what* – may I ask?' said Molly. 'I can't say I'm too happy about all the whispering.'

'Nan!' snapped Marilyn. 'Who d'you think you're talking to? And who are you to lay down the law? For a start the rent book's in Dad's name, and secondly you didn't have a problem with the bent gear you shifted this morning!'

'I've been around a long time, Marilyn, don't forget that. I know fear when I smell it.' Molly looked from her grown grand-daughter to Albert and Stanley, hardened men when out in the world but a touch intimidated when in Molly's black books. They stood there like boys summoned to stand in front of a fierce headmistress.

Dressed as if they were going to do a house move, they certainly looked the part of two honest men. But it wasn't furniture they were planning to shift that day – rather, the safe from a Japanese loan company in Bishopsgate. And Johnny was supplying his dad's van for the job.

'Give us a break, Molly, for fuck's sake,' pleaded Albert. 'Stanley's gran was made a widow no more than four weeks ago. We're moving her out of that dump where she's living all by 'erself now that the old chap's gone.'

'Well, how was I to know that?' said Molly, defensively. 'You never explain yourselves. You just and come and go – and that's how it should be with family, I suppose. But not on a Sunday. This is our holy day . . . And talking of family, the only thing that stops you being part of ours is that neither of you has put a gold band on any of my two granddaughters' left hands yet.

You've got your feet under the table and not one wedding ring to be seen! Never mind a nice big diamond solitaire. These two gangster's molls should have 'ad at least one each by now. Either a solitaire or a nice thick cluster of diamonds to show off. What are the pair of you? Cheapskates?'

If nothing else, Molly had brought total silence to the room. They were speechless, waiting to see what she was going to do or say next. It was Jim who broke the ice when he came in from the front room followed by Johnny, whom he had invited to stay for dinner.

'Hello, Cath,' said her boyfriend, smiling and blushing a little. I just fetched Dad's van for the boys to borrow. It's parked up round the corner.' He looked from her to Molly and smiled. 'Just trying to help out a bit – that's all.'

'Well, I think that's really nice of you, love,' said Alice. 'Really decent. And don't you worry. There's plenty of dinner to go one more.' She looked over to Jim and added, 'Open a bottle of Guinness, love. Johnny looks like he could do with a drink.'

'Thanks,' said Johnny, 'I wouldn't mind. And that roast smells lovely. I *will* stop, if that's all right with you, Cath.'

'Course it is,' said Cathy, very happy to see him again.

'Right. So we're all sorted out then, are we?' said Ava. 'The boys can go now, can they, Nan?'

'What you asking me for? I'm not stopping 'em. They can stop or they can go. The day that I interfere—' Molly was stopped mid-sentence by the sound of the doorbell yet again. 'Now what? Jim's right – this place really *is* more like a railway station than a home.'

'That'll be George, Molly,' said Stanley. He looked across to Albert and raised one eyebrow. 'Ready?'

'As ever I will be. It's that lovely smell of roast potatoes that's making me wonder if I should stop right where I am,' replied Albert. This was a ploy to avoid any sign of pre-performance nerves.

'Rosie's George?' said Molly, her eyes narrowed. 'He'll be helping you to move the old man's furniture as well, will he?'

'That's right, Molly,' said Stanley as he eased Albert out of the doorway and into the passage. 'Keep the teapot warm.'

'Something's not right,' warned Molly when she had heard the street door shut. She now feared that her first instincts had been right and turned her attention to Johnny, who was being quiet for one of two reasons – either he was shy in Cathy's company, or he knew that Albert, Stanley and George were going out on a job.

'You wouldn't be keeping anything from us, Johnny, would yer?' asked Molly.

'Course not. They gave me a bell this morning and asked if they could borrow the van and so I fetched it round.' This wasn't quite true. He knew exactly what the van was going to be used for, and this wasn't the first time he had supplied it for them.

'All I know,' said Alice, 'is that I want to dish up our Sunday dinner and enjoy a bit of peace and quiet. It's worse than working in Woolworth's on a busy Saturday.' She glanced at Johnny, who was looking a bit shy. 'Go on into the front room, Johnny, love. I expect Jim's waiting to have a beer with you.'

'Oh, right. Of course,' he said, his face lighting up. 'I can't take the heat so I'll get away from the kitchen,' he joked, then made a quick exit.

'Love him,' murmured Alice. 'He's such a nice, polite boy.'

'Yeah,' said Molly, 'but I still reckon you have to watch the quiet ones. I wouldn't mind betting he's on the team.'

'What team?' enquired Alice as she drained the cabbage water into a jug. 'Football?'

Molly went quiet, shaking her head as she threw a few lumps of coal into the fire. 'Let's see what the wind blows in with them lads when they get back. If you ask me, they're out on a job. And I don't mean nicking the takings from Woolworth's neither.'

'Shush, Mum. Marilyn and Ava are in Cathy's room and that's directly above us.'

'Oh, what . . . and you fink I don't know that? She glanced up at the ceiling and said in a loud voice, 'All I know is that a few quid should go on our table when they get back. I know when there's a planned job on – I wasn't born yesterday. I wouldn't mind betting it's a safe job an' all!'

The sound of Ava's boot heel thumping above brought a smile to Molly's face. 'See? I told yer. There was a message in that heel tap.'

'And what was that?' Alice asked.

'It's no Mickey Mouse job.' She raised an eyebrow and shuffled six white china plates on to the table ready for the roast lamb. Smiling to herself, she pictured Arthur Wood sitting in the chair by the fire waiting for his Sunday dinner . . . and felt a glow in that part of her where the sun had not shone in a very long time.

4

After the Sunday roast followed by Molly's famous apple crumble and custard, and the washing up done and dried, the house in Tillet Street was still. Other than the low sound of an old movie on the television, which was absorbing Marilyn, Ava, Cathy and Johnny, it was quiet. This cosy kind of winter afternoon with a fire burning in the grate was the rule rather than the exception, as was Molly, Alice and Jim's Sunday afternoon nap, which they were enjoying upstairs in the undisturbed part of the house.

Snuggled up on the sofa with Johnny, her shoes off, Cathy was more content than she ever imagined she could be. Starting her new job the next day drifted into her mind on and off, but she was no longer worried about going into a completely different world from the one she had been used to at Gottard's. She knew she would look the part, because Molly had steam-pressed her best clothes for her.

The movie, *Curse of the Werewolf,* told the story of a poor beggar who had been imprisoned unjustly for years by a villainous Spanish aristocrat and who, by the time he had made his escape, had degenerated into an animal. The beast then raped a servant girl who later gave birth to a werewolf. The dialogue was accompanied from time to time by the sound of Johnny gently snoring as he dozed on and off. Peaceful though he looked, unbeknown to the others, he was worried because the previous day he had taken a loan from a moneylender to make up for his loss on the horses, then tried to win it back but with a disastrous outcome. He was getting himself deeper and deeper into debt, owing money here, there and everywhere.

So gripped were they by the horror film that the girls didn't hear the van pull up outside the house, so when the doorbell suddenly rang the three of them jumped out of their skins and Johnny woke with a start, saying, 'Look out for its claws . . . !'

Laughing at his bewildered expression, Marilyn dragged herself up from her armchair and went to open the front door to the men. Eager to return to the film, she hadn't noticed that there was not one smile or hello as the guys walked through to the small living room at the back of the house. Out of duty rather than zeal she put the kettle on, but then told herself that they weren't helpless little boys. 'Make yourselves a pot of tea and tuck into whatever you fancy from the cupboard,' she said. 'Fruit cake, biscuits, whatever. Only I want to see the rest of the film.'

Back in her armchair in the front room with her legs curled under her, Marilyn sensed that things might have gone wrong with the little expedition but felt it best to leave the men to themselves. If things hadn't worked out she knew they would prefer to talk together in private. Suddenly, however, her beloved Albert appeared in the doorway. 'I don't suppose there's any left-over dinner, is there, Marilyn? We're starving.'

'We kept some meat back for sandwiches, and there's a sliced loaf in the bin. Help yourselves,' she replied, unwilling to trade the action on screen for domestic duties.

'Right. I suppose we'll make do with a sandwich, then. Where will I find the horseradish?'

'In the little kitchen cupboard, sweetheart – over the sink.' The butter's in the dish on the mantelshelf, so it should be soft enough for spreading.' She looked into her bloke's face and could see by the expression in his eyes that he was worried. He was sporting his little-boy-hurt look.

'No rush, darling,' he said, a touch sarcastic. 'All in your own time.' He nodded at Ava, who was giving him a black look for disturbing their film, and then left them to it, sighing loudly to convey the message: 'I might as well be dead for all you care.' The girls had seen it many times before so it went right over their heads. If he wanted to persuade himself that he was neglected just because he was in a mood, this was fine by them.

'Something's gone wrong,' murmured Marilyn, once he was out of earshot.

'Leave 'em to chew the fat,' was Ava's preoccupied reply. 'It won't be the first time. They don't plan things properly – that's their trouble.'

Molly, who had been lightly dozing in her bedroom with a hot water bottle under her shoulder which was giving her hell, had heard the guys come in and was on her way downstairs. She wanted to be in on the animated conversation that usually followed a break-in. Through the open door of the front room she could see the unruffled scene of her lazy granddaughters and Johnny, who was half asleep with his legs under the table. 'It didn't take him long,' she mumbled, chuffed to bits that he was in the fold. She liked Johnny, gambler or not. He was a lovely guy.

The men's low, serious conversation came to an abrupt stop as she walked through the back living room into the kitchen to make herself a cup of tea. It had taken only seconds for her to clock that something had gone wrong. As far as Molly was concerned, George's presence was the biggest clue. Whenever they had pulled off a job successfully there were smiles all round and George would have gone straight in to Rosie to give her the good news.

Too fucking bad, thought Molly. They were going to have to talk while she was there, whether they liked it or not. They could include her in it or ignore her, but she had no intention of missing out on the chit-chat because she liked to know what was going on. And in any case, it was obvious that they had a serious problem and probably needed a bit of advice from an old veteran like herself. Molly had, after all was said and done, been nicking stuff since she was old enough to toddle off to the corner shop by herself when her family lived in a narrow back street in Wapping.

She could see that, even though the coals in the grate were still glowing, the fire needed a top-up, so she had a good reason to be there. 'Everything all right, boys?' she enquired, chirpy and wide awake as she poked the glowing embers. 'Go well, did it?'

'Wouldn't mind a sandwich, Molly,' said Albert. 'We've not 'ad a thing to eat all day.'

'I guessed that might be the case, which is why I've got up from my lovely comfy bed in the middle of my afternoon rest . . . once you'd woke me up. I heard the door go. I guessed you'd be hungry.

Albert, quieter than usual, said, 'I take it Johnny's in the front room, Molly?'

'He is, yeah,' Stanley answered for her. They're in the middle of watching the Sunday film – *Curse of the Werewolf*. It's a pity Johnny's not doing a bit of casual labour to pay off his gambling debts. He owes me a ton.'

'*Curse of the Werewolf* . . .' Albert chuckled. 'I loved that film first time round. I forgot it was on again today.' The room fell silent again.

'So what was it then?' Molly persisted. 'Alarm go off? Security guard on duty? Or did you go to the wrong address like your favourite films stars would have done – Laurel and Hardy?'

'Don't know what you're talking about, Molly,' said Stanley innocently. 'You've been reading too many of them crime paperbacks. We told you, we've been shifting furniture as a favour.'

'Yeah, I'm sure.' Molly smiled broadly, unable to ignore the funny side of it. 'You've cocked up, boys – why not admit it, eh? You won't be the first. Either get it off your chest or get up off them chairs and go 'ome. You've brought a depressing atmosphere in wiv yer and I ain't 'aving that. Don't forget Jim's bad heart.'

'All right. If you must know, we couldn't manage to blow the door off of a little safe.'

'Ah . . .' Molly nodded slowly, 'I thought as much. You 'ave cocked up. Well, I s'pose that's definitely a good reason for the long faces. How wrong can a job go? Come on, then – own up. Who's responsible for that little mishap, then?'

'It's not exactly the end of the world, Molly. It's just a bit inconvenient, that's all,' muttered Albert.

Rolling himself a cigarette, George slowly shook his head. 'That's the understatement of the fucking year!'

Stanley said, 'It wasn't our fault, Molly. And anyway . . . all is not lost.'

'Meaning?' enquired Molly, showing no sign of emotion one way or the other.

'We didn't manage to blow the door off the safe . . . but we know a man who can do it – no problem. Trouble is, he's in Scotland.'

'And we're in England. Well done, boys. Good judgment that, wasn't it? How many times have I told you to use people on your own doorstep? Fucking Scotland! What was you thinking?'

'Molly – you've never told us that,' remonstrated Albert, quietly laughing at her.

'Well, then, excuse me for slipping up! So . . . it was all a waste of time. What a pity.' She looked at each of the three men in turn. 'You can't go back a second time. So don't even think about it. You're gonna have to take it like men . . . because history has proved time and time again that only fools go into a no-win situation twice. You're just gonna have to accept failure and wipe the egg clean off your face, boys, whether you like it or not.'

'There's no need for us to go back, darlin',' said Stanley, irritated. 'The safe's in the van.' Then he shut his eyes tightly to block the stream of verbal abuse he was expecting Molly to throw at them.

Surprising them, a touch out of character, Molly was silenced by this little bit of news. She looked at the faces of these hardened criminals, waiting for them to grin and say it was a wind-up, that they wouldn't even think of daring to bring trouble to her family's doorstep – especially since they were nearly family themselves, coming and going when they felt like it.

'Tell me that's a joke,' she said. 'A joke that's hilarious, but only when it's told years after the incident and not at the time. Tell me that even you three wouldn't do such a stupid, risky thing.'

'Don't worry about it, Molly,' said George. 'It's all under control. That's the trouble with you women – you go into panic mode when it's not necessary. My Rosie's just the same. Born worrier.'

'Born worrier?' Molly laughed. 'She'll wring your fucking neck if you really 'ave brought a safe back here. Tell me Stanley was joking, George. That it never 'appened. Tell me you couldn't get into the building so you came away quietly and no burglar alarms went off and no police cars chased you to our door.'

'Don't be silly, Molly,' said Albert, giving her a wink. 'We've not been caught yet, 'ave we?'

'No? Well, how come you spent two years in Parkhurst? That's hardly a boy scout's prison, is it?'

'That was years ago. When I was young and tough and too big for my boots.' He smiled and winked at his partners in crime. 'The safe's in the van waiting for the man who could pick the lock to the crown jewels, should it take his fancy. It'll cost us, but there you go. There's a little fortune in that safe, so all our pockets will be lined at the end of the day. Your purse as well.'

Visibly taken back, Molly was momentarily lost for words. Then, her voice almost a whisper, she said, 'Are you honestly telling me that parked outside this house is Johnny's dad's van with a safe full of money? A safe that you can't open?'

'Yeah. That's about the picture, Molly, in a nutshell. The only little problem we've got is that my contact won't be able to get down from Scotland till Tuesday.'

'Tuesday? So the van'll be sitting out there for two fucking days and two fucking nights with the Old Bill on the lookout and fingerprints all over it?'

'We wore cotton gloves, Molly,' Stanley assured her. 'And it's just an ordinary van. Who the fuck is gonna take any notice of it? Take a couple of your menopause pills and calm down.'

'In the normal run of things, sweetheart, I would crack up at that joke. But somewhere, not too far away, a safe has gone missing. A safe with a good few grand in it, I would think. A safe that's got to be got rid of once it's empty. And I'm wondering, even in my menopausal state of being, where you're gonna dump the thing. In the Cut? Or will you leave it in our back yard? Is this your brainy plan?'

'Course it's not! We had to fetch it back 'ere!' barked Stanley. 'We could 'ardly park it up in a bus station, could we? Is this what you'd 'ave suggested?'

'No, it's not. But you can fucking well go and park it up somewhere else now. Anywhere other than on our doorstep. And thinking off the top of my head, I'll tell you of a nice dark secluded place where you could pull in and hide the evidence for a bit.'

'Well, go on, then,' said Albert. 'What have you got in mind?'

'I'll tell you after a cup of tea. Then we'll go for a little ride, boys. One of you can drive the van and George can drive his car, with me in the front showing you the way.'

'Where to?' demanded Stanley, irritated but with a glimmer of hope in his voice.

'That's for me to know, sweetheart, and you to find out . . . once we're in the car. All right? Me and George will lead and you and Albert can follow us in the van. But first, as I said, we'll have a nice cup of tea and a cold meat sandwich. How does that suit yer?'

'Where are you thinking of taking them, Nan,' asked Marilyn, who had just appeared in the doorway.

'Mind your own business! Go back and watch your Dracula film, darling.'

'It's not *Dracula* – it's *Curse of the Werewolf*. And it's finished. Me and Ava are going back to our flat.'

'Come on, Molly,' said Albert encouragingly. 'You can't expect us to just follow like little boy scouts. What 'ave you got in mind?'

'A very dark yard in Cutler Street. In a corner where the stalls are stacked ready for next Sunday – under tarpaulin that won't be looked at or disturbed *until* next Sunday. We take the safe and leave it there till your man comes down from Scotland?

The room fell silent until Albert started to laugh. 'If that doesn't take the biscuit, nothing will. That is fucking brilliant, Molly. You are one clever old cow on the quiet.'

'I know. And brilliance gets it due reward. I want ten per cent of your takings.'

'Sod off,' said Albert, laughing at her. 'You can 'ave a couple of 'undred if it all works out. And only because you're family.'

'No, sweetheart,' Molly smiled. 'I want a grand.'

'You can 'ave five 'undred, Molly,' said Stanley, 'and think yourself lucky that we love you or you'd get sweet fuck-all. We can make our own way there – it's hardly miles away, is it? And Jock McLock will 'ave that safe door open by tomorrow night – no problem.'

'Not if I make a little phone call,' said Molly. 'And you're not family *yet*, sunshine.'

'Oh, give 'er what she wants,' sighed Albert, and then, 'All right if I use the phone, Molly?'

'Course it is, Albert. And thanks for backing me up. As it happens, you *can* go without me. You know where the yard in Cutler Street is, don't yer?'

'Should do. Your old boyfriend's got a stall there with under-the-counter goods for sale.'

'I know 'e 'as. I've always known it,' she fibbed. 'Anyway, how come you go slumming down Cutler Street?'

'I pop in now and then to see a man about a dog, Molly, that's all. A canny old jeweller who's got a pawn shop there. And you know Jews love to do business on a Sunday. I go from old man Maurice once I've done a little bit of business with 'im to old man Arthur and a cup of tea from the travelling café parked in the yard. Tea and toast. Lovely.'

'So that's a hint, is it? Tea and toast?'

'It wasn't, darling, but now you mention it . . .'

'You can have both with pleasure – but then you can move like lightning and put that safe to bed.'

'They'll have a cup of tea only,' Marilyn broke in. 'You go and watch the telly, Nan, and keep your voice down. I don't want Dad worrying over this. Let's not forget his bad heart, eh?'

'You don't have to remind me of that, darlin'. It's for the sake of your dad and his condition that I'm master-minding this bit of clumsy business that your boyfriend cocked up. Talk about sending a boy out to do woman's work!' With that Molly turned to leave, saying, 'Next time you plan a little safe job – come and talk to me about it first.' Then she stopped in her tracks and turned to face them. 'And you leave young Johnny out of your wheeling and dealing. And not just because he's still wet behind the ears, but because he's our Cathy's sweetheart and too young to be involved with you lot.'

Once Molly was out of earshot, Stanley quietly sniggered. 'Wet behind the ears? Johnny was pinching bars of chocolate from off the counter in Woolworth's before he was five years old. Ask his mother. She loves to tell the story.'

'He's all right,' said Albert. 'He can cut his teeth on his first job with that lorry load of tinned salmon. He's trusted in the docks, so it should be a piece of cake. I'll have a little chat with him before I go – see if he's up for it on Friday.'

'Here comes the boy with the good looks,' said Stanley, his voice raised to get the message across that Johnny was, as it happened, on his way in from the passage.

'The removal job go all right, then, did it?' Johnny smiled.

'Not exactly, Johnny, not exactly. But sit down and have a

cup of tea with us. Spending all your time in there with the women – what's wrong with you?'

'I was watching a film, a good old one.'

'Oh, well, it's all right for some. Look at us, still in these bloody overalls and the job's not finished yet. Don't ask why.'

'Why?' said Johnny, his warm sense of humour easing the tension in the room that the men weren't even aware of. They weren't as relaxed about the safe as they would have others believe.

Stanley closed the door into the passage, then sat back down again at the small dining table. He looked from George to Albert with a question on his face, and received a nod of approval for him to do the talking. 'So, Johnny,' he began, giving him a wink and smiling, 'you're skint and need to borrow a tenner.'

'Yeah,' said Johnny, 'to see me through to payday.'

'And what about your debts, son?' asked Albert. At forty-three he was the eldest of them and felt he was entitled to play the part of a father figure. 'Because from what I gather you've not been all that lucky on the racetrack. Your little dog hasn't come in for a while.'

'My luck's gone from bad to worse. It's gotta change soon, though, eh? Always does. Can't have a losing streak for much longer. I was eighty quid up this time last month.'

'I'm gonna lend you the money, son,' said Albert, 'to tide you over till payday. Now you keep out of the betting shop and away from the dogtrack this week. If you do, you can come in on a job that's being arranged. It's in Canary Wharf and it should see you with a tidy little sum. Not a fortune – but good for a novice.'

'What's my part and how much and when?' said Johnny, cutting through the flannel.

'Tins of prime red salmon. A container's due in on Friday and all you have to do is drive it away from the docks, up Commercial Street, to pull in left at Gardeners Corner into a side turning. A driver'll be there waiting to continue the journey out into the countryside. Then you just catch the bus back to work and slip in through the gate as easy as you like. If you get pulled, say you nipped out to put a bet on. You'll have a betting slip from the bloke who you pass the lorry to. And who knows? You might even get lucky. He might 'ave backed you a winner.'

'Ingenious,' Johnny smiled. 'So the time on the betting slip, should anything go wrong, is my alibi.'

'Exactly.'

'And what's the payout?'

'Two grand.'

Johnnie's face lit up. 'You're 'aving me on! Tins of salmon?'

'A lot of tins of salmon and a few other bits and bobs in between that you don't need to know about. Do you want the job or not?'

'Course I do. I've been a long time waiting, lads. It's good to know you trust me. My only question is, why me? I know we all 'ave to start somewhere, but there are enough blokes out there that would be up for this who've got a track record.'

'We would 've brought you in sooner, son,' said Albert, 'but your reputation as a loser when it comes to gambling lets you down. Go too far down that road and you make the wrong kind of enemies. So that's the deal if you want in with us. Walk past the betting shops from now on.'

'Fair enough. I'm in.'

'Good . . . I hear you're a bit soft on Cathy,' said Stanley.

'Soft? It's more than that. I'm bowled over.' He looked from Stanley to Albert and grinned. 'Thanks, guys. I appreciate this.'

'Well, there's no more to be said, then.' Albert slipped a hand into his inside pocket and pulled out a wad of notes. 'Give this to your dad for the loan of the van. He knows it's coming to him, so don't get tempted to try and double it – because you're out in the cold if you do.'

'I won't. Don't you worry.' He slipped the money into his

inside pocket, gave a wink and a smile and went back to his girlfriend in the front room.

Once the door closed behind Johnny, Albert stretched out in his armchair and took out a cigarette. 'Let's hope he pays off his debts after the job's done and dusted. He owes money to lads in the docks who'll kick the shit out of 'im if he don't pay up. I'm surprised Jim let 'im get his feet under the table and his backside on the couch next to Cathy. A compulsive gambler's worse than a drug addict.'

'No more favours for friends if it goes wrong, Albert,' said Stanley. 'You're too fucking soft by half. If he falls apart on that job we could all go down.'

'You're getting more like an old woman every day, Stanley.' Albert quietly chuckled and winked at his mate. 'Stop worrying. Ten minutes and we're off to Cutler Street. Right?'

'Sounds good to me,' said George.

Half an hour or so later, the downstairs of that terraced house in the back streets of Bethnal Green exhibited a more sombre mood. Jim and Alice were still having their nap and Molly had gone in to keep Rosie company. Marilyn and Ava were on their way home and the men off to Club Row. So Cathy and Johnny had the front room to themselves. With the door closed and the small coal fire glowing, the lights low and a record playing softly on the turntable, the lovebirds were stretched out on the sofa, wrapped in each other's arms. They wouldn't have known or cared if bombs had been dropping outside, because Cathy and Johnny were making love to the voice of Fats Domino singing 'Blueberry Hill'.

Johnny, of course, had no inkling that his dad's van had been driven to the yard in Cutler Street and was at that precise moment pulling into an ideal dark corner where the men could lift the safe out of the back and hide it under one of the open-fronted sheds. One thing that the men had forgotten was to bring a torch with them, but eventually they found one in the van after shuffling tools around. Molly, as usual, had been bang on right. There were plenty of tarpaulin covers, some in a tall neat pile and other thrown carelessly into a pile in the corner. Although it pained the men to leave the safe with all that money inside, they knew they had no choice for the moment.

Once out of the yard, as they moved slowly along Cutler Street they saw a tart propping up a semi-drunk punter who was singing 'When Irish Eyes Are Smiling'. A common enough sight in that neck of the woods – but the pair had turned into the yard to conduct their business. As they drove away, the men could only hope that the woman was a hardened prostitute about to give a five-minute quickie against the wall, and not one going in search of a makeshift bed to accommodate her customer.

'Drop us off at the girls' place, would you, George? They'll sulk for a week if we don't let 'em know all's well.'

'If I must,' grumbled George, obviously pissed off by the request. 'I feel as if I've been on the move all day with nothing to see for it. Now you want me to go to Victoria Park. Great.'

'Stop fucking moaning. You're like an old woman at times,' said Albert, breaking into quiet laughter. 'Your face'll soon light up once we've got that door off.'

'I'd sooner it was already lit up, to tell you the truth.' George swerved the car round a corner to take a short cut through the back doubles. 'I can't stand it when the work's only half finished.'

'That's the way it goes sometimes,' said Stanley. 'It's the nature of our profession.'

'Tell me about it.'

'Hark at 'im,' Albert laughed. 'You've got a good voice, George. Give us a song instead of all the carping. You'll be taking tea wiv Molly next and going on about the rising price of eggs and what they used to cost in the old days.'

'You reckon? Well, if I'm the old woman you're the Girl Guide. I mean, who was it couldn't blow the safe door off, then? Who's had to summon some geezer down from Scotland to get it open?' It's fucking crazy and you know it. We can't even be certain if the safe's full, from what you said earlier on.'

'That was a joke, for fuck's sake! We're looking at around thirty grand. And before you ask, yes, the inside information is a hundred per cent. With a bit for Johnny for the loan of the van and a bit for Mac the Knife from Scotland, it'll be a nice little earner for all of us.'

'So what was all that gob earlier on about, then? Whether the payday at the firm's been changed from Fridays to Thursdays?'

'A bit of drama from the girl on the inside. My sister the drama queen – you know what she's like. She turns a crisis into a drama whenever she can. Thrives on it. She only left that company six months ago . . . they're hardly gonna change staff payday from a Friday to a Thursday all of a sudden. Stop tormenting yourself.'

'I just don't like cock-ups, that's all.'

'Nor does Mac the Knife. Don't forget he'll be coming all the way down from Scotland and taking a risk by going to that yard. D'you reckon I want to get in his bad books? He's a nutter. Upset him and we'd all 'ave to get on the next plane to Spain. If that safe's empty I'll leg it to the airport while I've still got legs. They might be white and hairy but I've grown fond of 'em.

'Very funny,' said George, trying not to smile or get nervous at the thought of the Scotsman in an ugly mood. But, smiles being contagious, it was only seconds before all three of them were laughing and all the stress had melted away. The adrenalin rush was part and parcel of thieving, after all was said and done.

'I just wanna get Johnny's dad's van back and put my Rosie's mind at ease.'

'You'll never do that, Georgie boy,' Albert chuckled. 'Women love to worry just so they can feel nice and easy once a problem's solved. That's when they go all soft and suggest an early night.

★   ★   ★

With the curtains drawn, and only the glow of a table lamp in the front room, Cathy was playing her favourite record, 'When a Man Loves a Woman'. She and Johnny were relaxing on the sofa, with their feet up and her head snuggled into his shoulder, and Cathy, having just made love with him, was content to let time stand still. She had lost her virginity at fifteen, experimenting with a lad at school who had been a friend of hers for years. He had suggested they try out this sex thing to see what it was like, and the result had been clumsy and hilarious. The experiment had done little for Cathy, but had instigated in him a habit of screwing any girl who was up for it. He had gone through the fourth year of senior school as if he were the only gander in a field of geese – and the girls couldn't get enough of it.

Now, having experienced love as it should be made, Cathy was delirious. It had been wonderful – and, more than this, she knew now that she and Johnny were in love. If it hadn't been for the sound of Alice coming downstairs after her Sunday nap she would have remained on cloud nine with no thoughts for the morrow. But there were other people in their world who had their feet firmly on the ground.

'I don't want to disturb you two lovebirds,' remarked Alice as she poked her head round the door, 'but don't you think it might be an idea if you pressed your clothes for work, Cathy? You'll want to look and feel good on your first morning.'

'Nan already did that for me, Mum. Steam-pressed my two-piece and hung it in my cupboard with the blouse I'll be wearing. And I've polished my boots . . . and my winter coat's on a hanger and not chucked over my bedroom chair.'

'Boots? Don't you think you should wear your best shoes?'

'My boots *are* my best shoes, Mum. Stop worrying. They're all polished up and look brand-new and they go with everything else.'

'Well . . . I suppose that's as much as you can do, then. I'm just about to make a pot of tea. Would you like a cup, Johnny, before you go?'

'Not for me, thanks.' Johnny glanced at his watch and pulled a face. 'Bloody hell – it's gone six! Dad'll be wondering where his van is.'

'They should be back any time,' said Alice, leaving the youngesters to themselves and going off to the kitchen.

Cathy and Johnny immediately slipped back into each other's arms on the sofa. 'Do you know something, Cath,' said Johnny, his voice quiet and husky, 'I think I've been in love with you for ages – ever since I started to come in to see your dad on a regular basis.'

'When Dad was first home from hospital . . . God, that seems like an age ago.'

'I know. I probably wouldn't 'ave met you if I 'adn't been next door playing cards with George and the boys that night. It came up in conversation that your dad – who I only knew from working in the docks – lived next door. We all thought a lot of Jim before 'is 'eart attack, Cath. He was one for 'elping young dockers fresh in, like I was. Showed us the ropes and that.'

'I know he did.'

'The thing is . . . I'm two years older than you and I'm not sure 'ow 'e'll take it – us going out seriously together.'

'He'll be fine,' said Cathy. 'In fact he'll be more than fine. He already sees you as part of the family.'

'Anyway . . . you'll probably lose interest in me once you've met them posh journalists at work. They're bound to ask you out for a drink. You'll probably 'ave a lot more in common with them than with me – just a labourer working in the docks. I'm never gonna be a white-collar worker, Cath.'

'Johnny – I'm from a long line of dockers. What are you talking about?'

'Yeah, but . . . you're different. You've always worked in an office.'

'But practically all the girls from my class left school before they were sixteen, and most of them got office jobs. Some better than mine and some not as good. None of us took O-levels. Not out of choice, admittedly, but—'

'What are you trying to say, Cath?'

'That just because we're working-class it doesn't mean we're bound to work in a factory or a shop. Nor does working in a factory or a shop make any of my mates any different from me. Except that they earn more money than I do, what with piece work and overtime on top. We all do what we're best at or what suits us – that's all I'm saying.'

'That makes sense. So how about us going to the pictures after work tomorrow?'

'Not really. It's my first day, don't forget. Let's make it Tuesday or Wednesday, eh?'

'Suits me. What time do 'ou finish anyway?'

'Half five or thereabouts.'

'Well . . . I could meet you from work on your first day and we could go for a coffee and you can tell me all about it.'

'Sounds great. Yeah. Let's do that.' She kissed him on the cheek, looked into his eyes and without thinking said, 'I could fall in love with you if I'm not careful.'

Johnny slowly drew breath and then only just managed to say, 'Do you really mean that, Cath?'

'Of course I do. I loved every second of what happened this afternoon.' She looked into his blue eyes and felt herself melting as he smiled that handsome smile of his. 'If you want the truth – I've never felt like this before, Johnny.'

There was no need for any more words. The new love of her life drew her close and she could feel his heart beating against her breasts. 'I love you, Cath,' he whispered. 'I 'ope you don't break my 'eart.' Then the doorbell broke into their private little world and he let out a sigh. 'That's probably George back with Dad's van.'

Just as he was about to leave the room Cathy stopped him. 'You will kick the gambling habit, won't you, Johnny? Only my family mention it now and then when you lot aren't around, and it's got me worried now.'

Johnny peered at her, puzzled. 'I don't 'ave a gambling 'abit, Cathy. I just like to try my 'and at a bit of luck now and then.

Let what they say go in one ear and out the other. I'm getting a bit fed up with 'earing it, to tell the truth. Don't take any notice of what they say.' He smiled and winked at her. 'Love you loads.'

'Love you too.' said Cathy. 'Get out of here before I nail your feet to the floor.'

'I'll phone you once I'm back 'ome – if that's all right?'

'Of course it is.' Cathy then kissed him tenderly, before murmuring, 'I'll be waiting for that call.'

5

With butterflies in her stomach, Cathy walked slowly along Bethnal Green Road. She had allowed herself more than enough time to get to Moorgate station, which was on the Central Line and only one stop before Farringdon, her old weekday haunt. But today she would be moving in a completely different world from the one she had been used to at Gottard's.

Fortunately this late January day was sunny, and with her thick coat and warm scarf around her neck she couldn't have wished for a better morning to begin working for her new employer in publishing. Glancing through the ornate black iron railings into the park where she had played so often with her friends as a child, she remembered how sweet the drinking water from the old stone fountain had tasted when she had been hot and thirsty. Cathy had first been taken to the park when she was five by her dad to join the children's library there, and after that had gone there with him most Saturdays. One thing that had always stayed with her was the bit of history that Jim had related about the building and the time when it had been a lunatic asylum, which was why the place was known locally as Barmy Park. He said his grandmother had told him how sad it had been to see some of the poor souls wandering around in the old days, looking lost and in a world of their own. But this didn't stop her from loving the beautiful, well-kept gardens and the stunning rose beds in summer.

Once on the platform Cathy knew she wouldn't have to wait long for a train, but would still have to squeeze herself into a packed and sweltering carriage because this was the rush hour.

Today, instead of her normal dull Monday morning feeling, she was actually excited at the thought of going to work. But apprehensive, too. Getting out at Moorgate, she smiled happily to herself as she walked through unfamiliar streets on her way to pastures new.

Once inside, on the first floor of Johnson's in the reception area, she was surprised to find nobody about. The place wasn't bustling, as she had expected, but very quiet and a touch eerie. She was fifteen minutes early, true, but even so it was nine-fifteen. By now, had she been still at Gottard's, she would have been at her desk typing for three-quarters of an hour, with all the staff in every office silently working away too. Looking around herself in the quiet, she took in her surroundings. The reception desk that she would be sitting behind seemed much grander than on the day of her interview, when the place had been buzzing with people. The plush gold carpet looked magnificent, reflected in the full-length mirrored doors of the coats cupboard. On the highly polished reception desk, which to Cathy looked more like an elegant dining table, was a beautiful display of fresh flowers in a plain but stylish white vase.

Going into the ladies' powder room, Cathy was pleased to have some spare time to check on her make-up. On either side of a row of six sparkling white basins with shiny chrome taps hung beautiful framed prints of tranquil river and forest scenes. This room made her feel as if she were in a hotel instead of at work. Looking into the bevel-edge mirror which ran the length of the washbasins, she smiled at her reflection. 'This is more like it, Cathy,' she whispered. 'This is the place to be.'

No sooner had she touched up her mascara and swept on some lipstick than a girl of around her own age arrived – she looked like the singer Sandie Shaw, with hair the same dark colour and swinging pageboy style. Smiling at Cathy, she asked if she was the new receptionist and introduced herself as Pauline.

'I can hardly believe this place,' said Cathy, talking to her new acquaintance as if they had known each other for ages. 'It's fabulous compared to the stuffy dump where I used to work.'

The friendly girl looked into the mirror, checking that her eye make-up hadn't smudged. 'You wait till you meet the blokes. If I wasn't already engaged I'd be having a whale of a time.' She glanced at Cathy's left hand.

'I'm not engaged,' responded Cathy. 'But I do have a boyfriend.'

'That won't put the guys in this place off, trust me.'

'Morning, each,' another girl greeted them as she came bounding in, her long brown curls all awry and falling around her freckled face. She immediately introduced herself as Margaret and asked Cathy what she thought of her new pale apricot lipstick as if they were bosom pals.

Pauline answered for her. 'That colour really suits you, Margaret.' She then lit a cigarette and blew smoke rings. 'I love it.'

Delighted by their relaxed mood, Cathy said, 'When is everyone expected to start working?'

'Somewhere between nine-thirty and ten, except for the day when a paper or magazine goes to print. Then we all get in early and work our socks off. Fridays are usually quiet . . . and that's when the guys play tricks on us. It's all to do with give and take. No one is looking over our shoulder, but we could be called in to see the personnel officer if we don't come up with the work on time. She keeps us young ones in order. If she didn't, there'd be a lot of snogging going on in the dark room where the press photos are developed.'

'I think I'm gonna enjoy working in this place,' said Cathy. It was worlds apart from what she was used to.

'So,' enquired Pauline, 'are we going to the pub with the journalists for a welcome drink after work, Cath?'

'I don't wanna be a damp squib,' she quietly answered, 'but my boyfriend's going to meet me outside – this being my first day. And I've only just started to go out with 'im, so—'

'Fair enough,' said Pauline. 'We'll go tomorrow after work.' She looked into Cathy's face and chuckled. 'You won't be able to get out of it. It's your initiation into this place. The lads will play all kinds of tricks to test you, as well. So be warned. They'll hide your handbag in the gents, they'll put salt in your coffee and a fart cushion on your chair, and they'll leave mysterious love notes on your desk.'

'You're in the newspaper publishing world now,' Margaret chipped in, 'so enjoy it while you may.'

'I will – and thanks for the tips. But what am I supposed to do now?'

'Sit behind that posh desk in reception and wait for the typing to come in from the journalists, as well as greeting visitors and letting the MD know when they arrive. Important visitors, Cathy, and don't be surprised if you see politicians come in that you might have seen on the telly.' Then, checking her appearance in a full-length mirror, Pauline murmured, 'It's a good place to work – don't get us wrong. Just don't take the flirting from the boys too seriously.'

It hadn't taken Cathy long to see that the girls were right about the boys. But they were fun and not in the least bit lecherous, and only drifted in now and then as she typed up edited copy for the journalists. She also greeted guests and directed them to the appropriate managerial staff as well as taking phone messages. But even though she was busy there was no sense of grind to it. It was light and bright, and everyone who worked in the building seemed happy. This wonderful atmosphere was worth all the nights of anxiety she had endured when she first decided to leave Gottard's and then constantly wondered if she was doing the right thing. Now she knew for sure that she had done exactly the right thing. It was a demanding but brilliant job and the day flew by, and before she realised it was time for her to leave and meet Johnny.

True to his word, he arrived on the dot of five-thirty in

reception – to find Cathy surrounded by young guys flirting with her. Quickly up and away, the couple walked hand in hand away from the building and had no idea that there were at least twenty young staff at the picture window of the first-floor general office looking down at them. 'There goes love's young dream,' sighed one of the guys. What they couldn't possibly have known was that Cathy, oblivious to the fact herself, had conceived that first time they made love and was now pregnant with Johnny's baby.

As a small celebration of Cathy's first day in her new job, Molly had made a light fruit cake that morning and given it a thin layer of white icing decorated with little silver confectionery balls spelling out the word 'Congratulations'. With a few hours to spare before her youngest granddaughter came home, and with the cake hidden in the sideboard, Jim out on a visit to a mate and Alice not yet back from work, Molly had the place to herself and time to think.

Relaxing in a comfortable chair with a pot of tea, she tried not to think about something that had been worrying her of late – something that she had told no one about. The dreaded thought which had been pervading her mind was cancer. Lung cancer. She knew of two people in their mid-fifties who had died from it and she was nearly seventy, so what chance had she of surviving? If cancer was the cause of the agonising pains just below her left shoulder and going through to the front, then she had to face the fact that she might not have as long in this world as she would like.

She wondered if it was time to go and see the doctor. In the early hours of that very morning she had been woken yet again by a severe and sudden attack, which gradually settled into a dull ache as if someone was slowly pulling a long needle through from below her shoulder blade and down into her back. The strongest painkillers she could buy over the chemist's counter had not always eased this pain, let alone made it go away. She had picked up a secondhand medical paperback from a stall in the market and it was from this that she had deduced, according to the symptoms given, that her pain could be caused by cancer. She had suffered excruciatingly at times when her family believed she was just having an afternoon nap. But night-time attacks were far worse and lonelier: sometimes they lasted all through the night, with stabbing pains piercing right through her left lung.

To an onlooker, Molly might easily have looked a sorry soul, but once she had pushed her health fears to the back of her mind she started to enjoy her solitude. She cast her mind back to the time when she had met her late husband and fallen in love with her head in the clouds – in the same way that Cathy was doing now. The difference between herself and her granddaughter – and Molly of course had no idea – was that she hadn't given herself to her man so early in their courtship.

The nagging worries returned with the sudden thought of herself being discussed in hushed voices – it made her go cold, as it had done a few times before. If she *was* seriously ill she didn't want or need a great long debate over what was best for her. Until a few months ago she had been rudely healthy and had taken for granted that she would live to be a hundred. The trouble was that she couldn't help overdoing things. If it suddenly took her fancy, Molly would give all the paintwork in the house a good wash down and not stop, other than for a cup of tea every so often, until the job was done.

Going into the garden for a breath of fresh air, she sensed that Henry was up in his room at the top of Rosie and George's house and watching her from his window. Molly glanced up and gave him a nod. It was her way of saying, 'I know you're watching me, son, and I don't mind.' He was a sensitive soul, and in a way she was part of his lonely world.

Walking back from the market that morning with two heavy shopping bags, filled with fruit and vegetables, she had felt that familiar deep burning sensation in her back. So, once she had unloaded her shopping bags, she had taken it easy.

In the market she had passed two lots of people in wheel-chairs being pushed along by family members, and had nodded and smiled at them. But this was not what she wanted for herself. No way.

An independent woman by nature, Molly could not bear the thought of having to rely on somebody else to get her out of bed, wash and dress her, and be responsible for her welfare for the rest of her life. She couldn't imagine not being able to rush here, there and everywhere or boss people about, which was one of her greatest pleasures in life. Her worst nightmare was to have to be put to bed by one of the family or to have a visiting carer come in to wipe her backside. Glancing at her reflection in the window, she smiled faintly as she murmured, 'If you're dying, Molly, and if this is what it's like . . . it's not half as bad as you thought it would be.' She then commended herself on the fact that she carried no guilt, had done her best by her family and had no unpaid debts.

Draining her teacup, she decided to go for a nice stroll to the Bethnal Green gardens and the library to sit quietly in the reading room and look through one of the big heavy medical reference books that never went out on loan. This was a first for her, because she had always considered the reading room as a place for young students and old people – which she didn't, of course, consider herself to be. But the urge to find out what was wrong with her was stronger. She took her coat with its fur-lined hood from the cupboard in the passage and pulled it on, smiling when she recalled where it had come from – John Lewis's. One of her thieving granddaughters had lifted it the year before as a Mother's Day present for Alice to give to Molly.

Once in the reading room she selected a medical book with lots of helpful pictures and found what she was looking for – a section on the lungs. Soon she was so absorbed that she didn't notice her old friend Arthur come in. He had been strolling through the park on his way to pay her an impromptu visit at the old house in Tillet Street when, from a distance, he saw her going into the library. And now, pulling out a book on antiques to read while he sat at a small table in the corner of the room, he smiled inwardly. It amused him to see Molly in this place – and especially in this room which he had always thought was out of their realm. Indeed, he was pleasantly surprised at how comfortable and at ease each of them was. Not only that, but it was also lovely and warm. Arthur decided he was quite content to wait while his lifelong friend swotted up on whatever it was that had taken her fancy.

Molly for her part could find little to indicate that she was a victim of the ferocious disease she feared after all. She hadn't had a persistent cough which produced a small amount of sputum sometimes flecked with blood, although she did sometimes suffer shortness of breath after walking for a half-hour or so. But this, she reasoned to herself, was to be expected, since she tended to walk too quickly for her age. It was something she was prepared to change if needs be.

She did discover something, however, which fitted her symptoms – especially those sharp, fierce, needle-like pains attacking her from the back. It was pleurisy, the incredibly painful ailment that had caused her sweet grandmother's death. She read through the symptoms more thoroughly, and there it was as clear as the day. This was without question what she had been suffering from intermittently, and she knew from experience how to cope with it. All the advice that had been given to her old granny now came flooding back. Don't exert yourself in any way. Remember your age. Let others lift and stretch for you. Don't suddenly decide to whitewash a wall. And she would need medication from her doctor, too.

Molly smiled as she remembered her old gran. When it came to temperament they were like two peas in a pod. Her gran too had thought that she could do as much as a man could: fix shelves, dig the garden, move furniture, paint walls. And her gran had been doing heavy work of this kind right up until she was in her seventies and one attack of pleurisy had been just too damaging. After suffering a collapsed lung she spent three days in hospital on a ventilator before dying. Molly was not saddened by this flashback but filled with relief as she saw her gran in her mind's eye. Just before she was taken to hospital in the old-fashioned ambulance she had winked at her and whispered, 'You wait till I get to 'eaven, Molly love . . . I'll kick a few people in the arse and get my own back.'

Molly realised she was going to appreciate her son-in-law's company more than ever now she had to take it easy. She loved playing cards, dominoes and Monopoly with Jim, and best of all studying the horses, so they could put on their little two-shilling bets. So, relaxed now in the knowledge that she had a condition which, once given the respect it deserved, could be kept at bay, her worries floated up through the ceiling and out of the library window. She leaned back in her chair as the winter sun shone through the stained glass window and warmed the cockles of her heart. She was not dying.

'Well I never 'ad you down for a scholar, Molly. What a dark horse you are!' said Arthur who had appeared behind her and was standing hands on hips.

'What the fuck are *you* doing 'ere?' she whispered, unable to hide her pleasure at seeing him. In his old-fashioned but clean and well-pressed suit, white shirt and paisley-patterned tie he looked quite handsome.

'What I'm always doing 'ere,' he fibbed. 'Studying the antiques books so I don't miss anything that looks like rubbish – but is worf a pot.'

'A pot to piss in?' she said, baiting him.

'No. Not that. Oh no. A pot of gold. Come on, I'll walk you 'ome and you can tell me why you're searching through that medical book and 'ow long you've got to live.'

Pulling herself up from the chair, she said indignantly, 'I'm as fit as a fiddle, Arthur, whether you like it or not.'

'Course you are,' he said. 'I could 'ave told you that. Wasting bloody time looking in that bloody doom-and-gloom book.' He glanced down at the page to see the piece she had been reading and the caption. Pleurisy, eh? A drop of camphor oil in hot water—'

'I know exactly what to do, Arthur! I used to prepare a little enamel bowl of inhalant for my gran.' She slipped her arm into his. 'Now tell me the truth. Why are *you* in this place? Studying antiques? If that's not a load of bollocks I don't know what is. You know all there is about what's worth a few bob and what isn't. And do you know why?'

'No . . . but you're gonna tell me. I can sense it.'

'Because you've got a nose for it. Just like your dad, his dad and all of the dads before him. Rag and bones it might 'ave been once, but what little treasures they did discover in their time, eh?'

Walking with Molly into the gardens, he said, 'And we found it all out for ourselves without 'aving to look in library books. My great-great-grandfather was the first person in the trade to discover that beneath the surface of black metal was solid silver and a valuable hallmark.'

'So you've said before.'

'And all it took was a bit of elbow grease and rubbing with the 'em of 'is old overcoat to discover that little fact . . . which earned him a few gold sovereigns over the years.'

'I know, Arthur – you told me.'

'Antique dealers? What the fuck do they know? It's in the blood, Molly. In the blood.' He sniffed and held his chin high as he said, 'Fancy a cup of tea and a cake in the tea rooms?'

'That would be very nice, Arthur,' she said, 'but there ain't any tea rooms round this way.'

'Course there is. The little Italian café at the top of Globe Road.'

'Oh, yeah,' she said. 'I'd forgotten about that place. That's what we'll do, then. Very nice, too. But I'm not paying.'

'My treat today, Molly. My treat. And do you know the best way to check how that pleurisy of yours is doing?'

'I'm sure you're gonna tell me anyway,' said Molly.

'No, I don't expect you do. I'll let you into a little secret. Another bit of information that never came out of one of them family medical books. Do you wanna hear it or not?'

'Have I got a choice?'

'No. This is it. You draw in as much air as you can and you slowly go through the alphabet, and as you're doing it you mark how far you've got till you 'ave to stop for a breather. You write the letter down on a bit of paper, and that way you'll see how things are going. I can still get to W before I have to let go and breathe again. I used to be able to go right through the alphabet and start again and get to G. Try it when you're in bed at night.'

'I'll try it when I think I will, thank you.'

'That's my girl,' he said, grinning. 'Full of the same old gusto but always takes my advice when I'm not looking. It's a funny old world though, innit? Eh? The way life pulls you back and then pushes you forward again. We shouldn't take anyfing for granted, Molly. Life's too precious.'

Stopping dead in her tracks, Molly peered into her mate's face. 'What are you going on about? Doctor's given you just a few months to live, 'as 'e?'

'You must be joking.' Arthur laughed. 'Fit as a fiddle, me. But you wanna watch that pleurisy. That pain can be nasty.'

'Tell me about it,' she said, slowing down a little. 'It's like an old elastic band being stretched from thick to thin from the back of my shoulder right through to the front and then – ping!'

'And 'ow often d'yer get it?'

'About every four to six months, I suppose. When I overdo things. This time it came on after I'd washed all the paintwork in the 'ouse. I thought I'd do it before spring cleaning time came and beat all the other neighbours to it. My windows sparkle in the sun, you know.'

'And give every Tom, Dick and Harry a clear view into your front room. You're getting soft in the head, Molly. Keep the winder grimy and let nobody see your business. I'm surprised at you, gal. I thought you 'ad more sense than that.'

'I never said anything about the front room window. But as it happens I do keep them sparkling nowadays. Now that we can afford lovely net curtains to stop the nosey parkers from peering in. People who have nuffing to do and can't be bothered to use their brains and sleep far too much. People who busy themselves with the wrong things such as idle gossip and chasing make-believe fantasies.' Molly glanced sideways at her friend to see that he was more thoughtful than usual.

'You're not listening to a fucking word I'm saying, are yer?'

'As it happens, for a change I *was* listening Molly. And do you know what I think? I reckon the way to get any kind of sense out of this life is to put as much into it as you can and a little bit more than you expect to get back. And the way to do that, as far as I can see, is to look out for those within your own realm. Family and neighbours. If everyone did that there wouldn't be any problems, would there?'

'Well, it wouldn't stop a war, Arthur – but it would help locally, I'll give you that. And I must say that's a bit ripe, coming from you!'

Ignoring her or not listening, Arthur murmured thoughtfully, 'If all people, in all countries, took that stance there might not be any wars.' He scratched the neck around the starched collar of his shirt and went all thoughtful again.

'Where would this planet be if there were no world wars to blow it about a bit and fuck it up?' said Molly.

Quietly laughing at her, Arthur paused for thought. He was patting himself on the back for having made this unplanned trip today and even more pleased that Molly had walked back into his life on that fateful Sunday morning. He felt that life, his life, was on the up and up, and that there just might be a reason for him still being alone and well. He and Molly had seen almost seven decades come and go. Here they were now, strolling along as happy as you like towards Globe Road and the Italian café, with neither of them feeling as if they had to chat – and he couldn't think of anything nicer. Molly wasn't bothered by the silence; in fact she felt very comfortable in it.

When they arrived at the café, true to character Arthur pushed the door open and stood aside to let Molly go in first. The wonderful smell of pannetone cake baking in the kitchen out the back, not to mention the smell of percolating coffee, brought a smile to both their faces. Taking a table for two by the window, the couple looked as if they were married and had been for donkey's years.

Her voice lowered, Molly leaned forward and said, 'Why d'you reckon they always seem to 'ave red and white tablecloths in their cafes, these Eyeties?'

'Bright and cheerful, that's why,' replied Arthur, as he removed his cap and placed it on a nearby shelf. 'If I 'ad a wish, Molly, it would be to 'ave been born Italian. Lovely people. I wouldn't 'ave left Rome to come to London, though. So I s'pose that must be their weakness, eh? Not satisfied with what they already had – sunshine and juicy grapes galore.'

'I don't think the Baroncinis are from Rome, Arthur.'

'Manner of speaking, Molly. Manner of speaking. This lot are from the countryside. But still potty to leave it behind for Bethnal Green.'

'Don't talk rot. London's a famous place – East, West, South and North. Now go up to the counter and put the order in. Save 'em 'aving to come to us. They're run off their feet by the look of things.'

'No way. Sit back, girl. Sit back and be waited on. We've turned seventy, don't forget.'

'You might 'ave done,' said Molly firmly, 'but I'm still sixty-nine until next November – and that's months away.' She glanced at the menu pinned on the wall. 'I think I'll 'ave a slice of hot sausage pizza and a cup of tea.'

They gave their order to the sixteen-year-old grandson of Mr Baroncini, the old boy who mostly sat in the corner like the old Godfather while his sons ran this successful café.

Arthur looked across to the man he had known for donkey's years and winked. The old boy smiled, nodded and gave a thumbs up sign, showing off his solid gold watch. This family had been in Britain for as long as Arthur could remember, and amongst the younger generation the accent had disappeared. They had become the well-off Italian cockneys, and deservedly so. Arthur, when living in his old house in Whitehead Street, off Cleveland Way, had known Edie Birch from way back when. Her mother had committed suicide after her father had left the family for another woman. Later on, Edie's daughter Maggie had married one of the Baroncinis and their son was the lad now serving them, Peppito.

Once the young man had taken their orders Arthur, with folded arms and a smile on his face, asked how his great-aunt Naomi was – a woman whom, had she been younger, he would like to have swept off her feet. 'Still driving everyone mad, is she, son?'

'No. She's too old for all that. She's eighty-eight, you know.'

'So she's not organising all of your lives then?'

'No. Not any more. She tries to now and again, though.'

'See what I mean, Molly.' Arthur tapped the side of his nose. 'Some women know how to rule the roost without being overtly loud about it. That crafty cow still runs the little Barcroft estate club for old folk from what I've heard – never mind the Baroncini family.'

Peppito quietly laughed but had to agree with him. 'It's her fault that I'm being put through college,' he said. 'I'm training to be a structural engineer.'

'Well, you've not nuffing to moan about then, 'ave you, son?' said Molly. 'There's money in that. Engineers earn a fortune, I bet. Naomi knew what she was doing all right. Tell her that Molly sends 'er love and remind 'er that she knows where I live.'

'I will,' he said gladly.

As they walked back to Tillet Street past the Bethnal Green fire station, with Arthur bending Molly's ear about a large old

Victorian house he'd been asked to clear in Hackney, Molly's thoughts were elsewhere. She had seen one too many over-flowing dustbins in the back streets because of the imminent dustmen's strike. 'All it bloody well needs is for the fire service to come out at the same time as the dustmen,' she murmured to herself.

'Never mind that,' said Arthur. 'You wait till the three-day week comes. This country's on the slippery slope, I reckon. Postmen'll be next to come out. And all the young can fink about is pop festivals, smoking marijuana and flower power!

'Load of blooming 'ippies. It's football them lads should be immersed in, Molly, not flowers in the barnet. They should've been at Wembley for the World Cup final, when England beat Germany instead of loafing about on the grass picking daisies. What's happening to our men? Eh? That's what I'd like the answer to. Gawd knows where it'll all lead to,' he moaned.

Arriving at her front door, Molly turned the key in the lock to the sound of raucous laughter from inside. 'The thieving granddaughters are here already,' she sighed, as pleased as punch beneath the surface.

Chuckling, Arthur followed her through the passage to the living room at the back. 'Don't knock it, Molly,' he said.

Nodding hello to Ava and Marilyn, he shook Jim's hand warmly. 'All right, mate?'

'Not so bad for seeing you, Arthur. Our Cathy was chuffed that you gave her Molly's old lamp. Good to see you again, mate.'

Arthur removed his cap, pulled a chair from under the dining table and sat down to look from Marilyn to Ava. 'Haven't seen you two in a while . . . got anyfing to show me 'ave yer? Anyfing hot that you can't shift and I can? On my stall?'

'Not right now, Arthur,' said Ava, while touching up her lipstick in her compact mirror. 'But we'll keep you in touch now that you're back in the fold.' She snapped her compact shut and winked at him, happiness shining out through her eyes. 'You've put a rosy glow back into Nan's cheeks for us.'

'She'll end up in fucking Holloway she will,' said Molly, blushing. 'And I won't be going in to visit with fruit and sweets.' Hiding her true feelings, she went through the open door into the adjacent kitchen to join Jim who was boiling the kettle. Leaning close to her son-in-law she whispered, 'What's put the smile on her face then?'

'A job – and one that sounds a bit risky to me,' he whispered back. 'All the lads are involved. Our Cathy's Johnny as well. And that's what worries me. The boy's not a criminal, Molly. A bit of tea-leafing now and then, that's all. But he *is* a gambler – that's the trouble. Gambling debts lead to thieving so as to pay people back.'

'Yeah, all right. It's those two molls and their fucking boyfriends who've pulled him in. I'll have a word in ginger Albert's ear. Tell 'im to gently drop the lad.'

'It's a bit too late for that. The job's done and dusted. The lorry came out of the docks this afternoon. It's garaged up in Norfolk on a derelict farm in the Fens – parked up in one of the outbuildings until things cool down.'

'Oh . . . right. So how much are we talking?'

'A good few grand, from what I can gather.'

Molly stared at Jim, lost for words for once. All she could manage was, 'Never!'

'It's true, Molly. But it's a bit of a risk. There's always a grass around looking for a backhander from the law. Especially in the docks. And look at them two in there. Glowing like Belisha beacons. It wouldn't take a pro five minutes to see that their blokes have pulled it off.'

'Well, let's hope they've all been professional enough not to have left a gap for a grass to squeeze through then, eh? Does our Cathy know about Johnny being involved?'

'No. Apparently he just jumped for it when the boys approached him. He wants to buy our little girl an engagement ring.'

'Do what? They've only known each other five minutes. Are you sure?'

'Shush. Keep your voice down,' said Jim, checking that the

others in the next room were still busy laughing and joking. 'Albert asked Johnny if he wanted to drive the lorry from one end of the docks to the other, and then out of the docks and pass it on to the contact in Aldgate.'

'Silly bastard!' whispered Molly. 'He's still wet behind the ears. But what the fuck was Albert thinking of – letting a kid take that on?'

'I don't know, Molly. But shush. Marilyn's clocked us whispering.'

'I don't care what she's clocked,' said Molly out loud, turning around and glaring at her granddaughter. Hands on hips, she said angrily, 'All right, are you, Marilyn? Only you've got a strange expression on your face. I think it might be guilt.'

'You can't make a baby crawl if it wants to get up and walk. Remember that one, Nan?'

'So you know exactly what I'm thinking about, then.' Molly pointed a finger at her grown granddaughter. '*You* should've known better. This is your baby sister on the line, Marilyn. She loves that boy and they're planning to be married.'

'Oh, shut up, Nan. They've not known each other for five minutes.'

'I know that. But I also happen to know that the only reason he's going on that job is so he can pay his gambling debts before he pops the question.' She was telling white lies but her granddaughters had got her goat up.

'All the more reason the boy should join the men,' Ava joined in. 'It's none of our business, Nan – and it's not something for you to poke your nose in, either. There's been a lot of time invested in this job. So just stay in the kitchen and do what you're best at – get out the cake you've made for our Cathy.'

'Leave it be, Nan,' said Marilyn. 'Let it go. It's got nothing to do with us. Dad shouldn't have told you. And not one word to our Cathy when she gets in from work, either. In a week's time we'll all be smiling. Trust me.'

'Trust you?' said Molly. 'I wouldn't trust you to change a baby's nappy, your head's so high in the fucking clouds.'

'Possibly, Nan . . . but my feet are firmly fixed on the ground.'

'Which explain why your neck's so long,' rejoined Molly. 'I always said you were a bit of an ostrich.'

While all this bit of banter was going on between the women, Becky Hanovitch was sitting by the fire in her small sitting room next door, thinking about her past and wishing she had never gone to Buckhurst Hill in the first place. Wondering what her family was like, and if any of them were worth the trouble she had gone through to track them down, she felt a kind of revulsion towards them, if only for the actions of the younger generation. In truth, all she really wanted was to know more about her mother.

Knowing how disturbed his wife had been by the humiliating incident, Leo was making her a nice cup of tea with a spoonful of honey in an attempt to ease the nasty episode out of her mind. As he poured boiling water into the pot he spoke to her through the open doorway.

'You know what your trouble is, Becky? You raise your hopes too high. And in any case, who's to say you'd have liked the family? All this rubbish about family ties and blood relatives. Who gives a toss? If you had a sister, who's to say you'd like each other? All I know is both my sisters hated each other with a vengeance when they were alive. They were always competing and bitching about this, that or the other. You're better off without relations, if you ask me. Friends are more important.' He glanced at her to see if she was paying attention, and knew that he had her listening.

But despite what he was saying out loud, in secret he had written to the woman of the house in Buckhurst Hill, letting her know what had happened and asking if she could find it in her heart to write to Becky to apologise.

'Funnily enough, I was just thinking the same thing, Leo,' replied Becky. 'But what I don't understand is why they sent those boys to do their dirty work. One of them could have written to say hello and goodbye and don't come again. I can take a hint – never mind plain talking. But a brick? Had you or I have been sitting in the front room it could have killed us.'

'Well, it didn't, so stop wasting your time thinking about it. Do you want a jam tart with your cup of tea?'

'I can't eat anything. It would stick in my throat.'

'Please yourself. But I'll say this and I'll say no more. They've succeeded in what they set out to do. Look at yourself. You're letting the lowest type of a person upset you. We don't need those kinds of people.'

'I know we don't *need* them. But it would have been nice if they'd let me know that they weren't interested by sending a card with a flower on saying hello and goodbye and good luck.'

Coming into the room, Leo sat down opposite his wife of so many years, gutted to see her unhappy like this. 'We've got each other, Becky, and after all these years that must count for something?'

She raised her eyes and gently smiled at him. 'It means everything. I still think the world of you – even though you nag all the time.'

'And I think the world of you. So there we are . . . Can we put this business to bed now?'

'No. I can't do that. I want to go back. I want to face one of them and ask why – why they let those lads do such a thing.'

Leo sighed, got up and went back to the kitchen. What could he say? He glanced out of the window at his tiny back garden and the small grave of their beloved cat, and thought he might go down the Lane at some point to buy his wife a new kitten to help her get over their loss. To help her and himself – they were both missing Pongo, even though neither of them was saying so . . . Then, seeing Henry stretch a leg over the fence and go into Jim's back yard, he smiled. The lad was a sight for sore eyes any day of the week, and again he thought how lucky he and Becky were to have such friendly neighbours who were more like family. He quietly chuckled as he remembered the old saying, 'You can choose your friends but not your relatives.'

Standing in the back doorway of Jim's house, Henry quietly coughed to let the family know that he was there. Molly came out and looked at him, saying, 'Come on in, sunshine, and tell us how much of our conversation you heard.' They had continued to debate the odds of what Ava and Marilyn's men were up to.

'Molly,' replied Henry with a smile, 'I hear more when I'm serving in the shop – and from both sides of the counter – than you could possibly hope to compete with.' He then turned to Jim and said, 'I've left a lad in charge until Jerry's wife relieves him.'

Molly ignored the muffled laughter of her granddaughters and knew exactly why the dirty cows were laughing. She gave them a warning look, knowing that the double meaning of Henry's innocent remark had completely escaped him. 'Who's Jerry when he's at home?' she demanded.

'The new owner, Molly. I suggested that it might be a good idea if we were to put leaflets through doors in this area, letting our customers know we're under new management and offering them a free newspaper this Sunday . . . But actually, Molly, I did come to have a quiet word with Jim. So if it's all right with you and you don't mind, I'd like to conduct my business and be on my way – I'm rather busy at the moment.' Turning to Jim, he asked, 'Do you want to keep on with the *News of the World*, Jim, or would you rather change to a more serious paper. The *Sunday Times*, perhaps?'

'No, son,' said Jim. '*News of the World* has always been my bit of Sunday reading. It'll do me fine.'

'New management?' said Molly, refusing to be put off. 'Since when? I never heard a word about this. You don't think you might have got your facts a bit crooked, sweetheart?'

Henry slowly shook his head and lowered his voice as he said, 'The information that I have just passed on to you, Molly, is *confidential* information. I've known for a while – of course I have – but I was asked not to disclose it. And who am I to question the way the wheels turn within the business sector?' He looked round the room at the others and said, 'I trust you will all keep this to yourselves.'

'Not a word will pass our lips,' said Ava trying to keep a straight face. 'Scout's honour.'

'Thank you. I appreciate that. And Molly – I do have something to ask of you. A favour.'

'Well, go on then, Batman. What is it?'

'Becky has asked me to go with her to Buckhurst Hill. No matter how much I've tried to persuade her otherwise, she wants to knock on the door of her long-lost relative's house and ask why they sent the boys to warn her off.'

'Ask her if she'd rather we sent the boys to ask them why those little bastards broke the window,' said Ava.

'I don't think that would solve anything for her,' said Henry, slowly shaking his head and letting out a low sigh. 'And I have to say that I'm surprised at you. We're talking about an old woman who wants to link up with her family, not frighten them away. Now . . . under normal circumstances I would gladly go with them – of course I would. But with my sudden promotion at the shop from assistant manager to manager, I simply don't have the time.' He looked at each of them in turn, ending with Molly. 'It was my considered opinion that *you* should go with the old couple, Molly, and I'm pleased to tell you that they agree with me.'

'Of course I'm gonna go with them. They already know that. Me and Rosie are gonna take them when they're ready for it. D'you think they might have forgotten that we said we'd go?'

'Possibly. But I'll just say that you've asked me to remind them about it, shall I?'

'Whatever you think, son. Only don't let it get too complicated, eh? Tell them to let us know when they want to go to Buckhurst Hill. If it's during the week, Rosie'll have to know so she can take time off from work.

'Of course. I'll have a word with them.' Henry smiled graciously and departed the way he had entered, via their back door and garden and then over their fence.

'I don't believe that lad at times. He behaves as if he's the general manager in charge of the whole street!'

'I think he's brilliant,' said Marilyn, smiling. 'I've never met anyone like him. And do you know what, I'm sure he's a step ahead of us all of the time. He always gets what he wants – our attention.'

6

It was a beautiful sunny March day when Cathy arrived at Johnson's, sank down into the chair behind her desk and covered her face with both hands. She had felt awful on the tube, and thrown up outside Moorgate station. This was the first time it had happened since she had felt she might be pregnant, having missed two periods. Luckily, even though she was fifteen minutes late for work instead of her usual ten minutes early, no one was in reception to see how pale and ghastly she looked. The go-slow on the underground by workers who were pushing for more pay meant that most people were getting in later than usual. The building was quiet and she thanked God for it, even though she knew that in fifteen minutes or so it would be buzzing.

She loved her new job and had made lots of friends there, girls and guys of her own age and some older. They all seemed to enjoy their work, even though one of them might suddenly rush around in a fury on the day a magazine or newspaper went to press if an important article wasn't ready or a half-page advert was about to miss the deadline. It was a place that she looked forward to stepping into each morning instead of dreading it, as she had done towards the end of her time at Gottard's.

After a few moments to collect herself she ran through in her mind the events of the previous evening, when she had confessed to her sister Marilyn that she had missed a second period and thrown up in the lavatory at home in the mornings. Feeling guilty and anxious in the knowledge that she would soon have to break the news to her parents, and having gone over a million times in her head how she would broach the subject, she sat staring at nothing, confused and scared. When the door of the ladies' powder room opened and her friend Pauline called her name she raised her eyes to the girl with the Sandie Shaw look-alike hairstyle and big brown eyes who was in on her secret.

'Did you do the test?' she asked in a loud whisper.

'Of course I did. Thanks for going to the chemist and getting it for me. I won't forget that.'

'Never mind that . . . what was the result?'

'Positive.'

Pauline opened her mouth wide and closed it again, then murmured, '*Jesus Christ!* What are you gonna do?'

'There's nothing I can do, and before you and Margaret get together on it, no, I'm not going to even think about an abortion. This is me and Johnny's baby growing inside me. Marilyn's the only one – apart from you – that I've told so far, and only because she was round ours last night and probed. She picked up on my worry even though I thought I was putting on a brave face and fooling them all into thinking I was going down with a stomach bug.'

Pauline sat on the edge of the desk and looked into Cathy's sorry face. 'What about Johnny? What does he want to do?'

'Get married as soon as possible. I phoned him last night with the result.'

'And?'

'He was actually pleased, could you believe? All he kept saying was, "Cath, we're gonna have a baby." It's what I want now that it's definite – don't get me wrong. But I hate the thought of us having to get married. This is what's upsetting me more than anything.'

'Why? You'd have got married in any case. You're crazy about each other. It's just been forced forward a bit, that's all. So . . . what kind of a wedding will you go for?'

'Small, quiet and discreet. I've never been one to dream of a big white wedding cake – or dress, for that matter. No. It's to be a small affair and I don't intend to tell anyone at home until it's done and dusted. Marilyn won't let on. She knows my nan and mum are bound to interfere – never mind Johnny's family. His sisters will want to get in on the act and I don't like them. Neither does he. They're miserable and bitchy, and do you know why?'

'No.'

'Because they eat twice as much as a man and it's made them both overweight and they can't live with that – but neither can they live without eating all day long. Jam doughnuts and chips are their favourite food.'

'So you'll make all the arrangements and tell them at the last minute?'

'No. I'll tell them once I'm married. After the ceremony.'

'Well, good for you.' Pauline laughed. 'Bloody well good for you. I wish I had your mettle.'

'It's not a case of having mettle, Pauline – it's a case of having no choice. Will you be my bridesmaid without the long frock and bouquet of flowers?'

Taken aback, Pauline broke into a lovely smile. 'I would *love* it!'

'Good. I'm gonna ask Margaret as well. I want just you two there, and Johnny will do the same – have two friends he can trust not to let the cat out of the bag until the ring's on my finger.'

'When's this all gonna happen?'

'As soon as possible.'

There was no more to be said. Cathy was determined to try and smile over the situation she was in and not cry about it – to celebrate her baby, not condemn it.

That evening, once she was home from work and had eaten her evening meal, she sat in the back room gazing into the flickering flames of the fire while her mum and nan washed and dried the dishes. She knew the two of them would want to be the first to know that she was going to have a baby, but trusted Marilyn to keep her promise not to say anything. Yet whether from inner guilt or gut instinct, Cathy felt that Molly, who had been giving her strange looks, might have guessed that something was up with her.

Even so, as far as Cathy was concerned Johnny was the most important player in this little scenario, because it was his baby she was having. His and hers. She knew that he loved her too much even to think of walking away once he knew she was pregnant. Instead of frowning with dismay, he had been chuffed to bits. It made no difference, he insisted, whether they married because of their situation or waited and saved for a traditional white wedding. He had said over and over that he loved her and that he wanted them to be married. Gazing into the fire, she recalled his wonderful smile and the look of pride on his face.

'What's up, Cathy, love?' said her dad, coming into the room and sitting at the small dining table. 'Johnny chucked you, 'as 'e?'

With her mum also close by, Cathy felt it was a case of now or never – get it over and done with, or hold on to her original plan of not telling them until after she was married. But just as she was about to speak, the doorbell rang and Molly shot off to answer it.

'Who's Nan expecting?' said Cathy. 'The royal family?' She was relieved to have been given this little intermission before she made her confession.

'Arthur's coming to play cards with me and Molly. I think the pair of them are getting more than just a bit sweet on each other. Who'd have believed it at their age, eh, love?'

'I don't even wanna think about it, Dad. It's too weird.' They both quietly laughed as they heard Arthur rambling on about some radios he was selling and the quality of them as he followed Molly through the passage.

'Are you all right, Cath? Only I've been a bit worried about you,' said Jim.

'I'm fine, Dad,' she said. 'There's been some sickness and

diarrhoea at work and it didn't pass me by entirely. But I think I'm getting over it.' She cocked an ear and smiled again. 'Listen to them two in the passage. Anyone would think they were an old married couple already.'

'I couldn't 'alf do with some fish and chips, Molly,' said Arthur as he came into the room. 'My stomach's rumbling. But I suppose you lot 'ave already 'ad your grub.'

Molly rolled her eyes as she said, 'Course we 'ave! But sit down and I'll chuck a few bits and bobs in the frying pan.'

'Oh, cheers. That'll be lovely – as long as it's no trouble.' Arthur winked at Cathy. 'Just what I fancied, a bit of a fry-up. Egg, bacon, tomatoes and beans, a bit of fried bread, and all washed down with a big cup of tea. Lovely.'

The vision of a plateful of fatty food turned Cathy's stomach. She got up quickly and muttered an excuse about having to get something from the corner shop so that she could make a sharp exit and be sick in private away from the house. Outside in the street she drew in great gulps of fresh air and rested against the brick wall until the sense that she was going to faint passed away. She decided to walk to the corner and back again to make the most of the fresh air.

Back in the house the usual banter was going on. 'Show me what's in your bag,' said Molly to Arthur, 'because if you 'aven't got anyfing in there that's going cheap and worth my while, I'm not feeding yer. You can go out and get the fish and chips you fancy.'

Settling himself into a chair, Arthur removed his cap and said, 'All in good time, Molly. All in good time.' Grinning at her he gave a little wink – and from this anyone with any kind of a brain would figure out that he held a secret that he was longing to tell.

'Well, go on then, Arthur,' said Molly. 'Spit it out before you burst a blood vessel.'

'Spit what out?' he said, all innocent and teasing.

'What do you know that we don't? And it 'ad better be worth the telling.'

'Don't know what you mean,' he said, leaning back and stretching his legs out. 'Unless of course you're referring to something that I heard when I bumped into somebody today?'

'I'm not referring to anyfing. It's you who's excited, not me.'

'Oh. It shows then, does it? Well I s'pose I am a bit chuffed. I mean to say, it's a bloody compliment when someone gives you a treat just because he finks you're a good old boy. That's respect that is. It's not everyday you get a twenty pound note pushed into your hand beneath a handshake.'

'Hark at it,' said Molly. 'Handshake. The Lord Mayor of London, was it?'

'You could say that.' Arthur laughed. 'It was Albert as a matter of fact.'

'Oh, right. So Mac the Knife 'as been and gone. Well, I'll be looking at more than a twenty pound note, Arthur. And don't ask me why or how much cos that's for me to know and you to find out.'

'I'm not really bothered,' he sniffed. 'I'm more than content with my little treat. Which was given to me just because I'm a lovely bloke. Nice that, innit? Lovely gesture. Not everyone can say that they've—'

'Did Albert say anything about a bloke called Mac coming down from Scotland?'

'Yeah. He did as it just so happens.' He then burst out laughing. 'Blew a door off a safe that was tucked away in the yard. My yard – where I run my stall from. I cracked up when he told me about it. Ingenious plan.'

'And what happened to the safe after the door was blown off?'

'Eh?'

'You heard. Stop fucking about.'

'It's on its way to Scotland to be dumped.' He gave Molly an all-knowing look. 'You're granddaughters will be up West by now – shopping for England. But that's all I'm saying.' He then tapped the side of his nose and winked at her. 'Mum's the word.'

'Too right it is,' said Molly, her blue eyes sparkling. She then looked down at the floor and Arthur's big old worn leather bag.'

'I might have some goods in there to interest you – and then agen I might not,' said Arthur, teasing his friend of old whose mind was actually on higher things. Things that she could buy from the money that would be coming from Albert, Stanley and George. By the sound of things it had all worked out nicely in the end and all because of her quick thinking with regard to Cutler Street being a perfect hiding place for the safe. She couldn't wait to tuck a thick wad or two of twenty pound notes into the secret place at the back of her underwear drawer. But, she was still in the mood for wheeling and dealing and wanted to see what was in that bag.

As it happened Arthur had brought with him a dozen small up-to-the-minute portable radios at a rock-bottom price of fifteen shillings each. They agreed she could ask for almost double the price and they would still go like hot cakes. Settling into a chair at the table, with Jim opposite, Arthur was ready for a game of rummy for pennies. It was a very nice homely scene accompanied by the sound of bacon sizzling in the pan in the kitchen.

'That smells lovely, Molly!' said Arthur, pulling out a tobacco tin from his inside pocket to roll himself a cigarette. 'So how's the old ticker these days, Jim? You look all right. Not too much colour in the cheeks. That's the tell-tale sign, I reckon. Red cheeks means high blood pressure.'

'I'm all right,' replied Jim. 'A bit slower than I was because of the new tablets they're trying out on me, but I can live with that. What about you? Still no sign of aches or pains?'

'Nar, fit as fiddle me. I've never drank spirits, though, 'ave I? For no other reason than I don't like the bloody taste of the stuff. But then you're not a big drinker yourself, are yer?'

'No. A beer now and then does me. I used to like a drop of whisky, but it's not worth the risk to the old ticker. I wouldn't mind a drop of stout, though.'

From her place in the kitchen with the connecting door wedged back as usual Molly could hear the men going on as if they were old women, and it gave her a nice warm feeling inside. Her son-in-law, who was more like a very close friend, was getting on so well with Arthur, who was becoming more like family.

Molly dished up and put the plate on the table, saying, 'Sorry, you two, but there's not a drop of ale in the place.'

'Don't you apologise to me, girl,' said Arthur. 'No. This is lovely. Don't you worry.' He shrugged and splayed his hands, a knife gripped in one and a fork in the other, as he addressed Jim. 'What we gonna do with her, eh, Jim? She cooks me a lovely dinner like this in no time at all, so what does it matter if she forgets the fried tomatoes?'

Playing along with his game of guilt-making, but one step ahead of him, Molly said, 'I ain't worried, Arthur, I'm just annoyed with myself. I promised Becky and Leo that I'd give 'em a couple of tomatoes, and I've only just remembered they're still in a brown paper bag in the cupboard waiting to be delivered. She wants 'em to go with the calf's liver she's cooking for their supper.'

This was one of Molly's white lies to enable her to get out of the house, and also part of her well thought out plan. The old lady had known that Arthur was bringing the radios with him that day, and had already found a buyer for the lot at one pound fifteen shillings each. She felt it imprudent to let on just how easy it was for her to sell goods at a better profit than could be realised by any of those in her flock, and since her reliable friend and fence, a canny market woman, lived not five minutes away she knew she could be there and back in no time at all. The radios were still in the bag in the cupboard under the stairs and ready to go.

'Well, you'd better go and give Molly and Leo my tomatoes, then, 'adn't you? I'll be all right. A nice thick slice of bread and butter and I'm as 'appy as Larry.'

'I'll cut you a slice,' said Jim, knowing when not to push

Molly's buttons too hard. He could see that Arthur was in a tormenting mood.

'I'll just nip round to Becky's, then,' said Molly, smiling.

'There's no rush, is there, gal? Sit down for fuck's sake. You've been on the go since I turned up. You're not getting any younger, y'know.'

Jim rolled his eyes as he looked to heaven with a wish and a prayer: *Don't let Arthur wind Molly up too tight.* He caught Arthur's eye and shot him a warning look that meant he was overstepping the mark.

'Say 'ello to the lovely old couple for me, will you, Molly?' Arthur quickly added, if for nothing else but to keep the peace.

'No, I won't. It wouldn't 'urt you to pay 'em a visit now and then and say 'ello for yourself. They 'ad a brick through their window, y'know.'

'So you told me – three or four times. I don't suppose you could put a bet on for me while yer out, could yer?'

'Don't tell me you 'aven't already placed one – it's the Grand National!'

'I know, but I've changed my mind and I wanna put two quid each way on Gay Trip.'

'Well, in that case – no. Stick to whatever you've chosen. In any case *I've* backed Gay Trip, so one way or the other we'll be crying or laughing together, won't we? So talk about football or boxing instead of the gee-gees. 'Cos that's what you men live for, ain't it?'

Leaving them to stare after her, Molly shut the room door, quietly drew her holdall out of the cupboard under the stairs and was out of the house in a flash. She was about to receive twelve pounds above what she had paid to add to the bundle of money she kept hidden in a secret compartment in her underwear drawer – a place that no one would think of looking even if they were inclined to.

Not too upset that she had gone out and left them, Arthur ate his meal with relish. 'She's a proper live wire is your mother-in-law, Jim.'

'I know. She said she was gonna buy me a poster of Joe Frazier for my birthday. But then Molly's always having a dig about my passion for watching boxing on the telly. I don't think I'd want a poster, though.'

'Poor old Jimmy Ellis, eh?' said Arthur. 'Joe knocked spots off him in the end.'

'No . . . Ellis put up a bloody good show. Thinking about that makes me go cold. Freezing cold,' said Jim. 'D'you fancy a fresh cup of tea, Arthur?'

'I do, as it happens. I'll finish this and then clear the table while you make it. How does that suit yer?'

'It suits me fine,' said Jim, shuffling together a few old newspapers into a pile before placing them on the sideboard to make space for their card game. He then carried the dirty crockery into the kitchen and put it in the sink. A comfortable and contented man, Jim enjoyed Arthur's company – it also made a nice change for him to have a man to talk to since he was mostly surrounded by women.

'Talking about the Grand National makes me think of poor old Arkle,' Jim sighed. 'The greatest racehorse ever bred, in my opinion. February 1970 will always be a day to remember. Sad. Very sad.'

'Yeah, well, animals don't live as long as they should do, unfortunately,' commiserated Arthur, shuffling the cards. He didn't want to get into a chat about the tragedy of a lifetime and Arkle no longer being around, so changed the subject. 'What d'yer reckon to Edward bloody Heath declaring a state of emergency when you dockers staged your first national strike? That's the kind of a thing a woman would do.'

'Whatever made you think of that? And don't forget I'm not a docker any more, Arthur – worse luck. Cathy's boyfriend Johnny knows all the ins and outs of what goes on in Tobacco Dock and Canary Wharf. He's bang up-to-date on it. Young blood, you see. If you ask me it was 'im and his generation that pushed to accept the increased pay offer. Old-time dockers, like I was, are a bit on the stubborn side if truth be told.'

'Ain't we all, Jim, ain't we all.' Arthur was satisfied that he had given Jim an opportunity to talk about his old world, the docks. But the sudden long ringing of the doorbell stopped him short.

'Who the hell's that? That's no ordinary ring, Arthur.'

'Probably a salesman trying to get rid of a set of encyclopaedias. I'll get it. You stay where you are. Your cheeks are flushed as it is. You wanna be careful, Jim boy, with that damaged heart of yours.'

Arthur went through to the front to open the door, while Jim sank back in his chair and wondered if his friend had second sight. He had, for some strange reason, been thinking that, even though things were going fairly well in their realm, Alice had been promoted to assistant store manageress at Woolworth's which meant that she would have more responsibilities and worry. It wasn't as if they needed the extra cash, and with both Ava and Marilyn continuing to earn a decent living from ill-gotten gains there was always a bit coming in from them for treats and perks.

Of course, he would rather his girls weren't thieves, but nothing was going to change them. They loved the life they led, and from their flat close to Victoria Park enjoyed running their little illicit buying and selling business, dealing in anything that happened to come their way through the network. Their men, Albert and Stanley, who were of course partners in crime, were rising in status as local friendly villains and were now driving around in Jaguar saloons. The sad thing about it all was that Cathy's boyfriend, Johnny the docker, was being initi-ated into their world.

Wondering why it was taking so long for Arthur to come back in, Jim wandered into the passage to hear muted voices from the front room. Someone was crying and it sounded very much like his beloved daughter Cathy. From the open doorway he saw her sitting on the settee, Arthur next to her, one arm around her shoulder and wiping her tears with his sparkling white handkerchief. Jim could hardly believe his eyes and felt his heart lurch. Drawing breath with difficulty, he only just managed to say, 'What's happened, Cathy, love?'

She raised her red and swollen eyes and started to weep again. 'You're gonna hate me for what I've done.'

Taking a long, slow breath, Jim shook his head. 'I couldn't hate you, sweetheart. You should know that. What's happened?' By the look on Arthur's face, Cathy had confided something to him. Having been sick again at the corner of the street, her defences were down. So when Arthur had placed an arm round her shoulder and said, 'Come on, sweetheart. Nothing's as bad as it seems if you share it with someone', share it she had. Her troubles had come pouring out in one long rush.

'Anyone would think she's the only one it's 'appened to. I told 'er, Jim, I said, what difference do it make whether you put the gold ring on the finger before or after you've started to grow a little Dean? More the merrier, eh?' It was a brave attempt to soften the blow.

Jim could hardly believe his ears. His Cathy. His baby . . . was in the family way? Surely not? Without thinking he said, 'I suppose it's definite, Cathy, or you wouldn't be in floods of tears. Does Johnny know?' He was speaking the words as if they came naturally to him, but inside he was gutted. Gutted, angry and badly let down by someone he had trusted his girl to.

'It *is* definite, yeah. And of course Johnny knows.' Cathy, still tearful and red around the eyes, looked at her father and only just managed to say, 'Don't be cross with him, Dad. It's my fault as well as his.'

Dropping into the small fireside armchair, Jim slowly shook his head. 'How mad can it get? I've got two daughters who should have families by now who aren't interested, and my youngest daughter, who's far too young, *is* expecting a baby.'

Arthur glanced at his watch and raised an eyebrow, feigning surprise. 'Jesus Christ – is that the time? I'd best be on my way.' He squeezed Cathy's shoulder and said, 'You take care of yourself and that godson of mine. And if it *is* a boy you'd better fucking well name it after me. After all, I did give you your nan's lamp back, didn't I?' With that he winked at Jim and made a sharp exit before Molly got back. He didn't want to be around when she heard the news.

Once outside, he surreptitiously looked both ways to make sure the street was clear of Molly. He guessed that she hadn't gone into Becky's but was out there somewhere, passing on the radios to a fence and making more on them than she had let on. Wheeling and dealing was in her blood, and she was better at it than anyone he knew. The fact that she was making more than he was didn't bother him one bit, because he now had a plan – a plan for the pair of them that he was keeping close to his chest . . . a plan for the two of them to set up together.

Walking along the street, he smiled to himself at the thought of a double wedding: his and Molly's, Cathy's and Johnny's. He had seen a nice ruby and diamond dress ring in a pawn-shop owned by a mate in Whitechapel and was on his way there to do business. As far as he was concerned he and Molly should have married decades ago, when they courted each other and danced in local competitions. Nobody could tango like Molly, and he considered himself a fool to have let go of her to one of his mates in the early twenties. And after all was said and done, Molly had been his first and she Arthur's – so they had something in common with Cathy and Johnny, he reckoned.

Back in the house, his arms around his daughter's shoulders, Jim said quietly, 'You're gonna have to tell your mum you're pregnant, Cath. Once she gets in from the hairdresser's.'

'I'm really sorry about this, Dad. I don't know—'

'It's all right,' he said, not wanting to think about it. 'Are you sure? Absolutely sure?'

'Yes. I've had a test done and it's positive. I'm growing a baby, Dad – try and accept it. I know what you're thinking – that I've not been going out with him that long. And you're right. We just got carried away—'

'Yeah, all right, love. Let's leave it at that, eh?'

'I'd still feel ashamed if I'd been going out with him for a year. Mum's gonna be so cross with me. And Nan will hit the roof.'

'Well, you're going to have to take that on the chin, sweetheart. But don't blame yourself for it all. You've had boyfriends before Johnny and you never went over the line with them, so I know where the blame is gonna be cast.'

Letting that go, since Johnny hadn't in fact been her first, she said, 'Don't be too hard on him though, Dad, eh? He *is* gonna be your son-in-law, after all. His mum and dad might want a flashy traditional white wedding and we're not planning to do that – so we're not gonna tell them anything until we're married.'

'But is marriage what he wants, sweetheart? Or what *you* want, come to that? I mean to say, between us we could help you bring up the baby.'

'Dad . . . Johnny loves me. We love each other. Of course he wants to marry me. He's coming round soon to see you. He feels really bad about it . . . that he's let you down. We planned to both be here in the front room when he asks for my hand in marriage.'

Jim quietly chuckled. 'Bit old-fashioned, innit, love?'

'No! Things that important don't go in and out of fashion – I can't believe you said that!'

'All right, all right. No need to get aerated.' Jim leaned back into the settee and drew breath. He was going to have to let his little girl go . . . his little girl, who was now a child-bearing woman. It felt a touch like bereavement. 'I'll make us both a nice cup of tea, love,' he said. 'How does that sound?'

'That sounds lovely, Dad. Perfect.'

Once by herself in that cosy little front room Cathy began to feel more comfortable about things, now that she had told her dad and Arthur knew too. She guessed they would pave the way for her when it came to her mum and her nan.

The person whom Cathy would have liked to go to for advice once she had missed her first period was Rosie. But she hadn't felt able to, since her friend and neighbour had been trying so hard for a baby herself and Cathy bemoaning her own pregnancy, she thought, would be like a slap in the face. It would be even worse now that Rose had finally had it confirmed by the fertility specialists that she would not be able to have children.

Feeling better now that she had offloaded her worry, Cathy laid a hand on her stomach and smiled for her baby. 'We'll be all right. We'll be more than all right with our family rallying round us.'

The sound of a key in the door brought her sharply out of that nice warm maternal mood, and from the familiar little kick to the bottom of the door she knew it was her nan back from wherever she had been. Through the small gap in the room door she saw that Molly was in a good mood as she strode along the passage. Taking the bull by the horns, she pulled herself up from the settee and cautiously made her way into the back living room where Jim was pouring tea from their big blue teapot. Molly, as usual, was doing all the talking, quizzing Jim about Arthur. How long had he been gone for? Did Jim think he might have followed her out and seen where she had gone?

'No, Molly,' said Jim quietly. 'You and your crafty wheeling and dealing were the furthest thing from his mind. He left because he could see that Cathy and me needed to be by ourselves.'

Coming into the room, Cathy said simply, 'I'm pregnant.'

The wind taken from her sails, Molly was clearly knocked for six. 'That 'ad better be a joke, sweetheart,' was all she could think of to say.

'It's not a joke.' Cathy looked from Molly to her dad, who was smiling sadly but managed to give her a supportive wink.

'You can't be up the spout?' said Molly, going immediately into denial. 'You're too young, and you've not been going out with that soft soppy sod for long enough.'

'How old were you when you were first in the club, Nan?'
said Cathy, braving it.

'That's neither here nor there. So what is it, then? You're a
couple of days over, is this it?'

'Molly,' said Jim, 'our Cathy is gonna have a baby, like it or
lump it. Now calm down, so that when Alice comes in the
tension in the air right now will have drifted up the chimney.'

'Mum should have been the first to be told, Nan. Arthur
knows, Dad knows and you know. So don't make a song and
dance about it. I've got myself in a mess and I've only myself
to blame, but as it happens I don't think it's the end of the
world. I love Johnny. He loves me. We'll get married soon and
be just another couple like a lot of others who've been in the
same boat.'

Molly slumped down in her chair and slowly shook her head.
'What on earth could Dr Phillips have thought of you?'

'I've not been to see him.'

'Well how the fuck do you know you're pregnant?' Molly
shook her head in disbelief. 'I don't believe this. She finks she's
up the spout and she's not even been looked at.'

'I've not seen a period since the beginning of January,' said
Cathy.

'You what? January? What was it . . . an immaculate concep-
tion? You weren't even courting at the time.'

'Yes, I was. Johnny and me started going out together the
first week of January, if you remember rightly.'

'Stone me dead!' said Molly. 'It didn't take 'im long to stick
'is cornet into the ice cream, did it?'

Leaving silence to hang in the air, both Cathy and Jim waited
for the next piece of oratory from someone who was known
to have been a bit of a nymphomaniac in the Roaring Twenties.
Unable to keep her mouth shut for five seconds, Molly was
quickly off again, and this time on a slightly different tack.

'Just as well 'e did join the criminal fraternity. I suppose
that's what must 'ave turned him from a boy into a man. My
only honest-to-goodness granddaughter! Little fucker. You wait

till I see 'im. This is gonna cost a fair bit. The Deans aren't gonna 'ave a second-rate wedding . . . so if you're finking about a quiet do, you can forget it.' Molly gave Cathy the once-over. 'At least you're 'ardly showing. What are you? Three months gone? Well, you can start eating for two. That's my great-grandchild in there and I'll most likely be dead and buried before another one comes along. So just sit yourself down and let your dad cook a nice big fry-up for yer.'

'I don't want a fry-up, Nan,' protested Cathy, nauseated at the very thought of it. 'I chucked up when you were cooking for Arthur. And I was sick in the ladies at work this morning. In fact I've been sick in the morning on and off since the beginning of February – and now we're almost in April.'

'You can't beat bacon and eggs—'

'If Cathy doesn't want a fry-up, Molly, I think we should respect that.'

'Oh, and you're the expert on pregnant women now, are you?'

'Nan, please. Don't do this. Don't start fussing over me as if I'm ill. You've got enough on your plate as it is.'

'In what way?'

'You're gonna have to help pave the way when Mum gets in and we tell her. You know you're good at—' The sound of the doorbell stopped her short. That'll be Johnny now. And don't you dare go on at him!' Cathy looked from her nan to Jim. 'Tell her, Dad. Tell her not to swear at him. I'll take him in the front room and then come and get you.'

With that Cathy left the room to go to her sweetheart, knowing he would be anxious to know the response to her confession. Even though they had planned it this way, for her to come home early so as to break the news to her dad and her nan before her mother arrived home, she was nervous. She felt sure that Alice was going to be angry as well as upset, and could only hope that Jim and Molly would act as a kind of a buffer.

But it wasn't Johnny at the door. It was Albert and Stanley. They followed Cathy into the back room looking sheepish and said, 'All right, Molly? Jim?'

'Bright as a new penny,' said Molly. 'What's up, then? Come to tell me that my granddaughters have been caught nicking gear, 'ave you?'

'If you keep on saying things like that, Molly,' Jim warned, 'you might just make it happen!'

'Well, by the look on their faces I'd say there's an ill wind blowing.'

'You'd best sit down, all three of you.'

'Is it something serious to do with Marilyn and Ava?' said Cathy. 'Because if it's not, I'd rather go upstairs for a five-minute lie-down before Johnny gets here.'

'Well, that's just it,' said Albert. 'Johnny might not be coming round. He got a message to me via one of the dockers to let you know he might not be able to make it.'

The room fell silent. Jim and Molly looked at each other, fearing the worst: that these two had got him involved in something big and he was too wet behind the ears not to have been caught red-handed; that their Cathy was about to be badly let down and face bringing up her baby as a single parent, shamed and snubbed by the neighbours. 'Well, spit it out then, one of you,' said Jim, placing an arm around his daughter's shoulder. 'Broke a bone, has he?'

'No rush,' said Stanley. 'Let's sit down a minute, eh? My feet are killing me.' They weren't, of course, but he wanted Jim with his bad heart to be in a chair when they said what they had to say. Cathy too, for that matter.

'Fair enough,' murmured Cathy as she sank into a fireside chair. 'What's my Johnny been up to, then? It must be serious or you wouldn't both be here. Right?'

'You've got it in one, sweetheart,' said Albert as he sat down opposite her. 'We've each been pulled in for questioning at one time or another, darling, as you know. And now it's Johnny's turn.'

'Johnny's been arrested?' she asked, not really taking this in. 'Why?'

'Because of a little job he was involved in.'

'With you and Stanley?'

'That's right, babe. But don't worry over it. They might not even bang 'im up for the night. We're going round to Wapping nick now to see if we can bail 'im out.'

'Well, why come 'ere first?' demanded Molly, fury showing in her eyes. 'What the fuck are you doing in this room when you should be there?'

'We're doing what Johnny wanted us to do, Molly – get word to Cathy ourselves before one of his bloody loud-mouthed sisters comes round. That's where the Old Bill will go first, to search 'is 'ouse and find out on the quiet what they can about his movements. We've seen it all before, don't forget. But we'll get 'im off, don't worry.'

'Bent solicitors don't always come up trumps,' said Molly. 'Don't start raising 'er 'opes. What 'ave they pulled 'im in for?' Molly was in her straight-talking, no-nonsense mood.

'Nicking tins of salmon, would you believe,' said Stanley, breaking into false laughter that was not in the least convincing.

'Yeah – and the rest? I know what goes on. What was slipped inside one or two of those crates? Cocaine?'

'Don't be silly. It's a little job that's gone wrong, that's all. The dock police 'ave been told to clean up and they're pulling more than one gang in, trust me. Johnny just 'appens to 'ave been seen driving a lorry out of the docks and coming back without it. So they've pulled him in for questioning. That's all.'

'Okay,' said Molly, 'fine. But would you mind telling us few, within these walls where no one else can 'ear us, 'ave they got a case? Did the law pull in the lorry that Johnny was driving?'

'Yes,' said Stanley, having had enough of the old woman. 'It happens all the time, Molly. You're over-worrying.'

'Well, then, I'll stop worrying.' She sat down on a chair at the table. 'I'll stop worrying and start working out how long he'll get. Because, no matter which way you spread the butter, the lad's been picked up and 'is fingerprints will be all over the steering wheel. And we're not talking about a load of tinned salmon – we're talking about the drugs that was slipped in between which 'ave no doubt been found by now. How much was there? What was it worth?'

'Not a lot. Twenty grand, if that.'

'Well, that's a fortune as far as I'm concerned. And did Johnny know exactly what was on board?'

'No.'

'Well, cheers for that, Stanley. Thanks a lot. You've stitched up our future son-in-law,' said Molly, angrily pursing her lips.

'Oh, I've 'ad enough of this,' said Albert. 'You're being a drama queen, Molly, and it's not like you. Come on, Stan, we've got more important fings to do. We need to get our mate the solicitor to go and get Johnny out on bail.'

Stanley turned to Cathy and gave her a comforting wink. 'If he can't get him out of there for you, no one can. He's the best there is.'

'Yeah . . . and known to be bent,' added Molly.

Albert looked from Stanley to Jim, who he could see was trying not to appear worried. 'We'll give you a bell as soon as we know anything, Jim. All right?'

'What did the lad do, Albert? Tell me again so I can get it straight in my head.'

'He's gone and got 'imself involved with amateurs. You know we wouldn't touch a lorry-load of fucking salmon. And we certainly wouldn't touch drugs.' He was lying, and doing so convincingly. 'He drove a container lorry out with tinned salmon aboard. That's what they'll charge 'im for in the end. They won't be able to pin the other drugs on him. He's as clean as a whistle, don't forget. This was his first job, and it shows – and the Old Bill knows it. He must 'ave acted guilty when he went through them gates and they had him marked. When the salmon failed to arrive at its true destination, that's all they needed. If he goes down it'll only be for eighteen months at the most.'

'The dock police are coming down 'ard on all the thieving that goes on,' said Stanley. 'Unfortunately for Johnny there was more than salmon aboard. That's the way it goes.'

'So where's Johnny now? Did you say he was in a cell at the police station?' asked Cathy, having listened to it all but not really able to take it in.

'Wapping police station. He was picked up early this morning. But don't worry, Cath, we'll get 'im out on bail.'

'When?'

'Tomorrow, if not this afternoon. Leave it to us – we'll pull a few strings. Anyway, I've put a message out to a bent copper working in the right places. We wouldn't have bothered you, but Johnny got word to us that this is what he wanted. He didn't want you to think he'd run out on you, love.'

'Well, that's all right, then,' said Cathy. 'No need to be solemn. I'm going upstairs to put my feet up. I think I might have flu coming on – I've got a bit of a headache.' None of this was true, but she was still feeling sick and in any case needed to be by herself. 'Don't worry about Johnny,' she added, smiling at them. 'They'll know he's not one of you lot. He's my Johnny. My gullible guy tried to be one of you lot, but failed. He's got a clean record. He won't go off the straight and narrow after this. Maybe it'll shock him out of gambling his money on the horses and dogs as well.'

Leaving them to it, Cathy went upstairs, closed the door and then lay on her bed to stare at the ceiling as the gravity of what she had just been told sunk in. Johnny had been arrested. Her Johnny in a prison cell? It couldn't be possible. Not with all the professional criminals out there driving around in Jags and wearing gold watches and cufflinks. She told herself that they wouldn't send him to prison for stealing tins of salmon – even if he was guilty, having probably been roped in by Albert and Stanley.

She shook off her worry and sighed as she laid her hand on her stomach and thought about the baby growing inside. Her baby. Her and Johnny's baby. With tears soaking into her pillow, Cathy closed her eyes and whispered a prayer: 'Please God, don't let them keep Johnny locked up. Please let him turn up at my door a free man.'

Downstairs, knowing that Cathy was settled above, Molly looked sternly first at Albert and then at Stanley. 'Now tell us the strength of it. Is he guilty or is he covering up for someone . . . and will he go down for it?'

'He drove the lorry out knowing about the salmon though not about the cocaine, but he'll still get time. The question is, how long. This'll go to the Bailey.'

'The Old Bailey?' said Molly in disbelief. 'Gimme a break. Tins of fucking salmon?'

'We told you, Molly,' said Albert. 'It doesn't matter what the load is. Even if it was just the salmon. They're clamping down and looking to set examples. Harsh examples. If he's found guilty he could be looking at two years because they'll probably offload a few other jobs on to him – it's part and parcel.'

'No way,' said Jim. 'You're talking out the back of your head. Six months at the most.'

'Whatever,' said Stanley. 'But the important thing is that we've delivered the message. He told us about Cathy . . . and . . . well, you know.'

A silence filled the room as everything sank in. 'If your lawyer can't get 'im off there won't be a wedding till he gets out,' said Jim. 'Great. That's all we need.'

'No, but Cathy will get to see him while he's out on bail. And that could be for a month or so. That's better than nothing . . . Anyway – we'd best be going. Sorry to be the bringer of bad news. Give us a bell if you need us.'

Once they heard the front door slam shut behind the boys Molly leaned back in her chair and let out a heavy sigh, feeling sick inside as tears slowly trickled down her cheeks. This was bad news whichever way it was viewed. Even though it was good of the boys to come and tell them what had happened, she couldn't help feeling that they might well have been the ones who had arranged the job that Cathy's boyfriend, the father of her baby, was going down for. For some reason her mind flashed back to the time when she was young, when her family had been poor but life was so much less complicated. Tonight she wished she could turn back the clock and start again.

'Why has the shit suddenly hit the fan? What's it all about, Jim?' she murmured. 'Why have things gone all topsy-turvy? When I was six my dad's health broke down and he lost his job at the chemical factory in Hackney. We were poor, but we never got into trouble with the police.'

'Maybe you were just lucky then, eh?'

'We nicked stuff – of course we did. Who didn't? But nothing like this! It was either to put a meal on the table or a warm coat on our back. Thieve or go hungry and freeze in the winter. But this generation's not content with what they've got – they always want more. Look at the cars that Stanley and Albert drive around in. And the clothes that Marilyn and Ava wear. And now Johnny'll be locked up in a cell. What's this gonna do to Cathy and that baby?'

'She'll be all right. It's a different world now, Molly. We have to face that. She can live with us and we'll all rally round. You know, you'd love it once the gossip stops and the neighbours get used to the idea. She won't be the first unmarried mother, will she?'

Feeling a bit light-headed, Molly drew breath and picked up a folded newspaper with which to fan her face. 'My old gran and my mother worked into the wee hours to earn a few extra shillings, sitting at the kitchen table and addressing envelopes for sevenpence a thousand. And they took in a lodger who slept in the attic room of their rented house in Jubilee Street. But they didn't do it so we could 'ave luxuries like this lot 'ave got. Just to get by, that was all.'

'I know what you mean,' said Jim. 'My mother used to do a day's work at the clothing factory, then go home to hand-stitch the hems of dresses that were delivered by the dozen from the factory. Sometimes she had to work right through the night to get an order in on time. She used to make me and my sisters clothes on an old clumsy treadle sewing machine, using offcuts she slipped into her knickers at the end of the working day.'

'I know fings were cheaper then,' said Molly, 'so we didn't need as much money as we do now – but still it doesn't seem to add up. Gas was cheap . . . I don't think we put more than a penny or two a day into the slot meter if we were careful with it. Frugal, I believe, is the word I'm looking for. We only lit the gas mantle when it was too dark to see by natural light coming in through the window.'

Jim noticed the faraway look in his mother-in-law's face and felt concerned about her. 'You all right, Molly? You look a bit pale, mate.'

Fanning her face again, she replied, 'It's thinking about the old days, Jim, I suppose. When 'fings were hard – but easier in a way than they are today. Nowadays we all seem to want more and more, and I'm just as bad. I s'pose that's the way it goes. The more you get, the more you want. And now our Cathy's gonna be left a single mother bringing up her baby while the father's in prison. What's 'appening to our family, Jim?'

Molly gazed into her son-in-law's worried face as a million white stars filled her head and his voice came through a tunnel a long way off. He was calling her name but she was unable to answer him and, feeling as if all her life and spirit had drained away, she crumpled to the floor with a thud.

Off his chair quicker than he had moved in a while, Jim placed a cushion under Molly's head as she lay on the old patterned rug. He knelt beside her, holding her hand and rubbing it to get the circulation going. He was gutted to see her like this, white as a sheet and not talking. Molly always talked. As her eyelashes fluttered and her lids gradually opened, he said quietly, 'Try and relax, Molly, love.'

'What's 'appening, Jim?' is all she could manage to whisper.

'You passed out, old love. But don't you worry. You just lie there and I'll fetch you a glass of water. Don't try and get up. I take it nothing hurts badly?'

'No,' she whispered, her eyelids drooping. 'I don't think so. I'm not all that with it, though, Jim . . . let me stop down 'ere for a minute or two, there's a good chap.'

'Of course you can stop there. It's what you should do. The trouble with you, Molly, is that you keep your worries inside.' From the kitchen he kept an eye on her as he filled a glass with cold water from the tap. 'You can't tell me you weren't brooding over our Cathy,' he said, talking more to himself than to Molly.

'I can't brood over something that's on our doorstep, Jim,' said Molly, slowly easing herself into a sitting position. 'Brooding comes from worry over what might 'appen, but this is right on our doorstep.'

'I suppose you're right,' said Jim, coming back with her drink. 'Do you want to sit there or shall I help you into your chair? There's no rush.'

'She's pregnant and the young lad, the father of her baby, is in prison.'

'Not prison, Molly. In a cell in the police station being questioned. There's a big difference.'

'Help me up, Jim. I've made a right bloody fool of myself. And don't let on to the girls. They'll put me to bed for a week, knowing them.'

7

Once in her favourite chair at the table, Molly took a few long, slow breaths. 'I will say that this has shocked me, Jim. I will admit that. Me, the one person you all thought was unshockable. She's no more than a girl, is our Cathy. Our little girl.'

'I know,' he said, placing a cushion behind her back, then turned as he heard tapping on the back window. It was Henry, who in a strange way was a comforting sight, bringing a bit of normality back into their world. 'I don't think we should say anything in front of him,' warned Jim as he waved him in.

'I've brought in the *East End Advertiser* for you to look at,' said Henry, coming into the room. 'There's an article on the docks, Jim, and how the police are clamping down on the organised stealing of goods shipped in or those meant to be shipped out. I thought you might find it interesting since you were a docker. And since Cathy's boyfriend is one.'

'That's good of you, Henry. Leave it on the table, son, and I'll have a read later on.'

'Of course, this isn't the only reason I've come in.' Henry smiled at them and there seemed to be a different kind of expression in his eyes – a proud and pleased-with-himself look. Jim glanced at Molly and the look on her face said it all. Could he have heard what had been said that afternoon through the open kitchen window?

'And what might that be, Henry? This reason for you coming in?' By the tone of Molly's voice she was almost daring him not to mention private family business that he might have overheard.

'I've got some good news and some bad news.' He paused in his usual way, waiting for a response.

'Well, get it off your chest then, Henry, son. We haven't got all day,' said Jim.

'The bad news is that I shall be moving away from the best neighbours and friends anybody could wish for.'

A silence filled the room. Henry moving on? It didn't seem possible. 'Well, I must say I'm very sorry to hear that, son,' said Jim. 'Very sorry indeed. Where were you thinking of going to?'

'Stratford East. And now for the good news. I've been promoted.'

'Stratford East?' repeated Molly quietly. 'Well, at least that's not too far – just a bus ride away. But I don't know why you'd want to go there, Henry. You'll 'ave all kinds of people around you. All sorts have moved into Stratford, son. Hippies as well as different nationalities. The West Indians are all right. I get on well with them – they bring sunshine in on a dull day. You'll miss the village feel of old Bethnal Green, though.'

'I realise all this,' said Henry. 'But it's promotion. I've been offered a position as manager in a tobacconist's-cum-confectionery shop, with accommodation above. Two flats. My flat on the first floor will go with the job and the other, at the very top, is to be let. But only to someone whom I feel is honest and trustworthy. This, of course, will mean that I shall have to conduct interviews. I would rather take the loft conversion because I prefer to be at the top of the building – which, as you know, is something I'm used to in Rosie and George's house. But I shall make do with the one-bedroom flat because that's directly above the premises.'

'I don't see what the difference is, son,' said Jim, doing his best to pay attention to him if only to take his mind off his daughter who he guessed would probably be weeping in private upstairs.

'Well, well, well,' said Molly, shaking her head. 'This *is* a day for change. Whatever next? Becky and Leo are gonna miss you, as well as Rosie, George and us lot.'

'I know. And I shall miss all of you. The old couple have been like grandparents to me ever since I can remember – and Rosie and George more like parents than landlords. But I shall come and visit every single week. The 253 bus stops right outside the shop and there's a parking space out the back for when Rosie and George come. At least there's been no more trouble from those boys who threw the brick at Leo and Becky's window, so my mind is at rest there.'

'Well, just so long as you've thought long and hard about this, Henry, because good friends and decent neighbours are often worth more than family,' said Jim.

'I realise this and I've weighed it all up – but I've come to the conclusion that it's time I made my own way in the world.'

'What's the flat like, Henry?' said Cathy as she came into the room, yawning after her short nap. 'Not the one you'll be taking, but the other one?' She presumed that the thump she had heard from her bedroom, and which had disturbed her nap, was Henry coming in via the back door. This was because Molly, as would be expected of her, showed no obvious sign of having fainted other than the fact that her face was still a ghostly grey.

'Actually it's the nicer of the two but, as I said, I need to be directly above the shop – that's so I can hear should a burglar get in below. Normally, yes, I would prefer to be at the top, closer to the sky and further away from street noise . . . Now, the reason I've come to tell you this is that I would like some straight advice.'

'Fire away then, Henry,' said Jim. 'Fire away, son.'

'What is your honest-to-God considered opinion now that I've laid it all out? Do you think I should take the new position offered and the flat, surrounded by strangers but independent – or stay where I am and where I feel at home?'

'Take it, you daft thing,' said Molly, a little colour coming back into her cheeks now that she saw her beloved Cathy looking better. 'You'd be a fool not to. And don't come all that rubbish about the devil you know is better than the devil you don't, because it's all bollocks. None of us know what the fuck's gonna happen to us next. Grab the opportunity with both hands is my advice.'

'Yes, I can see where you're coming from, Molly,' said Henry rubbing his chin thoughtfully. 'It *is* the chance of a lifetime. And you don't feel that Rosie and George will think me rather selfish for leaving them after the kindness they've shown me all these years? They opened their doors to me out of sheer kindness, let's not forget. I was fine living with Becky and Leo, but they were old even then and I was younger than I am now, of course. Younger and less ambitious or – if we're to be perfectly honest – more lacking in confidence and self-esteem.'

Without even trying he had touched their hearts and brought tears to Molly's eyes. 'You're a lovely lad, Henry,' she only just managed to say. 'Don't you start thinking of changing. Take the job and the flat – but stay just as you are, son. You don't need to be any more than what you are.'

'Thank you for that, Molly,' he said. He then glanced at Cathy and smiled warmly. 'This is an opportunity for me to be totally independent, don't you think?'

'I do, Henry. Go for it. Get in there before someone else does. Take the job and take the flat.'

Henry slowly nodded and then looked at Jim. 'And *your* honest opinion?'

'Take it in both hands, Henry. Grasp it and relish it, son.'

A huge smile spread across Henry's face, lighting it up in such a way that none of them had seen before. This was pure happiness shining through.

'This other room you mention,' said Cathy, moved by his innocent little boy expression and still hoping to get an answer to the question she had put earlier. 'Have you seen it?'

'I didn't say room, Cathy, I said flat.' A touch of his familiar would-be authoritarian manner was back.

'So you did,' she said, feeling happy for once instead of irritated by his tone. 'And what does the flat consist of?'

'The one I shall be taking, or the one at the top?'

'The one at the top.'

Henry rubbed his chin thoughtfully as he remembered. 'A fair-sized, comfortable sitting room. A spacious bedroom, with one wall almost taken up by a partly leaded stained glass window that casts rays of coloured light into the room. The kitchen is small but compact, and the bathroom has a matching white bath, sink and lavatory pan. A touch old-fashioned, but clean and undamaged. There is also a small box room which someone could fit a single bed into and would be fine if you were to have a guest to stay overnight.'

'And how much a week is the rent?'

'Four pounds ten shillings.'

'And it's in Stratford East, close to the market and shops?'

'Cathy . . . it's on the High Street, above a large tobacconist's and confectionery shop. So what does this tell you? That it's in a dark and narrow back street?'

'Point taken.'

'Next question?'

'And both flats, yours and the other one, have their own front door?' asked Cathy.

Henry slowly shook his head and sighed. 'Of course each flat will have a separate entrance. I will have to share the staircase and landing, but that's all. I shall be in the first-floor flat, which is smaller and cheaper, at four pounds a week minus two pounds allowance for it being part of my position as manager of the shop. This also suits me because I shall eventually decorate it right through to suit my taste, so one bedroom will be less work than two. I also intend to furnish it gradually with things to my own liking. I'm not one for frills and fuss, as you have probably gathered.'

'It'll be an expensive move, then, son,' said Molly. 'If you've got to decorate and furnish it. And don't forget you'll have to do all your own errands and cook for yourself.'

'I won't *have* to decorate or furnish straightaway. It's already furnished with old stuff and wallpapered in a clean but flowery pattern that I shall emulsion in different colours that blend.'

'And you've thought about things such as utility bills?' said Jim.

'Yes. I've worked it all out on paper.'

'And when does your landlord need an answer about the top flat? The one with the spare bedroom?' said Cathy.

'It's vacant possession, Cathy, that's as much as I know. But why ask? I've already told you that I intend to take the one below it.'

'I might be interested in renting,' she said, 'if you think you could cope with me as a neighbour.'

Henry was clearly pleased at this suggestion, but tried not to appear too eager to have her living so close to him. 'It would be the best of all things as far as I'm concerned, Cathy – to have someone I know and trust in the building. But why would you want to move away from your home and your family?'

'Same reason as you. A bit of independence does nobody any harm.' The last thing she wanted was for him to know right then that she was pregnant. 'I'm not saying I *will* go for it. I'm interested, that's all.'

'I don't think that's a good idea, Cathy, love,' said Jim quietly. 'You're gonna need every bit of help and support you can get.'

His discreet remark was lost on Henry. 'Answering your question, Cathy . . . without wishing to tread on toes, of course I will put your name forward if this is what you want – and I can't think of a better neighbour to have living above me. And, as I've been advised by my elders – which is appreciated – you too will need to be sure you can afford it given the cost of living these days.' He then glanced at his watch, every bit the businessman with a tight schedule. 'Rosie will be in from work soon and I want to tell her about this straightaway. She might feel hurt that I've broken the news to you first, so if you could keep this to yourselves . . .'

Neither Jim nor Molly was any longer paying attention to him – their thoughts were all on Cathy. 'And what about when you have to give up work, Cath?' said her caring nan, trying to keep the worry out of her voice. 'Because you 'ave to consider that Johnny might not be around to keep you and the baby.'

'I'll go to the Assistance Board and get benefits and I'll have my children's allowance.' Suddenly realising what each of them had said in front of Henry, Cathy gave Molly a look that told her she needn't keep her mouth shut. The cat was out of the bag now, so she continued. 'I'll come back here every Saturday, stay overnight, have my Sunday dinner with you and then go back to my pad. I can go down and keep Henry company if I get lonely, and he can come in and see me if and when he wants.'

'And look after the baby by yourself?' said Jim, going along with Cathy and talking openly in front of Henry as if he were part of their family.

'I think I could manage it, Dad. And I know you'll all come and make sure I'm all right. Especially Marilyn and Ava. They'll bung me a few notes to make sure I don't go without – you know that. They'll be the best aunts in the world. It'll give me a chance to be responsible for myself. I got myself into this mess, and I think it'll be better for me if I can make it by myself – so long as I know you're all there behind me.'

'But you'll be lonely, love,' said Jim. 'It sounds like Johnny could go down for an eighteen-month stretch according to the boys.'

'Exactly my point, Dad. I've got to make my own way now, so as to get the hang of being independent once the baby's born. I won't say no to a treat from any of you when you feel like shopping for me. Stock up my cupboard and that. And I'll have my friend Henry for company.'

She looked from Jim to Henry, who for once in his life had been stunned into silence. 'Thanks for coming in and telling us what your plans are – and I'll let you know as soon as I can about the other flat.'

Still unable to recover from his shock, Henry simply nodded and then looked at Jim, saying, 'Thank you for hearing me out, and for the advice, Jim.'

'Think nothing of it, son. You take the bull by the horns, lad. Go for it.'

'I agree,' said Molly. 'And good luck to yer, boy. We'll miss yer, no mistake, but you've got yer entire life in front of yer.'

Henry had stopped listening and was thinking. Thinking about Cathy. Cathy, who was by the sound of it carrying a child. The child of a young man whom he considered to be a touch on the flash side in his Italian suit. He was shocked and disappointed, but hid it well. He had come to think of her as his closest friend. Almost as his own girlfriend. 'Thank you again for your advice, Molly, and yours, Jim. I *will* take the flat.' He then glanced at Cathy. 'Let me know for sure if you want to rent the other flat . . . You obviously have private family business you need to discuss, and if I came in at the wrong time I apologise for the intrusion.' He was so sincere that each of them wanted to give him a little hug, but this wouldn't have been the right thing for Henry who was about to take a big step – from being a sad and lonely soul to being someone setting out on his own. It seemed as if he had gone from boy to man overnight.

'You can let the landlord know that I *do* want the flat, Henry. Take it as a positive.'

'I will, Cathy – you have my word.' With that, Henry bade them goodbye and departed through the back door.

Once he was out of earshot, Molly, who up to this point had been uncharacteristically passive, said, 'What's wrong with you, Cathy – apart from being up the spout with your hormones all over the place? You can't possibly manage on your own! A single parent? It's fucking mad.'

'Plenty have to do it, Nan – when needs must.'

'Needs must? What kind of rubbish is that? The father of your child is facing a prison sentence! Forget the flat. You'll 'ave to stop 'ere so we can 'elp you along till Johnny does 'is time and gets back 'ome.'

'He might not get time, Nan.'

'I think he probably will, Cathy,' said Jim. 'You heard what the lads said. There were drugs amidst them tins of salmon, and apart from that examples are being set. Eighteen months is a long time to be on your own with a baby to take care of.'

'Well, if he does go away, Dad, then he does. I'll make it work. You can get on a bus and come and see me – Stratford East's not that far away, is it? And Johnny's family live in that area, so I expect his mum and dad will pay me visits to see their grandchild. Hopefully not his sisters, though. They don't like me. They think I'm stuck up.'

'What makes you say that?' said Molly, already on her guard to protect Cathy.

'He took me round there one Saturday afternoon to introduce me.'

'And?'

'They deliberately looked me up and down and then eyed each other with their noses turned up. And I know why. I'm not daft. Envy. They're both fat as pigs and don't get off of their lazy arses for anyone. They just stuff their faces and watch telly all day long.'

'Oh, come on, Cathy, don't exaggerate. They must be out at work during the day,' said Jim.

'No. One's collecting sick pay because of a leg injury – she broke it, true, but it healed ages ago. Yet she still limps and says she's in pain to get her doctor to keep on signing medical certificates. And the other one, whenever she's sent for an interview in a factory or shop, behaves as if she's a halfwit and a bit deaf so that she can stay on the dole.'

'Fuck me,' said Molly, blowing air. 'I thought our girls were bad enough for nicking stuff for a living – but at least they work their socks off at it. What about Johnny's mum? Is she the same?'

'Nope. And neither is his dad. They both work full-time.'

Molly glanced from Cathy to Jim. 'Does Johnny's dad work down the docks?'

'No. He used to, but he left to help a mate who started his own little business in the print. Doing all right as well. So Trevor earns a decent wage. I think he all but runs the print room while his mate, who's really his boss, runs the business side. It's hardly big business, but not a bad living.'

'Well, I don't fancy meeting them lazy sisters of Johnny's, but I think we should invite his mum and dad round for Sunday tea, don't you, Jim?'

'Yeah. But let me hint at it to Alice, eh? It should be her idea, really.'

'You'll like 'em, both of you will,' said Cathy eagerly. 'Nice, decent people just like Johnny.'

Molly raised an eyebrow, her expression saying it all. Johnny had got Cathy pregnant and was about to leave her to get on with it. Decent? Not quite. She was just about to say so when Cathy cut in.

'Nan, Johnny did what he did because of our situation. He'd been approached before by the boys, and put it on the back burner because he wasn't really interested. But once we knew I was in the club he went back to them and said he was in on whatever came up.'

'I'm not saying any different, am I?' said Molly, knowing when to stay her criticism. 'He was thinking of you, sweetheart, and your baby. Of course he was. But I will say this, and then I'll say no more. I did hear through the grapevine that his sisters are always rude to the neighbours and shouting at each other, as if there's one continual row going on.'

'Oh, so you did do your homework, then, Nan?' said Cathy, smiling. 'I should have known you'd do that, shouldn't I?'

'Too right. I've only got three granddaughters. And even if they don't appreciate me I'm always in the background making sure they're all right.'

'We know you are, Nan. And we love you to bits for it.'

Later that evening, in the soft glow coming from her small bedside lamp, Cathy thought about how far she had come in such a short time. And how her mum, once she had been told, had accepted her daughter's predicament. On the surface Cathy still hoped that Johnny wouldn't go to prison, but deep down she knew, from all that had been said, that he probably would. Albert had phoned soon after Henry had left to say that Johnny would be home once certain papers had been signed. Albert's inside contact at Stepney police station had found out from Wapping station, where Johnny was being held and questioned, that he would probably be released next day once the thousand-pound bail had been paid by Albert and Stanley.

Cathy's mind was still at sixes and sevens, one minute visualising herself, Johnny and their baby in the flat in Stratford East, and the next picturing herself living hand to mouth with a baby to breast-feed and no Johnny to hold and love her. She knew that with the help of her dad and Arthur she could make the flat look lovely, but everything had happened so quickly that she could hardly think straight, let alone take it all in.

She knew she was going to miss working at Johnson's, as well as the social life when she went with her new friends for a drink at the local City pubs after work. Even though she was madly in love with Johnny, she had quite enjoyed the lads' flirting and silly tricks. But this would soon be all over, because since she was beginning to show she was going to have to leave. A pregnant woman on reception in a successful newspaper publishing company was not on the cards, and she respected this. In any case, the idea did not appeal to her one bit. She was going to have to hand in her month's notice. Thankfully, the hourglass figure and the fashions to match it were completely out of vogue, so she could easily cover her growing stomach with the new look of loose tops over flowing skirts.

Pushing all this from her mind, she thought about Henry and the flat and telling Johnny about it as soon as he was out on bail. When the sound of the doorbell broke into her stillness she wondered if it might be Albert or Stanley or both of them come to give an update on Johnny's release, so she was out of her room in a flash and running down the stairs to get to the door first. Nothing could have shocked her more than

to find Johnny standing on the doorstep, dressed in his best
suit and looking as handsome as ever, but not smiling.

'Hello, Cath,' he said, struggling with his emotions. 'I'm sorry,
darling. Really sorry for what I'm putting you through.' Cathy
opened her mouth to say something but was lost for words.
'You gonna let me come in then, or what?'

She stood aside and, almost trance-like, waved him in. Once
inside the house with the street door shut, Johnny took her in
his arms and they stood locked together. No words were necessary. When they finally broke apart to look into each other's
faces, he said again, 'I'm really sorry, darling. Really sorry. But
I will make it up to you. I promise.'

She gestured to him to stop, fearing that she would burst
into tears. Together they went through to the back room.

'Well, here's a sight for sore eyes,' said Jim, standing up to
welcome his future son-in-law. 'Oh God, Johnny – it's so good
to see you. When did they release you, son? How long have
you been out? Did Albert and Stanley turn up with the bail
money, or what?'

'Dad . . .' Cathy quietly laughed. 'Let Johnny get his second
wind.'

'Sorry, son, sorry. Only I'm not 'alf pleased to see you.' He
stepped back and looked at him. 'They didn't knock you about,
then?'

'Course not,' said Johnny, relaxed and smiling.

'He's seen too many Hollywood gangster movies,' said Molly.
'Silly fucker. But give us a hug in any case. I'm not too old
for a cuddle.'

'Anything to oblige,' said Johnny, grinning.

Alice, privately sighing with relief, went into the kitchen to
put on the kettle. This was more than she could have asked
for right then: to see Jim relax again and Cathy not only smiling
but with that look of happiness back in her lovely dark blue
eyes. Questions were being fired at Johnny but she blocked it
out. She didn't want or need to know the ins and outs or think
any more about what the future might hold for her pregnant

daughter. Johnny was in the same room as Cathy. It was enough.

'Albert reckoned we wouldn't see you for another day,' said Jim.

'Did someone come forward and admit it wasn't all your fault?' asked Cathy.

'The lads paid the bail, I take it,' said Jim.

All of this and more Alice heard, and let it go above her head until she finally insisted, 'Leave the poor sod alone!' This made Johnny laugh.

'Sorry, son, sorry,' said Jim.

Molly for once was quiet, content just to watch the scene in that room which had gone from misery to joy within minutes. 'Wouldn't you two prefer to be on your own?' she suggested, catching Cathy's eye and giving her a knowing wink.

'You're right, Nan,' she replied and then turned to Johnny. 'Would you rather have a pint of beer than a cup of tea?'

'Would I ever!' he said, picking up on the chance to escape and be by himself with Cathy.

'Right. Come on then, babe. Let's go.' Cathy gripped his arm and pulled him towards the door. 'Let's go for a walk and a drink.'

Once outside, they looked at Johnny's car, then at each other and linked arms, each with the same thought: to walk and not ride, and make the most of everything while they could. While Johnny was still a free man. Strolling along as close to each other as possible, they carried on through the back streets to Cambridge Heath Road, alongside the black railings that separated them from the Bethnal Green public gardens. Without any plan or design they headed towards the Blind Beggar, a five-minute walk away.

Sitting in a quiet corner of the pub that was so familiar to them both, they avoided talking about anything other than their marriage and how they could arrange it before he went away. The fact that he would be found guilty at the forthcoming trial was taken as read. 'If we do it in church we could have a word with the vicar at St Peter's,' said Cathy after her second Babycham. I'm sure he'd bring it forward for us because of the circumstances.'

'A lightning wedding!' said Johnny. 'He probably has more of those than he has planned ones.'

'Probably. It's not that unusual around this way for the bride to be pregnant before the marriage, is it?'

'Not where my mates from schooldays are concerned,' said Johnny. 'It's part and parcel to be pregnant first.'

'I know. But it's not what I wanted, though.'

'Nor anyone, nor me. But there we are. It just seems to happen. Love comes before caution, that's what my nan used to say. We know it should be the other way round, Cath, but it hardly ever is . . . I just want us to make one little vow before the big one in church.'

'And what's that?'

'Not to ever talk about me and the case and all that. Never again. Not a word.'

'That suits me,' said Cathy. 'It suits me right down to the ground.'

'But before we do, I want you to know that part of the payoff for not grassing is that my gambling debts are gonna be settled for me. As well as the deal that Albert and Stanley 'ave struck for a payoff to stay silent.'

'That's good . . . and it'll be great once I'm settled in the flat.'

'Flat? What flat?'

'One in Stratford East that's available at a good rent . . . But that's it. No more talking about anything other than our wedding plans. A deal?'

'A deal,' said Johnny, giving her a gentle kiss on her beautiful lips.

Cathy had already heard from Albert and Stanley that her financial welfare would be taken care of, as had Johnny. So there was no point in going over it and, providing he adhered to the code of silence within the underworld, he would be financially rewarded once out of prison. Cathy, of course, would receive a lump sum from the boys straightaway.

'So what it is you want, Cath? White wedding or registry office?'

'I think I'd like to be married in St Peter's. A small wedding, though, with the reception held in the church hall. And I'd like Rosie's husband George and his band playing in the evening. But I'd equally like to get married in secret at Stepney registry office without fuss or frills. What about you?'

'The second option – because of circumstance. But I honestly don't mind.'

So, in a private corner of the Blind Beggar, they discussed and debated everything until Cathy, in between sipping her Babycham, said, 'I'd like to get married as soon as possible. And not tell anyone in either of our families about it until it's done and dusted. But if we do go down that route no one must know, Johnny, because if it leaks out beforehand my sisters will try and stop it even if the rest of them go along with us.'

'Would they really twist your arm?'

'Yes. I'm the baby of the family, and Ava and Marilyn will want the church wedding and it will have to be a bit of a do. True East End-style.'

'I can see what you're saying, Cath. But you're under twenty-one, darling, and you'll need your parents' permission and their signature on the application form for a marriage licence.'

'I know. I've already worked that one out. I'll forge Dad's signature and I'll ask my two mates from work – they're strangers to our family – to be witnesses. They're called Pauline and Margaret, and they've already said they'd do it and not breathe a word to anyone. Once we're married we'll go and tell my parents and then yours, and hope that they'll all laugh at the nerve of it. We can do it, Johnny – and it's what I want. I'm beginning to show, and I'm definitely not wearing a wedding dress designed to cover my belly up and be a giggling stock for the gossips.'

Johnny too preferred to keep it as low-key as possible. He

had always hated ceremonies, and in any case the thought of his sisters interfering or getting drunk on the day made him go cold. So he admitted that everything Cathy was saying was what he really wanted, and that he was simply giving her the freedom of choice. White weddings, to his mind, were for the sake of the bride and not the bridegroom.

'I thought it was every girl's dream to be a bride in white satin and lace,' he said.

'It's our baby, that's the most important thing. I don't want to try and hide it away as if it's a bad apple – and as I said, I definitely don't want to try and hide my bulge under a big flouncy white dress. I want us to be proud as punch that we're gonna have a baby.'

Too gutted to say anything, Johnny leaned across the small table and kissed her lightly on the lips. 'I love you, Cath, and I can't bear the thought of being away from you for so long. And as for getting married – I'm happy to do whatever you want. And I'm sorry that I've let you down so badly.'

Cathy swallowed against the lump in her throat and only just managed to say, 'I'll live to tell the tale, babe, while you're away.'

'Maybe it won't be so bad. The lawyer reckons that with good behaviour and my clean record I might not have to serve the full eighteen months that's on the cards. And I'll be a model inmate, trust me. The lawyer reckons I'll do most of my time in an open prison because I'm a first-timer.'

Cathy's face broke into a gentle smile. 'Well, there we are, then. We've got the rest of our lives to look forward to, so what's a year and a half to us?'

'A lot . . . but we can do it. So what about this flat in Stratford, then, Cath? Do you want me to put a month's deposit down?'

'There's no need. Nan will do that for us. She's already offered it. And we can't afford to look a gift horse in the mouth. So keep your pride in your pocket for when you're standing in the dock at the Old Bailey. You're gonna need every bit of it.' She reached out and took his hand and looked into his eyes.

'If you let me arrange it all, we can be married and in our own place in three weeks' time.'

'That quick?'

'Yep. I've checked it out.'

'Well, I've only got one problem with it, Cath, and that's your family. I don't think it's fair not to tell them what you're doing.'

'They'll do their best to stop me. I know they will.'

'Who exactly? Your mum, your dad, your nan, your sisters? Think about it. Take your time and imagine each one of them and how they're gonna react.'

Staring out at nothing, Cathy did as Johnny suggested. She started with Alice, and in her mind's eye could see her mother nodding thoughtfully and then agreeing with her – because of the rush for one thing, her expecting a baby for another, and because they were a small family who had had hardly any contact with the few aunts or cousins on her side since they had moved out of the East End years ago. She knew that her dad wouldn't be bothered because his only sibling, his brother, had emigrated to New Zealand in the mid-fifties. That left her nan, Marilyn and Ava, and she knew that Molly wouldn't mind in the least.

But her sisters would without doubt kick up merry hell, as she had already told her best friend at work. For one thing, Marilyn and Ava would be deprived of dressing up to the nines – and they loved the idea of a wedding ceremony so long as it wasn't their own. Each of them had said that the day their baby sister got married the whole of the East End would come out to watch, because it would be as good as any royal wedding. And the bride would go to the church by horse and carriage or in a Rolls Royce.

'Okay,' said Cathy.

'Okay, what?'

'I'll talk to Mum, Dad and Nan and ask them not to let on to my sisters. They won't like not being there, Johnny – but if it's what you want, I'll do it.'

'It's not what *I* want, Cath. It's just that I think you might regret it if it does upset them more than you realise. We could make a compromise and just invite them—'

'No. Absolutely not. My sisters will simply take over and invite whoever they want. You have to trust me on this one, babe. I do know what they're like. Drama queens who love the limelight, the pair of them. I still think it's best to be cheeky and announce the news after it's done and dusted and we've still got a bit of confetti in our hair.'

'You mean the evening of the day we get married?'

'Yeah. After our wedding dinner with your two friends, who will each be a best man, and my two friends from work who can be our bridesmaids but without the frocks and bouquets.'

'No. I don't think that would go down well at all.'

'All right. Second option. I'll put it to them beforehand. Tonight, in fact. Not the sisters, though.'

'I think that would be best,' said Johnny as he gazed into Cathy's beautiful face. 'As for me – all I want is for you to be mine for ever and a day extra. And to prove that, a little present I got you before I was pulled in. I was keeping it for the right moment – I'll give it to you now.' He slipped his hand into his jacket pocket, pulled out a small red velvet box and flicked the top open to reveal a secondhand small diamond cluster engagement ring. He then got down on one knee and quietly said, 'Marry me, Cathy. I love you.'

Once back at home after the surprise announcement that they were now officially engaged had been made and the beautiful modest ring admired, Johnny left the family of four to themselves. He felt that Cathy should tell them in private, and in her own way, their plans to marry without any fuss and in a registry office.

'So my little girl is engaged to be married,' said Jim, as proud and pleased as any father could be. 'One out of three's not bad, I s'pose,' he joshed.

'Oh, don't you worry.' said Molly, 'Once the other two see

that ring they'll be on at Stanley and Albert, you can bet your bottom dollar. And then the race will be on between the two of them as to who gets in first with the big flashy white wedding.'

Cathy slowly raised her eyes to look at Molly, the words 'big flashy white wedding' floating in her mind. Was her nan giving her a message that she wasn't in favour of it? Or was she trying to draw her granddaughter in? Cathy wasn't sure, and she wanted to be. She wanted to win this little battle and without any upset, if that was possible.

'The trouble is, we need to get our skates on,' said Cathy. 'I don't want to walk up the aisle with a big belly, do I?'

'You surely don't mean the aisle of a church, Cath, do yer?' said Molly incredulously. 'Not in your condition!'

'And why not?' snapped Alice. 'She's hardly showing.'

'Nan 'as got a point there, Mum. I never thought of that. I already can't do up the top button of any of my skirts or jeans and I'm only just over three months. And it's gonna take another two months at least to book and plan everything.'

'I don't know why you don't get married in a registry office,' sniffed Molly, all nonchalant.

'I'd love to, Nan, but Mum and Dad wouldn't want that. It wouldn't be fair on them.'

'Don't be daft,' said Jim. 'This is your big day, love. You do what makes you happy. You're gonna have a hard time of it as it is with Johnny going away. And in your condition you'd be well to do without all the rushing around organising everything.'

'That's true,' said Cathy. 'There's the flowers, the wedding dress, the bridesmaids, the catering, the hall to be booked—'

'I know, love, I know,' said Jim. 'Don't go on – I'm already feeling tired at the thought of it.'

'Why? What will you have to do?' said Alice indignantly. 'It's the women who arrange everything, not the men. They just turn up on the day.'

'Well, I think Molly's right,' Jim insisted. 'There's nothing wrong with a nice respectable registry office wedding.'

'No? I don't agree. Cathy's the only one who deserves to get married in white. The other two have been living in sin for God knows how long. She gave herself to Johnny when she shouldn't have done, but at least she was a virgin before he took advantage.'

'Mum? How can you say that? It takes two to tango – remember? Your words, not mine. You've said that more than once. I'm just as much to blame as Johnny. And it was in our front room that it happened, don't forget. I was hardly led astray by him, was I?'

'All right, Cathy, don't rub salt into the wound!'

'What do you mean? Whose wound is this? I'm the one in the club, and Johnny's the one who's going to prison because of Albert and Stanley! I think Johnny's the victim here, don't you?'

'Victim? What do you mean: victim?' Alice was proving to be far from the thoughtful, compliant mum Cathy had envisaged. 'Next thing I know you'll be telling me you made him make you pregnant in our front room! He should think himself lucky he's not had a slap round the fucking face from me or a punch on the nose from your father!'

'Now then, now then. That's enough, girls!' said Jim.

'Enough?' said Molly, smiling. 'This is only the beginning. It happens every time with a white wedding. I used to work in a factory, don't forget – a factory filled with young girls who get married. The rows and fights and break-ups over wedding arrangements were phenomenal. Fucking stupid, if you ask me.'

'Well, I'm not asking you, Mum, am I?' snapped Alice. 'I'm the mother of the bride and I'll say what is and what isn't gonna happen. And my daughter is getting married in a church, like it or lump it!'

'It's funny you should say that, Alice,' said Molly, leaning back in her chair and gazing up at the ceiling. 'I think I remember saying something similar myself, when you and Jim told me and your father that you were gonna do the self-same thing that I'm now suggesting for your daughter. Funny how things that go round come round, innit?'

'That was different. It was 1940 and there was a war on, if you remember.'

'I do remember. But you could've married in a church – had you had the time and inclination to arrange it before you showed too much.'

A deathly hush filled the room before Cathy started to laugh. 'You *are* joking, Nan, surely?' She looked from Molly to Alice, who was blushing madly.

'Everything was different then. We never knew if we'd be blown up in the night or not. And your father was a soldier lucky to get leave now and then.'

'That's enough of this,' said Jim, firmly. 'What do you want to do, Cathy?'

'Get married in a registry office with just us there, and no friends or other relatives on either side. Johnny's or ours.'

'We haven't got many in any case, love,' said Jim sadly. 'But Johnny's from a very big East End family. You'll have to hire a hall all right – and even then they'll fill it.'

'Who says they will?' snapped Alice. '*We're* the bride's parents. *We* choose who comes to the wedding and who doesn't.'

'Not really, Mum,' said Cathy. 'It's equal both sides, I think you'll find.'

'Course it fucking well is,' said Molly. 'You either do it properly or you don't do it at all. And as far as I'm concerned I'd rather give the money to Cath to bank for a rainy day than spend it on Johnny's family having a Knees Up Mother Brown.'

The room fell silent as this sank in where Alice was concerned. She was a bit of a snob on the quiet, and the vision which Molly had cleverly placed in her mind was making her go cold. 'Well, it's up to you, Cathy. Do what you think is best.'

'No, Mum. No way. I'm not gonna do something that you disagree with.'

'I never said I disagreed, Cathy. I was just giving my opinion – but I do have more than one opinion, unlike some people that I could mention. I'm not against a small, quiet registry office do. I'm happy so long as you are.'

'Oh, right,' she grinned. 'So if we go off and marry in Gretna Green, you won't mind that either?'

'No, I won't. You do whatever you want, darling, and don't let your nan or your dad sway you any which way.' Cathy looked from her mother to her nan, to receive a little wink. Sometimes she wondered if Molly did have a sixth sense and was ahead of all three of them. She had just given her granddaughter the best wedding gift she could have – she had paved the way for her to do what she wanted, to get married in secret. Nevertheless, even though Cathy had now been given a free hand, she knew that her sisters wouldn't be able to resist trying to turn a small wedding, albeit in a registry office, into a flashy turnout. And of course if they were at the wedding then Johnny's sisters would have to be invited too . . . and it would go on and on from there.

Johnny's, as Molly had pointed out, was a big, close family with cousins, aunts and uncles galore. So the following week, after talking about it with Johnny and getting his wholehearted agreement, one lunchtime Cathy caught a bus from Moorgate to the Stepney registry office. Here she picked up the necessary form and filled it in once back at work, forging her dad's signature. She hated going behind his back, but knew that he would understand why she was doing so once she explained it on the day she was married, after the ceremony.

The excitement in the reception area of Johnson's was at fever pitch once she broke the news to Pauline and Margaret and asked if they would go with her to John Lewis's to choose a spring dress and coat and hat to match. The next day she went to visit her sisters to ask if they would lend her forty pounds, which she had decided would be her budget. She told them she needed the outfit for a big wedding she had been invited to by one of her friends at work. As expected, she had to go through the ins and outs of Johnny's arrest, bail and likely sentence, but she didn't mind. The more it was discussed openly among her family, the less severe it sounded. Wanting to see a smile on their baby sister's face, they made the most of the fact that the payoff from the small gang of professional villains inside and outside the docks – Albert and Stanley included – would see the young couple all right financially. And smile Cathy did. She had no guilty feelings over telling them the white lie or that she was marrying in secret, because she knew that they would laugh out loud once it was done and announced and the gold band was on her left finger.

8

On the day before Cathy and Johnny were to be married in secret, Molly and Arthur, with no inkling as to what was going on, were in the back room going through the pros and cons of a registry office wedding for her granddaughter or a white one. They discussed the time it would take to make all the arrangements and just how much she would be showing by then. They knew that the cost of the wedding, either way, did not come into the scenario: Molly had every intention of giving Ava and Marilyn the bill to hand on to their guys, who could well afford to pay it.

Molly, sitting at the table opposite Arthur, was drawing up a list and estimating costs. And Arthur – despite Molly's plans for who was going to foot the bill – was telling her every now and then of people he knew who could do a good job on the cheap: florists, caterers and a mate who worked in an off-licence. He even knew a woman who lived in Jubilee Street in Stepney who made wedding dresses better than could be purchased in Harrod's and at a fraction of the cost. The dress had been at the top of Molly's list, marked with three stars to indicate priority. She wanted her granddaughter to feel really special on her white wedding day – if this was what she opted for in the end. Every time Molly had broached the subject, at least twice a day, Cathy had said, 'I'm not sure, Nan. I don't know whether to have a white wedding or not.' She knew exactly what she was going to do, of course, but had to keep it a tight secret if she was going to pull it off.

'You know what?' said Molly, sipping her tea. 'Of my three granddaughters, Cathy's the last one I ever imagined would get 'erself in the club and have to get married. The other two 'ave been foot-loose and fancy-free for years, and yet she's the one who cops it. And how can I condemn Cathy, when I was in the family way myself when I got married?'

'We'll see she's all right while Johnny's away. A sensible lad like him's gonna behave while he's doing 'is time and get parole before you know it.'

'She'll still be by 'erself when she has the baby, though, won't she?'

Arthur burst out laughing before saying, 'Some chance! You lot will be fussing around 'er and the little one twenty-four hours a day if she was to let you.' Then, looking away for a moment, he scratched his chin and wondered whether this might not be the right time to present her with the little gift he had in his pocket – if for nothing else than to take her mind off Cathy and the bloody wedding plans Molly kept on making and re-making. He had done his best to be a good listener, offering suggestions now and then, but a little diversion was necessary as far as he was concerned. Yes, now was the time for the secondhand ruby and diamond ring, which he had bought at a knock-down price, to come out of the dark. This had been his little secret that made him smile when he woke up alone in the mornings in his house in Jubilee Street. He intended to propose to Molly and have her move out of Jim and Alice's place into his lovely little terraced palace. But the one thing he wasn't going to allow her to do was drag the old stained glass table lamp with her. All of this was running through his mind as Molly continued to prattle on about white weddings.

'My mother used her Christmas club money to pay for my sister's wedding frock year ago,' she was saying. 'It's a pity no one can be bothered to run them thrift clubs any more. Your ex used to run a committee, didn't she?'

'Yeah. That's right. She did,' he said, sorry that Molly had brought his former wife into his thoughts. 'But she ran away with the money,' he joshed, hoping to end it there on a light note.

'Don't tell pork pies. She ran off with *your* money – and more fool you for not keeping your eye on things. Too bloody soft by 'alf, you were.'

'Tell me about it. Anyway . . . I never saw the point of loan clubs. The women paid five shillings a week and then borrowed a fiver out of the funds which had to be paid back over twenty-one weeks with five bob on top of the usual five shillings and five bob on top of that in interest. Why not save up your five shillings in a post office account? How long would it take? No more than twenty weeks to save up the fiver.'

'But that interest mounted up and was then shared out at Christmas. I thought it was a good idea.'

'If you can trust the one who's banking the money, I suppose it might be. How many of the treasurers legged it with the cash before payoff? Several. I think you'll find I'm right.'

Molly shrugged. 'I couldn't care less anyway. If the dozy sods can't pick out a dishonest face that's their own fault. When it was run properly, it worked well.'

'If you say so,' sniffed Arthur. 'It made Christmas time more special for the working classes to know they had extra money to spend on food and toys, I suppose.'

'Course it did. And do you know what the best bit about Christmas is?'

'No. But you're gonna tell me.'

'Tangerines, oranges, mixed nuts and them gold-wrapped chocolate coins that we hung on a tree, Arthur, that's what.'

'We still do hang them on the tree.'

'Yeah, but it's different now. We can afford all the bits and bobs. It's not as special as it was,' said Molly.

'Well, that's because you're rich. Whereas most of us are poor.'

'Rich? Do me a favour! Now then, shall we forget the wedding plans for a while and play snakes and ladders?'

Arthur burst out laughing. 'Snakes and ladders?' He leaned back in his chair and remembered his boyhood. 'Go on, then. Go and get the game if it keeps you smiling.' He leaned back in his chair and studied her face, which, though now lined, to him was as beautiful as ever. She still had lovely blue eyes and well-shaped lips.

'I take it you wouldn't want a church wedding if you got married again,' he suddenly blurted out, surprising himself, never mind Molly.

'Married? I'm a bit past that, Arthur. I'll be seventy next year.'

'You're never too old to have a bit of the other, though, are yer?'

'I wouldn't know. It's been a bloody long time going cold. Why? What are you suggesting? That we try out a bit of the other? Because if you are – I'm up for it. You can thaw out my frozen pasty any time.'

'I wasn't hinting at that, as it happens.' Then, without thinking too much about it, he felt in his pocket and brought out the ring. 'What d'yer reckon to that, then? They might be only small, them there diamonds and rubies, but they're good ones. I looked at every stone through a magnifying glass.'

'I bet you did! But it's no good looking at me. I'm not in the market for dear stuff. Not everyone's a moneybag like you.' She glanced at the ring again and then said, 'I wish I was, cos I would keep this little gem. How much did you pay for it?'

'That's for me to know and you to find out. Hold out your left hand. Let's see how it looks on a finger.'

'And what if it gets stuck once it's over my knuckle? You gonna cut my finger off?'

'Either that or let it stop there,' said Arthur as he slipped the ring on to the third finger of her left hand, above the wedding ring from her first marriage. 'Look at that sparkle! Lovely little ring, innit? That'll shock everyone, won't it? What say we get married when it's convenient and you join me in my little house in Jubilee Street? What d'yer say to that?'

For possibly the first time since he had known her, Molly was speechless. 'That's taken the wind out of your sails innit?'

'Is this meant to be a joke? Because if it is, I'm not gonna take that ring off.'

'Course it's not a joke. I've been waiting for the right moment to ask if you'll marry me.'

'At our age?'

'Why not? I intend to live until I'm ninety, just like my old dad. And you run about as if you're still a young woman, buying and selling nicked gear.'

'You're not messing about, are yer? This isn't costume jewellery, is it? Because if it *is* a daft joke I won't find it very funny.'

'Does it feel like costume jewellery or like a fifteen-carat old gold ring with diamonds and rubies?'

'So it's secondhand then?'

'Secondhand? That's an *antique*! I'll have it back if you're not satisfied.'

'No, this'll do me,' smiled Molly. She held out her hand and wiggled her fingers, admiring the ring again. 'You've got an eye for good stuff, Arthur, I will say that. I s'pose you want a kiss, then?'

'Well, that's up to you, Molly. But an appreciative hug would be nice.'

Molly stood up and held out her arms to him. 'Come here, you silly old sod! You should 'ave done this years ago. Fancy leaving it this long.'

'Yeah, well . . . I had to play the field a bit once I was a free man again, didn't I.' He cupped her face with one hand and smiled. 'You're still a lovely-looking woman, even though your face is lined more than mine is. I don't suppose we could slip upstairs, could we?' he pleaded, a hopeful glint in his eye. 'Only my old soldier ain't 'alf standing to attention.'

'Is that right? Well . . . I think we'd better do something about that and quick. Come on. Let's get up there before you lose the urge.' With no more ado, laughing and giggling like a couple of teenagers, Molly and Arthur climbed the stairway to heaven.

★   ★   ★

Dressed in her new turquoise blue dress and coat, with a beautiful spray of fresh orchids pinned on to the lapel, Cathy looked lovely as she arrived at Stepney registry office. Johnny for his part was smart in a new navy serge suit, white shirt and carnation pinned on to his lapel. Their only guests were Cathy's two friends Margaret and Pauline, and two of Johnny's mates who didn't work in the docks and didn't know Cathy's family. It was important to the couple that only those who were strangers to both sets of parents were there to see them married in secret. This way they could, with hand on heart, say they hadn't invited anyone other than outsiders.

Having stored her lovely new outfit in Johnny's best friend Tony's bed-sit down by St Katherine's docks Cathy had got herself ready there, with Pauline and Margaret to give her moral support. Once suited up himself, Tony had driven the three girls to the registry office to meet up with Johnny who was waiting outside with his best man.

The wedding ceremony, in a flower-filled room, turned out to be just as moving as if it had been held in church, and when Johnny slipped the gold band on to Cathy's finger she smiled radiantly at him, overjoyed and watery-eyed. It hadn't taken them long to become man and wife, but in its own way their marriage was not only romantic but also fun and exciting because of the secrecy and daredevil nature of it. After a local photographer, compliments of Cathy's two friends, had taken the wedding pictures the six of them went off in a taxi to the Great Eastern Hotel for a special three-course meal laid on by Johnny's two friends as their wedding present. At the end of the meal the head waiter brought a bottle of champagne and when Johnny raised his glass and proposed a toast to his beautiful wife it brought tears to the eyes of all three of the girls.

'I don't think I could ask for more than this,' he added. 'My best friends and Cathy's best friends at the table, and nobody else.' He then looked into his young wife's face and said, 'I never thought in a million years that the girl I'd been too shy to ask out would be sitting here now with my ring on her finger.

I love you, Cathy, and I've fancied you for ages. Thanks for
marrying me!'

Later that day, a little tipsy and very happy even though the
problems facing them still hovered like a dark cloud, Cathy
and Johnny took a black cab to her house ready to face her
parents and Molly. They had rehearsed how they would explain
why they had decided on the lightning registry office wedding,
but once inside the house trepidation set in. Going through
the passage on their way to the back room where they could
hear Jim, Alice and Molly quietly talking, they looked at each
other expecting the worst, but quietly laughing nevertheless.

Still wearing their smart clothes, with the telltale orchid and
carnation pinned on their respective lapels, it was obvious that
they had been to their own wedding and it didn't take much
for Cathy's family to guess what they had done. Molly was the
first to react, and with a suppressed smile rather than shock
and anger. 'They've gone and fucking well done it!' she
exclaimed.

Then an awesome silence filled the room as Cathy looked
at her mum and Johnny checked the expression on Jim's face,
which was one of astonishment. Johnny quickly got in before
questions began to fly, saying, 'It was the only way we could
do it, Jim, without all the drama from my family.'

Cathy, standing next to him, clasped her hand in Johnny's
as she offered her reasons in a rush. 'We couldn't go in for a
proper wedding – which I know is what you all wanted –
because it would take too long to arrange it all and I'll be
showing too much and in any case Johnny hasn't got long
before his trial and sentence.'

Johnny followed up. 'Once I'm out of prison,' he said, his
throat suddenly dry, 'we can take our vows again with Cathy
in white and make a really cracking show of it.'

'Please don't be too cross with us,' said Cathy, gripping
Johnny's hand so tight that her wedding ring was digging into
his fingers.

'I want to spend the rest of my life with your daughter, Jim. Will you give us your blessing?'

Jim opened his mouth to say something but couldn't get the words out. He simply shook his head slowly in silence while Alice and Molly just stared at the young couple.

Cathy made the most of the continued silence, adding, 'I'm gonna keep our little home fire burning till Johnny comes out, but I'll need all of your support to help me through until then. Moral support and hugs, that is, not money.' She then turned to face her new husband and they instinctively kissed each other lightly on the lips as if they had just made their pledge at the altar before the family.

'You look beautiful, Cathy,' Alice managed to say as a warm smile spread across her face, surprising the young couple. Of the three of them, she was the one they thought would be aggrieved the most.

Tears welling in her eyes, Cathy murmured, 'Oh, Mum . . . that's just what I wanted to hear you say.'

With no more to be said as far as she was concerned, Alice, with tears in her eyes too, stood up and opened her arms wide. 'Come here and give me a hug, you beautiful little daredevil.' Mother and daughter held each other tightly, each of them softly crying tears of love and warmth, not repentance.

Molly, almost lost for words for a change, quietly said, 'Well, at least you won't be gossiped about in church, sweetheart.'

All eyes were then on Jim, who was still in his chair looking at his daughter. He was neither frowning nor smiling, but watery-eyed. 'I won't say I'm not bowled over by this,' he just managed to say, 'but congratulations, the pair of you. It must have taken a lot of courage to do a thing like this.'

'So you're not angry with me then, Dad?' asked Cathy.

'Course I'm not, sweetheart. If you're old enough to vote, you're old enough to choose the way you get married. Good luck to the pair of you.' He stood up and offered Johnny his hand. 'Things are not gonna be that easy for you, son, with all that's happened – but we're right behind you. We'll take care of your little family while you're a guest of Her Majesty. Congratulations.' He spread his arms and gave Johnny a bloke's hug.

Molly, who remained in her chair, looked from one to the other, thinking that if she had used all of her guile she could not have made a better job of it than Cathy had. It was done and dusted, with smiles all round. They were tearful smiles, and no doubt there was a touch of sadness behind them, she felt. But it didn't matter. Her youngest granddaughter had, in her own sweet way, taken the load from everyone's shoulders.

'I blame the government for giving you kids the vote at eighteen instead of twenty-one. You'll be running the country between you, next thing we know.' Molly looked from Cathy to Johnny and pulled an envelope from her Marks and Spencer's cardigan pocket. 'Albert pulled up in his car yesterday just after I'd got off the bus after doing a little bit of shopping. He asked me to give this to you, Cathy, to pass on to Johnny. I should think there's a few grand in there but I haven't counted it,' she fibbed. 'Now, which one of you shall I give it to?'

Johnny looked at the bulging envelope and knew exactly what was in it: his payoff. 'Give it to Cathy. She's gonna need it while I'm away.' He looked into her face with a warm smile. 'You can pay a year's rent in advance on the flat and still have a bundle left.' This was his compensation for shouldering the blame for a crime in which he had only been a small player, and true to promise the envelope contained three thousand pounds.

It's a funny thing,' said Molly, back in her chair, 'that Albert should want to hand that envelope to me to give to you, Johnny. Why d'yer reckon he did that?'

Johnny blushed a little and then sheepishly said, 'There's no fooling you, is there? He and Stanley asked me if I wanted it now or whether they should give it to Cath on the day I go down, to cheer her up. I said I'd rather they gave it to you to give to her now.'

'Why was that, then?' Molly sniffed.

'Because you rule the roost on the quiet and you've got all of our respect.'

'Nice one, son.' Jim laughed. 'Very clever. Keep the bird at the top of the pecking order happy and it makes for a peaceful life. I think you've taken a leaf out of my book. Now, who's gonna give George and Rosie a knock and tell them to come in for a drink? Becky, Leo and young Henry as well.'

'Henry won't be there, you daft sod. He moved out and into his flat last week, didn't he?'

'Course he did. I forgot. But then it doesn't seem right not to include his name somehow. He's part and parcel of our little world.'

'He still will be, Dad. And I'm really glad that he'll be in the flat below ours. He can keep me company during the long winter evenings. And now that we've got the money, me and Johnny can make the flat look nice and live in it together for a few weeks before the inevitable.'

'Do you think it might be a good idea to pack in your job sooner rather than later, Cath? It's not as if you're gonna need the money to make ends meet. I know full well your nan's got a bit put by for you.'

'She knows that already,' said Molly. 'She knows I wouldn't let my only honest granddaughter go short. And I agree with your dad, Cathy. I think you should give up work now.'

'I've already handed in a month's notice, Nan – I did it the day before yesterday. The company's happy to give me a month's salary on top of my wages – in fact they're obliged to – but in their own friendly way they've asked me to go straightaway. It's because I'm already showing, which doesn't look good in reception. So at least me and Johnny will have all of those days together in our flat before he goes away.'

Choked by this lovely warm family reaction, Johnny shook everyone's hands, told them all that he would look after Cathy for ever and that he was sorry for getting involved in a crime that was way above his head. 'I'll make it up to Cath, I swear it – and once I'm away I'll be on my best behaviour and do everything I can to get early parole.'

'And that's how it should be,' said Alice, tears rolling down her cheeks. 'Onwards and upwards, sweethearts, onwards and upwards.'

Molly was the next up from her seat, a touch slower than usual and not from ill health but more from shock. As she held out her arms to Cathy without saying a word, her granddaughter fell into them and hugged the warm fleshy body of the old lady she dearly loved, whispering, 'Thanks for being a brick over this, Nan.'

A few days into Johnny's trial at the Old Bailey, Alice and Molly sat either side of Cathy in the hushed but stern atmosphere of the court room, with wigged and gowned barristers and the judge in formal robes and an even heavier wig. Their expressions hardly ever changed from serious and severe. It was awful, and yet so unreal that all three of the women felt as if they were in a movie, especially when Johnny came in and stood in the dock a frightened and somewhat broken young man.

This was one time when Cathy could have done with her elder sisters by her side and, if asked, Molly and Alice would have said they felt the same. But, given the means by which they and their blokes earned their livings, this was no place for them to be seen – and recognised. Unfortunately for Cathy, Johnny's sisters *were* there, giving her black looks that she could have done without. Doing her best to forget they were there, she focussed on Johnny's barrister – the man she was pinning her hopes on to get him off with a light sentence. Soon after the proceedings commenced Cathy badly wanted to slip outside for fresh air, but she managed to hold on for two and a half hours until there was a one hour break at midday and she, Alice and Molly, went to a nearby café for lunch.

Once they had ordered sandwiches and hot drinks inside, and seated themselves around a small table they began to relax a little. 'Well, there's one thing we can be thankful for, Legal Aid or not, that's a very good barrister fighting Johnny's corner,' said Alice, smiling. 'He keeps on the way he's going and he'll persuade that jury that our boy's as innocent as a little lamb.'

'Don't bank on it,' said Molly. 'He's not fighting to get him off, Alice, but to get a short sentence.'

'True,' said Alice, tersely. 'But for driving the lorry out and believing there was only tinned salmon on board.'

'So? What does that tell yer?' said Molly, all knowing and a touch snappy.

'You tell me, Mum. You're so certain.'

'That he'll get time! Clean record or not. Ignorant that there was drugs on board or not!'

'Keep your voice down, Nan.' Cathy firmly whispered.

'Tell your mother not me. My voice was low.'

'By your standards maybe but not by the rest of the people in here,' said Alice.

'Stop it. Both of you,' Cathy whispered. 'Let's just wait and see and look on the bright side. That's what both of you have preached to me in the past.'

'Sorry, sweetheart.' Alice patted her daughter's hand and smiled warmly at her. 'We're on edge, that's all.'

Back in the courtroom after their break the three of them sat waiting for the trial to resume. Once things were moving again the time sped by and no one could have been more pleasantly surprised than the three generations of women when at the end of the hearing came the announcement of a 'hung jury' and a re-trial. Cathy, whose eyes were fixed on Johnny's face as he stood in the dock didn't understand what was happening but his smile as he looked at her lifted Cathy from the dark gloom. She smiled back at him as tears filled her eyes.

'My God. That beggars belief. Would you credit that?' murmured Alice. 'The jury's come out in our favour.'

'Not all of 'em,' said Molly, 'but enough to call for a re-trial. Johnny must have a bloody good guardian angel is all I can say.' Her voice, fortunately, was drowned by the sound of muttered talking everywhere as various people discussed the surprise ending of this trial. It all brought a smile to Cathy's face because her sweetheart was going to be let home on bail and so would be around for her for another two weeks until the second hearing. She could hardly believe it and neither could Johnny if expressions were to go by. His face seemed to have lit up as he looked at her before being led out of court.

Precious time of course speeds by and before Cathy and Johnny knew it the two weeks were up, and now, after spending as much time as possible together, he was back in court with the same three women there to support him. Early enough and more used to the place this second time, they secured seats as close as possible to where Johnny would be standing to give as much moral support as possible. The sense of him getting off with a caution was high on Cathy's list of possibilities. But this time things did not go as well as in the first hearing. Johnny's barrister left the courtroom mid-way through the trial because he was due at another more serious hearing within the same building. 'So much for Legal Aid,' said Molly. 'Bastard.' As the trial drew to an end with the judge's summing-up, Cathy badly wanted to slip outside for fresh air, but managed to hold on until sentence was pronounced. Found guilty as charged, Johnny was given sentences totalling five years to run concurrently, which at the end of the day meant that with good behaviour, and taking into consideration the fact that this was the first time he had been in trouble, he would serve at the most the eighteen months that Albert and Stanley had predicted.

Just before Johnny was led out of the dock, he looked up at Cathy and mouthed the words, '*I love you.*' She returned the silent message and smiled at him before blowing a kiss. The room then filled with hushed conversations as it began to empty, but Cathy wasn't ready to go just yet and asked her mum and nan to go on ahead. It had all gone so quickly, as if Johnny had been just another customer in a queue at a railway station waiting to buy a ticket. Once the room was clear of everyone other than the lawyers, Cathy wanted to scream at them that they were fools. That they had got it wrong. That Johnny was just a small pawn on the chess board.

Suddenly realising that she was standing there glaring at a small group of men and one woman wearing black gowns and wigs, smiling and congratulating each other on the outcome of her husband's trial, Cathy composed herself. She had always been told by her dad that self-respect and dignity won the day, and she had remembered his advice and dressed smartly that morning for this occasion.

None of the legal people took any notice of Cathy as she drew close to the group and stood there, arms folded and defiant, until she broke into their chit-chat and said, 'Well done! You've just sent the wrong man to prison. That's my husband and I'm expecting his baby, and he's never been in trouble before now. And all you can do is congratulate each other. I wonder what your parents would think if they could see the whole picture. Shame on you!' That said, she turned away and walked out, holding her head high.

Angry and hurt at the way the men and women of the law had been smiling and shaking hands, she had trouble keeping her chin up. But her determination held out and she did not cry. Johnny was going to Wormwood Scrubs, which at least was easy to get to by train. Joining Alice and Molly outside the Old Bailey, she declined an offer to go to the nearby tea rooms. 'I just want to go home,' she said. 'I need a hug from my dad.'

On her very first visit to Johnny in prison Cathy had gone alone because she wanted him all to herself. Marilyn and Ava had done their best to persuade her otherwise, saying that she would need some moral support, but she stood up for herself and refused. She had no idea what it was like to see someone she loved in a prisoner's uniform behind a toughened glass partition during a visit, but her sisters did: the pair of them had been on numerous visits to Brixton, Wandsworth and Wormwood Scrubs at one time or another to see their blokes. Too clever to be caught breaking the law themselves, they hadn't even had a whiff of Holloway, the women's prison where Molly was often telling them they would end up.

Finding her own way Wormwood Scrubs, and only having to ask a policeman directions once after she had got off the train, Cathy soon arrived at the wide entrance gate that led up to the main door. She rang the bell and was let in through a much smaller door set into the huge arched surround. After showing her pass she went into the waiting room, which was packed with visitors of all ages. Some had children who were playing together, while others sat shyly on their mothers' laps. It all seemed a very ordinary and everyday situation. Although it was austere, it was also a place for making friendships, because people met up on a monthly basis when visiting their loved ones. Cathy, however, didn't strike up a conversation with anyone, because she wanted to think about Johnny. She knew she was only going to be allowed to see and talk to her sweetheart husband for twenty minutes.

So she sat there quietly and thought about everything to do with Johnny, right back to the first time he came through the passage into the back room and asked if she fancied going for a drink with him. So engrossed was she that she didn't realise her name was being called by one of the prison officers. After all, she hadn't been married long and wasn't used to her new name. 'Mrs Catherine Dean!' came the second, louder call to which she responded, 'Yes! That's me.'

She then had to wait with another couple, parents of a young man inside, while a few more visitors in her group were called before they were led through a passageway and courtyard, with gates unlocked and then locked again once they had gone through. Eventually they arrived in the block where she would be allowed to see Johnny.

Entering the long, narrow room, she saw on her left a row

of cubicles behind toughened glass, each with a prisoner in grey waiting for his visitors. Walking slowly along, she stopped when she saw Johnny smiling at her, rested her arms on the narrow wooden counter and pushed her face close to the glass. 'Hello, sweetheart!'

Johnny grinned, telling her that despite the thickness of the glass partitions there was no need to shout because they contained special sound equipment. 'How are you, darling?' he said, a touch choked to say the least. 'I can't tell you how I've been looking forward to your visit.'

'I'm fine, Johnny . . . Are they feeding you properly?'

'Yeah. Canteen food – but who cares about that? Listen . . . I saw my social worker this morning first thing and she reckons I'll be transferred to an open prison within a couple of months. Ford, like I told you I might. And it's in the country-side. I'll let you know as soon as they've told me for sure. God, I can't tell you how pleased I am about that. I just can't wait for you to visit me there. It sounds like a good place as prisons go.'

'What do you mean, two months or so? I'll come to see you here next month, silly.'

'No, Cath. I don't want you to have to come to this place. It's horrible. And don't say it's not, because it is. It's degrading and you shouldn't have to be visiting me. Wait until I'm at Ford. By all accounts it's a smashing place. I'll be able to play cricket there as well. Don't come back to this dump, Cath. Say you won't, for my sake.'

'All right, Johnny. I'll wait until they move you.' She went quiet and touched the glass with her fingertips. He did the same from the other side and mouthed the words, 'I love you.'

'Me too,' she said, desperate not to shed a tear. 'And baby.'

Johnny broke into a lovely smile and quietly laughed. 'Is our baby kicking yet?'

'I think so . . . in fact I'm sure of it, but I've not said anything to Mum or Nan in case they laugh at me and say it's not possible – that's it's too early. But I feel it move all of the time.'

Her eyes glistened with tears of joy. 'It's nearing the end of May and I'm five months gone, so I suppose it's possible.'

'I can't wait for the end of September when it's due, Cath. I just wish I could be there for you when your time comes. Someone in here told me they give compassionate leave, so I might be able to visit you in hospital – escorted, of course.'

'I wouldn't do that, darling,' said Cathy bravely. 'I'd rather you saw our baby at home once you're back for good. It won't even be a year from now, darling, and we've got decades together, you and me. And this won't be our only baby, will it? There'll be another one or two later on and you'll be there for us, with a regular job – no more gambling or getting involved with my sisters' crowd. And I promise I'll send regular photos of baby from the day it's born.' She smiled at him and said, 'I love you so much.'

Gutted by her loyalty, he pinched his lips together and then looked at her questioningly. 'Why did you say that it won't even be a year from now, Cath? I'll be in longer than that – you know I will.'

'Albert doesn't think so, babe. He's still fighting your corner with his solicitor. He now thinks they'll let you out on parole even earlier than he first reckoned – after you've served just a year. *If* you prove an excellent prisoner on your best behaviour all the time. So our baby will only be a few months old when you come home – home to our flat which by then will be lovingly furnished throughout.'

'Well, if that's the case it's brilliant news! But don't bank on it, Cathy, in case you're disappointed.' He pushed his hands into his face and took a deep breath in order to compose himself and then said, 'How's your dad? This hasn't had an effect on his heart, has it?'

'He's fine, Johnny. Everyone is. Me too. The only thing I'm not sure about is you not wanting me to visit next month. Are you certain this is what you want?'

'Positive. My sisters 'ave written a note nagging for a visit, so I'd rather get that over and done with. Mum and Dad too.

I wrote and told them not to come this month because I wanted to use every second looking at you.'

'I wonder how that went down?' she smiled.

'Not all that well – but that's too bad. I couldn't ask for more than you there in front of me right now. Even if there is a sheet of glass between us. At least I'll be able to hold your hand at Ford.'

'That will be wonderful – and you're right. Let's wait for that. And I'm glad your family will be here for you next month.' A bell rang to indicate the end of visiting time. Each placed a hand on the glass as if they were touching each other and whispered their goodbyes, with the promise of lots of love and kisses to come.

Over the next few months, with time on her hands now that she was no longer working, Cathy began to buy clothes to put in the bottom drawer for her baby. Making the most of her independence and free time, she got to know Henry better and they spent many evenings in each other's flats. She had bought herself a few cookery books, and loved trying new things out on him. Ava and Marilyn had already bought her a cot from Mothercare, which was installed in the bedroom next to the one which housed Cathy and Johnny's double bed. Alice, Molly and Becky were looking forward to the new addition, and knitting bootees and matinee jackets. It hadn't been easy for Cathy to break the news to her neighbour Rosie, whose inability to have children had given her a sense of failure as a woman. But as it turned out, Rosie was as thrilled as anyone else that her friend was going to have a baby – and happier still when Cathy asked if she and George would be godparents.

So, with her sisters, parents, nan and Rosie coming to visit her in the flat in Stratford East, Cathy could not have wished for better under the circumstances. More than this, she was glad of Henry's company on a daily basis, especially when she felt a little lonely. Sometimes she went down into the shop and chatted with him for ten minutes or so during the day, or sat outside in the small garden at the rear of the antique shop next door, where the proprietor, Stewart, offered free coffee to customers. Stewart liked to wear kaftans and other Eastern inspired garments, and rolled his own cigarettes which Cathy suspected rightly did not contain tobacco. Still, that was his business, she reckoned. One day she was chatting to him when she admitted, 'My husband's in prison. He was a bit naughty down the docks where he worked and got caught out. He won't be around for a year or so.'

'How very bold of you to say so,' was Stewart's immediate and friendly response.

Innocently she had replied, and only because she wanted to keep up friendships she had made, 'You must come in for a coffee at my place some time. I might even make you a meal. I've been studying a cookery book or two and I can now make Hungarian goulash, which is great with rice and a side salad.'

'Sounds delicious,' said Stewart, gazing into her face. 'I shall look forward to that, Cathy – and indeed to dropping in for a coffee. Later on this afternoon . . . or this evening, perhaps?'

'No . . . I've got things to do this afternoon. And this evening I'm going with Henry and Helen – you know, the girl who works with him in the tobacconist's – to the Prospect of Whitby. We're in for a sing song, if the pub's reputation is anything to go by.'

'What a coincidence,' said Stewart. 'I've been meaning to take a look at the place myself. Do let me know what you think of it, Cathy,' he said, smiling warmly at her. She saw the attention from this handsome, self-assured man as flattery, and no more than that.

Later on that evening, while she was putting on her make-up to go out, someone knocked three times on the street door. It was Stewart, smiling and holding out a bottle of red wine. His presence sent a flash of worry through her. Had she led him to believe that she wanted his company? She invited him up to the flat, of course – it would have seemed rude to her to do otherwise – but she reminded him on the way that she was due to go out in five minutes or so with her friends.

'I hear the old tavern's very much in vogue now – mostly used by medical students and a few old East Enders who live in Wapping. It sounds absolutely marvellous,' he said persistently.

'Well, if you want to, Stewart, you'd be very welcome to come along.' What else could she say? He seemed a bit of a loner, even though he would be a catch for any free young girl.

'I'd love to come,' he said.

By the time they had been in the old tavern for fifteen minutes or so, Cathy found that for some reason the company of Stewart, Henry and Helen helped her feel more at ease with the medical students who were crowding the place. It was such a contrast from the pubs she used to frequent with her friends before she had started courting Johnny, with their whiff of high living from ill-gotten gains. Girls and lads in the Prospect didn't seem to care how drunk they were as they downed one pint of ale after another to create a party-like atmosphere without the dancing.

On a good night, as this obviously was, the students were relaxed and more easy-going than Cathy imagined they would be, and when they broke out into what was obviously a favourite ballad everyone joined in – Cathy felt sure they could be heard all around Wapping. The ballad was a touch repetitious when it came to the chorus, but deliberately so: '"Oh Sir Bastian, do not touch me" – as she lay between the lily-white sheets with nothing on at all!'

With each rendition a word was dropped until just two remained, to be sung more loudly: 'Oh . . . Sir!' It was fun, and Cathy liked the set of people she had come with. She could tell that Henry was comfortable too and didn't look out of place the way he had among the East End boys done up to the nines in their Italian suits and shoes. It was almost as if he had been born into the wrong family in the wrong place. He was a studious young man and always had been, and the more she watched, as he blended in quite uninhibited with the medical students, the more she understood him.

Henry hadn't at first taken to Stewart because of his direct approach, but as time wore on he had begun to accept him as someone who, when he himself was otherwise engaged, would be company for Cathy whenever she got lonely up there in the flat. But he needn't have worried. Enjoying her evening out, Cathy was happy in the knowledge that with her sisters calling in every so often, as well as Jim, Alice, Molly and Arthur, she was hardly an abandoned soul. Best of all, in August, Johnny was being transferred to Ford open prison.

After taking the bus from Stratford along the Mile End Road to get off at Cambridge Heath Road Cathy strolled through her favourite Bethnal Green gardens on her way to pay her parents a weekly visit. At the Tillet Street house she pressed the door bell briefly and then let herself in with her key. To her delight Leo and Becky were in the back room of Jim and Alice's house sharing a pot of tea made by Molly, and they were equally pleased to see her – to get an update on how Henry was making out.

'Hello, you two,' said Cathy. 'Where're are my parents then?'

'Your mother's not back from work yet and your dad had to pop out. He shouldn't be five minutes. And Molly's upstairs getting ready to go out with us.'

'Oh right,' she smiled. 'You popped in and dad popped out. Henry sends his love.'

'Why doesn't he come to visit?' asked Becky. 'We miss him. And we have some news to give him. It's to do with the brick being thrown at our window, which I know had a bad effect on him. Tell him from us that we've had a very nice letter from the woman on my mother's side of the family, and we're going to Buckhurst Hill.'

'She answered a letter,' Leo chipped in. 'This silly cow sent a little card with a picture of flowers on the corner, asking if the boys who threw the brick were part of the family.' He said nothing about the fact that he too had sent a letter.

'What does it matter who wrote first, Leo?' said his wife. 'She answered me, didn't she? That must tell us something – that the woman doesn't bear a grudge.'

'Why should she bear a grudge?' said Leo. 'She's the one in the wrong, not you.'

'She wrote to say that she'd given the lads a good telling-off, Cathy.' Becky smiled. 'She grilled them, and they confessed. The boys had overheard some conversations in the house and taken things into their own hands.'

'I know what I'd like to do to them,' said Leo, 'and not only the lads. I could read between the lines of that note. The woman's afraid we'll make trouble, frightened that her neighbours might hear from us what kind of people they are. You can bet your bottom dollar that's the only reason she got in touch. At least the little bastards won't be back. At least that's something.'

'Maybe it was worth going to Somerset House, after all,' commented Cathy. 'If you don't try, you don't know – that's what my dad always says, anyway.'

'Sandria. What sort of a bloody name is that?' said Leo, talking to the air before turning to Cathy again. 'She signed her name Sandria . . . It's Becky who wants to go back again. A waste of bloody time, if you ask me.'

'No, it's not a waste of time, Leo. Stop being an old moaner,' said Cathy.

Becky laughed and slowly shook her head. 'We miss you, Cathy, you know that? But at least you come once a week to see all of us. And look at you – what a size! You don't think you might be carrying twins?'

'I know I'm not. The welfare clinic would have picked up on that if I was. I'm eating too much pie and mash. Can't get enough of it.'

'Well, it's a lovely meal and very cheap too,' said Leo. 'You can't beat it.'

The sound of the doorbell brought Molly down from her room where she had been getting ready. She opened the door to Arthur, who of course was now a regular visitor. He gave her a kiss on the cheek and then made his way through to the back room where he could hear Cathy talking to the old Jewish couple.

'Hello, Becky, ducks. Where you off to, then? You're all done up like the Queen.'

'We popped in because we knew that Cathy was coming to visit. Then we're going to Buckhurst Hill with Rosie and Molly,' said Becky. 'Rosie's taken the day off specially – we're just off to collect her. What does that tell us about friends and neighbours, eh? Wonderful.'

'Yeah . . . that's very nice. So you're off to meet your long-lost family, are yer?'

'They wrote me a letter—'

'That's right,' he said, reminding her in his own gentle way that she had already told him three or four times. 'Did you want me to run you there in the car? Save getting the tube?'

'No, thanks,' said Molly. 'We'd like to get there in one piece. You don't know the way, and I've been in the car with you when you don't know the way. It's a fucking nightmare. Poor Becky'll have a heart attack before she gets to see her kith and kin.'

The journey to Buckhurst Hill took no more than forty-five minutes, which was just as well because poor old Leo needed the gents. From the way he half-walked, half-ran to the lavatory once they had got off the train it was obvious he was bursting for a pee. The three women waited outside the station for him to reappear, taking in their surroundings and appreciating the air which seemed much fresher and a touch colder than in the East End. Rosie in particular was surprised at the sense of being in the country when they were only just on the edge of London. She glanced at the large tall Victorian terraced houses opposite, which had huge trees in the front gardens.

'Sorry about that,' said Leo, arriving at his wife's side. 'The bladder's weaker than it was when I was a young man.'

'But you got there in time?' said Becky, her face serious.

'Of course I bloody well got there in time. What's the matter with you? You think I'm senile and can't do a short train ride without wetting my pants? Silly cow.' He sniffed and looked around. 'Now, if my memory serves me right there isn't a tea room or café close by, so it's into the Railway Tavern for a drink afterwards.'

'No, we're gonna be given tea when we get to the house,' Becky reminded him.

'So do we turn left or right?' enquired Molly as they stood in the street like lost souls.

'We turn right,' said Becky.

'Good. Let's go, then.' Molly glanced at Rosie, who was covering a smile.

'First right, straight across the road, down the hill, left down The Meadway, then right and right again. Number fourteen Little Dove Way.'

'Nothing wrong with your memory, is there, Leo?' Rosie laughed. 'How come you remember it so well?'

'Easy,' he said, strolling along with all the confidence in the world. 'Forget the names of the streets. You just remember what I just said: right, across, left, straight ahead, right and right again. And you say it over and over until it's fixed in your brain.'

'This is a really lovely part of the world,' said Rosie, as she glanced at the Stradbroke Grove sign, once they had crossed the main road and were walking down the hill. 'Stradbroke Grove. I wonder why that rings a bell.'

'Because I mentioned it on the train. I said if I were to live in such a place as this I would choose Stradbroke Grove, a lovely tree-lined road. Can you imagine what these trees look like in spring, with blossom everywhere?'

'I can't believe how quiet it is. This is like being in the country properly – in a village.' Rosie was very impressed and a look of happiness was shining out through her eyes. 'I feel I could live here,' she said.

'Right, here we are,' said Leo. 'Turn left.'

'Sounds like a bloody sergeant major, doesn't he?'

'Leave 'im alone, Becky. I'd sooner 'ave someone leading us to the exact place than getting lost. Because if we'd left it to Arthur he'd still be driving us round the mulberry bush. What time did they say for you to arrive?'

'Three-thirty.'

'Well, you're bang on with your time, Leo. You said it was only a ten-minute walk, so we've got five minutes to spare. In other words, slow down a bit for fuck's sake.'

'Molly, please,' said Becky, her eyes full of expression. 'Please don't swear while we're in this area. And don't for God's sake swear once we get there.'

'Hark at her,' said Leo. 'She reads me the Riot Act as well. Last night and again this morning. I'm not allowed to say "bloody" in Buckhurst Hill, can you believe? Anyone would think we were visiting royalty. Turn right at the end.'

'What I like about the area,' said Rosie, 'is that none of the houses are the same. There was that row of four terraced cottages. Then two groups of semi-detached with detached ones in between. I could definitely live here.'

'No, you bloody well couldn't,' insisted Leo. 'It would cost a fortune to buy one of these places.'

'It wouldn't,' said Becky. 'It's always cheaper to buy in the suburbs, because it's not exactly the countryside with posh mansions everywhere, and then again if you're commuting to London to work you've got the journey both ends of the day.'

'Hark at her,' said Leo. 'All of a sudden she's an estate agent.'

'You're dead right, Becky,' said Rosie. 'I wonder where the shops are.'

'From here?' said Leo, pausing for a moment for breath and to get his bearings. 'From memory I would say, left out of The Meadway, up to the main road again which I believe is called Palmerston Road, then we take a right, past the children's home, cross over Palmerston, go down a little alleyway and come out into Queen's Road. And you'll find every bloody shop you need. The pavements are fairly wide and the road quiet and narrow at the top because the turning's been built on a hill. There you'll find one of the best little libraries you could want. Nice and cosy.'

'He's right. We went into a tea room next door to it and then popped in to have a look around,' said Becky.

'And there's a baker's halfway down called Hobley's. I'm telling you now, you won't find bread like that man makes anywhere in the world. Wonderful bread.'

'And cakes, Leo. You remember the lardy cake we fetched back home with us?'

'Sliced with a little butter, it was delicious. Never tasted anything so fresh. And do you know why it's a success, with people queuing outside every day? Because the man and wife who own it do all of their own bloody baking, that's why. Out the back of the shop. You can smell it for miles around. One of the last few real bakers, more's the pity. Turn right again and we're in the right place.'

'What was that you said about a children's home, Leo?'

'A bloody huge double-fronted house. It doesn't say it in big letters . . . keep walking straight . . . the house is the big one at the end. It doesn't say "Children's Home" in big letters, like I said, but I saw a couple of happy faces peering out the window, which made me smile. And then I noticed the polished brass plaque on the wall by the front door. I have a feeling the children are from the East End. Don't ask me why . . . But then again it stands to reason,' he said, 'because there's always been a very big children's home in Wanstead – and I know of another one in Chipping Ongar where a few kids from my turning went before the war. So it stands to reason that there would be one or two smaller homes in this area. In between Wanstead and Ongar.'

Molly cautiously eyed Rosie and knew what was going through her mind. 'I don't know why you and George don't move to a place like this. What would a three-bedroom house cost, d'you reckon?'

'Seven thousand pounds, if you wanted one of those we've

just passed in The Meadway – a three-bedroom spacious semi-detached. Thirteen thousand if you fancy a big detached chalet bungalow with a third of an acre garden out the back and a lovely front garden, double-gated. That's what I'd go for if I were a rich man. The one in Stradbroke Grove. Number thirty-six.'

'How the fuck do you know that, Leo?' said Molly.

'Because when we walked down the hill of Queens Road the last time we were here we looked in the window of an estate agent – which, if my memory serves me right, was called Ambrose. For thirteen thousand you could own a beautiful detached chalet bungalow with leaded light windows and a third of an acre garden. That's the one I'd go for if I was still a young working man. Or I'd go for one of the little two-bedroom terraced cottages in The Meadway at five and a half thousand.'

'We're here,' said Becky suddenly, her voice quiet and trembling. 'This is it.'

'Fuck me!' exclaimed Molly. 'It's a bloody mansion.'

'It isn't a mansion,' said Leo. 'It's a six-bedroom detached.' He stopped in his tracks and the other three followed suit. 'So? Are we ready to go into the lion's den for tea?'

'I feel sick,' said Becky feebly. 'I don't feel well at all.'

'I'm not surprised you feel sick, with Leo giving us a bloody running commentary on the housing market.' Molly placed an arm around the old woman's bony shoulders and squeezed her. 'You'll be all right, darling. You've got us. And don't you forget that. They might be your blood relatives, but we're your lifelong friends.'

'Thank you, Molly. And you're right. Why should I be afraid? I did nothing wrong.'

'No. But their spoilt kids did. They put a brick through your window, don't forget, and this is your family's way of saying sorry.'

'But who would have put the lads up to it? It could only have been the parents – the ones I sent the letter to in the first place. I've never been able to forget those words: "I take it you are happy to live next door to the poor Jew?" I only wrote the letter in the first place because I needed to fill in the blank spaces. You remember that I told you this? I wanted to know my roots.' She looked from one to the other of them. 'Suddenly I had a brother and sister that I knew nothing about. Maybe I shouldn't have interfered? What do you think?'

'What are you talking about, woman? They wrote and invited you to meet them, didn't they? They want to see you for one reason or another,' said Leo. 'Stop worrying.'

'That's true. And they know I'm going on eighty. I didn't ask for anything in the letter. I just said I would like to see my brother or sister. Do you think they will be there? All my family? My brother and my sister? What if they don't like me?'

'And what if you can't stand them?' said Molly. 'You give us the nod and we're out of there like bullets from a gun.'

'Molly's right,' Becky murmured. 'Let's get it over with. Nothing lost if nothing's gained. That's what you're always telling me, Leo. And don't say it's not true, because it is.'

Opening the latched gate into the extensive front garden, Leo stood aside as if he were the lord of the manor and, with a sly smile on his face, swept a hand through the air as if inviting them on to his land.

Giving Rosie a wink, Molly moved close to her and whispered, 'I think this is gonna be a bit of an eye-opener, don't you?'

'We'll see,' said Rosie, keeping her thoughts to herself. She had already picked up bad vibes and they weren't even inside the house yet.

'Why she wants to find her bloody brother and sister beats me,' moaned Leo as he followed them up the wide entrance path. 'She discovers she has a half-sister and a half-brother, so she has to say hello – after almost eighty bloody years.'

'Shut up, Leo,' whispered Molly. 'We're here now, so behave yourself.'

Leo shrugged, sniffed and waited for the solid oak door to

open. When it did, his heart sank. There stood a woman in her late forties, dressed up to the nines in what could possibly be regarded as smart day wear – a midnight blue silk top above perfectly tailored navy linen slacks. On her feet she wore gold Cuban heeled shoes. Her fingers were almost hidden by rings and the dozen or so fine gold bracelets on her arm clashed nicely together.

The woman, her hands clasped together, offered Becky a film-star smile as she said, 'You must be Rebecca. Do come in – all of you. I am Sandria.' She stood aside and waved them into the ostentatious hall with its sparkling chandelier hanging above the black and white tiled floor and ornaments filling every surface.

'That's an unusual name,' said Molly, 'Sandria . . . and yet, funnily enough, you're not the first one I've met with it. Was you christened Sandra as well?'

The woman smiled patronisingly at Molly as she looked her up and down. 'And you are?'

'Molly, love. How do you do? It's lovely to meet someone from the East End who's made a few bob and does their best to live amidst them that are born to it. Bloody well done, girl. Shop in Harrod's for that top, by any chance, did you?'

'Well, as a matter of fact I did. But how on earth could you know that?'

'Because the one you're wearing looks very similar to a dozen or so others that I sold in our neighbourhood on the cheap a couple of winter seasons ago. Course, the labels were cut out,' she said, giving the uppity woman with working-class roots a wink.

'Very amusing,' said Sandria.

'I live next door to Becky here. Ain't she beautiful? Age couldn't damage her lovely looks even though she's had a very hard time of it.'

Knowing that Molly was behaving like this because the woman had instantly got under her skin, Rosie gave her a little sly kick before offering her own hand to the woman. 'Hello,' she said, smiling warmly. 'I live next door to Becky and Leo on the other side. They were really pleased when you wrote to invite them for tea. Where are the rest of her family? Hiding so they can surprise her with a big welcome hello?'

'Well, actually, it's just me. And even though we're not strictly related, I was only too happy to volunteer. Do come into the morning room . . .'

'Why?' said Leo. 'It's the afternoon, isn't it?'

'Well, yes, it is, but I think you would feel more comfortable in there than in the drawing room.' She led them through with a graceful wave of the hand and a grimace that only Leo saw. He gave her a grin back to match it.

Once she had invited them to sit down on the brightly flowered loose-covered sofas she glanced at her expensive gold watch and asked if they would prefer orange juice or tea.

'Tea, please,' said Molly, flopping down on to one of the sofas and placing her feet on a footstool. 'And if it's all right with you, no fish paste sandwiches for me. But if you've some smoked salmon that would be a different kettle of fish entirely.'

'Oh, I see. You didn't have lunch before you left home,' said the woman, cupping her chin and trying to show a little grace as well as perfectly painted manicured nails and a flashy ring or two. 'I have to say that I wasn't actually expecting there to be four of you – and certainly not here for a meal.' She smiled falsely. 'But I'll open some peanuts and crisps . . . I have something the family wish to give to you, Rebecca, which is the reason why I wrote and asked you to come.'

'A glass of orange juice all round will be fine,' said Rosie, giving Leo the evil eye. 'We plan to go on to Epping – to the tea rooms, for coffee and cake.'

'Oh, how lovely. It's such a Dickensian little place. But rather expensive, I think you'll find.'

'We're not planning to buy the place,' said Molly. 'Just have a cup of coffee and a piece of cake.'

'Of course,' said the woman, with a carefully stage-managed smile. 'I'll just fetch something to drink, then.'

'I thought my half-sister and brother would be here,' said Becky, a look of scepticism on her face. 'Couldn't they make it? You wrote how old they were – and they're younger than I am.'

'Well . . . as a matter of fact they're abroad at the moment. In the family villa in Spain. But they send their good wishes.' She withdrew a small white envelope from her pocket. 'They asked me to give you this. It's a little something from all of them.'

'Is it tickets?' said Becky, a more hopeful look on her face. 'Plane tickets to Spain? For a holiday with my family?'

'Well, no . . . actually it's pocket money – to spend on yourself. They were all so horribly upset to hear that you had spent time in an orphanage. Your existence did actually come as a bit of a shock. The family knew that there was a skeleton in the cupboard, but didn't really want to start opening doors. I do hope it wasn't too awful . . . your upbringing.'

'I didn't know any different,' said Becky, thinking that this appalling woman was just a nosey bitch. 'Just like the others I scrubbed part of the block clean each day. Maybe the kitchen, or the lavatories.'

'Scrubbed clean? How marvellous – at least you weren't living in a dirty place.' She handed the envelope to Becky with a wide smile, then drifted out of the room muttering something about possibly not having any fresh orange juice and that it might have to be lemonade.

Leo looked across to his wife as she held the envelope in her hand. 'Well, open it then and we can go. Maybe it's a cheque? Personally, I've seen and heard enough. She can stick her lemonade up her arse.'

'Give us that envelope, Becky,' said Molly.

'Why? You're not going to make a fuss, are you, darling?'

'Course I'm not. I just want to take a butcher's.'

Becky held it out and Molly stepped away from them to open it. Inside were two crisp ten pound notes and a greetings card which looked a touch jaded. She decided to let Becky see it. Let her see what these people were like and realise that their absence in her life was no loss. The printed words in the card read, 'To a Special Person', and it was signed, 'Sandria'. On the front of the card was a single red rose – Molly was no fool and guessed that it was a Valentine card which had been purchased at one time or another and not used. She slipped the money and card back into the envelope and, letting her head rule her heart, offered it to Becky because she felt that this was no time for false sentiments.

Taking it from her, Becky read the words in silence and then slowly withdrew the two notes to draw a quivering breath. The expression on Leo's face suggested he was already sharing his wife's hurt and humiliation. He knew she had been looking forward so much to seeing her family, and all she had found was this ghastly woman who had married into it. But he stayed silent, because even he knew that this was neither the time nor the place for one of his usual quips.

'I didn't come here for this,' said Becky softly. 'This is not why I came.' She looked at Molly and then at Leo. 'Will you nag me if I tear this money and the card into pieces?'

'Keep the money and tear up the card,' he urged, his voice soft and tinged with affection.

'No. I want to rip it all to bits.'

'Keep the notes and give them to charity. What you haven't had you can't miss. Tear the bloody card to pieces.'

Coming back into the room with a small tray containing four glasses and a bottle of lemonade, Sandria spoke with false sincerity. 'So sorry to have kept you waiting. I had to go into the store room for the lemonade. The bottle in the refrigerator was only a quarter full.'

'Or three-quarters empty,' said Leo.

The woman looked from him to Becky as if he hadn't even spoken. 'It's a pretty little card, isn't it?'

'Tell me something,' said Becky, looking directly into her hostess's face. 'The boys who threw the brick. What relation to you are they?'

'My young nephews by marriage and one of their friends.'
She placed the tray on a coffee table and then shrugged. 'The
rogues were given a good ticking off for going into the East
End without an adult. I dread to think what might have happened
to them.'

Molly ran this sentence through her mind, and it confirmed
her first thoughts about the woman. 'Well, if that's the case,
Sandra,' she said, 'I would have thought that you would have
wanted to give the little fuckers a stroke of your old man's belt.'
She gave the woman a knowing smile and then added, 'I would
say . . . from the cockney twang beneath your voice that Wapping
and around the docks is where you're from, sweetheart. Now
tell me I'm wrong?'

'I've lived in Essex for such a long time that I feel that my
roots are firmly fixed here.'

'Molly,' said Becky, 'don't even bother to spar with this
woman. Don't waste your breath. Thank God there's none of
my mother's blood running through her veins. The worst sort
are those who struggle to climb the social ladder. They make
me sick . . .

'And with my Jewish nose, inherited from my father, I can
smell such people a mile off – and this room stinks to high
heaven of snobbery. You should learn how to use perfume,
sweetheart. You reek of it, when there should only be the merest
hint and even then in the evenings and not during an ordinary
day . . .

'Let me give you a little advice. Advice that you might like
to pass on to your friends with whom you no doubt take tea
in the afternoons. Money talks a thousand languages, but it
doesn't open doors. You could have all the best diamonds on
your fingers but will always be seen as ostentatious because you
can't carry it off, sweetheart. My mother's roots were in the
East End and my father, who used her, was from a well-to-do
Jewish family in Shropshire. Did you know that?'

'I didn't actually – but how interesting. Now if you would
all like to drink up,' she said, glancing at her watch.

Becky looked from her to Rosie, who was smiling and said, 'Are you desperate for the lemonade?'

'No,' said Becky, 'but I *am* desperate to get out of this place. I've never seen such a pretentious room in all my life. And I've been inside a few homes in my time, for one reason or another. All this cut glass and gilt . . .' She sailed a hand through the air. 'It's so over the top it makes me want to puke.'

'I quite agree. Come on. Our business here is finished.' Molly looked into the woman's heavily made-up face and said, 'If those boys should come into my street again I will phone the police and your local newspaper to give them the story. Don't forget that I know the family name. Your family name. What a story it would make round here, eh?'

Leo, leaving Becky to speak for herself, was looking at a long reproduction Sheraton sideboard crammed with ornate silver-framed photographs and a sepia one of a woman who looked very similar in the face to Becky, and who had obviously dressed up specially in satin and lace for the studio picture. 'Look at the silver-framed photos, Becky,' he said, grinning. 'This could easily be your mother.'

'So . . .' said Sandria, a patronising smile on her ghastly face, 'it's been lovely to have met you but I do have another appointment . . . at the hairdresser's.'

Molly watched as Becky moved towards the sideboard, placed one hand at the end and swept all the framed photographs on to the floor. She then turned to her hostess and said, 'I'll give the money to charity – I wouldn't want to even wipe my arse with it. You can choose your friends, sweetheart, but you can't choose your family. And I have the best friends and neighbours a person could wish for. But I'm glad I came and I saw, because now I can bury the past and be glad of it. You are a woman who should be ashamed of what you have turned into – deeply ashamed! I spit on you!'

'Come on,' said Leo. 'Let's get out of this bloody house before I shit my pants. I've seen enough. I've heard enough. Come on.'

Becky wasn't quite finished, though. She looked into the woman's raddled face and said, 'Twenty pounds and a faded card? You should be feeling guilty, but I don't see any sign of it. Take a good at yourself in one of those bloody mirrors. I know you've only married into this family – but that's no excuse. You think I don't know a cockney accent when I hear it? My friend here is right. You weren't to the manor born, by any stretch of the imagination – and do you know what? That makes it worse.' Becky then tore the card into tiny pieces and let them float to the floor.

'Don't bother to see us out.' Looking over her shoulder at the others, she said, 'Get me out of this fucking shit-hole. We've wasted enough of our time.'

This was new – a side of Becky they had never seen before. Even as she walked out she had more to say, and she turned to look at the woman again. 'I thank God that I came. That I saw. That I may leave and not look back!' She then spat over her right shoulder to give the most insulting signal of all – she was symbolically spitting on the woman's grave. With that she left the room, the others close behind her.

'I'm glad I went to Somerset House,' she said, calmer now as she walked along the front path. 'I'm glad I found out what kind of people they are. Let them keep their bloody thick-pile carpets, gold drapes and gilt-framed mirrors. It stinks of affectation!'

Walking by her side, Leo said, 'The old-style Jews from Hungary, Poland and Germany have good taste. God only knows where that lot are from. So you're not sorry, then, Becky? Sorry that we won't be seeing any more of that woman or the family?'

'Sorry? Good God, no. I'm glad I came, though.' She started to laugh quietly. 'You should see what I've got in my pocket.'

This stopped them all in their tracks. Becky stealing something? Never! 'So which piece of family silver did you lift?' enquired Leo, hoping it would be something solid and worth a few bob.

'A picture frame. An ornate silver picture frame. I've got what I came for. I've got a picture of my mother.'

Much happier now, the four of them walked back by the same route they had come along, discussing whether to get on a train straightaway or go for afternoon tea somewhere. 'She never even offered us a biscuit,' said Molly indignantly.

'I don't know why, but now, with her picture in my pocket, I feel as if I can smell my mother. Is that mad or what?'

'Mad,' said Leo, 'but what's new?'

'Her smell is what I remember. Lavender, but not from a bottle. I think she must have worn a spray of it when she breast-fed me. From what I learned later on, they banished her from the paupers' home when I was four years old. That's when I was sent to the Bethnal Green children's home. I remember her hugging me and crying and saying she would come back for me one day. But she never did. I waited and waited, until I began to think of one of the women who worked there as my mother. It helped a little. But it doesn't matter any more because she's in my pocket . . . I have a photo of my mother in my pocket. I can't tell you what this means to me. I recognised her. Can you believe that? I recognised her, and yet I was so young when they sent her away. I can't wait to get home and put her on the sideboard where I can look at her every day. That's all I want now. I'm happy. Let's get back to our own area. To Bethnal Green. To one of our cafés. My treat.'

'Maybe we'll go to the Italian café, then, if Molly and Rosie agree,' said Leo. 'You can have a nice cup of real coffee and cakes and sandwiches. How does that sound?'

'Wonderful. I also want a bit of East End sunshine on my face.'

Arriving at the turn-off into The Meadway, Rosie, who had been quiet through all of this, said, 'Would you mind if we took a slightly different route to the station, Becky?'

'Of course not, darling. Why would I?'

'That's just what I was thinking, Rosie,' Molly smiled. 'I'd like to take a look at that children's home to make the journey really worthwhile. They might even let us go in.'

'It will make for an even better trip,' said Leo. 'Look at my beautiful wife's face. It's like a black cloud's gone from it. Thank God for it. I won't have to listen to her going on about her bloody roots any more.'

Becky laughed out loud and then said, 'I think it would make a nice ending to this little outing if we were to drop by the children's home. You would make a wonderful mother, Rosie. Let's go take a look at the place.'

And so the four of them arrived at the double-fronted house on Palmerston Road which ran from the high road right through to Chigwell. At the front gate Leo, ever the gentleman, pushed it open and stood aside as the three women stepped on to the short path leading to the front door. Glancing up at a window for no particular reason, Becky saw the thin, pale face of a little girl looking down at them and memories of the worst time of her life came flooding back. She had not stayed in such a lovely place as a child; but she had been a face at the window, waiting for her mother to come and get her.

Molly pressed the brass bell on the old brick wall next to the door, and within seconds it was opened by a gentle, smiling woman in her fifties who asked if she could help.

'We hope so,' said Leo. 'We were wondering if we could come in for five minutes and have a chat with one of the staff. About the children. About bringing some presents next time we come on a visit to Buckhurst Hill.'

'What a lovely thought. Come on in,' said the motherly-faced woman. She was the Matron of the home and introduced herself as Valerie – an ordinary name for an extraordinary woman who had devoted her life to children in need.

'We shan't take up too much of your time,' said Becky. 'I'm sure you must be very busy one way and another.' She was deliberately being the leading light so that Rosie could be left to make up her own mind once she saw the children, without advice or comments from any of her friends.

'We're always busy,' said the Matron. 'But never too busy for the good-hearted. Come up to my office.'

The four visitors filed into the spacious hallway from which a wide staircase led up to the five bedrooms, each of which slept four children. Sitting down in Valerie's office, they learned that people were welcome to visit as long as they did so on a regular basis.

'The thing is,' said Valerie, 'the children look forward to visits and it's healthier for them if they know that certain people will turn up on certain days. That stops them watching out all the time for a familiar face, and then being disappointed.'

'I can understand that,' said Becky. 'I was in a children's home when I was very young and so I know what you mean. What if we were to come once a month? Do you think this would be all right?'

'Of course it would, but you have to be practical. Once every four weeks is quite a responsibility to take on. Every two or three months is probably more of a reality, I would have thought.'

'Two months,' said Molly. 'I think we'd like that, don't you, Leo?'

'Absolutely. And I'll put it in writing.'

'Good. Would you like to come and say hello to our children?'

'We'd like that very much,' said Rosie, her cheeks glowing pink and a sparkle in her blue eyes.

Valerie eased herself from her chair behind the desk. 'I'll just go and fetch one of the aunties,' she said.

'What a difference from the place where I was all those years ago,' said Becky. 'There's a lovely atmosphere here!'

'Yes, there is,' said Valerie, coming back into the room. 'Here we are, then. This is Auntie Barbara, who will take you to meet our children. All twenty of them.'

Rosie didn't go with them. She stayed in the office because she wanted to talk to the Matron about fostering and adoption. She found it very easy to talk to the woman, telling her that she had been on a fertility drug programme for a while but had been told by the specialists that there was sadly nothing doing for her. Because of that, she explained to Valerie, she and her husband, George, had decided to adopt if possible, and felt they were now ready. Valerie stressed that taking on someone else's child was a huge commitment.

'I realise this,' said Rosie. 'I've already spoken to the welfare office in the area where I live, and we've been through everything. I would be just as happy to take on a slightly older child as I would a baby, and so would my husband. It's what we want to do. What we really want to do. What we will do.'

'And meanwhile you'd like to visit us with your friends so as to get used to the concept of it? Before you start to look into the ins and outs of adoption?'

'If you think that that would be all right – I would, yes.'

'Of course you will have to contact the local authorities if you do decide that you want to foster or adopt a child,' she said, offering a warm smile.

'I know I would. But I'd really like to come back with my husband if that's all right? I know it will all take time. I'd like to come by myself sometimes, and at other times with my husband.'

'So, you've obviously talked things through a lot. Why not come along together, just the two of you, in a couple of weeks' time?'

'That sounds good. We'll do that.' Rosie smiled and for the first time in a while felt happy. Really happy.

Valerie then handed Rosie a small business card and said, 'Give me a call when you're ready and we'll arrange a time for you to come with your husband.'

Once outside in the crisp fresh air, Rosie felt like crying. When she had started out on this little trip she had absolutely no idea that she would be going home with a resolution. To stop pondering and get on with looking after babies or children who needed love and a home. She glanced up at the windows to see a little face smiling at her and waved back.

On the homeward-bound train they had to split up, with

Leo and Becky together and Molly and Rosie side by side a little distance away. Molly, who had been deep in thought about Cathy and her situation, suddenly said, 'What do you reckon about this bloke Stewart, Rosie? You know, the one who sells a few antique bits and seems to be a bit of a hippy. He's got friendly with our Cathy. What do you reckon he's after?'

'I'm not sure he's after anything. He's living in cloud cuckoo land, I think, just like the rest of the Love, Light and Peace brigade. The type who suddenly disappear off to India, put on robes and wear beads round their necks and flowers in their hair and then kill themselves with drugs. Take that American woman, Janice Joplin, with that beautiful strong voice. She killed 'erself stone dead a month or so ago. Took an overdose.'

'And you reckon it was deliberate? That it was suicide?' said Molly.

'I don't know. She overdosed on drugs whether she meant to or not. It was a tragedy. A young white American with a black woman's voice . . . and now she's dead. And not from some fatal illness, but from taking drugs. Tell me where the sense in that is. Because I don't know.'

'Well, let's hope Cathy won't be influenced by that bloke and start smoking marijuana.'

'Oh, gimme a break, Molly. Course she won't.'

'Well, you say that . . . but how many others have thought that one of their own wouldn't be that stupid. I'm just saying that this bloke who skulked his way into Cathy's little flat with a bottle of plonk needs to be checked out.'

Both women fell silent, Molly still worrying about Cathy and Rosie thinking about the face of the child looking out of the window. A child who was pinning all her hopes on a new mummy and daddy coming along and adopting her. 'I can't get that children's home out of my mind, Molly. They're loved so much at that place, but they want a mum and dad. I wonder what's going through Becky's mind right now? Talk about dragging all the past up.'

'It's what she wanted. And don't forget it was Leo who led

us to the children's home afterwards. We helped Becky to do what she truly wanted – to lay a ghost. That's what she's doing. And who are we to knock it?'

They travelled the rest of the journey in silence until they were approaching Stratford station when Molly suddenly said, 'I'm getting off at the next stop. I want to see my granddaughter.'

'Fair enough,' said Rosie. 'I'll come with you. I'd like to see my friend as well.'

'That's fine by me. But what about Becky and Leo? Will they be all right to go the rest of the way without us looking out for them?'

'I'll go and see.' Rosie made her way along the gangway to have a quiet word with the old couple, who insisted they would be all right.

'What are we?' said Leo. 'Invalids or an old couple who've lost all their marbles? Of course we'll be all right. We do use public transport, you know. We go to Forest Gate regularly by train, and to Mile End if we fancy seeing an afternoon film.'

'And you're okay, Becky?'

'Sure . . . but I thought we were going to Baroncini's café for coffee and cake?'

'Another time, sweetheart. Another time,' said Rosie and gave her a wink. 'Molly wants to see her granddaughter since we're passing through Stratford. You know what she's like.'

'Of course I do,' said Becky, smiling. 'And you want to see her too. Don't worry about us. We'll be fine. And thanks for coming with us today. I can't tell you how pleased I am that I went. I mean, really pleased. You understand what I'm saying? Apart from letting go of the past, we went into that lovely children's home. Wasn't it a nice place? We're going to go regularly. Tell her, Leo.'

'We're going to go regularly,' he sniffed, his old, laid back humour always in place.

The sparkle in Becky's eyes said everything, and there was an expression on her face that Rosie had not seen before.

She looked as if a huge weight had been lifted from her shoulders and there was a relaxed and contented look about her. Giving them each a peck on the cheek, Rosie winked and left them to themselves. But when the train pulled into Stratford East she glanced at them before getting off, just to make sure they were all right. They waved and smiled back at her, their expression saying it all – they would be fine.

During the ten-minute walk from the station to her granddaughter's flat, Molly told her young friend about the little bit of something that fell off a shelf in Sandria's sitting room and into her shopping bag. She slipped her hand into her coat pocket and pulled out a beautiful antique solid silver inkwell. 'What d'yer think of that then? She won't miss it for a while. It was the nicest bit in the collection on one of 'er sideboards.

'I don't believe you.' Rosie laughed out loud. 'You're better than the men at thieving.'

'Flattery will get you anywhere,' said Molly. 'Now then, don't let me lose my rag if the pansy's slouching on Cathy's settee. Pinch, punch or nudge me if I look like I'm losing it.'

'Will do.'

Arriving at the street door to the two flats above the shop, Molly rang the bell and said, 'I don't know why she couldn't have stayed at 'ome with us. Still, there you are. She wants to be independent.'

The street door, creaking as usual when it opened, revealed not Cathy but one of Johnny's sisters, short, stout with long, straight, dark hair, a pale face and small brown eyes. 'Who are you?' she said, curling one side of her top lip. Taken back by this greeting, Molly had to check that she was at the right door.

'We've come to see Cathy,' said Rosie.

'Well, she's not seeing visitors at the moment. Jot your names down on a bit of paper and pop them through the letter box, and she'll talk to you on the phone another time.'

'I don't think so,' said Molly as the woman was about to close the door on them. Leaning forward, she said quietly, 'I don't know who you are, darling, but if you don't step aside you'll feel the weight of my hand right across your arse. I might not look, it but I'm old enough to be your grandmother.'

'Oh, right . . . you must be the Molly the Dolly who prances about as if she's a teenager. I'm still not letting you in, though. So it's up to you, lady – either move your foot or I'll smash it to smithereens when I shut this door on it. All right?'

'Leave it, Molly,' said Rosie, ever the peacemaker. 'I'm sure we can get to the bottom of this without falling out.' She eased her friend out of the way and said to the woman, 'Has something happened to Cathy that we should know about?'

'No. But me and my sister aren't leaving our brother's wife with a fancy man. We caught her with her knickers down – almost.'

'What's that supposed to mean?' said Rosie.

'She had a bloke in here when we arrived. That's what it means, darlin'. My brother's not been inside five minutes and she's having an affair. Nice family she's come from,' she said, eyeing Molly.

'It's all right, Rosie. I can see why the girls are upset. I would be as well if I'd got the wrong end of the stick.' She gave a smile to the woman and a nudge to her mate. 'I expect you mean the family friend, Stewart.'

Molly's little bit of fast thinking seemed to do the trick. Not that the woman was appeased, by any means – she just didn't quite know what to make of it. But at least the wind had been taken out of her sails. 'Well, she never told me and my sister that he was a family friend and she looked dead guilty when we confronted 'er. What does that tell yer? That she's innocent? I don't fucking well fink so.'

'Never mind,' said Molly, moving the woman aside and going into the passageway and up the stairs. 'I'll soon sort this out. If I think the man's been sniffing around her I'll have his guts for garters.'

'The trouble with that sister-in-law of ours is that she thinks she's better than she is. A snob is what I'd call 'er. I don't know what our Johnny saw in 'er.'

Once in the flat, Molly could hardly believe her eyes. There was her sweet-natured granddaughter on the sofa crying into her hands while Johnny's other sister, the ginger-haired one, stood over her, arms folded and looking as if she could kill.

'Shall I put the kettle on, then?' enquired Rosie, hoping that this might ease the tension a little. Cathy looked up at her and nodded before she began to weep again. 'A nice cup of coffee is what you need, babe. Two sugars.'

'Yes, please,' murmured Cathy, a faint smile on her face.

'Who're you two?' demanded the sister on guard.

'I was just about to ask you the same thing,' said Molly, fuming. She jerked her thumb at the door and added, 'Outside in the passage, ginger nut. I want a word with you and your sister.'

'You'll get more than a fucking word, lady, if you talk to me like that! Say what you 'ave to and say it now, because I'm going nowhere. Ask this little tart why I'm fucking angry.'

'Little tart?' cried Molly indignantly. 'That's my granddaughter you're defaming. Now you either take that back or get out. Suit yerself.'

'Excuse me, lady, but I *am* Johnny's sister. And this tart is, sadly, his wife. And don't tell me she's not a slag before you know the ins and outs. We came in and caught her sitting with a geezer drinking coffee and there was a distinct smell of marijuana in the air. She's a drug addict and so was the guy – who legged it once we appeared on the scene. I wouldn't mind, but we came round to see if she was lonely! My brother was locked up because of her – because this tart was pregnant and he needed money for the wedding, which we wasn't invited to.'

'I think you'll find that's wrong,' said Molly. 'I believe your brother got involved in the theft to pay off his gambling debts. And as for the wedding, none of us were invited because your brother knew that you'd show him up if there was a family do. So if you've finished, we'll leave it at that, shall we?'

'Finished? I 'aven't even started yet. I think you'd best take this whore home with you. I'll stop here and wait for lover boy to come back, then give him a kick in the balls to make sure *he* doesn't come back.'

'Over my dead body you will,' snapped Molly. 'Get out – now!'

'Oh, right . . . so you applaud her for having a fucking man in while my brother's doing time? Doing time because of your family. Cathy's whoring sisters and their lover boys dragged our Johnny into their world of crime. But did we shout the odds over that? No. But I'm not standing back while this whore entertains men in my brother's home. That's a bit too much to ask, wouldn't you say?'

'I don't entertain men,' Cathy broke in. 'Both Henry and Stewart are mates. I'm allowed to have friends! I could write to Johnny and tell him about this before you poison his mind but I wouldn't want to waste a stamp! If he walked in and heard you he'd laugh at you and then throw you out on to the street – he can't stand the pair of you in any case!'

'Lies. Fucking lies! You fucking whore!'

'Listen, you,' said Molly, pointing a finger. 'She's entitled to 'ave friends, and it's your brother's fault that she's in the situation she's in. She never gambled and owed money to the wrong sort. But your brother Johnny did! All right? Now fuck off out of 'ere before I really lose my rag.'

'I bet she 'elped him spend 'is winnings though,' said the second sister, who had been smugly standing in the background, puffing on a cigarette. 'Just like she spends the treats *our* parents give 'er! They worry more over you than they do us! Popping round with a fresh baker's loaf and buns for yer! I bet you take money off em an' all!'

'Your brother is a compulsive gambler, sweetheart, and your parents know it and they're thankful that our Cathy will help mend his ways. He'd spit in your face if he knew you were in this flat 'aving a go at his *pregnant* wife. You've got a mind like a sewer if you think she'd have an affair in her state you silly mare!'

'Nan, please don't argue with them,' said Cathy, covering

her face with both hands. 'They're not worth it. Just chuck the pair of 'em out.'

'You're dead right, sweetheart.' She pointed a finger at one sister and then the other saying, 'You and you . . . out! Go forth and multiply!'

'Don't worry, we're going. We know she's a slut, pregnant or not. And one day once our bruvver's out, we'll tell 'im what she's like! How *soiled* her bed sheets are!'

'We could send a telegram to Johnny,' said the other sister, the smug look still on her face. 'Tell him about this little whore. You can smell that man in this room. Never mind the fact that we caught him 'ere with his feet under the table.'

Molly was no longer listening because she knew the girls wouldn't dare send a telegram. Albert and Stanley had already told her that they had made a social call to Johnny's parents asking them to keep the girls off Cathy's back. She looked at Cathy who was covering her face with her hands again and clearly wishing it would all go away. Then Molly flung the door wide and ordered the sisters out. This time, seeing the fury in her eyes, they went – not exactly like little lambs but using every swearword in the book because they knew they had lost their battle. Once they had gone, Molly hugged Cathy while Rosie went into the kitchen and made a pot of tea.

'What were they on about, Cathy? How much truth is there in what they were saying?'

Her head lowered and her face hidden behind her hands, Cathy said, 'They came in and me and Stewart had been talking and laughing and, yes, he was smoking one of his funny roll-ups – but that was all. How could they even think I'd have an affair? I've not long been married. I love Johnny, and in any case look at me – aren't I carrying our baby? Those girls have got disgusting minds.

'Stewart's antique shop is only next door. I got talking to him when I went in to look at some of the nice things in there and we got on well. That's all there is to it. I do get lonely for people now and then. I'm seven months gone. I can't go out to do even part-time work like this, can I? And then there are the evenings in this flat by myself with only the television for company. Henry comes up now and then, but Helen's his girl-friend now and he's got her to think of. 'I get lonely, Nan. I'm not used to being by myself.'

Pushing her hand through her hair, Molly felt like crying. 'I said you should have stayed at 'ome with us. Living 'ere by yourself is mad. Your 'usband's doing time and you're preg-nant. It's fucking crazy. You should be with us so we can take care of you.'

She turned to Rosie and asked, 'What do you think, Ro? D'you reckon she should come back 'ome with us?'

'Only if she wants to, Molly. She's not your little girl any more.'

'Those horrible sisters said they were gonna ask for a special visit to see Johnny and tell him that I've moved a man in,' said Cathy. 'That is such a lie!'

'Take no notice, love. The welfare office at the prison won't let them in to see Johnny without a pass,' said Molly. 'And besides which . . . Albert and Stanley have their own way of doing things and they know Johnny's sisters and how to clip their wings. They can't stand the pair of them. They only have to open their mouths and people flinch away.'

'I don't know about you two,' said Rosie, 'but I couldn't half do with a cup of tea and it's ready to pour. Do you want one, either of you?'

'I'll do it,' said Molly. 'You two sit down and have a talk. I'm still raving mad over them two. Either that or I'm too long in the tooth for all this.'

By themselves on the sofa, Rosie spoke in a low voice. 'What's going on, Cath? Has that hippy made a move on you? Because if so, I think you shouldn't let him in any more. Personally, I don't think I'd trust him. And now I know you're lonely I'll come round more often. I've got loads to tell you. About me and George possibly fostering children from a home in Buckhurst Hill.'

'That's great, Rosie. I'm really pleased for you.'

'Even though you're not smiling?'

'I'm sorry . . . I just feel sick inside over what's been going on here. I can't tell you how horrible they were to me before you arrived. I was really scared.'

'The trouble is that sometimes things like this start off with people being good mates. But you're not daft, and you're old enough to know what's what. You keep Stewart as a friend. Sod us worrying over you. I trust your judgement and I'll persuade your nan to leave you to choose your own friends, male or female.'

'I do like Stewart. He makes me laugh when I go into his shop. He's only been in here once or twice. Okay, he does smoke pot – but so do a lot of people. And I love Johnny. I love him so much that it hurts.'

'Just as well, Cathy,' said Molly coming in with a tea tray. 'And it's not you I don't trust, sweetheart, it's men in general. They use their dick like a searchlight.'

Laughing at her nan, Cathy said, 'I'm feeling a bit tired. Do you two mind if I lie down after this cup of tea?'

'Course not, Cath,' said Rosie. 'We'll be gone in five minutes. And if the ugly sisters come back, just pick up the phone. You don't have to put up with that kind of a thing. Right?'

'Right.'

'Promise?'

'Promise. But I'm still gonna be friends with Stewart and I'm going to apologise to him for Johnny's sisters. Right?'

'Right,' said Rosie, smiling.

9

In September, with just two weeks before her baby was due, Cathy woke in the night with a low and painful backache and wondered if she had overdone things. For some reason that day she had felt she had to make absolutely certain that there was no dirt in the flat which could possibly harbour infection, so she had scrubbed and bleached the kitchen sink, the bath, the basin and the lavatory pan. She also mopped the floors where lino had been laid and vacuumed the carpet and curtains, and then cleaned the windows. Exhausted and yet still energetic, she had put her feet up to enjoy a nice fresh cup of tea and relaxed into a sudden calm mood. She had felt her baby moving more than ever before and then nothing. But now she was experiencing severe pain coming and going.

Unable to believe that she was in fact in labour, she nevertheless walked slowly to the cupboard where she kept the small bottle of medicinal brandy supplied by Molly, who had instructed her to take a tablespoon once the pains started. She unscrewed the bottle top, swallowed what she thought to be the right amount and felt instantly better as the golden liquid warmed her chest. Then she was immediately gripped by another and fiercer labour pain.

She staggered to the telephone and dialled Henry's number, hugely relieved that he picked it up after just a few rings. 'Henry, phone for an ambulance!' she managed to gasp before another pain struck and her waters broke. She replaced the receiver, then managed to make her way to the front door and open it. Within no time Henry was bounding up the stairs, moving more quickly than she had ever seen him do before.

'Cathy, you should be lying down,' he insisted, his face pale and frightened. He placed an arm around her waist and helped her towards the armchair. 'The ambulance will be here soon,' he assured her.

'I hope so, Henry, because I'm definitely in labour. My waters have broken.'

Pacing the floor and wringing his hands, he was trying to remember what he had read in one of his encyclopaedias about delivering a baby in an emergency. He kept glancing at Cathy, then going to the window to watch for the ambulance, until he could just hear the siren in the distance. 'Ah . . . ,' he said, breathing more easily. 'It's on its way. I'll go down and tell them to fetch a chair up, shall I?'

'I don't know,' said Cathy, moaning in pain. 'This is fucking painful, Henry! I don't want this baby! I don't want to be having a baby! Get help!'

'Breathe deeply, Cath!' he commanded. 'Take deep breaths.'

'What do you know about it? You're a man! I want my mum! Where is she?'

'Just hold on, Cathy. I'm going to let the ambulance men in. Just hold on.' He rushed out of the room and down the stairs while Cathy screwed both hands up into fists and held her breath, then released it when the two ambulance men entered the room with Henry.

'Come on, my dear,' said the taller and broader of them, 'and don't you worry about a thing. We'll soon have you in a nice comfortable bed in hospital.' They took an arm each to get Cath to her feet and walked her slowly towards the door, then assisted her down the stairs, telling her to take her time and assuring her that nothing was going to happen for a few hours yet. She was, they told her, one of hundreds of women they had seen in this stage of labour, so they recognised exactly where she was at and everything would be fine. Their soft, persuasive voices helped a great deal. And by the time she stepped into the back of the ambulance she felt safe and even managed a weak smile.

Within no more than two minutes Cathy was on her way to the London Hospital in Whitechapel, with blue lights flashing and the siren wailing. Two hours later, she gave birth to an eight-pound baby boy, who was going to be named after Rosie's George, who of all people was there in the hospital room with her when she gave birth. Henry in his wisdom had dialled Rosie's number and not that of Cathy's parents while he was waiting for the ambulance to arrive. He felt that a call such as this could affect Jim's damaged heart. This had been Henry's priority – this and getting Cathy to hospital as quickly as possible to deliver her beautiful blue-eyed boy into the world.

After ten days of rest in the maternity ward with her friends and family coming and going as well as Johnny's parents, Cathy with her little suitcase packed and her baby wrapped in a shawl, walked out of the hospital. A very happy young mother was then driven home to her flat by George. In the back of the car with Cathy sat Rosie who was there to comfort her, and be with her future Godson, baby George. Alice, who was to stay at the flat for a month or so to help her inexperienced daughter look after the baby, was radiantly happy and very proud of Cathy. Both women knew that Molly was at the flat waiting for them to arrive and would at that moment be busy arranging the many flowers that had been sent, placing them in vases begged, borrowed or bought for the occasion.

By the time they arrived at the flat it looked lovely, filled not just with the scent of the flowers but with an atmosphere of love. Carrying her first grandchild, wrapped in a lovely white shawl, Alice was thankful that friends and family were there to look after Cathy. Thankful and pleased too that dear sweet Henry was there and not far away if she needed him, just one flight of stairs away. Once in her favourite armchair by the little fireplace with her precious baby wrapped in her arms, Cathy was wishing that Johnny could be there by her side.

Before Cathy knew it, Christmas was drawing near. The streets and shops were ablaze with white or coloured lights to encourage people to shop for presents. She hadn't seen quite as much of her family as she would like, but at least she had her friends. Henry and Helen had popped in often and Stewart had been a brick, fetching her a small box of chocolates a couple of times a week and talking with her by the fireside about all kinds of changes that were going on in and around London. She had come to rely on his visits, but had decided not to mention this to her family in case they got the wrong impression about their warm platonic relationship.

Molly and Arthur were due to arrive in an hour or so to baby-sit while she went out with Henry and Helen for a quiet drink. There was a lovely calm atmosphere in the flat, and the sound of the doorbell made her jump. Believing that the old couple had arrived early, she went to open the door to find Stewart there with a bottle of white wine, hoping to spend an hour or so with her by the fire. She invited him in but as they walked up the stairs said, 'I can't ask you to stay, Stewart, because my nan's coming to baby-sit while I go out with Henry and Helen to the Prospect for an hour or so. But you can open the wine if you want and we'll have a glass each.'

'No problem, Cathy,' he said, speaking in a quiet, husky voice. 'I wouldn't dream of spoiling your plans, and in any case I'm a little exhausted. I've been running around all day looking for a nice room to rent for a month or so while my flat above the shop is being renovated.'

'Well, if you're stuck let me know. I don't mind if you lodge with me and baby for a few weeks. The spare room's small but it'll do for temporary lodgings. Let me know,' she said.

'That's really thoughtful, Cathy, and if it did come to that I'd willingly pay you a decent rent.'

'Oh, that won't be necessary. You can pay the electric and gas bill if you want. But let's wait and see, shall we? Hopefully you'll find a place.'

Leaving him in the sitting room, she went into the kitchen to place in the fridge baby George's bottle of Cow and Gate formula that she had made up and had now cooled down. This was for Molly to warm up and feed him later on while she was out. No sooner had Stewart settled by the fire with his glass of wine than the doorbell went again. It was Molly and Arthur, there a little earlier than arranged. When she came into the sitting room Molly peered at Stewart, to whom she took an immediate dislike born of instinct and long experience. Arthur politely shook his hand while studying his face. He had heard about this young man who had befriended Cathy and was using his guile to sum him up, knowing from experience that first impressions do count. He raised an eyebrow at Molly and waited to hear what she had to say about this fellow once they were by themselves.

Molly didn't care for the way he slumped back in the armchair, too much at home for her liking. His long legs stretched out, taking up too much of the small space. She put it down to the fact that his eyes were somewhat glassy and so he might have been smoking dope before he arrived at Cathy's. And Arthur wasn't happy about the way he had gone into the kitchen to refill his glass with wine from the bottle he had brought with him. 'Are you sure you won't join me?' he asked. 'I'm sure we've got some more glasses in the cupboard,' he added, almost as if it was a flat that he and Cathy shared.

'No, that's all right, son,' said Arthur. 'Stout or a drop of brandy is our drink, and we've fetched some with us. You might as well take the rest of that bottle with you when you go. Don't want it to go to waste, do we, eh?' he smiled. Ten minutes later Stewart made his excuses, claiming he had to be at an important meeting with a customer. After shaking hands with Molly and Arthur he took his leave, and soon afterwards Cathy went down to Henry's flat to join him and Helen for their evening out.

By themselves, with baby George sound asleep in his crib in the bedroom, Molly and Arthur discussed the hippy over a glass of beer. 'I wouldn't mind if he tried to look like a normal bloke,' said Arthur. 'But he seems to deliberately behave a bit on the girly side to me. Long wavy hair tied back in a pony tail and a pink shirt? What next? High-heeled shoes?'

Slowly shaking his head, he added, 'It's all the rage, I suppose. Girls looking like boys and boys looking like girls. But it'll soon pass, this flower power and all that rubbish. Every time you look at a newspaper there's something in there about it. Spiritual regeneration's what it's called.'

'Load of bollocks,' said Molly. 'My old mum would turn in 'er grave.' Thoughtful for a moment, she then said, 'You don't think that Cathy's having a romance with that drip, do you?'

'Course she's not! What d'yer want? Our Cath to be a sad, lonely soul with no friends?'

'She was four months or so when she moved in, and from what I know he's been in and out ever since then. So if he found her attractive with a big belly he might well make a move on her now that she's all slim again.'

'But he also might be one of them blokes who like to have girls as mates. And Cathy needs all the friends she can get. She's got Henry, thank God, but what if he hadn't been in when she went into labour? Maybe the poof would have been the one she phoned?'

'All right, point taken,' said Molly. 'And try and keep your voice down or you'll wake up baby George.'

'Oh, right, yeah. I forgot about him for the minute. Are we allowed to 'ave the telly on, then? Or will that disturb the little prince?'

'Course we're allowed to watch it. But keep the sound down.'

Arthur rested back in his chair and smiled, content to let her have the last word. He saw himself as a patient man and took the fact that she ruled the roost in Jim and Alice's house in his stride. But she wouldn't be in charge under his roof once they were paired up in his lovely little house in Jubilee Street – after he had given her a nice long run so as to be sure that the old engine wasn't about to pack up.

'I wouldn't mind going to the Prospect once next summer comes round, Molly,' said Arthur. He was thinking of a nice warm evening on the little deck that overlooked the river. It was a place where a chap just might pop the question. 'It's always been a romantic little spot, from what I gather.'

'Romantic? Wapping? Never!'

'By the river, it is. Think of a moonlit night . . .'

'Whatever you say, Arthur, whatever you say. Now, you know I never miss *Coronation Street,* and I want to see it *and* listen to it.'

'Well, I'm not gonna talk, am I? Got nothing to say.'

'Good.'

'It's full of history, that place, though . . . I was a lorry driver at one time, going in and out of the various wharves and yards – and if truth be known I did miss it a bit when I gave it up to go back to being a rag and bone man. We used to go down to the Prospect and belt out all the First and Second World War songs. Sometimes there was a solo performance by a drunk with a good voice – but never anyone playing a bit of classical music on a guitar like nowadays. A lovely old pub it is, and only a stone's throw from what my old granddad used to call the Stepney Marshes.'

'I couldn't give a toss, Arthur. Ken Barlow doesn't look all that well. They'd better not kill him off, handsome little devil!'

Arthur slipped deeper into his fireside chair as he remembered his local history. 'Course, when King Edward III lived at Greenwich his hounds and spaniels were kept on the marshes.'

Her curiosity piqued, she glanced sideways at him to see if he was making all of this up. 'Tell me about it later on, eh?'

'A waterman was murdered on them marshes. By all accounts his faithful old dog wouldn't leave his body till hunger forced him to swim over to Greenwich in search of food. Back and forth it went all the time until it led a bloke to his murdered master. Then, the following week, the dog snarled at a bloke he'd singled out. Another waterman. The man was taken to one side by the other men and finally confessed that he'd killed the dog's master. And it was at that point that it was named the Isle of the Dog . . . which eventually became the Isle of Dogs . . . Course, Millwall is easier to fathom—'

Molly glared at Arthur. No words were needed to make him keep shtum – but not before adding one more interesting fact to show his defiance at having to watch the soap on the telly. 'There were seven windmills there at one time, you know. But you won't wanna hear about that.'

'Correct,' said Molly firmly.

'When they were digging the docks they found traces of early man, elephant and deer. But you don't wanna hear all that. You love *Coronation Street*. You know you do.' He stretched his legs and yawned. 'You won't mind if I doze off, will yer?'

'Do what you like. I'll stop the night if I 'ave to. Don't bother me one way or another.'

Within seconds his head was resting back and he was snoring. But then just a few minutes later he suddenly woke up and blurted out, 'It's a pity all them ancient blocks of flats was pulled down. They 'ad character, Quinn's Buildings.'

Shaking her head in wonder, Molly ordered him to go back to sleep and not start talking about damp old Victorian fleapits with hundreds of stairs and no lifts and only a bucket to pee in. His eyes closed again, but still he quietly rambled on to himself while drifting off. 'Them cocky bastards from South London used to come over, tapping a stick with a nail in it trying to intimidate us lads. I had a good few decent punch-ups with that lot. Could do what you liked in them days. It's all we had to keep ourselves amused.

'Pearcy Place was my favourite haunt. I used to cut through from Globe Road to see the old Welshman, Mr Evans, the dairyman who let me watch while he milked his cows and then poured the warm milk into them big churns in the alleyway.

'That was a smashing corner to play in, though, wasn't it, eh?' Arthur murmured, to the sound of the music that indicated the end of *Coronation Street*. 'It was a pity when the old boy moved to Three Colts Lane, taking his cows with him. He ended up with twenty-three in all, you know. Could 'ave grown into a nice little business that – if the war hadn't started up in nineteen-fourteen and caused him to sell his livestock.'

Molly lifted herself from her chair and leaned over to switch off the television set. 'Come on, then. We'll wrap baby up, put him in the pram and go for a walk to the Prospect.'

'Eh? Do what?' said Arthur, a touch panicky.

'You 'eard me. You don't want to watch television, so we'll go for a nice long walk in the dark to your favourite part of London.'

'No,' said Arthur, all serious as he leaned forward and switched the set back on again. 'You love your telly. You sit down and watch whatever you want while I 'ave a little doze in this armchair. I'm not gonna spoil your evening.'

By the time Cathy came home that night at just gone ten-thirty Molly had bottle-fed the baby and was ready for her bed. She was going home in Arthur's secondhand light blue Ford Anglia car, recently purchased at a car auction in Aldgate. This acquisition was his pride and joy that he kept as shiny as a new pin, cleaning and polishing it every Sunday morning come rain or shine.

'Baby George slept for most of the time, Cathy,' she proudly announced. 'I gave him his bottle when you said I was to, and then after winding and changing him we enjoyed a little bit of baby talk while he was on my knee looking up at me. Looking up and smiling.'

'He wasn't smiling,' corrected Arthur. 'He was burping.'

Cathy wasn't listening to their banter but looking at her bundle of joy lying in his small blue cot, fast asleep. Once they had their coats on she gave Arthur a farewell hug, thanking him for not only putting up with her nan but helping to look after the baby.

'Any time, Cathy, any time. I'm pleased you went to the Prospect – it's a nice little pub. But don't get too stuck on the company. They're not our sort. And neither is that pretty boy from the antique shop. I can't remember 'is name.'

'Stewart,' said Cathy.

'Oh, well – that says it all, doesn't it? *Stewart*.' He rolled his eyes and then gave her a peck on the cheek. Cathy knew what he was getting at. He was telling her not to get involved with another man while her husband was doing time.

'You can't go far wrong with your Johnny, Cath,' he said. 'And we all reckon with good behaviour and all that he'll get time knocked off 'is sentence.'

'Don't you worry, Arthur. I'm waiting for the day. But I do need company and friends now and then.'

'Course you do. Anyone would. But trust no man to come too close, that's all I'm saying! Because you're a lovely-looking girl, Cathy. Beautiful. And there'll be more than one crafty bastard out there that'll vie for yer. I'm not saying you've gotta act like a nun, but keep a long arm's length, eh?'

He pushed his shoulders back, an old habit from when he was young and a bit of a spiv, to add brightly, 'Keep both legs in one stocking and you won't go wrong.'

'I will, don't you worry. I'm going to see Johnny on Monday.'

'Oh, yeah? And who's going with yer?'

'No one. It's me he wants to see and only me. He said so in his letter.'

'Good. And don't you let them sisters of his sway you otherwise. But if you want me to give you a lift, I'll leave you at the gate and pick you up again after your visit. Give me the nod if this is what you'd like.'

'Thanks, Arthur. The only thing is,' she whispered, 'if you did that, Nan would want to come along for the ride – and I don't think I could cope with her telling me what to say to him and what not to say.'

'Tell me about it!'

'And you'd have to tell her, wouldn't you, if you did take me?'

'Course I wouldn't,' Arthur sniffed and pushed the shoulders of his jacket back again, a habit that he would probably never get out of. 'I just let 'er *think* I tell her everything. Now then, Johnny's parents – do you think they're keeping in touch with you as much as they should do? Doing their bit, so to speak?'

'Johnny's dad sends a postal order each month for twenty pounds which is from all of them, and his mum drops in once a week during her lunch break from Yardley's soap factory where she works. She always brings things for baby George with her. I think she's keeping her eye on me.'

'Nothing wrong with that. You need all the support you can get. And remember, family first, friends second. Especially *new* friends who haven't been tried and tested.'

'Yeah . . . I've got the point, Arthur.'

'Only I'm not sure about that poofy-looking bloke. He might try it on, you know. Now then, would you like me to give you a ride to see Johnny?'

'I would *really* like that. So long as you don't mind not being able to visit him. His mum's got the other visiting card so—'

'What do I wanna go inside a bloody prison for – whether it's an open prison or bloody Parkhurst? I've spent my entire life being clever enough to stay out of jail, on and off the Monopoly board.' That said, Arthur gave her a wink and patted her shoulder as if she were a child. 'Give me a bell and tell me what time you want me to pick you up.'

Pouring milk into a small saucepan, Cathy suddenly felt lonely in the quiet room now that the television had been turned off and the old couple had gone. Waiting for the milk to come to the boil so that she could have a mug of cocoa as well as make the baby's bottle up for the night, she thought about her 'arty' friend Stewart. She did like him, and wondered why Henry and Arthur had each in their own way reacted against him. He was sweet and considerate and she felt comfortable in his company. His only downside where her family were concerned was that he was good-looking and therefore a threat.

On the day of Cathy's next visit to the open prison Rosie was in her flat. They were going over the final instructions about baby George's feeding times when Rosie casually said, 'Did I tell you that the adoption papers have come through for me and George to read and sign?'

'No, you didn't. So it shouldn't be that long, then, should it?' Cathy smiled.

Sitting in the armchair with Cathy's baby awake and resting on her knee, Rosie gazed into his face and began to hold a one-sided conversation with him. Here was someone who wanted and loved babies and couldn't have any of her own, and was nursing baby George who hadn't been planned. The situation seemed tragic to Cathy, and yet Rosie never complained but just carried on in her own sweet way looking at other women's babies and hoping that one day she could, one way or another, be a mother.

After rushing around to make sure that she had left everything out that Rosie would need for her day of baby-sitting, Cathy just had time to flick on a little mascara and lipstick before the doorbell rang. She quickly grabbed her black maxi coat that reached her ankles and snatched her handbag off a chair by the door. She then kissed baby George goodbye and rushed down the narrow flight of stairs to open the door to Arthur.

Seeing his smiling face, she felt her shoulders drop as all urgency melted away. 'God, you're a sight for sore eyes,' she said, brushing a light kiss on his rosy cheek.

'So are you,' he said. 'You look like a Hollywood film star!'

Respecting her desire for little conversation, Arthur told Cathy to turn on the car radio if she wanted to listen to songs from the hit parade. She declined this with a smile and shake of the head. 'Peace and quiet is fine by me, Arthur. I might even doze off, if that's not too rude. Baby George was a bit unsettled during the night, so I never got that much sleep.'

'Well then, you doze off, gal. I'm happy to drive in silence.' And for the best part of the journey from London to the open prison in Sussex this was the way of it – a comfortable easy ride in between little meaningful exchanges. When they arrived at the big wide open gates that led into the prison which was to remain Johnny's home for at least another nine months, Cathy felt her heart lurch. She couldn't have wished for a better place for him to have been sent to serve his term, but even so facts were facts. He was locked away from the outside world.

'Now don't you worry about me,' said Arthur. 'I'll go and have a pint in that little corner pub we passed and then go for a nice walk once it's closed for the afternoon. If it closes.'

'Well, make sure you relax while you're having a drink – and don't get lost afterwards,' she said before closing the car door between them. Then, with mixed feelings of excitement and trepidation, she walked off in her high-heeled, knee-length boots, the cold wind blowing in her face, towards the prison entrance. Even now, after a few visits, she still could hardly believe this was happening. One year ago she was planning to leave Gottard's for a bright new career, having no idea that her life had already been mapped for her.

Seeing Johnny again in these surroundings, which were as pleasant as an open prison could be, Cathy was warmed by his handsome smiling face. Of course he wanted to know everything about his baby and Cathy was only too pleased to go through it all in detail – how he looked like his dad, how he smiled when he burped, how many hours he slept and how beautiful he was. Then she listened to Johnny telling her how involved he was in the various leisure pursuits and training programmes, proving to her that he was not going to allow himself to be a cabbage in there and that he was okay even though Christmas was drawing near. He told her about the carpentry classes he loved, and gave her the latest gossip on his fellow inmates, some of whom were famous and received visits from people in the world of film and rock music.

In his own way he was letting her know that the place wasn't full of scar-faced thugs and that he was in decent enough company. Gazing into her beautiful face, he promised her a better future as he gently squeezed her hand. 'I did wrong, Cath,' he murmured, 'and I'm really sorry. I shouldn't 'ave got involved in crime to pay off my gambling debts. There's no get-rich-quick solution. I know that now.'

'No, there's not. And that includes gambling. You've learned one of life's important lessons, Johnny,' she said. 'And that's the best thing to come out of this, as well as learning not to trust anyone other than your own.'

'You're right there, darling,' he agreed. 'And I swear to you and I swear on our baby's life, that I won't ever gamble agen. Ever. Not even for a bit of sport when the Grand National comes round. And I won't go anywhere near the dog track either. Once I'm out of here I want to do what I'm good at. I'm gonna be a furniture maker, Cath. It'll be a while till I get to that stage, but meanwhile I'll be able to get a job as a qualified carpenter, once I'm back home with you and the baby. I'm spending every bit of free time I get in the carpentry class.'

'That's great, Johnny,' she said, squeezing his hand.

'Woodwork was something I really enjoyed at school and what I wanted to take up, but once we were fifteen we lads were expected to make a decent wage so as to put a bit back into the pot at home. But I don't need to tell you that.'

'Of course you don't.' She gripped both his hands in hers and leaned over the tiny Formica table as if they were the only ones in the visitors' room, taking no notice of other prisoners or their visitors. 'Johnny . . . it would really please me if you do come out with a trade. I would love it.'

A happy smile on his face, Johnny produced a small wooden jewellery box with her name carved across the hinged lid.

'I started this after our last visit. What d'yer reckon? Is it any good?'

'Oh, darling . . .' Cathy murmured, her eyes filling with tears. 'It's beautiful. I love it. And I love you.'

The visiting time flew by, and before she knew it Cathy was walking away from the prison building towards the gates, the soles of her boots crunching on the gravel again – a sound that would stay with her for ever. She was really pleased that Johnny was taking the carpentry classes. Old timber floorboards and joists purchased for next to nothing and turned into furniture were now all the rage, and Stewart had explained to her how they could be bought cheaply from large houses that were being demolished. She had seen hand-made furniture from reclaimed timber in his antique shop, and once stripped and waxed the wood looked fantastic.

Dropping Cathy off outside her flat, Arthur gave her a friendly squeeze of the arm and made her promise that if she was ever short of cash she would go to see him. He had confided to her during the drive back to London that he had some decent savings put by from all of his wheeling and dealing over the years.

Once Arthur had pulled away Cathy mentally crossed another month away from her Johnny off the calendar before she let herself in and ran up the stairs, eager to see her baby and Rosie.

'My little ward has been as good as gold,' her friend said. 'He fell soundly asleep soon after you left, woke up bang on time for his next feed and then gurgled and smiled at me until I put him down again.' She raised her eyes to Cathy's and smiled. 'I love your baby as if he were my own.'

'Well, you are his godmother,' she said, and then dropped into an armchair and burst into tears. 'I'm sorry, Ro,' she apologised, drying her eyes. 'This always happens after a visit, once I'm back home and reality hits. I get so lonely at times, especially when I'm in bed.'

Rosie didn't know quite what to say to her other than, 'I'll make us a cup of tea and you can curl up in the armchair and tell me all about the visit – the place, the people, and what Johnny's been doing to help pass the time.'

'That sounds good.' She showed Rosie the jewellery box that he had made for her. An hour or so flew by as they talked, and then the doorbell went. Cathy went down to open the door, believing it to be George arriving to collect his wife. But she was wrong. It was Stewart standing there, holding a small bunch of late autumn flowers to cheer her up after the ordeal of having to go to visit a husband in prison.

Following her up the stairs and telling her that he had just picked up at a bargain price a fantastic Victorian bedside cabinet, the joy on his face disappeared when he saw Rosie there. Rosie was not in the least impressed by the flowers he had brought Cathy. This young man looked like someone who was practised at getting a girl into bed, she felt sure. Looking from Stewart to Cathy, she saw that her friend was blushing. The doorbell went again and this time it was indeed George, there to pick Rosie up.

'I'll go straight down, Cathy,' she said, grabbing her coat and handbag. She didn't want George to walk into this cosy little scene with a handsome stranger in Cathy's flat. She nodded politely at Stewart, gave her friend a peck on the cheek and then said, 'Oh, and by the way, I'm going back to Buckhurst Hill to visit the children's home I told you about. Let me know if you want to come with me for a break. The fresh air will do baby good.'

'That sounds lovely, Rosie. I'm really pleased. Let me know how you get on,' said Cathy.

This response sent a cold wave through Rosie. Cathy either hadn't taken in properly what she had said, or she was all too eager to see her out. 'Well, I guess you'll be calling in to see your mum and dad, Cath, so you can catch up then, can't you?'

'Of course I can. Say hello to George for me.'

Rosie showed a hand, hid her true feelings and said no more as she let herself out of the flat. Halfway down the flight of stairs she stopped and mentally shook off the worry in her mind because, as sure as apples grew on trees, George would pick up on her concern over the way her close friend might be taken in by Stewart who behaved as if he already had his slippers under the bed. She knew that, should Johnny's family find out, all hell would break loose.

'All right, sweetheart?' enquired George as she settled herself in the front seat.

'I'm not sure, George. I need to think.'

'Fair enough,' he replied. He too had seen Stewart going up to the main entrance to the flats while he was waiting to manoeuvre into a parking space on the busy main road. It was obvious that it was Cathy he had gone up to see, since he was carrying a bunch of flowers.

Back in the flat sitting cross-legged on the floor and slowly rolling a joint, Stewart glanced at Cathy as she relaxed with her feet up on the sofa sipping a mug of coffee. 'I have a feeling that your friend was not too happy at my arrival,' he said. 'That she might have been reading too much into things, as some of the folk in this area tend to do.'

'Don't talk daft. Rosie's all right. She knows that I need to have friends, Stewart. If I can't have people coming to visit I might as well go back home to Mum and Dad and Nan. Are you rolling one of those for me?'

'Do any of your family know I use that spare room from time to time?'

'No, of course not! They'd go berserk. And if it ever got back to Johnny's family, that could be the end of my marriage. I think you'd better not stay again, Stewart. I'm sorry.'

'If you wish it, then I shall stay away altogether.'

'No, you don't have to do that. Just don't come with your overnight bag any more.'

'I absolutely agree. I wouldn't want to fall out with your grandmother. Now then, I suggest you share this with me. A few puffs are all you'll need to de-stress. Why not make us a herbal tea? Too much caffeine is bad for the blood, you know.'

'I've only got camomile or lemon grass.'

'Lemon grass will do nicely. Liven up the taste buds. I thought I'd treat us both to an Indian takeaway this evening. How does that grab you?'

'Fantastic. A good hot curry. But let it be my treat. I'm celebrating the lovely visit to Johnny I had today.' Cathy dragged herself up from the comfortable sofa and went into the small kitchen to switch on the kettle.

Stewart stretched his long legs and propped a cushion from the armchair between his back and the wall. 'Whatever. Whenever. I'm too exhausted to think. I bought four marble fireplaces today from a Georgian house which will soon be bulldozed to the ground.' It was a lie.

'Where was that?' asked Cathy, speaking through the open doorway while she waited for the water in the kettle to boil.

'Woodford Green, on the outskirts of Essex.'

'Really?' said Cathy. 'That's only one stop before Buckhurst Hill, I think – the place that Rosie was just telling me about. Our old neighbour Becky has relatives there. Relatives who are a bit on the snobby side.'

'That doesn't surprise me. It's one of those little places tucked away in a time warp. But, I have to say, I'd love to find a little bargain cottage in one of the lanes where one could ignore the aspiring new middle classes,' he said, stretching out his arm to offer her the roll-up. Taking it from him, she slowly drew on the twisted end and then handed it back so as to attend to the tea.

'This really is a lovely little flat you've got here, Cathy. I envy you well living in it, and I'm sorry that you feel badly about my stopping over now and then. But I do see your reasoning for it. And it does make sense.'

'Good,' said Cathy, coming back into the room and taking the reefer from him again.

Stewart sipped his tea and then said, 'Your friend who just left – is she a close chum?'

'Yes, she is. She's also a family friend and next door neighbour and my baby's godmother. Rosie's all right. Brilliant, in fact. If you picked up a sense of suspicion from her, that's because she's worried in case I get drawn in by someone who might not be trustworthy. She's only looking after my welfare.'

'Well, she can stop barking up this tree, Cathy. We're not *all* looking to bed a woman, you know. Some of us simply enjoy the company of someone as natural and lovely as you.'

Cathy looked directly into her new friend's face and said, 'Thanks. That's a really nice thing to say.'

'I meant it. I'm not trying to get you into bed. I'm here as a friend. Although of course it would be heavenly . . .'

Cathy quietly laughed at him and his theatricals. 'I never said you were trying to get me in bed. I'm sure there are plenty of girls who would kill a cat to go out with you.'

'No, as a matter of fact. Now why not put on some music? The Sam Cook LP you were playing the last time I called in out of the blue to help fill your empty, lonely evening.'

'No, you do it – and keep it down really low so as not to wake baby up.' She curled her legs under her, smiling. 'Roll me one all to myself tonight. I've been to a prison to visit my man, after all's said and done. I need to unwind.'

'Of course you do,' said Stewart as he gazed across the room into her face. A face that looked even more beautiful in the light of the low flames of the gas fire to the sound of Sam Cook singing 'You Send Me'. As far as he was concerned there was no more to be said. He withdrew his tobacco pouch from his inside pocket and decided to go a little heavier with the weed because he felt like laughing and he felt like making love, and as far as he was concerned this would be the night for it.

Cathy felt so relaxed in his company, so safe and secure, as they listened to love songs. In some ways he reminded her of Johnny: the way he was gentle without trying, as well as his penetrating blue eyes. Of course she couldn't possibly have known that Stewart had a wife who had left him, taking their small child with her and going off to Scotland hoping never to see him again. Nor could she know that he was on the brink of bankruptcy and owed three months' rent to the landlord of the antique shop. Stewart certainly had no intention of telling her.

'Cathy,' he murmured, gazing into the flames, 'will you do something really special for me tonight? Will you come here and hold me? I had some awful news about a grandparent today which I don't want to talk about – but I so need to be held.' More lies.

'Oh, Stewart! Why didn't you say when you first came in?' said Cathy, going over to sit on his lap and look into his sorry face. 'You daft thing – you should have said so straightaway. I couldn't bear it if anything happened to my nan. She's been like a second mother to me.'

'Mine too,' said Stewart, gazing into her beautiful blue eyes. 'Yet another thing that we have in common, my darling girl. I don't suppose it would be all right if I were to brush a kiss across your cheek, would it?'

'No, it wouldn't, Stewart,' Cathy giggled, the marijuana having well and truly taken effect. 'But then again, I can't say that it would be wrong.' There was no more to be said. Stewart closed his eyes as he gently drew her head forward until their lips were locked together . . . and all to that wonderful sound of Sam Cook and 'Unforgettable'.

Her sense of guilt having dissolved, Cathy, with her baby sleeping peacefully in the next room, enjoyed the touch and musky scent of a man's body against hers for the first time in so long. They eased themselves down onto the floor and made love.

Later that night, once Stewart had left with a promise that he would take care of her every need until Johnny came home, Cathy made herself a mug of cocoa, hardly able to believe what she had done. Made love with another man. It all seemed like a strange and bizarre dream that could turn into a nightmare. She curled her legs under her as she sat down on the sofa and gazed at the floor. As she re-lived the evening in her mind she couldn't understand why it had felt so right or why she felt no heavy sense of guilt. When the nearby church clock struck the hour of midnight she realised just how tired she was. She switched off the lights and went into her bedroom to climb into bed too intoxicated to be bothered to even clean her teeth and the moment her head sank into the feather pillow she was asleep.

The next morning, however, as the early sunshine streaked in through a gap in the curtain, Cathy slowly opened her eyes with a soft pounding in her head and the sound of her baby waking up. Slightly disorientated for a few moments, having dreamt that she was in her old bedroom in Tillet Street, she lay still to take in her surroundings and acclimatise and to see if baby George would do as he often did on first waking and go back to sleep. When all went quiet again she slipped from her bed, longing for that first cup of coffee. As she waited for the kettle to boil, she smelled the scent of Stewart still on her skin and remembered what had happened the night before and she felt her heart sink. She could hardly believe she had let another man make love to her and could almost touch the guilt that was pervading her entire body as well as her mind.

Wishing that it had all been a dream and no more than that, she sat on the sofa and in the silence of the room once again she gazed at the carpeted floor where she had given herself to another man. Then, as the details of the previous evening returned to her, she remembered promising Stewart that she would go in and say hello as soon as she had bathed, dressed and tucked Baby George up in his pram. Then, with no warning, Johnny's face came into her mind and she could hear her friend Rosie's advice when Cathy had mentioned Stewart to her and she had said, '*Be careful Cathy. Don't let this turn into something dangerous.*'

'This isn't love, Rosie,' she murmured, as if her friend was in the room. 'This is two lonely people enjoying each other's company, that's all.'

A couple of hours later, after she had fed, bathed and dressed her beloved infant, taken a shower and dressed herself, she, with baby George in his small navy and chrome pram, was outside in the fresh mid-morning air with the winter sun on her face making her way through the narrow courtyard next door and into the back of Stewart's shop. To her relief, she found him sitting on a high backed chair with his legs outstretched as he sipped fresh percolated coffee and smoked a filter-tipped cigarette, every bit the contented young man. When he saw her he smiled and waited to see what her response might be and was not disappointed. He could see no sign of shame on her face. To his mind it was far too early in the day to have to console a guilty conscience.

'Cathy . . . what a lovely sight for sore eyes you are, my sweet. Even at this early hour.'

'It's eleven o'clock, Stewart.' She smiled back at him. 'Hardly the crack of dawn.'

He knew that there were no customers in the shop but still he glanced through the open doorway to be certain before he placed his cup onto a small antique mahogany side table and lifted himself from his chair to gaze into her face. As he held out his arms to her, he spoke quietly, saying, 'I seem to have been dreaming about you all night long.'

Cathy, showing caution, said, 'We have to forget what happened last night, Stewart. It was wrong. We got carried away.'

'Never say wrong, my darling. But I shall pretend to forget that it happened if this is your wish.' He stepped closer and placed his finger under her chin to tip her face so as to look directly into her eyes before kissing her gently on the lips. Warming to him again Cathy placed her hands on his shoulders and lightly kissed him back, until the sound of the shop door closing behind someone, brought her to her senses. Pulling away from him she heard the shrill voice of one of Johnny's sisters pierce through the otherwise silent place.

'I fucking well knew it!' said the sister with the ginger hair. 'She's been laid by the long lanky shit-face!'

Cathy, blushing madly, was stunned and silent as she stared into the faces of Johnny's sisters, lost for words.

'Third time lucky!' yelled the second sister pointing a finger at Cathy. 'We've been keeping an eye on the pair of yer! And this time you've been caught with *his* hand in *your* drawers! We saw you sneak in the side entrance you little fucking whore!'

'And to fink that we were almost ready to agree that you weren't sleeping around! We was gonna be good sister-in-laws! Can you believe that? We was gonna ask if you wanted to come to the pictures wiv us. You scumbag.' She then turned on Stewart, her eyes boring into his. 'And what 'ave *you* got to say for yerself, dozy bollocks?'

Holding up both hands to offer a gesture of passive surrender, he backed away, saying, 'Far be it for me to interfere in family quarrels.' He then offered a faint smile as he walked a touch regally to the front of the shop and turned the *Open* sign on the door to the *Closed* side before turning the key in the lock.

'I wonder if you three ladies would mind leaving via the back way . . .' I've just seen the rent collector for these premises and would rather turn off the lights,' he lied, as he looked from one of Johnny's sisters to the other. 'It's not just the housewife who must dodge such people. I'm two months in arrears, I fear.' With that he firmly ushered the three women out into the back-yard and closed and bolted the door behind them having avoided what could have been a distasteful scene.

Cathy, with Johnny's sisters looking at her as if she were something the cat had dragged in, turned her face away from their scowling expressions to take the handle of her baby's pram and walk away as they swore and name-called behind her. Deeply ashamed and embarrassed, Cathy turned into the high street and kept on walking until she could no longer hear them shouting accusations after her.

A couple of hours later, back in her flat, she was crying while her baby slept. She could hardly believe the way Stewart had treated her, as if she was part of a horrible family that he wished to have nothing to do with. She had all but given up hope of him calling in to explain himself. He had been so kind, honest and sincere and not in the least bit predatory, as far as she could tell. They had spent other times together at the Prospect of Whitby with Henry and Helen as well as in her flat talking for hours and he hadn't once made a pass.

When the doorbell pierced the silence, she all but jumped out of her skin for fear of it being the sisters returning with Johnny's mother in tow to confront her. Knowing she had no choice but to go down and open the door and get it over and done with, she took a deep breath and went to answer the second ring of the bell. But it wasn't the sisters standing there. It was Stewart.

'Thank goodness my quick thinking worked,' he said. 'I take it the ugly wenches have not returned?'

'No they haven't, Stewart,' said Cathy, puzzled by his gentle smile. 'But why did you see all three of us out? Why didn't you stick by me?'

He smiled again. 'Did it not work? My on the spot plan? Did they not leave you to escape to your little sanctuary?'

'Well . . . I suppose so . . . in a way. I did manage to shake them off . . .'

'Which is exactly what I would have expected from you. You knocked spots off them my love, I'm sure.' He then tipped his head sideways and said, 'May I not come in? Would it not be good to show those ghastly women, should they return, that we have nothing to hide? That we are just good friends?'

Cathy didn't entirely think so but beckoned him in and then closed the door. 'They saw us kissing, Stewart. We can't get round that,' she said as she climbed the stairs.

Once inside the flat with the door shut, Stewart looked at her, slowly shaking his head and smiling. 'It was a peck on the lips, Cathy, and I had my back to the door. They could hardly see anything. And even if they did, it would look far worse if we suddenly stayed away from each other – don't you think?'

'So we should carry on with you coming and going and brazen it out?'

'Precisely. Henry will vouch for the fact that we are friends and no more than that. And your family are very close to him from what you've told me. So stop fretting, my love.'

'I suppose you're right,' said Cathy, biting her lip.

'I am. Trust me. And if you really want to put your mind at ease, all we have to do is spend more time in this flat, with you not only entertaining your good friend, yours truly, Stewart, but Henry and Helen too. We could play a game of Monopoly or cards. And I would be the first to leave. On one or two other evenings, or an hour or so in the afternoons, we could be alone.

And why not? I'm sure Henry is in here sometimes with you by himself.'

'Of course he is. But he's a family friend.'

'He is also an attractive young man.'

'I take your point,' said Cathy, still biting her lip. 'I suppose we should just act naturally.'

'Precisely.'

'But no more making love. Just be good friends.'

'If you think we could manage that, then of course that's all we'll be.' Stewart looked into her eyes and smiled as he gently laid his hands on her shoulders. 'You have the expression of a scared rabbit wondering if the fox is about.' He then gently pressed his lips onto hers which turned into a passionate kiss from which he gently drew away, saying, 'I won't break your heart, Cathy. And I shall disappear into the void should you ever wish it.'

'And you know that we can't be forever?'

'Of course I do. But is not a few months, if this is all there is, better than nothing at all?'

'I belong to someone else, Stewart. Never forget that and I s'pose we're not harming anyone . . . so long as Johnny doesn't find out.'

'We're harming no one my sweet. What the eye does not see the heart cannot grieve over.'

This said, he held her in his arms and Cathy felt she could hear the beating of not only her heart but his too. With no more thoughts about Johnny's sisters she pulled gently away from Stewart to check that her baby was all right before she made them both a much needed cup of coffee.

However, Johnny's sisters were not satisfied in the least bit and in a high temper, they had jumped on to a bus and travelled two stops to get off close to the Red Lion pub, which they knew to be one that Stanley and Albert often frequented. And they had found them there. At the bar, enjoying a drink that very lunch time.

Once they had told the boys what was going on in Johnny's flat, the girls left without being offered a drink but having been told in no uncertain terms to keep their traps shut and to stop spying on Cathy. They had responded angrily to the under-lying threats until Stanley whispered curtly into the ear of Johnny's ginger sister: 'Your fucking locks'll be cut off and your head shaved and painted red if you don't stay out of Cathy's life.' She then left the pub like a lamb, with her sister in tow.

Not satisfied that this threat would stop the witch hunt, Albert made a mental note to let Molly know what was being said and tell her to keep an eye on things. To his mind, if Cathy needed company while her chap was locked up, it was nobody's business but her own. The interloper could easily be got rid of before Johnny was released and then it would be up to him and his young wife to sort out their own relationship. On the other hand, Stanley knew that his own fiery woman, being Cathy's sister, would kick the shit out of him should he get it wrong and the hippy fucked up Cathy's life. The boys were going to have to handle this carefully and show a blade to the guy called Stewart before things got too out of hand.

At the end of November, when Cathy's next visit to Johnny was due, there had already been a light fall of snow. Molly, sitting by the fire in the back room of the little house in Tillet Street, was thinking of her granddaughter and wondering about Cathy's friend Stewart. He always seemed to come up in conver-sation when she was with Cathy, even popping in now and then when Molly was there – only to pop out again within minutes once he saw her.

Today she was waiting for Arthur to arrive and take her in his car to see Cathy and baby George, picking up pie and mash on the way for all of them. She had been thinking about Henry, too, and how much she missed his to-ing and fro-ing through their back door and the way he made her smile with some of the things he came out with. Her thoughts then moved on to her thieving granddaughters, Marilyn and Ava, who were due to drop in. She wondered what they would be bringing with them today and whether there might be some decent stuff for her to sell on. Molly valued money more than ever now, because she had not only Cathy to think about but her little great-grandson as well. Mother and child weren't on the poverty line, by any means. But Molly wanted this child to have the best that life could give, and knew that thick wads of five pound notes in her bottom drawer was the best way of making sure the little boy would not go without.

Marilyn had phoned earlier to say that she and Ava would be dropping by even though Alice was at work and Jim would be at a friend's house that day playing cards with a few mates. She had sounded chirpier than usual, but gave nothing away. When the doorbell rang long and loud Molly guessed it would be them rather than Arthur. 'You're late,' she said. 'I'm just on my way out.'

'What, with your slippers on and no coat, Nan? You'll freeze to death,' said Marilyn as she all but fell into the passage with her huge bulging carrier bags. Once in the back room and seated, the girls eased off their knee-length boots which were wet with slush.

With an eye on the heavy bag that Marilyn had put down on the floor, Molly said, 'I hope you've not got anything in there you need to get rid of in a hurry – because I won't be able to give you much this week. I'm skint.'

'Nothing in there to interest you anyway, Nan,' replied Marilyn. 'I'm gasping for a cup of tea – put the kettle on.'

'When did your last servant die?' grumbled Molly as she went into the kitchen. 'You're both gonna come a cropper one of these days – when I'm dead and buried and can't give you advice any more.'

'You wait till you see what we've really got in our bag, Nan,' said Ava. 'Watches for starters.'

'Rolled gold or plate?' enquired Molly from the kitchen.

'Neither. Both are solid gold.'

'Both? Oh. Only two, then. Lot of good that is. This time of the year you'd 'ave been better off nicking a few dozen cheaper ones. More profit in the long run.'

'And we've got some real silk scarves as sold only in Liberty's. The delivery van broke down on the way and a whole boxful fell out of the back while the driver was changing a wheel.'

'Yeah, right. Had a puncture, did he?'

'We've got gas lighters, rolled gold, gentlemen and ladies!'

'That's more like it! How many and how much?'

'Four dozen. They sell in the shops for four pounds. You can have 'em for two.'

'Oh, yeah? You'll be lucky to get a pound each for 'em. Go and ask Fanny the Fence at number fourteen. She's been here, there and everywhere with the self-same thing at ten bob a go – and they're not selling like hot cakes, neither.'

'Stop telling lies, Nan,' Ava laughed.

'I'm not, sweetheart. The market's flooded with the bloody things. But since my contacts are better than hers I'll pay ten bob apiece and make a dollar on each one if I'm lucky. And I'm only gonna take them off your hands because it's Christmas coming up.'

'You'll get a pound each for them easy, Nan. We were thinking of popping round to see Cath if you fancy a ride. She's not phoned for a week or so. Have you heard from her?'

Molly came into the room with a laden tea tray. 'Rosie popped in earlier. I think she's a bit worried about the company our Cathy's been keeping.'

'The man from the funny farm,' said Marilyn, lighting a Rothman's cigarette. 'I shouldn't worry, Nan. He's out of his skull on pot.'

'Oh, right. And that makes it all okay, does it? The fact that someone we know nothing about 'as snaked 'is way into Cathy and baby George's little world. That doesn't matter?'

'She's a grown woman now. A mother.'

'Which is more than we can say for you, Marilyn, it's true – but Rosie thinks the drug addict has got his feet under your sister's table. Then again, if you're not bothered I won't worry myself over it. You know best.'

'And what has our Cath got to say about it?' said Ava.

'I've not asked her. But you seem to know who I'm talking about, so I'll tell Rosie not to worry and that all's well.'

'We're already on the case, Nan. Rosie mentioned it to George, who had a word with Albert and Stanley, who said they were aware of it via their own source and that everyone's talking about our sister, who hasn't even put a foot wrong yet – as far as any of us know.'

'Oh,' said Molly, 'that's nice of Albert and Stanley. It just shows you. Beneath that tough and sometimes mean face they both like to put on, they're as soft as anything.'

'You should know that by now, Nan,' said Ava. 'I've told you enough times that both of them are Robin Hoods on the quiet. They make sure the folk in the old people's home in Stepney Green don't go cold or hungry, and they put up Christmas decorations for them every year as well as supplying fruit and chocolates. But for Christ's sake don't say I've told you. They prefer to do what they do without being labelled do-gooders – they do it because they want to.'

'It doesn't surprise me,' said Molly. 'Albert's old granny was in that 'ome, I do believe. I suppose it was going in there to visit her that made him think about things.'

'Whatever,' said Ava. 'But . . . if you're asking our opinion about our Cathy, we think it's best to leave things well alone. She's doing all right. She's not only doing all right – she's being a bloody good mum to baby George.'

'We should be thankful she's making new friends,' added Marilyn. 'And don't forget that Cathy's got Henry living on her doorstep – and even he's found a soulmate there. A little shy girl called Helen who works in his shop. Henry and Helen. Rolls nicely off the tongue, don't it?'

'Well, if you ask me,' said Molly, 'it all sounds a bit too pink-tinted round the edges. Too perfect. Anyway, in answer to your question whether I'd like a lift, Arthur's due to turn up soon.

We're going over in his car to see Cath and the baby. So I'll work it out for myself.'

'Oh well – we'll go tomorrow, then, to spread the visits out . . . You might find a big fat black man in her bed, though.' Marilyn grinned cheekily.

'Or a skinny Pakistani,' Ava chimed in.

'Ah, right . . . so she's got two on the go, then. Catching up with you two. And I couldn't give a fuck what colour they are so long as they're not German or Japanese, and I'm sure that even you two can work out why.'

'Right,' said Marilyn. 'Time to go. That was a lovely cup of tea, Nan. We'll leave the gear here, if that's all right, and you can go through it. Sort out what you think you can shift and shove the rest under Cathy's old bed.'

'What's the rush?' said Molly.

'Time is money, Nan,' said Ava. 'That's what you taught us.' She took a couple of biscuits off the plate and popped them in her pocket. 'We're off to collect five cases of best champagne brandy for a client in Mayfair from a client in Shoreditch.'

'As you know, we love to hear about the war and the Germans and the Japs, Nan,' said Marilyn. 'But you're gonna have to tell us another time.'

'Who said I was gonna go on about the war? You two aren't too old for a good wallop, you know.'

'We believe you, Nan,' said Marilyn, making a sharp exit with Ava in her footsteps. 'We'll see ourselves out!'

Once she heard the front door slam shut, Molly was off her chair like a shot and delving into the girls' bag to assess the quality of the goods she would be selling on in a day or so. When she pulled out a small cellophane bag containing some classy-looking soft leather handbags she pulled both hands into fists and shouted, 'Yes!' The colour was perfect. Pale camel. Not only that, but on the corner of each in tiny gold script was the word 'Harrod's'.

'Crafty mares!' she laughed. 'They knew what they were doing leaving me to find these little gems.' She knew she could ask top dollar and make a very good profit for herself. Chuckling, she carefully placed the expensive quality items back into the cellophane bag and squeezed it oh so carefully into her faithful old holdall.

The watches were okay, as were the lighters – but those Harrod's bags were little gems that her old contact in Stratford East whom she hadn't seen for a while would be able to sell on with no trouble. All she needed now was for Arthur to drive her there. This had been a good day so far, and now she was going to see her adorable great-grandson as well as conduct a little business. Soon enough, three knocks on the door told her that he had arrived.

'You're gonna 'ave to let me 'ave a key, Molly – it's bloody freezing out 'ere,' said Arthur, giving a quick shiver for effect.

'Yeah. I must remember to get one cut.'

'You always say that,' he moaned as he followed her along the passage. He didn't want a key to the door – this was just a little game they liked to play. Both long in the tooth, they were making absolute certain that each of them could put up with the other before they tied the knot. They teased and they goaded, but could never quite manage to have a real row or one of those long tense silences that most couples seemed to think were part and parcel of the married state.

'I've got a bit of business to do in Stratford today,' Molly told him, 'so while I'm out you can stay with Cathy. Have a chat with her about the hippy, because word's got round – flown, in fact – and now Albert and Stanley are on the case. Best get this nipped in the bud now if there's any nipping to do, don't you think? Before there's any blood spilt on her doorstep.'

'Not really, no. Cathy won't go off the rails. She's got a sensible head on them shoulders.'

'I agree, but she's only flesh and blood, sunshine, and her hormones are probably all over the place. That Stewart's a handsome chap beneath all that pony-tail stuff.'

'Well,' said Arthur, 'if you want him sent packing the boys

will soon take care of it. But she's got the baby to look after night and day. A bit of company might be a good thing.'

'You'd better not mean that, Arthur!'

'Not sex or that – I'm talking about company. That's all.' He had only just managed to wriggle out of saying the worst thing he could have to Molly.

'Do you know what,' said Molly, all thoughtful. 'I think I'll stop round Cathy's tonight, keep her company. I don't really know why none of us have thought of that before. Not even her sisters. Why didn't you say something to me, Arthur? What's wrong with you?'

'Me? What d'yer mean, Molly? What 'ave I done wrong?'

'You should have bucked my ideas up! You should have told me to stay with my granddaughter now and then. She's got a spare room, ain't she?'

'Yeah. All right. Keep your wig on. Stop tonight. You can give me a bell in the morning and let me know when you want me to pick you up. Right?'

'Right. This is more like it. I'll go and chuck a pair of pyjamas and a toothbrush into a carrier bag.'

Cathy couldn't have been more pleased to see her nan at the door brandishing her overnight things. This was more like it. This was what was going to turn her flat into a home, having her family come to stay over. Arthur would have none of it, though, and once they had all eaten the pie and mash that he and Molly had picked up on the way he was happy to leave the two women to themselves.

'You can stop over as well, Arthur, if you like,' said Cathy. 'I'll go on the settee and you can have my bed.'

'No. That's all right, ducks. You and your nan have a nice night in together – that's what families should do now and then.' With that he kissed her on the cheek, did the same to Molly and made his escape. He wasn't quite ready to spend a night under the same roof as his fiancée. Not quite ready. Not yet.

'I'm glad he's gone,' said Molly once she heard the front door shut. 'I like my own space in the mornings and to have to face Arthur rambling on would do my head in. Turn the telly on then, love. We're in for a nice evening.'

Cathy quietly laughed. 'I've got a bottle of white wine in the fridge. Do you fancy a glass?'

'I thought you'd never ask,' said Molly, happy as a lark.

Lying in the spare bed that night, having gone to bed early at ten o'clock, Molly ran the past year through her mind. What a year it had been! Had someone told her that she would be lying in this bed in this flat tonight with a little great-grandson in the cot next to her, her youngest granddaughter Cathy in the next room, she would have laughed in their face. She thought about the trip that she and her friends had made to Buckhurst Hill, and thanked God for that. Becky smiled more now than she had ever done before. And then of course there was Rosie, who had wandered into the children's home with them and turned her life around. Soon there would be a brother and sister aged five and six staying with her and George. Nicely tired after drinking half a bottle of wine, Molly relaxed happily between the white cotton sheets. Turning over, and snuggling her head into her feather pillow, she was surprised to hear a soft tap-tap on the door. Then it creaked open as Cathy whispered, 'Are you asleep, Nan?'

'No, sweetheart, I'm not quite there yet.' She pulled herself up on to her elbow and looked at her granddaughter in the half-light coming in from the narrow passage between the bedroom and the sitting room. 'What's the matter, love? Couldn't you sleep?'

'Nothing's wrong . . . I just wanted to make sure you were okay.'

'Oh, right, good.' She hauled herself up to rest on the padded headboard. 'So get it off your chest, then. We're both in need of a good night's sleep.'

'It's about Johnny's sisters,' Cathy began, sitting on the edge of the bed.

'Don't tell me they've been round again, Cath? Well?'

Smiling nervously at her nan, she said, 'What if they get a special pass to visit Johnny? What if they phone and tell the social worker there about Stewart coming to see me? It'll break Johnny's heart, Nan, and it'll break our marriage. No question.'

'But you've not slept with the bloke, Cathy. And Albert and Stanley had a quiet word with Johnny's sisters. They told the little cows that he's a pansy. Poofs like women's company. Some of my best friends when I was in my teens were queers.'

'I feel a bit of a fool, really. I was the only one who didn't see through him.'

'What do you mean, Cathy? I don't understand.'

'He's turned out to be a married man. Not only that, up to his eyes in debt and a bit of a con artist.'

'And where is he now?' said Molly her cheeks flushed with anger.

'Gone. That's all I've heard. That's all that Henry's heard. He did a midnight. So not only am I shown to be stupid for being taken in by him, but Johnny's sisters will tell him about it, twisting and turning the knife. I don't know what to do, Nan.'

Molly thought a moment and realised that this wasn't the right time to throw stones or criticise someone whom Cathy had been taken in by. Nor was it the time to hint that his disappearance was most likely down to the boys, who had seen to him in their own sweet way with no words other than a threat required. Molly also had a feeling that a confession was about to be made – she had found a bottle of men's aftershave under the bed and hidden it away so that she didn't have to confront it. If his sisters *had* been right all along, then Cathy's marriage was on the line. 'Your sisters said that Albert and Stanley were on to the drop-out, Cathy. But I can't say whether they gave him a hiding and saw him on his way, if that's what you're getting at, sweetheart.'

'The trouble is, there was a bit of truth in what Johnny's horrible sisters were saying.'

'D'you mean you slept with him?'

'More than that, Nan, I let him rent this room for a couple of weeks. But I never let him sleep in mine and Johnny's bed. Not once.'

Shocked by this sudden confession, Molly did her level best to cover it. 'I'm not gonna blame you, Cathy. The man was a confidence trickster and everyone but you saw it. And he wasn't slow to move in on you, was he? A young woman with a new-born baby having to fend for herself. What chance did you stand against all that charm and the wine and flowers he brought you? But don't worry – I daresay you won't see hide nor hair of that man again. His sort never return to a place they've soiled. And Johnny won't discover the truth – that's already been established.

'I feel so ashamed of myself. And I don't trust his sisters. They'll tell him, I know they will.'

'They won't. Trust me.'

'But how can you be so sure, Nan?'

Sighing, she slowly shook her head. 'You're like a bloody detective, you are. I know because I made a little phone call – that's why. Call it blackmail, call it what you fucking well like, but Johnny's family are more likely to send you a bunch of flowers and an apology than anything else. I know more of what goes on in that family than anyone. I made it my business to find out. I never felt right about that bloke so I put the boys on to it weeks ago. And they heard about it from another source too. You don't have to worry over it, I promise.'

'Honestly?' Cathy smiled. 'God's honour?'

'Yes, darling. God's honour. Now either go and get some sleep or fetch us two little glasses so we can have a drop of my Irish whiskey as a nightcap. What's it to be?'

'Irish whiskey.'

'Good. But before I forget – how's our Henry doing? Do you see much of him?'

'He's fine, Nan. He doesn't pop in as often but that's all for the right reasons. He's got more responsibilities now – managing the shop below and of course, there's Helen, his girl friend. They're so right for each other. But he's still my Henry from next door at Tillet Street. And not only that but a substitute brother at times. He still takes things as seriously as ever but we wouldn't want him to change would we?'

'No, Cath, we wouldn't.' Molly quietly laughed. 'He's funny without realising.'

The house quiet, and the baby and grandmother asleep, Cathy lay in her bed with the curtain open a little so as to let in the light of the moon. She did feel better after her confession, even though the guilt was still there deep inside. She couldn't understand now why she had gone along with it all. It was the drink, the smokes, the music that had got to her.

Her thoughts drifted back to the day when they were all in the front room at home watching an old movie: Ava and Marilyn, Johnny and herself. Each of them had been curled up in that cosy room with a fire burning in the grate, while her mum and dad and her nan had been enjoying their usual Sunday afternoon nap upstairs. She hugged herself, pulled her knees up to her chin and whispered, as tears trickled down her face, 'I'm sorry. I didn't mean to let him use our spare room. But he had nowhere to go.' She closed her eyes and pretended that she was back on the sofa with Johnny in the front room of the house in Tillet Street, watching television and holding his hand.

So much had happened in such a short time. She had gone from one world to another when she left Gottard's and said goodbye to friends and colleagues at work, got pregnant, married and was now living in this little flat above her old mate Henry. He would now be in his bedroom below, she knew; Nan was in the small bedroom next to hers with her adorable baby George in his cot sound asleep. The creaking of her door as her nan came in was a welcoming sound.

'Sorry, darling, but even with the whiskey I couldn't fall asleep for thinking. Do you know the worst thing that's 'appened this year, Cathy?' she asked.

'What's that, Nan?'

'They went and took *Mrs Dale's Diary* off the wireless.'

Cathy laughed and held out her arms. 'Give me a hug, Nan, and tell me you've forgiven me.'

'Course I forgive you and all you've confessed to me, even though you've not spelt it out. No one will ever know. And shall I tell you why I've really come in?'

'You will anyway,' said Cathy, wiping a tear from her cheek.

'Because this flat's got a room for a lodger . . . and I'm taking it until Johnny comes home. All right?'

'Oh Nan . . . I would love that. And I won't be lonely any more.'

'No, sweetheart, you won't be lonely ever again. I'm stopping right where I am until Johnny comes home. What goes round, comes round, sweetheart. You're a good girl and a good mother, and you'll be the best wife that he could wish for. Remember that, and forget all the stuff that's gone before. It's what's ahead of you that's the most important thing. Right . . . sermon over. Fancy a cup of sweet tea?'

'Oh, I do, Nan. And thank you. Thank you from the bottom of my heart.'

'You don't have to do that, sweetheart. I was just trying to think of a way to wangle myself in here with you and our little baby George. And now I've done it.' She gave Cathy a smile and a wink and went to put the kettle on, content that things were going to be all right from then onwards. More than all right.